SETH

In the Company of Snipers

Book 17

Irish Winters

COPYRIGHT

Seth; In the Company of Snipers, 17

Cover design: Kelli Ann Morgan, Inspire Creative Services
Cover image: Paul Henry Serres Photography, www.paulhenryserres.com
Cover model: Jérôme
Interior book design: Bob Houston, eBook Formatting
Editor: Linda Clarkson, Black Opal Editing and Proofreading

ISBN Paperback: 978-1-942895-57-2
ISBN eBook: 978-1-942895-58-9
Library of Congress Control Number: 2018941454

In the Company of Snipers

You can find Irish Winters on Facebook:
https://www.facebook.com/author.irishwinters

On Twitter: https://twitter.com/irishwinters1

For news on upcoming releases, sign up for Irish Winters' Newsletter at IrishWinters.com.

For more information about all my books, visit IrishWinters.com.

IN THE COMPANY OF SNIPERS

This series revolves around former Marine scout sniper, Alex Stewart, and his covert surveillance company, The TEAM, home-based out of Alexandria, Virginia. An obsessive patriot and workaholic, he created the company to give former military snipers like him, a chance at returning to civilian life with a decent job, security, and a future.

This is not a serial with each book ending at a cliffhanger. *In the Company of Snipers* is a collection of passionate love stories involving strong women and men who are tough enough to take on the world alone. Each is a stand-alone read, complete in itself.

Spoiler alert: Every story contains adult scenes including sexual situations (some explicit), language, and violence. I don't write sweet romance, so be forewarned.

Book 1, *ALEX*, reveals how The TEAM came to be, as well as how Alex met Kelsey, how they fell in love and fought all odds to stay together. Each of the following books is a complete romance in itself, where, in the course of an active TEAM operation, one agent comes face to face with his or her demons. The men and women I write about are all patriots and warriors, dealing with what they've lived through or mistakes they've made.

It's my hope that you will come to realize along with my heroes...

Love changes everything.

Prologue

It was a bright sunny day to be high in the sky. Perfect weather for the perfect flight home. After a grueling four-month deployment, this soldier-boy had two weeks of leave coming, and he was damned excited to be back in America. But flying over the patchwork quilt of Ohio's and Indiana's farms and fields below couldn't beat the thrill of his first glimpse of Chicago, standing brash and bold on the western shore of Lake Michigan.

Home. Seth McCray was nearly home.

Antsy to be on his feet again and with his family and fiancée, he drummed nervous fingertips on his armrest. Aisle seats at the rear of the plane afforded the barest view of the land that he loved, but he'd seen enough to know he was nearly home.

Mom had sounded good when he'd last talked with her, damned good and lucky to be alive. Now recovered from a scary bout with melanoma, he couldn't wait to see her for himself. She'd cry when he'd hug her. Hell, he might tear up, too, but he'd missed her. He'd missed all his family and they'd be waiting for him. The last leg of this journey always seemed like the longest. It dragged. *Can't this jet fly any faster?*

Seth drew in a belly full of air at the mere thought of Katelynn, his beautiful, soon-to-be wife, and the mother of his future children. His very best friend, and the woman he loved with every fiber of his body. Make that adored. His blood burned thinking what he wanted to do with her and to her, once he got her all to himself. Holding back might not be possible once he tasted her sweet lips. *God, I love her!*

Coffee caramel, that was what she'd tasted like the last time he'd kissed her. They'd spent their last minutes before his flight at the Starbucks kiosk in the same terminal, sipping coffee from the same paper cup, murmuring encouragement to each other despite their sadness. How could he forget? Katelynn had been in every one of his dreams these last months. Not once had he ended a day without chatting on-line with her or writing her. Yeah. He was one of those guys—a total sap.

He'd proposed to her on his last ten-day leave, but he couldn't wait, not one more day to get her in his arms. Mom and Dad would understand. He and Katelynn needed to tie the knot and be quick about it. A man wanted his woman in his bed when he finally made it back to the States, to have and to hold until death they do part. To love. All those things.

Since his first deployment, Seth had learned more than he'd ever wanted to know about death. With every beat of his heart, he now knew full well that every minute with Katelynn might be his last. Because of that hard lesson, he planned to spend the rest of his time on Earth wisely—with her. Damned if that didn't get his cock to saluting as if it heard reveille. *Down boy. Not yet. Maybe not even during this trip home. She's a virgin and she's not ready. She would've told me if she was. Wouldn't she?*

He didn't know. Seth chewed the inside of his cheek, worried that she hadn't answered his last email, but that was okay. He'd pressed send just as he'd cleared JFK airspace and lost the signal, heading for O'Hare. That was hours ago. Forcing an exhale, he stretched his six-foot three frame as much as he could without infringing on other passengers' space. He was in the land of the free now. Nothing to worry about here in America. Time was on his side.

At last, the pilot touched down at O'Hare, taxied to their gate, and the Jetway engaged. Out of his seat with his duffel on the floor between his boots, Seth stood in the galley and watched every last one of the other passengers prepare to disembark. Some of them took their dear, sweet time, locating their carry-ons from the overhead compartments, asking others to grab them, chatting. Impatient to be off the jet, he'd already disabled airplane mode and checked all incoming IMs, texts, and emails.

Katelynn still hadn't replied, not even with one of her cutesy emojis, so he shot a winking kitten to her. That ought to make her smile.

Still no response. Had she turned her cell off? Now? Today of all days? His boot set to tapping.

"Thank you for your service," the pretty redheaded flight attendant said at his elbow. "I know you guys probably hear that a lot, but I mean it. I wish I could do more for each and every one of you."

He nodded as he peered down at her. Folks meant well, but he was forever uncomfortable being thanked for doing his job. "Thank you kindly, ma'am, but don't worry about it."

He hadn't been drafted like the guys in the 1960s. Those were some shitty days to be Army, and America hadn't been a friendly place for GI's to come home to then. He'd seen the old news stories. Vietnam vets had been treated horribly by the press, the know-it-alls and do-nothings in Hollywood, and most college students.

But things were different now. People respected the men and women who served, and they should, by hell. The Armed Forces—believe it or not—had actually gotten smarter in how they handled their volunteer service members. The five-stars had learned a few things since the debacle called Vietnam. Not enough by a long shot, but they'd wised up. A little.

A pleasant blush colored her cheeks. "You sound like my brother," she said as the line ahead of Seth began to move. "He's a Marine and proud of it."

"He should be. Marines work hard, 'course not as hard as Army Rangers," Seth drawled.

Her brows lifted. "You must be a Ranger."

"Almost. I'm going onto Fort Benning next month to begin Ranger training. Looking forward to it."

A bright smile lit her face. "You must enjoy hard work and long marches then."

Seth dragged his duffel up from the floor, not wanting to be rude, but needing to get off this jet and his hands on his woman. "Not as much as I like taking the war to the terrorists and keeping it off American soil."

There was something about her, something innocent and unabashedly optimistic, that struck Seth. She was a lovely study in reds and browns with those cinnamon sprinkles across her nose, lush, moist lips, and enough positivity in her bright blue eyes to light the moon. Her fist came up as she leveled her knuckles and smacked his bicep playfully, a sure sign she had brothers. "As Cord would say, give 'em hell, soldier boy."

"Your older brother?" Seth asked, just to make conversation when the line ahead stalled yet again. *For Pete's sake, people. Exiting a plane isn't rocket science.*

She gave him a proud smile. "One and only. USMC Lance Corporal Cord Shepherd. You remind me of him."

"Oh, yeah? Where's he stationed?"

"Twenty-Nine Palms at the moment, but he'll get orders to deploy soon. Least he's hoping."

"Ah, California. You're a West Coast girl."

"I am, born and raised, but I live in Chicago now. You're from here?" A wistful tone had crept into her voice.

"Downers Grove, just east of the city." Finally. The last few stragglers moved to the front exit. "Take care of yourself, Red," Seth said by way of goodbye.

"Same to you," she told him, her blue eyes bright once more. "I don't want to see you on the news. No parades or headstones, okay?"

He sent her a grin over his shoulder. "Promise. See you next time."

"Plan on it."

Before he disembarked, Seth turned and called to her, "Hey, Red. What's your handle? You know, your name?"

The wide smile she volleyed back with was a good way to end this final leg of a long flight. "Devereaux Shepherd," she called from where she stood at the rear galley, chatting with another attendant. "What's yours, Ranger Rick?"

"Sergeant Seth McCray at your service, ma'am." He tipped two fingers to his forehead and told her, "Catch you on the flip flop."

"You take care now!"

With a cheery wave from his now-favorite flight attendant, Seth left the airliner behind and joined the other passengers filing up the Jetway ramp to the concourse. Making good time, and his heart light with anticipation, Seth passed them all as his long legs ate up the real estate between him and the baggage carousels.

Katelynn and his folks were waiting. Everyone needed to get out of his way! As usual, O'Hare's latest renovation ruled every corner. Dodging scaffolding and avoiding the workers and dust, Seth tried not to run, but a man coming home after four long months was a damned anxious man. *Move it, people! Move it, move it, move it! Happy soldier on leave coming through!*

He'd just cleared the corner at ground level, when—there they were, Mom and Dad, their backs to him, but a sight to behold nonetheless. His dad's hair looked a little grayer, but his mom looked real good. She'd survived cancer, and that was something to be proud of.

Breathlessly, he dropped his duffel, then walked up behind them and grabbed them both around their necks as tears stung his eyes. Nothing ever felt better than this moment right here. *Home, damn it. I'm home.*

His mother turned in his arms. "Seth. Oh, Seth. God, I'm… I'm so sorry." That was Mom, forever apologizing for things out of her control, like the rain or the humidity. Stuff like that.

"I'm home, Mom," he told her. "Two weeks. I've got two weeks!"

"Son." The way his father said that one word, stopped Seth's heart. Maxwell McCray had an inch on his son, but he seemed smaller today. Diminished.

Seth's mouth went dry. He stuck a hand on his dad's shoulder. "Dad? What?"

His mother choked a sob, the back of her hand to her mouth. "There's been an accident, honey. Katelynn and her parents… They were on their way to the airport, but…" Tears filled her eyes. "I'm so sorry. She had everything arranged. She wanted to surprise you. Bethie, her sister was her maid of honor. She'd asked Elliot to be your best man. You know how close you two are, and she thought… she thought…"

Maid of honor? Best man? Whose wedding was she going to today? Seth cut his mom's rambling short. Nothing she said made sense anyway. "Mom, where's Katelynn? She's supposed to be here." He glanced over his mom's shoulder to find his girl's pretty face in the crowd.

"Katelynn and her parents were in an accident on their way to the airport," his father said sadly. "I'm sorry, son, but she's…" He swiped a hand over his face, swallowed hard and said, "We just got word from Bethie. She was in the vehicle with Katelynn, too. Katelynn's… Seth, I'm so sorry. Katelynn's gone."

The concourse rocked with that one word.

Gone…

Gone…

Gone…

And Seth went down.

Chapter One

He groaned in his sleep like he had every night since it happened. Once again, the nightmare turned fluid and three-dimensional. Real. He could smell it. He could taste it. The walls of Uncle George's oceanside shack heaved, holding their breaths as if in anticipation. Even the ceiling had something to say, its groans guttural, almost threatening as it flexed and drooled down on him like a wet-mouthed fiend. Drawing close. Receding. Reminding. Forever reminding…

Groggy with little sleep, Seth batted the foul monster away. In its wake, the stench of beer, pizza, cigarette smoke, and sweat spilled like dirty water across a hardwood floor that wasn't really there. Not in Florida. Yet it ebbed and flowed. Forward and aft. Aft then forward. Always moving.

Seasickness threatened, yet the nausea was more of whiskey than of nightmare. Too bad that half bottle of Jack he'd commiserated with hadn't knocked him out cold. He could use a night off.

Seth drifted, lost in memories he couldn't avoid, no matter how much he drank or how hard he cried. All the Jack in the world had never kept *her* from coming back. God knew he'd tried. He just wished his nightly visitor were the woman he loved instead of—*her*.

Like always, the dream began in shadowy darkness. It was always too dim and nearly too dark to see beyond the faint glow cast from the amber-bubbled lampshades of Harry's cheap wall sconces. Groggy and mostly inebriated, Seth squinted though his eyes were closed, struggling to decipher the facts from the fiction of this never-ending dream.

Moving painfully slow, lighted figures emerged through the murk. Like the night it happened, these memories cast just enough light with just enough shadow to feel believable. Not like it wasn't hard to fool Seth. No sirree, Bob.

The noise from the packed beerhouse on Chicago's south side grated on the number ten migraine hammering inside his aching skull. His finger automatically reached for the scar on his brow. Damn thing itched when bad things happened. That was what made this dream seem real.

He was there again. Reliving the second most painful moment in his life.

"We shouldn't be here," he mumbled out loud to Elliot, the buddy responsible for Seth being at Harry's Beerhouse that night. He wasn't ready to socialize after Katelynn's funeral. Not so soon. But here he was.

"'S okay, bro," Elliot insisted. "You needed a night out. Chill. Have a couple beers. If you're not feeling it, we'll leave. I promise, man."

Once more Seth relented when he knew damned well he shouldn't be in any bar. But Elliot, one of those high-energy types, always strumming his fingers, tapping his toes, or bouncing his knee, was Seth's closest bud. After all they'd been through in high school football together, he was the one who needed the night out. Even now, his bright blue eyes scanned Harry's backdrop for good-looking women, chin nodding when one walked by their table, whistling under his breath if they passed his standards, which were low. Elliot loved playing the field and playing the game. Flirting. Just being good old Elliot.

Wanting to feel normal again, to feel something—anything—besides the freak show of grief and pain he'd sunk into, Seth had acquiesced under Elliot's nagging. So here he was sitting at a table in the center of the bar, more for his friend than for himself because that was what good friends did. They sucked up and they carried on. At least, they pretended to carry-on. What could one beer hurt?

Elliot had brought along three other guys Seth hardly knew, and that was fine. It gave him an out knowing that Elliot wouldn't be alone once he bailed. The four of them ordered a couple servings of club fries smothered in extra spicy chili, diced onions, handfuls of grated sharp cheddar, but hold the jalapeños, please.

In a big show of bravado, he ordered frosty mugs of Milwaukee's finest all around, then plussed them up with Tequila shooters, and encouraged his table to, "Drink up, mates!" Like he was a pirate on the high seas or something. Yeah. Elliot could be an idiot. Blind in one eye. Not able to see out of the other. Missing the greater picture.

Seth stared at his mug, not in the mood for the noise or the camaraderie but liking the beer. He wasn't sure he'd ever be in the mood for reality or normalcy. What the hell did anything matter? He swiped one thumb over the condensation dripping down his frosty mug, seeing Katelynn laid out in her casket. The mortician had done a good job. She hadn't been mangled in the accident, not like any of that mattered. She was still gone, and the hole in Seth's heart had fully eclipsed his need to live.

Yet, here he was, still breathing in and out. Still numb, yet in the worst pain a man could ever know. Nothing made sense, not why he was drinking or why he should live another day.

But right on schedule, like he had in every nightmare, Elliot complained the chili didn't have enough meat in it, that it was mostly beans. That Harry's cooks were skimping on the really good stuff.

One of Elliot's other buddies hadn't taken his eyes off his cell phone since he'd climbed into the rear seat of Elliot's king cab. The other guy stunk of cheap whiskey on top of rank body odor. A most wretched combination when mingled with the aromatic scents of beer and chili.

Then the night went bad.

A wiry, African American girl—she couldn't have been more than thirteen—ran into the place, shrieked a mouthful of ugly obscenities at no one in particular, pointed to the ceiling, and started shooting. Debris spattered over everyone. Beer spilled. Several amber bubble lights shattered. Tables and chairs overturned as most of Harry's patrons hit the floor. All except Seth. Like a white-boy Jack-in-the-Box, he'd jumped to his feet and stood there alone in the dark.

"Seth! Get down!" Elliot hissed from under his table. "She's gonna kill you!"

Seth just shook his head, not going anywhere. For sure not laying on his belly. Maybe because of his Army training. Maybe because he was still in shock and grief. Maybe because then was as good a time as any to die. He'd already lost his heart and his soul when Katelynn died. What did living without her matter?

The chick, who he now knew was Latoya Franklin, set her evil eye on Seth. A cruel sneer lifted her upper lip. She bared her teeth, and Seth thought she looked like a mad dog in that leather and chains outfit she'd worn.

Headed his way, she aimed and took two shots, but both went wild. At least that was what several witnesses said. Ducking her head like a cocky street fighter with a shitload of attitude, she'd swaggered up to Seth, and pointed her gun in his face.

But that was the law of the jungle for you, survival of the fittest. The fastest draw.

From sheer force of habit, he'd strapped on that night, his Glock tucked in the rear holster of his jeans. Little Miss Attitude failed to consider the possibility that he might be holding a forty-five caliber pay-back in his hand. It was that dark in Harry's that night, and a black, shiny weapon was easy to miss. Especially when you're young, stupid, higher than a kite on adrenaline, and packing a stolen POS gun.

She'd rolled her shoulders like she had something to prove, then snapped the pink-handled weapon under his nose. His muscle training took over. Like it or not, but yeah. All that hard-earned Army training saved his life. Didn't do much for her though.

The rest was history.

She went down with one in her forehead, another in her throat. But all Seth remembered was the terror in her chocolate brown eyes when the impact of his first round sent her flying off her feet. She flew backward, over tables and into the wall. Automatically, he'd fired again. The number one ROE, rule of engagement: Always make sure the person gunning for you is dead before you holster your piece.

But in that endless instant between impact and the cold hard truth, he saw the real Latoya. The one he'd never forget—right before the light went out of her eyes. Her tough bitch swagger and her attitude were just a juvenile mask. A disguise. A lie.

Latoya Franklin died scared and alone, something no child should have to do. She was simply a mixed-up, wayward kid in the wrong place at the wrong time, playing the odds, and believing the rampant lies told on the streets in her ghetto neighborhood. Her 'hood'. She should've been playing with dolls instead of with guns, but that was life on the hard streets of Chicago for you. A kid didn't stand a chance.

Five years. It'd been five long years since that godawful night, and you'd think after all that time, Latoya Franklin would finally leave him alone. But nooooooooooo. Every night, the lost little girl returned like one of Scrooge's three ghosts, to bug the living shit out of Seth.

An unearthly chill pushed into the room ahead of her like a warning from another world, his signal that she still had something to say. Icy dread came with her. Punching his pillow in groggy frustration, he groaned as her dirty bare feet dragged into his swept clean bedroom, scraping her heels, shuffling and whining, howling and moaning that she'd lost her shoes when he'd shot her.

Well, yeah, little girl. The power behind close-up ballistics tends to work like that.

The lament of the dead began with the usual, "It's all your fault!"

Yeah, yeah, yeah.

On and on she whined about how everything was *'that bastard Seth McCray's fault. Everythingggggg!'* How she'd never grow up like her *'girlfriendssssss.'* She'd never have babies or sweethearts, proms or a *'weddingggggg!'*

Not like she'd ever been decent mom or marriage material to begin with, not headed to prison like she'd been that night. In that respect, Seth and she were the same. Seth had no wedding in his future, either. Certainly, no babies. No sons or daughters. No darling wife smiling at him at the end of a hard day. Not even a dog.

Every last dream had died on Interstate 294's northbound center lane the day he'd come home. The happy times he'd been looking forward to with his girl? That kiss? Her hugs? Never happened. He hardly remembered the flight home anymore. Just the funeral. The viewing.

He didn't go onto Georgia for his much-anticipated training because he went to a funeral instead. He didn't become a Ranger, either, because he didn't have the heart. Everything good in his life stopped the day Katelynn died, and the night he got stuck with Latoya.

In his sleep, he scraped his fingernails over his head and ended up scratching the scars in his left brow, the ones he'd gotten in South America. He hadn't known Katelynn meant to surprise him in her wedding dress that day, nor that she'd arranged to hold their marriage ceremony right there in O'Hare, either. So, yeah. There was no joy to look forward to and none to look back on. Seth had no sweetheart and no girlfriend, no prospect of finding one, either. Those kinds of women, the good kind, came and went to other men. Never to him.

"You killed meeeeeeeee…" His lovely sad specter whined like pitiful *Moaning Myrtle* of J. K. Rowling's *Harry Potter* fame. Only, unlike Seth's ghost, Myrtle had never killed anyone, had she? Tonight's dire lament was more of the same, Latoya's avoidance of guilt and casting of blame. The bitching. That never changed. "I hate yoooouuuuuuuu…"

Yeah, well join the club. Most days I hate me, too.

It was funny how death changed a person, and not just physically. That night, all Latoya'd wanted was to kill, "F-ing white guys on her turf!" Now she wanted to talk. "I'm cold, and I'm lost, and it's all yourrrrr faaaaaault. Because of yoooouuuuuuuu, I'm still dead."

And yet you keep returning.

His mother's wise and often-spouted words sprang to mind:

If wishes were fishes, we'd have a fish fry.

And if bullshit were biscuits, we'd eat 'til we die…

Die.

Die.

Died.

Therein lay the problem. While Katelynn and Latoya had both died within days of each other, only this demented spirit—and he used the word kindly—Kept. Freakin'. Returning.

To chat!

"I've got news for you," he muttered out loud, stuck somewhere between REM, nightmare, and the haze of too much alcohol. "Good things don't happen to gals who kill people for fun. They get life behind bars, or they get dead." You'd think she'd have figured that out by now.

A new sound interrupted the ghostly rant. Footsteps shifted across the sand beyond his open door, telling on another nightly visitor. Latoya might walk the floors, she might pass through walls and windows, but until tonight, she'd never set foot on his beach. Well, technically Uncle George's beach.

Leave me alone already.

Another footstep answered him. Another muffled groan. Then a soft murmuring cry of distress. Real distress.

Seth jerked up from his pillow, his heart a pounding jackhammer inside his ribcage, his right arm automatically extended, and the nine-millimeter weapon from his nightstand aimed straight out the open door toward the sound of someone real.

Salt and sea, hibiscus and regret sifted past the billowing sheers, mingling in his head with the smoky, musty smells of that other night. Of other ghosts. Other deaths that never let him forget. Other footsteps. This might be just another part of the dream.

Canting his head, he drew upon his Army training and every bit of his sheer dumb luck to separate reality from nightmare. Long ago, he'd left home and Chicago in his rearview. Kabul was there in the dust, too. So were a handful of dead Taliban terrorists.

He shook it off as the memories of South America, another op gone sideways, returned. That easy mission had left him with more scars. Yet none of the people who'd died on those ops, not even his dearly beloved Katelynn, haunted him as regularly as this one little girl.

"I'm sorry," he told Latoya what he'd told her many times before, "but if you hadn't aimed that piece of shit pistol at me, I wouldn't have defended myself, would I? What'd you expect was going to happen? What'd you think I'd do? That I'd let you kill me, just so you could get more street cred? Hell, you had no business being in that bar. You weren't old enough. You should've stayed home with your mama" — the woman who, even now, regularly threatened to bomb Seth's family off the face of the Earth, if she ever stopped shooting up— "like a good girl, but no, you had to be bad like your bros. Guess you don't know they're all in prison now— where they belong. I'm sorry, but this death, *your death*, Miss Latoya Franklin, is on you. You drew first. Hell, you fired two shots at me! I defended myself. Get over it and leave me alone."

If only he could convince himself of that, she might go away.

Another non-Latoya-like moan hit his eardrums, only that one hadn't come from his not so friendly wraith. Un-huh. Someone made of flesh and bones was on his beach— sobbing.

Out the door Seth went, his weapon lowered, its barrel pointed down, but his senses flared, reaching out into the night for trouble. Could be nothing more than a couple college kids with a case of beer, or a pothead who'd lost his pipe. Could be a sloppy drunk who'd rowed himself in circles until he'd hit shore. The warmth of the Keys attracted plenty of vagrants, beach bums, and folks looking to get lost.

He'd nearly convinced himself that he'd been hearing things, that there was nothing to worry about, when a mournful, "He… he k-k-killed you," drifted across the beach.

He saw it then, a huddled mass of white beneath the shadowy cypress due east of his uncle's shack. A kid? A girl?

Hard to tell, but those possibilities drew him onward. Children and women had no business being out here alone. Too many bad things happened after midnight on these remote islands.

Lines of foam-peaked breakers crashed to his right. The full moon over his shoulder offered as much shadow as stark light. He approached the person stealthily. Quietly. From behind, just in case there was more than the one kneeling to contend with. It sounded like he, she, or it, was digging, the rasp of metal against sand an oddly comforting sound.

His six senses flared to detect an ambush or trouble, a habit learned the hard way after three deployments and one firefight in Chicago. Just because this was Florida and legally part of the States, didn't mean it was fraught with peace and goodwill any more than the murder capital of the USA, Chicago, had been. How well Seth knew. Hence the comfort of the Glock in his hand. It saved his life before. It would do so again.

His target, a petite woman now that he could distinguish form from shadow, knelt with her palms in the sand, her head down, and her shoulders heaving. Dressed entirely in white, a thick mop of silvery, shot-cropped hair topped the vision. A collapsible shovel lay at her side. Slowly, she pushed mounds of sand away from her, burying something or, God, not someone.

Not wanting to startle her or add to what already sounded like grief, he stopped short and coughed politely to announce himself.

Her head came up swiftly, and... holy shit. He'd come face to face with *Tinkerbell*. All this tiny thing needed was a pair of luminous wings and she could pass for Peter Pan's fairy companion.

Tugging at her short skirt, like it stood a chance of covering her knees, she scrambled to her bare feet. Her gaze fell to his weapon. As if caught and ready to bolt, she raked a hand over her hair.

"What do you want?" she bit out, hostile as hell, her bare feet spread, her weight shifted to run. Or fight. Hell, she looked ready to fly, and in that split second, he wasn't so sure she couldn't do just that. Her tiny fists came up as if she stood a chance of besting him in a donnybrook. Not hardly. He had her by a good hundred pounds and he was taller by a foot. At least.

Seth peered closer, not meaning to stare but needing to understand what he was seeing. Were those black streaks on her skirt blood or shadow? Was she bleeding?

Concerned for her safety, he lowered his weapon. "Excuse me, ma'am, but I'm not here to hurt you. Sorry 'bout scaring you, but I heard something, and I reacted. Are you hurt? Do you need help?"

"I had no choice," she told him, her chin up and her stance radiating defiance. "I had to bring him here. George wouldn't mind."

"George?" The lump at her feet wasn't very big. Couldn't be an adult, and the notion of her out here all by herself and burying a child, hurt Seth's tender heart. "Him, who?"

Her index finger stabbed where she'd been kneeling. "Him," she said, her voice trembling and tight, hoarse with what could only be grief. "He… he killed him."

Damn. She had buried a baby.

Chapter Two

Devereaux Shepherd stood ready to fight, not run. Never would she run from a bully again. Never! She knew she wasn't making sense, but she'd had enough of arrogant assholes to last ten life times. If this guy wanted his name added to the list, bring it on! She might be small in stature, but she packed one helluva punch, and she knew where to hit. Throat. Eyes. Balls. *Never strike first, but when forced to engage, always aim to maim or kill. Preferably to kill, damn it!* Cord's last words to her.

This guy didn't strike her as a bully, though, not the way he lowered that pistol and aimed it at the sand. But she'd studied life in the school of hard knocks. Looks were as deceiving as what came out of most men's mouths. They were all liars, but some were worse. This day had been the worst in a long time, and she wouldn't be shoved around one more time, damn it!

"You know George?" her midnight stranger asked, his head canted as if studying her for deceit. Let him look all he wanted. She wasn't the liar here, and she owed this jerk-off nothing.

"Everyone knows George," she told him tersely. "He owns this island. I haven't seen him around lately, but I know him. He's a nice guy." *One of few in the world.* "He wouldn't mind that I buried Gru here. He'd like that I thought of his island for something like… this."

Her lashes dropped to the packed mound of moist beach sand at her feet. She'd only chosen George's tiny island for Gru's final resting place because of its remoteness. George owned this tiny patch of sand and palms. Very few tourists, fishermen, or drunks visited it. Not only that, but this stretch of shore faced south to Cuba, and Gru would've liked that. And because she'd needed a quiet place where she'd be left alone for a day or two of fasting, praying, and tearing her hair out when her waitressing job allowed it.

A sob snuck up on her, lurching up her throat and out of her mouth before she could catch it. She'd failed Gru, and now he was dead because of her. Never in her wildest dreams had she expected to be burying his sad lifeless body, but now that she'd been caught in the act, she had to admit this was one of her crazier solutions for a life gone horribly wrong. Well, not completely horribly wrong. She still had Scottie. But Christ! She was in over her head, and so was Cord. He'd never admit to it, but she knew he was.

The guy eased his weight to the balls of his bare feet, still eyeballing the grave. "Who's Gru?" he asked, his voice devoid of the pushy authority most males in her life had led with when confronted with an angry woman.

Belligerently, Devereaux stepped into his line of sight. Gru deserved respect! Not ogling! "What do you care?" she bit out as harshly as she could. "Just go. This is none of your business. Leave me alone. I'll leave as soon as I'm ready." That ought to do it. Men—even armed men—hated mouthy women.

The annoying stranger wiped his free hand over his face like he was upset, but ended up cupping his chin, more like he was—thoughtful. Okay, that was different. Clean cut, wide-shouldered, and built like one of the panthers out of the Everglades, all ropey muscle and sinew, he took a step from her as well. "You're hurt."

The space he'd just relinquished spoke volumes. He might not be *just like all the others*.

"So?" she asked, annoyed she couldn't shake this guy, and that the mellow, baritone he'd used sent tiny shock waves coursing straight to her stupid heart. His voice seemed to have grown deeper. Kinder. *Well, too bad.* Once upon a time, she'd believed in fairytales, but no more. Men didn't wear white hats and they didn't ride in to save the day on dashing silver steeds. Every last one of them was an asshole in the making.

The guy stabbed both palms down his thighs as if searching for pockets, maybe his holster, but—he was wearing only boxers, probably because he'd been sleeping. He must've realized his state of undress the same moment she did. He took another step back, into moonlight. Seeing more of him was no help.

Her breath caught at the sheer wall of straight up male muscle. Moonlight glistened off the curve of wide shoulders, and instinctively, her nostrils twitched for the telltale hint of bug repellant or suntan lotion on that gorgeous expanse of exposed skin. Only manly musk, the slightest hint of tangy spice, and a definite hint of booze answered her call. Whiskey, maybe?

But those shoulders were massive and so was the thick neck between them. The weapon in his hand seemed to fit the image he projected. Capable. Confident. Not drunk, which only meant he might be a practiced alcoholic, adept at hiding his addiction in plain sight. That tender picture tugged at her heart. Proud men bragged about their drinking adventures, but she hadn't sensed that depth of ego from this guy. Yet.

The silver moon rising behind him cast his face in shadow, but she could see enough. Short, cropped hair topped his head, dark brown maybe, not black. Tattoo on his left bicep. No sleeve, just a simple—heart? She peered closer. Nine to one, she'd find 'Mom' inked in the center of that heart. *Who does that anymore? So, he's an alcoholic and a sap. Who cares?*

But scars. The moon also revealed thin lines of silvery white running down his biceps, forearms, and ribs. They webbed his massively muscled thighs as if someone had played a game of hopscotch there.

Calmer now, Devereaux looked with better eyes, finally seeing her intruder. He had scars everywhere. It was no wonder he drank—if he did. He'd obviously survived some horrendously painful event, an accident maybe, or an improvised explosive device, the bane of all American warriors in the sandbox—if he were military. Or torture.

Her heart softened at whatever must have happened to him. *Poor guy.* He still presented a definite wall between her and the ocean, though. Not that she'd run into the water to escape him, but she could swim to Molly's dock if she had to. She'd done it before.

Her tongue slipped over her swollen bottom lip as if it detected a tasty meal. This guy? Not hardly. So why was her brain sending wrong signals? Sympathy, maybe empathy for a stranger. Why the need to cradle him in her arms and tell him everything would be okay like she did with Scottie? Why should she care about this stranger now, here at Gru's grave?

Dev tossed her head at that notion. *I don't care about this guy. Not at all.*

He tried again. Patiently. "You're bleeding."

Devereaux shoved a hand through her hair, irked she'd been caught and had to explain herself to this, this—guy. How stupid was he? Stiffening her spine, she told him, "It's not my blood." *You're cute, but you're stupid.*

"Who'd you bury?" His question came out soft and curious instead of demanding or accusing. His shoulders shifted, angling his wide body to the side as if he meant to give her an exit should she choose to run.

That actually changed her mind. As big as he was, this stranger exuded concern for her and the sad crumpled body in the grave. There was genuine kindness glimmering in his eyes. This guy was no drunk or doper. He was just being nice, but she could use a dose of nice.

Devereaux decided she'd stay. "You know George?"

"Yes, ma'am, George McCray's my uncle. He had a stroke, so my dad and his other brothers put him in an assisted living home up in Pensacola until he recovers. Dad wants to take him home to Illinois. He can take better care of George, but he's worried the trip will be too hard on him. So, yeah. Pensacola."

Devereaux sank to her knees in the sand, the fight gone out of her. First Gru. Now George. He had brothers? He'd never mentioned family. "A stroke? When?"

"Three weeks ago." The gentle giant crouched in front of her, his hands dangling between his knees and the pistol now on the sand at his side, still keeping his distance and still too nice. That he'd placed his gun on the ground wasn't a smart move for a trained military guy. Cord's number one rule: *Care of your weapon comes first. Before downtime, grub, or games. You take care of your piece, it'll take care of you.*

But Devereaux suspected this stranger had done that more out of respect for her than for any other reason. He meant for her to trust him. What a startling revelation. Rude and crude, she could've dealt with. Not kindness and deferential treatment. Not from a guy.

"How bad was it?"

"Massive. He's paralyzed on his right side, and he's blind for now. But I'm not worried. Uncle George has always been the feisty one on my dad's side of the family. His brothers will take up the slack until he's on his feet. Just wait. He'll be back before you know it."

"Can he talk? Is he still sweet?" *Will he remember me?* Strokes were powerful game changers in a person's life, not only crippling once strong bodies with paralysis, but addling brain functions. Changing personalities. Destroying memories.

Devereaux wanted to cry for the gentle man who'd befriended her in her most desperate time. She'd met him when she'd first come to Florida to be near her brother. George had been her rock, and, yes, her salvation. *Why do bad things always happen to good people?*

His nephew's lips narrowed as if holding back more bad news. "You said he wouldn't mind you burying Gru here. If you don't mind me asking, how'd you know my uncle?"

She didn't blame him for not answering her questions, for withholding further personal information. Why should he? She hadn't revealed much, either. But lives depended on her discretion, and this guy was just here to wrap up his uncle's estate. He'd be gone the moment this chance meeting was over. Gone like the wind…

"I waitress at the Conch Shack. George is, umm, was a regular. *'One daily special, one extra-large conch chowder, and a frosty PBR, hold the glass, thank you ma'am'.* Everyday around four o'clock, he… he…" She bit back the words on the tip of her tongue. Everyone called him Uncle George or just plain George. He was the kindly older gentleman who'd looked out for her, and the first to tell her that she was a good girl who worked too hard. Who said she deserved better.

A tear got away from her, but Devereaux caught it before it let loose the flood she'd been fighting since she'd come home from swing shift to find a murderer in her backyard. Crying would make her look just as weak as expressing her feelings. The last thing she needed was this guy's misplaced pity. He'd already made inroads into her soul she hadn't been able to deflect. His kindness had to stop.

Yet when he turned to face the sea, the strong profile he presented struck her heart hard. This was no college kid come to play in the surf and sand. This was a proud man who seemed capable of taking on the world alone and whipping its ass. Square chin. Head held high. Shoulders back. A straighter-than-straight spine that indicated discipline and self-control despite his crouched position.

His nostrils flared to the scent of sand and sea, her personal favorite perfumes. His short hair spiked at odd angles as if he'd been sleeping, which stood to reason. It was well after midnight. His massive shoulders and biceps screamed power-lifts. He had to be military if that noble bearing meant what she thought it did. Cord looked that same way when he'd been in the Corps.

The guy turned, his gaze reconnecting with hers. "You stop by here to bury" —he cleared his throat— "things often?"

Her lashes hit the sand at his big bare foot, the other in the sand behind him since he was still kneeling. From there her gaze drifted up to muscular calves that supported the hefty weights his shoulders obviously loved to lift. No doubt this outstanding, entire male body was bronzed, tanned, and tasty, too. An inward cringe at what her tongue wanted to do with him rattled her self-control.

"I had nowhere else to take him," she admitted, her hackles flattened for the first time since she'd found Gru.

He extended his free hand, palm open as if it were a peace treaty. "Name's Seth McCray, ma'am. Sorry for not leading with that. If I had, we might've gotten off to a better start." The baritone notes in his easy statement rumbled over her last line of defenses. "My dad's Maxwell McCray. My other uncles are Michael and Matt, in case you want to check my story. Should be easy. They're old farts, but they've all got Facebook and Twitter accounts." Grunting, Seth scratched his eyebrow again. "Uncle Matt may even be on Instagram. I swear, the guy gets around almost as much as George did."

The mental image he'd just planted of three silver-haired elderly gentlemen posting Facebook memes curled the corners of her reluctant mouth. If he was as nice as he seemed, Seth McCray seemed like one of the very few good guys left in the world. He gave off no vibes of being a snake in disguise, so she took a chance and asked, "Maxwell, Mike, and Matt, huh? How'd you and Uncle George escape the M moniker?"

One side of his mouth tweaked into an endearing smile. "Mom's not into fads, and my dad always says Mom gets what she wants." Both shoulders lifted. "Or else I'd be Mark or Milton or..." Another shrug. "...something not Seth."

"Devereaux Shepherd," she said meekly, releasing a measured breath of relief. "My friends call me Dev." Why that blurted out of her mouth, she had no idea, but she couldn't call it back, so she grabbed the manly hand and squeezed it. He might as well know she always gave as good as she got.

The instant she made contact with his much larger and very callused palm, he had her. An electrical shiver slithered up her arm, over her shoulder, and down her spine. Her breath caught up high in her throat. *I should run,* she thought. Devereaux pulled her fingers out of his, blinking at the thrumming sensation that settled like a burning ember in the pit of her stomach.

How'd he do that? This guy wasn't dangerous—yet he was. Kindness. Like the sea behind him, the ebb and flow of his relentless kindness was on the verge of wearing her down. Pretty soon she'd think he actually cared, that she could rely on him, and it'd be downhill from there.

Seth seemed not to have noticed her reaction. He nodded at the fresh grave where one of her faithful friends rested. "You mind telling me who Gru is now that you know who I am? Uncle George must've meant something to you if you felt you could bury a friend... or someone, on his island. He was a friend, that guy you just buried, right?"

She nodded, the sadness of the night choking her. Whatever had just happened between Seth and her was frightening, but she *had* felt something more than male ego between them, not that she'd admit it. Not out loud. She was emotional. That was all. It had been a really long, hard day.

"When I first came to the Keys, he was the only friend I had until I met George." Gru was a hard-bought friend, at that.

She gulped, remembering. The ban on Americans traveling to Cuba had just been lifted. She'd always wanted to see the romantic side of Havana, so she'd foolishly saved her dollars and made the trip. Alone. How Cord had chewed her butt, when he'd rescued her, mostly from herself. Her and Gru.

A tremor rattled her bones at the memory of that last frantic dash to freedom. Now freelancing as an undercover agent, and rescuing women and children from the sex slave industry booming in Cuba, Cord had shown up with three of his former USMC buddies, one overloaded CRRC (Combat Rubber Raiding Craft), and a helluva lot of nerve.

She'd been so proud of him, yet scared for him, too. He'd taken out the three Spanish-speaking thugs holding her prisoner. They'd thought they were tough until Cord let loose on them. While he'd worked the guys over with his bare fists, his buddies extracted the three other women and four young girls Dev had been trapped within that filthy, abandoned warehouse basement. She'd barely had time to rescue Gru from the tiny wire cage he'd been stuffed in, waiting his turn for fun and games. Roland Montego, the master pervert behind those games, would've tortured Gru just to watch her squirm and scream. What a mess she'd made of her life, but every day now, she thanked God that she'd done one thing smart on that fateful excursion. She'd left Scottie at home with Trish.

"He came over with me from Cuba the one time I visited his island," she informed Seth. "We were a match made in heaven. He was quiet, watchful. I was Chatty Cathy." *And I still am.*

Dev swiped a quick finger under her eyelid to catch another stray tear. Gru had been pure joy and a true friend during her worst days. Realizing now that she'd never have that unique companionship again was a hard fact to bear.

"Listen. I have to go, but…" She bit her bottom lip, needing someone to confide in with all her beat-up heart and sad that it wouldn't be this guy. Cord would chew her ass if he knew she was out here by herself, talking with some stranger she'd just met and didn't really know. Again.

Seth's elegant brows dipped in a gentle V. "Shouldn't we at least give your friend a decent burial? Say a prayer or something?"

"No, he'll be okay." She gulped. "On a sunny day, he'll be able to see home from here."

Seth cocked his head at her as if he didn't understand. Endearing. That was the best word for Seth McCray. As ripped as his taut abdomen looked, as impressive as his fine, bare chest was, this tough man exuded a serenity she hadn't felt in a long while.

Plus, his boxers hadn't tented like most guys' underwear would have, which either meant Erectile Dysfunction or he wasn't attracted to women. Not that she cared. About Seth anyway. She had enough on her plate. But wasn't it sad when a gay man stole a woman's heart the way he did? Not that he'd stolen hers or anything even remotely like that, but still. Mother Nature had one twisted sense of humor.

Her silly mind wandered. Or maybe Seth was on some kind of medication that caused temporary ED. That would explain his lack of, umm, interest.

She breathed easier, relieved to be thinking about something as easy as a handsome man's libido for a change. But look at him. Seth was confident to kneel there so brave against a world that could be as harsh and unrelenting as a hurricane. The way he cocked his head as if he had to think about what she'd said. That adorable little boy glint in dark eyes she couldn't yet detect the color of. The way he'd squeezed her fingers firmly yet softly when he'd shaken hands, like he wouldn't think of hurting her. Like he was apologizing for frightening her. That, like it or not, he cared.

And that was the problem of the night. Seth McCray seemed to be as kind as his uncle, but he was too late to the game. What was done was done, and all the kindness in the world wouldn't bring Gru back. *Time to go.*

"You're a stubborn woman, Devereaux Shepherd," he said softly, his head canted again as if he had yet to unravel the mystery of her.

"Your uncle used to tell me that all the time," she admitted.

"But the authorities…" Seth murmured. "Shouldn't you at least inform someone that Gru passed away?"

"He didn't pass away. He was murdered."

"Okay, then, shouldn't we call the police to report his murder? You know who did it, don't you? Don't they deserve to be caught, arrested?"

Ah, this man. Dev's lip softened into a demure smile. "You think I'd drag a full-grown man out here? All by myself?" She should've led with that.

Seth's brows drew together thoughtfully. "That's what doesn't make sense. You keep saying you buried *him*. Was Gru, umm, vertically challenged?"

"You mean was he a little person? A dwarf?" She couldn't suppress the tease in her question.

"Not a child then?"

The sorrow that sparked deep within his eyes startled her. Dev hadn't stopped to think that he'd entertained such dark thoughts, that she'd buried someone as precious as a child. Out here? No one in their right mind would do that unless… Had he buried a child, his son or daughter? Was that why he wouldn't leave until he had an answer?

Reaching across the space between them, Devereaux circled his wrist with her fingers. Very quietly, she told him, "Gru's an iguana, Seth."

Chapter Three

"An iguana?" Seth sputtered. He hadn't seen that one coming. "You came all the way out here to bury a dead lizard on my uncle's island? That's why you're sneaking around here in the middle of the night? Because of a lizard!"

His sassy intruder withdrew her hand, which he shouldn't have noticed like he did. But it had been gentle and warm and—something else he couldn't quite define. One defiant shoulder lifted along with her brows. "For your information, I wasn't sneaking. How was I to know what happened to George or that you'd moved into his place?"

Point taken. "Okay, not sneaking. That wasn't what I meant anyway. But who buries a dead lizard on a deserted beach just so his grave faces south to Cuba? It's not like he can see it."

"I do," she declared, her chin up and a flash of something incredibly sexy in her countenance. "Gru liked to sun on this beach" —her index finger stabbed at the rolling breakers offshore— "when George lived here. Your uncle loved it when Gru and I visited him, and he wouldn't mind me burying Gru here. Why should you?"

She tossed her head and the sensual flame that danced over her face, lit Seth up. This woman had a fire inside and a temper to go with it. He conceded the match. "You're right.

That sounds like something Uncle George would do. And okay, I get it. I don't mind that you buried Gru here. I just wasn't expecting company in the middle of the night. This island's got nothing to offer but sun and surf. Where's your boat? How'd you get here?"

She folded her long arms in front of her, intertwining her wrists and fingers like a little girl. "I'm sorry I disturbed you, but it was the least I could do for him. Gru liked to run on this beach, and he came from Cuba. I left my boat tied to the dock, but he was heavy. I had to drag him." The tip of her tongue sliding over her bottom lip caught his eye, and he was hooked. The urge to bite that lip came out of nowhere. He couldn't look away.

"Damn, that's a long way," Seth hissed as his arm came up and his fingers raked over his skull. "That must be what I heard. You scared the freak out of me, and you're covered in blood. Least, the front of your smock is. I thought you'd buried a... a child."

"Did you...? Umm, I m-m-mean..." She stuttered as if no longer sure of herself. "Have you ever lost a... a...?"

"An iguana?" He shook his head. "No, ma'am. Had to bury my mom's Yorkie, but never a cold-blooded lizard."

"But a... a child?"

Oh, crap. She'd thought...? Because he'd thought...? Talk about reading each other's signals wrong. "I've never had any children," he assured her. *Wanted some, but that boat sailed with Katelynn. So, no. Never going to happen.*

Seth turned to stare at the endless surf crashing ashore, wishing he'd never come home that fateful day. Katelynn would still be alive then. But if wishes were fishes...

Yeah. No.

"Sorry," Devereaux said again, her voice as soft as the breeze off the ocean, pulling him out of his doldrums. "Gru might've been just a lizard to you, but he was my friend and I loved him, and I know he loved me. I owed him a decent burial."

Seth nodded, willing to give her that much. The loss of a pet was a big deal in his book, too. The tiny little grave under a stone marked 'Fluff' in his parents' backyard testified to the sap he was.

This gentle woman was still hiding beneath her earlier belligerence, though. Which posed the bigger question: Why the attitude? Was it just because he'd frightened her that she'd been so defensive? So rude?

She had the nerve to smile up at him. The look in her eyes hit him hard. The woman had legs from here to eternity beneath that short get-up, but the way she toed the sand and twisted her arms like a little girl hadn't gone unnoticed by Seth or his cock. Apparently, the alcohol had worn off.

But then she made it worse. "I can't believe he killed Gru. Scottie will be heartbroken when he finds out."

"Who's he and who's Scottie?"

Her lips thinned. "Scottie's my son. He's four."

Seth waited to know who that other 'he' in her life was, but the way Devereaux had ceased the information flow worried him. He was almost certain she was up against something or someone she couldn't handle, but she didn't yet trust him. He'd have to convince her.

"Never mind," she whispered. "I'm fine and Scottie will be fine, too. We've been through tougher times."

That didn't sound good. "Like what?" Seth asked. "Short of Hurricane Katrina, what's tougher than someone killing your pet? That's what you said, isn't it? *'He killed Gru.'* Who's bullying you, and why, Devereaux?" *And who do I need to talk to, as in with my fist in his face?*

A light flashed over her countenance, but just as quickly, her chin came up and the walls went down. She might've liked hearing her name on his lips, but she wasn't ready to share personal problems with some guy she'd just met. First things first.

"Coffee?" Seth asked, switching topics.

Her short, white-blonde locks swished against her petite skull like silver in the moonlight. "Another time," she said as she stepped one delicate foot forward. No shoes, like him, but that tiny foot was meant for a glass slipper, not long hours waitressing.

"Wait a sec. I'm wide awake now." He couldn't let her walk away. "The least I can do is see you home. Let me lock up. Be right back."

She shook her head. "No, Seth. I'm no weakling. I'm fine."

"And I said I'm seeing you home."

She huffed one short snort of—whatever. Indignation, maybe, but no woman was going to drop in on him like Devereaux had, then simply row herself home in the middle of the night.

She must've gotten the hint. With a tiny shrug which he read as compliance, she said, "Okay, but only to the dock shoreside. I tie up at Molly's. My place is a short walk from there."

We'll see about that short walk when we hit shore, won't we?

It took Seth no time at all to grab a shirt from his bedroom, slip into boat shorts and sandals, and lock Uncle George's shack, not that the flimsy hasp and padlock would've kept a determined scoundrel out. Uncle George had certainly lived a wanderer's life, but Seth intended to add smarter deterrents to the windows and doors while he was here. The world wasn't safe anymore. Hence the pistol tucked at the small of his back. No one needed to know he carried.

Devereaux stood waiting on the porch, watching offshore as the ocean breeze ruffled her hair. Now that she'd come out from the shadows, she looked familiar, but Seth couldn't place her in a specific time or place. Waifish and thin, she still looked like Tinkerbell, or maybe a surfer girl who ought to be riding the waves instead of digging up beaches burying lizards or stuck behind the counter of some fast food joint.

But her hair… Short, thick, and silvery blonde, it begged a man to thread his fingers into it, to cup her head and hold her close while he breathed in the scent of her.

And her lips. Drawn up in a perpetual pout, his tongue ached to lick them like a cherry *Tootsie Roll Pop*. Just once.

But that wasn't about to happen any time soon. Nodding at her blood-smeared hands and skirt to get his wayward mind back on track, he offered, "Want to wash up before we leave?"

Her head dipped as she took in the dark streaks down the front of her clothing. "I guess I should, huh? I don't want to scare anyone else."

Seth unlocked his humble abode once more, palmed the door open, and gestured her to enter. "I wasn't scared," he told her firmly, "but when folks poke around my deserted island, I respond."

"You're military," she said as she padded through his bedroom slash living room to the bathroom. He kept a nightlight near his bed, one of those motion-activated, light sensor, energy saving types that only flashed on when needed. Made watching her hips sway as she walked away from him a little easier. But those legs... Long. Lean. Tanned. And that butt swishing under her tiny skirt... Damn, she might as well have been wearing a matador's red cape.

"Army," he replied, dropping to the end of his bed and forcing a swallow down his dry throat. Everything about this woman tugged at his brain to remember—something. But it was too busy conjuring up sweaty images of him and her right here on Uncle George's bed. When the bathroom light snapped on, and she leaned over the counter to look in the mirror, Seth was presented with the perfect view of that tempting backside.

Don't look, his conscience warned. *Stop ogling. You love Katelynn.*

He nodded to himself. *I do, but...*

The faucet came on. "Are you still in?"

He shook his head, though she couldn't see him from where she stood, not with him still in the dark. "Gave up that lifestyle a few years ago," he said, ashamed at the growl in his voice.

Seth cleared his throat, surprised by the lust simmering in his groin. He wasn't a player. Never had been. Wasn't going to start now. He did love Katelynn. Always had. Always would. Yet his stiff neck still craned to see more of Devereaux. Her short skirt lapped at the curves of her buttocks, stroking one very fine ass and accentuating those long legs with every wiggle.

The shorts he'd just put on had grown exponentially tighter with every wiggle of the sweet butt bent over his bathroom counter. The sniper in his heart had already calculated distance and angle. He couldn't have peeled his eyeballs off her ass if he'd tried.

"Why'd you quit?"

Like a star-struck fool he asked, "Quit what?"

"The Army, you duck. Are you falling asleep on me out there?"

Never. Seth shook his head. *Oh yeah. The Army.* He swallowed every last one of his salacious thoughts. "I didn't quit. Took a medical."

That shut her up. Also shut down the rampant hard-on in his pants. Truth was, after Katelynn's death, he'd lost his nerve and his heart, and in that mess at Harry's in Chicago, he'd nearly lost his life. His dream of joining the 75th Ranger Regiment faded into depressing oblivion that resulted in a nerve-racking bout of Post-Traumatic Stress and one helluva long road to recovery. It wasn't until he'd landed a position with a surveillance company out of Alexandria, Virginia, The TEAM, that he'd finally felt like he was treading water again instead of drowning.

The guys and gals who worked for Alex Stewart were all former military, most of them elite snipers. They'd endured Seth's nervous twitches when he'd shown for work the first day. They'd even looked out for him in their rough, no-takers way. Best of all, they made him feel like he finally belonged somewhere again, that he was more than the POS he'd thought he was then.

Seth swallowed hard, remembering the first tough months with The TEAM, an innocuous name for a company as excellent as the one Alex Stewart had crafted out of a bunch of misfits. Two men stood out in the murk of that PTSD fueled nightmare: Alex Stewart himself, the former jarhead who owned the company and one badassed alpha in his own right; the other, Eric Reynolds, a former Navy Corpsman turned USMC scout sniper. They'd given him a chance and a hand-up, but more importantly, they'd respected him and his Army training. They'd helped him to believe in himself again.

Alex had a funny way of showing it sometimes, and not once did he hesitate to chew a new recruit's ass—Seth would know—but he never mollycoddled, and that made all the difference. From day one, he'd treated Seth like a man, not a broken-down has-been who needed a shoulder to cry on. The thought of any guy crying on Alex Stewart's shoulder made Seth smile. That'd be the day.

Eric had ridden Seth's ass hard those first few months, too. Kept reminding him what really went down at Harry's that night in Chicago. Kept him in touch with reality. Made sure he took his meds and never cut him any slack.

But it was the shootout outside Kabul, Afghanistan, a year later that had turned Seth back into the man he'd been before Katelynn's death. Something snapped inside him when he'd witnessed Eric take a direct hit and go down. He'd honestly thought his buddy had died.

In that godawful instant, the United States soldier deep inside of Seth had roared back to life with a vicious vengeance. Seth still remembered the blood-curdling scream that had poured out of his chest. It had burned like a roaring beast of fire—a dragon—igniting him from the inside out. He'd never heard anything so loud, so fierce, or so brave as the scream that came out of his gut that night. *His.* It was as if something had snapped to life inside him, and he knew damned well who he was—Army all the way!

He'd charged center-stage into that herd of sheep and the sneaking, bastard Taliban hiding amongst them. Seth didn't precisely remember how he got there, but he remembered killing every terrorist dumb enough to get in his way. Pissed at the world of liars and murderers, he'd dispensed a righteous load of American hellfire, and he'd saved Eric's life, damn it. Simply because that was the man Seth truly was. A buddy to the end. Not a has-been.

The other agents at the scene told him later that he'd killed quite a few Taliban once he'd let loose. They called him hero, said his reaction turned the tide on what could've been a massacre. Sadly, he'd also killed a few sheep. To this day, Seth still felt bad for the sheep. Especially the lambs. He was a gentle man by nature of his birth and the loving home he'd been raised in. He honored his mother and his father every single day. *But Lordy, Lordy, don't offend my family, my God, and for hell's sake, don't piss on my flag.*

A satisfied smile curled his lips at the thought of Alex, Eric, and the rest of the gals and guys on The TEAM. They inspired patriotism and a life that didn't suck every day. He had friends again. Okay, so he was still a loner and possibly a closet alcoholic, but yeah. Things were looking up.

Devereaux tipped her head and shoulders out the bathroom door to look at him. "What's with all the shoes?"

Seth glanced sideways at the stacks of boxes lining the wall by the door. "They're for kids. Know where I can unload them? A rescue mission? A women's shelter?"

She cocked her head. "You buy shoes to give them away?"

He nodded. "I don't buy them all, but yeah. I run a private charity. It's gotten bigger than I expected, but shoes are important. Little kids grow out of them fast. 'S no big deal."

"Saint Theresa's Church on Coral Avenue might be a good place to start." Her lips curved upward. "How'd you get tied up with shoes for kids? Weren't you going onto Fort Benning the last time we talked?"

Where'd that come from? "How'd you know?"

"I was on the same flight out of New York into O'Hare. We talked, remember?" She tossed a teasing smile across the room. "Don't tell me I'm that forgettable."

I thought you looked familiar. Cocking his head, Seth took another look at Devereaux. He never would've associated this version of her with the cute flight attendant who'd thanked him for his service all those long years ago. She'd lost weight since then, the once pleasingly plump figure he remembered filling out her airline uniform, now reduced to boyishly thin. Her long red hair was gone, replaced by a short, silvery bob. The bright, shiny innocence of that long-ago moment was gone, too. He recognized the somber darkness of a PTSD sufferer in her eyes. Whatever she'd lived through, she still carried it with her. He knew those signs, too.

"Your brother's USMC Lance Corporal Cord Shepherd. I remember now. He still fighting the good fight?" *Please, do not tell me he's in Arlington.*

"He's in Cuba, I think." Exiting the bathroom with a damp washcloth in hand, she looked through the sliding glass door and south across the sea as she took long steady swipes down her dress. No way was that stain coming out. It needed to soak overnight in cold water. "He was supposed to be back by now. He's been late before, only…" She drew in a deep breath, her tiny belly expanding with the effort. She turned and with a flick of her wrist, tossed the cloth into the bathroom, where hopefully, it landed on the counter and not the floor. "He's never been this late."

It was time to cut to the chase. "How did Gru die?" Seth asked, keeping his tone gentle but firm. "Who killed him and why?" *And what the hell are you involved with that you can't or won't talk about?*

"It was terrible. He… he…" She shook her head as the back of one delicate clean hand lifted to her mouth. "I never knew lizards could bleed so much, or that they screamed." Both hands lifted to her ears. "I… I can still hear him, Seth. He suffered, and there wasn't anything I could do to help him. I couldn't make him stop."

Make him, as in him, the lizard, stop screaming—or him, as in whoever killed him, stop? Seth wanted to know. Her teeth chattered at the end of that awful explanation, downright challenging him to step up. Lifting to his feet, he closed the distance between them and cupped her elbow. "Who killed him, Devereaux?"

She shook her head but didn't break away as he'd expected. "I shouldn't. You can't help me, and if he finds out—"

"If who finds out?" he pressed. "I can't help you if you won't let me. Tell me what's going on. Please."

"I shouldn't, but…" Her cheeks puffed with air before she blew out a deep sigh. "Sylvester Valentine," she whispered, glancing around as if merely speaking the creep's name would bring him into the shack with her.

It meant nothing to Seth, so he waited for her to elaborate.

Devereaux turned away from him to face the ocean. "Cord doesn't know this, and you can't tell him if you ever meet him. He's got enough on his plate, but…" Seth could hear her teeth grind before she said, "Sly's been coming around the Conch Shack lately, badgering me. He owns a couple bars on the waterfront in Key West. Beers-n-Babes and others, and he… he wants me to work for him." A shudder raced through her petite frame, shaking her so hard that she wrapped her hands around her biceps. Seth settled one firm palm to the small of her back—not to her ass, where it very much wanted to slide—but just to her back—to steady her.

"They're creepy, sleazy bars. I won't do what he wants me to do, only…" She bit her bottom lip long and hard enough that a tiny spot of blood welled off-center of the perfect Cupid's bow. "I may have no choice."

"Never give in to a bully," Seth told her, his focus stuck on that tiny, glistening bead of red that her lovely profile offered. "There's always a choice. I'm here now and if you need me to—"

Turning, she shushed him with one petite fingertip to his mouth. The tiny drop slipped over the edge of her lip and wound its way down her chin, unnoticed by her but not by him. "It's not your problem. It's mine. You've got your uncle to think about."

"So Sly killed Gru?" Seth asked around her finger.

She nodded. "I'd just gotten home after working the morning shift. I heard a squeal, then a strange scream. At first, I thought it was Scottie in the backyard, but when I ran out the door, it was…" Her breath caught. "My poor baby, Gru. Sly was half inside Gru's cage. He'd stabbed him. Blood was dripping off his right hand and knife. He looked straight at me when I came out my backdoor, and he said… he said: *'Tonight. Be at my place tonight or else.'*"

"Or else what?"

"I don't know, but I can't risk Scottie's life."

"You and Scottie can stay here with me," blurted out of Seth's big mouth. He licked his lips, wanting to lick hers. "Uncle George is in good hands. He won't mind, and I've got a spare bedroom. I can easily tend to his business while I help you."

She finally looked at him. The tough girl aura she'd projected faded into the soft feminine glow of a woman seeing a real man and possibly a friend, instead of a battered shell. Her eyes grew dark and too big for her face. Her lips pursed, in what he hoped was a prelude to a kiss, not that he'd act on it. *But I might…*

Katelynn's memory lingered, never more than a heartbeat away. He'd never sully the time he had with her, nor the promises they'd made to each other. True love linked lovers forever, and that was what he and Katelynn had had, a forever kind of love. He wouldn't have proposed marriage for anything less. Only… Devereaux needed his particular kind of expertise. He'd served as a bodyguard to other women on more than a few occasions. He lived to serve, and he very much wanted to serve—Devereaux Shepherd.

"I won't do that to you," she said firmly. "This is my battle. You can't just ride up on your white stallion and save every damsel in distress. Life doesn't work that way."

What he wouldn't give if it would—please—just for one day, work like that. "Maybe not, but I can cover your six and make sure this Sly fella doesn't hurt you or your son." *I can make the bastard pay.*

She shook her head, the tenderest gleam in her eyes. "No, Seth. Leave it alone. I can take care of myself."

The moment her lips pursed, Seth's pulse quickened. Like a sniper's scope, his vision narrowed in on the single drop of blood on her chin. He wanted to taste it. His head buzzed with temptation. Swallowing hard, he eased away and removed his hand from where it had no business resting. She wasn't Katelynn.

"You bit yourself," he told her softly, angling his head to one side, just in case. It'd been a long time since he'd kissed a woman, too long since he'd enjoyed even contemplating the act. Sure, there'd been the occasional grab-n-go at the local bar after a long day, but nothing and no one he wanted to repeat or think about later.

Her tongue slid over her bottom lip. "So, I did."

Softly, he wiped the offending spot away and squeezed it away between his finger and thumb. "You'd let me do that much for you, wouldn't you? Help you?" he asked, fighting the hint of hope in his tone. That'd make him sound desperate, which he knew he damned well was, but something about this fragile woman called to the warrior in his soul, to the better man. For the first time in years, Seth second-guessed the logic of having committed the rest of his time on Earth to a woman who no longer breathed. Did his undying devotion to Katelynn's memory make him noble—or insane?

"I should tell you to beat it, but…" Devereaux walked her fingertips up his shirt buttons to the hollow of his neck, her eyes on his throat. "I want to kiss you, Seth," she said, her whisper soft with need. "Now."

Chapter Four

Whoa, what have I done? Devereaux expected to be tossed on his bed and mauled with the pent-up lust simmering in his gaze, but Seth was something else. He closed the distance as if he were approaching a nervous filly. Not once did he rush her, but his mouth…

The man's mouth was made for sin and seduction, and she wanted it on her. Firm, moist lips glistened. He probably didn't know that he'd licked them as if already tasting her, but those simple gestures tantalized. Add to the mix the scruff on his chin, which jutted just enough to make him look determined instead of angry, and her stupid, stupid heart stuttered.

She'd had enough of angry men in her life. What was it about bad boys that attracted her like a moth to a raging forest fire that could never be tamed no matter how hard or how long she tried? Why did she continually put herself in this predicament?

His hands came up. Deliberately, he reached for her.

Devereaux had her fingers on his biceps even as she dropped her lashes, convinced she had a death wish the way she'd come onto a man she'd only just met. Seth McCray must think her no better than one of the many sluts walking the street, willing to spread her legs for any guy who passed by. But he felt too good. So strong. And willing.

Warm male breath skated across her cheek. "No, Dev," he whispered, the tip of his nose brushing over the curl of her ear. "This isn't what you want, and you know it."

Squeezing her eyes tight, she expected his tongue to make contact, wishing it would. Instead, he cupped her jaw firmly between both manly palms and tilted her chin up. "Look at me."

Shivering from the adrenaline spike that had just hit her system like a freight train, screaming at her to run like hell—as well as the delicious warmth of this guy's big hands on her jaw and at her throat—she lifted her lashes. Instead of the feral lust she'd expected, she saw the tender gleam of a question in his dark eyes. Maybe worry.

"I do know that," she whispered back, immediately contrite for her crazy heart. "I don't know what came over me." *You big fat liar. What came over you is your standard operating procedure. Your SOP. You trust too much, and you give yourself away too fast, girlfriend. Every time. One of these days, you're gonna get burned worse than you already have been.*

Dev silenced her inner diva with a mental, *This guy's different. I can tell. He's… nice.*

You said that last time, but look where you are now, hiding from James, stalked by Sly, but still ready to kiss some guy you just met.

Shut up.

Seth cocked his head, eyeing her lips because she'd foolishly run her tongue over the bottom one. "I'm not that guy," his mouth said, but the way his gaze fastened on her lips, she wasn't so sure who was lying to who.

His breath hitched. He blinked. With one swift step, he let go of her and backed away. "Are you ready?" he asked, his voice hoarse and tight.

By then her brain was as worthless as her rubbery legs. "Yes," she told him decisively. She'd taken chances before. Maybe this night with Seth would work out. *Three's a charm, right?*

He reached for her hand. "Good. Where's your dinghy? I'll take you home."

Oh. That. Flustered, she put her hand in his and squeezed to hide her embarrassment. What a fool she'd almost made of herself. She'd thought he'd asked if she was ready for sex, when he was merely ready to leave. "By the dock," she whispered, then forced a stronger tone. "I tied it at Uncle George's boat ramp."

With a curt nod toward the sliding glass door, Seth directed her out of the shack. Stepping on sand again, Devereaux drew in a deep breath of the ocean air while he locked up again. Striving to catch her breath, she stared at the wild ocean. Salt, sand, and freedom were what had brought her to the Keys. *Not sex.*

Gulping at the way the night of this damned long day was ending, she brushed a rebellious tear from the corner of her eye. No one knew better how sweet freedom tasted and how hard it had to be fought for than Devereaux. How elusive it was once you made enough mistakes. She hadn't been free since she'd hooked up on a layover in Denver with her ex-boyfriend, James Brand, a devilishly handsome co-pilot she should've avoided like the Black Death.

One night of sex with him had given her Scottie, but it also brought a migraine load of complications. James came from money. He hadn't needed to work. All he'd wanted was adventure and a way out of his parents' clutches. They wanted better for him. Not that he cared what they wanted any more than he cared about the child Devereaux carried. Not the high and mighty James Brand.

Devereaux sighed remembering. After avoiding her calls and dodging her at enough airport lounges, she'd finally caught up with him and told him he was a father. He'd argued, told her to prove the kid was his. When she did just that, he'd mailed her a check for one hundred thousand dollars. Told her to lose the kid, and then they'd talk. *The slimy worm.*

Talk nothing. She'd been smart enough not to tear that despicable check to shreds. For now, she'd tucked it in the simple white envelope taped to the underside of her top dresser drawer, safe and protected for the day he changed his mind and came after his son. Not that he ever would, but Devereaux couldn't take the chance. Sons of parents with money were self-centered, entitled, and unpredictable. She didn't plan to lose a court battle where influence and wealth could win over truth and motherhood.

In too few minutes, Seth crouched one knee to the weathered planks of George's dock as he dropped into her tiny boat. Turning, he extended a hand while the simple craft bobbed beneath his weight. Waves lapped at the timbers mooring the dock with nosy splashes. "Easy now. Step to the center. We don't want to capsize this thing."

That made her smile. "You think I don't know how to handle my own boat?" she asked as she accepted his fingers and climbed aboard. "I'm the captain here, remember?"

His face melted into a wide grin. Bathed in moonlight, he looked very much the epitome of a dashing and very handsome white knight. "My bad. I'm not used to women who can take care of themselves," he said as he released her grip.

She doubted that. "You didn't work with any female soldiers?"

His brows clashed. "Sure, but they're different."

"Do I need to carry a gun to prove I can take care of myself?" *Not that I've done a very good job at it, but still. I do know how to pilot my own boat—such as it is.*

"No guns," he said firmly. "You're the captain, I'm the bodyguard. I carry the gun. You drive."

"You have a gun? Where?"

"Always." Seth pointed a thumb over one shoulder. "I use a concealment holster at the small of my back. No one needs to know I'm carrying. Now, man the helm. Let's get underway."

That was unusually kind of him to let her handle the brand new, second-hand twenty-five horsepower outboard motor she'd recently purchased. She'd expected Seth to act like a know-it-all and take over all *manly* duties.

Dev took her place aft and grasped the tiller handle with confidence. The ocean was the place where she felt the most freedom and most like herself. She could dream out here under the capricious Florida sky, and this fourteen-foot fishing boat gave her that vacation from life every time she asked it to. With Sly bearing down on her, she needed those temporary escapes from reality. They kept her strong and optimistic. Best of all, Scottie loved their time on the ocean as much as she did. That little cutie pie was turning into a capable fisherman, too.

Shifting the engine into neutral, she inserted the emergency shut-off tab of the safety lanyard into the throttle control unit before turning the ignition key. As expected, her baby purred to life and churned water, bringing a small smile to Seth's lips. He nodded at her as if he was proud of her or something.

Devereaux gave him her biggest grin. It felt good to be seen as capable instead of weak. She'd learned a lot since she'd come to the Keys, but boating hadn't been one of those hard lessons, not at all. She'd always loved the ocean, and someday she'd be able to afford the rent on one of Molly's secured boathouses. No light-fingered thieves would steal her fishing poles then. She'd finally be someone.

"Hang on tight," she told him over *her* noisy outboard. Hers. Not the bank's, not Sylvester Valentine's, nor James Brand's. This little craft was all hers, bought and paid for, and that was quite an accomplishment for a single mom who worked an exhausting nine-to-five. Who owed her babysitter most of her paycheck. So, yeah. Dev might not be the best judge of men, but she knew a good boat when she saw one, and Bella was proof.

A chuckle lifted up from her heart at the name she'd given her boat. Bella, after Stephanie Meyer's damsel in distress, a girl who'd done extraordinarily crazy things, like dying for the love of a vampire.

Devereaux stole a sideways glance at Seth. He might not be a vampire, but the man had some serious, compelling charm. He wasn't thick in body or muscle bound like Hollywood portrayed military men. For sure, he wasn't John Cena or professional wrestling material. But look at him sitting there, facing the wind. His eyes didn't even water and his chin was up.

Yeah, Seth McCray liked the sea. She could tell.

Chapter Five

The moon lent adequate visibility and the ocean was smooth, but Seth kept an eye out for trouble. The short excursion from his uncle's island to Key West proved uneventful. Other than the joy glowing on Devereaux's pretty face, that is. The wind had tousled her short locks, bathing her forehead in moonlight with every wave they crested. She looked happy. Make that radiant.

Why her happiness meant anything, Seth wasn't sure. When she throttled down to an idle, the boat slowed as its wake caught up to it, lifting the small craft as it slid alongside a much larger boat on its way to the dock. He hated that this trip to shore was ending. Devereaux needed someone in her corner and he wanted that someone to be him, not whoever this Molly woman was and not Uncle George.

Yet Seth's promise to Katelynn had suffocated any hint of caring for Devereaux. They'd made vows to love, honor, and obey to each other. The marriage ceremony they'd never had would've been just a formality. That was how strongly they'd loved each other. To the moon and back. Lordy, Lordy, what kind of vow breaker was he?

Truth was he'd already broken those vows with a few illicit one-nighters. But they were nothing more than scratching an itch. He'd been drunk most days then, out of his mind with grief, and desperately grasping for something—someone—to catch onto in his downward spiral. He honestly didn't think those women counted.

Was he still faithful to Katelynn? In his heart, yes. That had never changed and none of those women meant anything. He couldn't even remember their names or asking in the first place. So, why'd Devereaux matter when those others hadn't? Better question, why were the vows he'd made with Katelynn in his head now when he hadn't dreamed of her once since he'd lost her? Latoya Franklin certainly had no trouble nagging him to death.

Maybe because he hadn't picked Devereaux up in a bar? Maybe because he wasn't drunk this time, and he knew precisely what he was doing? *Nah.* Seth shook those foolish conclusions off, convinced that once he knew Devereaux was home safe, she'd be on her own. He wouldn't interfere in her life. She didn't want him to.

The flashing turquoise and pink neon sign over Molly's Marina and Pub came into view once they cleared the larger, longer boat, which was actually a yacht, now that Seth could see it better. Long and sleek, its regal prow towered over Devereaux's tiny fishing boat. She didn't seem to notice. Deftly she handled the tiller, maneuvering her minnow of a boat into the empty space ahead of the whale of a yacht.

When she killed the motor, he glanced over his shoulder. Whoever owned that yacht moored behind her had better not run over Devereaux's boat on his way out to sea. Hers would be hard to see over that pompous prow. Again, it wasn't Seth's problem and he knew it. But still. She needed a fifteen-foot antenna posted somewhere on this little boat to announce her presence to the big guys. For that matter—he took serious stock of her bargain-basement conveyance—where was her ship-to-shore radio? A VHF transmitter? A walkie-talkie? The girl had no means of posting a mayday if the weather turned bad on her excursions.

"We're here," she said evenly as the motor cut.

"This rig licensed?" He had to know.

Her brows clenched. "Of course. What do you take me for, a—?"

"Then where's your radio?" he challenged, not believing what he was seeing. "Tell me you carry a portable with you every time you and Scottie go fishing. You do, don't you?"

Her chin came up and a smirk twisted her right cheek. "Look under your seat, smartass. I keep it locked up, right next to my bilge pump and my cold weather gear. Haven't needed them yet, but I'm not stupid enough to trust that some jerk walking by on the dock won't rob me blind."

Whew. Seth let out the breath he'd been holding, why, he'd never know. "I never said you were stupid. I was just… concerned." Concerned enough to bite her head off, this woman he'd intended to tell goodbye and never see again. *Good luck. So long. And all those other lies.*

Properly chastised for jumping to conclusions, he cleared his throat and politely asked, "How'd you keep this boat clean when you, umm…?"

Her bottom lip quivered. She knew what he meant. "I wrapped Gru in a plastic garbage bag, so he wouldn't bleed all over the place. It was all I had," she admitted, her tone flat and void of emotion.

He nodded, his nerves on edge now that he'd made a fool of himself. Scolding women wasn't his forte, but the image of Devereaux and her son alone on the water without any means of contacting the Coast Guard had made him uncharacteristically—tense. Yeah, that was the right word, certainly not possessive. Lordy, this little boat could sink in a heartbeat out there on the ocean, and no one would ever know.

None of my business? Bet me.

Chagrinned, Seth scrambled to secure the line, tying it good and tight while Devereaux tipped the business end of her outboard out of the water, removed the key, and slid its lanyard around her neck. He couldn't tear his eyeballs away as that shiny brass key disappeared beneath her stained white blouse to nestle—he guessed—between two small, but plump breasts. His cock noticed, too.

Forcing his stubborn male body to stand down, Seth offered Devereaux his hand. She grabbed hold, her fingers tight around his forearm instead of his palm as he'd expected. He gripped her arm accordingly. With an easy tug she cleared the boat, grinning when she landed off balance and one feminine palm made solid contact in the center of his chest.

And damn. Standing there looking up at him with the breeze whipping at her skirt, Devereaux was as slight as a water nymph, as ethereal as a goddess, and he had no business thinking what he was thinking. Everything ground to a halt. The planet. The waves lapping at the dock. His heart.

"Thanks for helping me tonight," she whispered, those fluttering fingertips echoing the pounding beat in his veins. For two cents he'd thread his fingers into her hair, pull her to his mouth, and kiss her.

"Night's not over," he reminded hoarsely, more to keep his mind on track than to warn her. They still had a short walk to her place, or so she'd said, and he wanted every last step of that walk with her. A tiny thing like Devereaux wasn't safe alone on this island or in this world, not at this time of night.

"'S okay," she murmured, her eyes gone dark and hooded, her lips pursed and moist and begging for a kiss. What was it about this woman that made saying goodbye to her not only difficult, but impossible?

Seth drew her into his arms. Devereaux turned her head and nestled under his chin, her ear over his heart. Unable to stop, Seth dipped his nose to the top of her heard, breathing her scent into his soul.

His love for Katelynn cried out, *'What are you doing?'*

Inhaling deeply, Seth answered honestly, *'Living. I'm just… living.'*

Chapter Six

Dev lifted her cheek from the masculine comfort of Seth's warm chest. He towered over her, but never had she felt more protected than here in his shadow. The universe seemed to have conspired against her, melting her resolve to be a smarter woman for a change and keep this handsome guy at bay.

"Kiss me," she whispered, begging again for something she had no right to expect from a stranger. Knowing his name made him no more a friend than the next guy she'd pass on the street, but could she tear herself away from this haven of masculine tenderness? Did she want to? Not. Yet.

He cocked his head and looked down into her eyes. His Adam's apple bobbed—just once—before he closed the distance. One big palm shifted to the nape of her neck as he covered her mouth with an oh, so tentative kiss.

Moaning from the sensual taste of aftershave mingled with whiskey, she let her tongue dance over his sealed lips. Not once did he squeeze her too tight or mold her to do his will. Not once did he push his body or his mouth at her. If anything, Seth was too nice. Too good. Until the barest manly groan rumbled against her breasts, inciting her nipples. Then Dev was in it to win it. Narrowing the tip of her tongue, she pressed it against those sealed tight lips. Playfully. But earnestly. This man needed a good hard kiss, and she meant to give it to him.

Clutching the back of his neck with both hands, she pulled him down to her level and leapt off the dock, wrapping her legs around his hips, matching her core to his belly. Surely he couldn't resist now. As if in answer, his palms cupped her ass, his fingers clenching both cheeks. Kneading her backside. Her libido soared.

Delirious with need, she kept up the assault on his lips until—at last—she breached his defenses. Just as she delved into the warm recesses of his mouth… Just as he groaned deliciously loud… She found her back pressed against one of the pier's uprights, and Seth's impressive erection against her belly. Sliding one hand over his belly to his shorts, she stroked him with the flat of her palm, impressed at the size and the heat of this man.

"Not here," he growled and that made her smile.

"Where then?"

"Who's watching Scottie?"

She liked that about Seth. He called her son by his given name instead of calling him *'the kid'* or something just as impersonal. "My girlfriend's watching him."

"Damn," Seth mumbled around her lips and tongue, one hand in her hair now, holding her head in place. "Guess your place won't work then."

Breathing hard, she mashed her mouth to his, needing his air and every last inch of his rugged male body inside hers. "Boathouse," she mumbled. "I have a key."

Seth took instructions well. With long strides, he cut the distance to Molly's Boathouse. After Devereaux fumbled the lock and nearly dropped the lanyard that held both of her keys, she managed to unlock the building. Hurriedly, he toed one of the barn-style doors open and ducked inside, bumping it shut with his hip. Soft lights glowed from one end of the boathouse to the other, bathing the placidly bobbing watercraft in dim, golden light.

Shivering with anticipation, she rubbed her nose into the hollow of Seth's neck like a cat with her very own catnip-man. The salt and the sea had never smelled so good as it did on his skin. Her senses flared, searching after every last atom of him.

He set her carefully on the padded storage bench that ran the inside wall of the boathouse, the perfect place for what Devereaux hoped happened next. Yet when Seth scooped her legs to the side instead of kneeling between them, when he sank to the bench and dragged her onto his lap instead of shoving her skirt over her hips, Devereaux's libido calmed. He wasn't as out of control as he needed to be. What was up with this guy?

"You taste good," he breathed as his tongue tangled with hers.

Arching into him, Devereaux gave Seth all he was willing to take, which seemed to be nothing more than kissing and heavy petting at the moment. His right hand now palmed her breast, his thumb strumming her nipple into a tight little diamond hard knot of hurry-up-and-kiss-me-now. But even that was done over her blouse and bra, not skin to skin. Except for her lips, he had yet to touch her like other men had. There was no groping or tearing of clothes. No sweating. No grinding against her like he had something to prove.

Aching for what she knew he could do to her, Dev rubbed her body against Seth, filling his hand with her breast and urging him to get down to business. She was no child and he was definitely all male. What would a little harmless sex hurt?

"No," hissed out around his busy lips. "I'm not what you need."

"Yes, you are," she told him, biting his bottom lip to prove she knew what she wanted. "You're exactly what I need." *Right here. Right now.*

"Devereaux…" he breathed.

Darn it! Seth needed to get with the program! Wiggling to face him, she lifted one knee over his lap and straddled his hips. Her skirt rolled up to her hips, offering him a look if he wanted to take it. *There, now. Much better.*

His dark, mercurial gaze drifted down her centerline to the dampening cleft between her legs and, ah. His throaty groan was music to her ears. Drenched and hungry for this timid guy, Dev launched a full-frontal assault, grinding her pelvic muscles up and down that fine rock-solid bone in his boat shorts. How on Earth could this big guy resist her now?

"I can't," he growled, his hips still telling her oh, yes he could.

"Why not?" she asked petulantly and annoyed to her toes. Obviously, he had no ED issues, and he certainly wasn't gay. What else could there—?

"Shit," she hissed, shoving to her feet, and fighting mad that he'd tugged her skirt off her ass. "You're married! You've got a wife back home and you… you're…" She covered her face with both hands, so damned sick of lying, cheating men.

"No!" Seth was on his feet. "It's not like that. I'm engaged only—"

"Jesus Christ!" She punched that big broad chest she'd just been seducing and let him have it. "One step away from the altar, and you're cheating on your future bride? You ass! How could you do this to me? To her!"

"I don't cheat," he said sternly, the anguish in his tone palpable. He reached for his forehead, scratching his left brow, the one with the scars running through it like a hashtag. "It's not like that."

Palms to her hips, Devereaux stood her ground. "You know what? I don't care what your noble excuse for cheating with me on your girlfriend is. Stay the hell away from me. I don't need the drama."

"Dev," he coaxed, his voice soft against the quiet sounds in the boathouse.

"No!" she screamed, stamping her bare feet to the dock, her eyes brimmed with tears that she refused to let fall. Not for this guy. The high and mighty Seth McCray wasn't worth her regret. She bit her lip and turned on him with one parting shot. "Go to hell, McCray. I was wrong about you. You're nothing like your uncle. God! Why do I always go for all the wrong men?"

Stomping to the double door, she flung it open and ran into the night. All men were bastards. They used, and they abused. They lied, and they cheated. By the time she cleared the end of the dock, she could hardly see through the torrent that her bitter reality had let loose in her foolish heart. She'd almost fallen for this guy. This creep! Worse, she'd been ready to give him everything. Like a slut, a desperate, needy slut. She sucked in a sob. *How desperate am I? Well, no more! From now on, I'm celibate. Like the "Flying Nun!"*

To make everything worse, she heard his footsteps on her trail. *Damn it, Seth. Why couldn't you be a good guy like your uncle? Why couldn't you take the hint and leave me alone?*

Furious and bawling her eyes out now, she curled her fingers into tight fists and whirled on the loser of all losers. Engaged! The asshat was engaged! "Leave me alone!" she yelled, blinking to see the idiot lurking in the shadows like the coward he was!

He stepped into the light. Only it wasn't Seth. Sylvester Valentine sneered at her. "Not going to happen, Baby Doll. I get what I want, and now you're mine."

Chapter Seven

It's complicated.

Seth closed the boathouse door and turned the knob to lock it. For the rest of his life, he had to be that better man. He'd follow Devereaux at a safe distance and he'd give her space, but he wasn't letting her go it alone, not at this time of night. He'd make sure she got home safe and then? He'd head for Uncle George's island. George moored a boat somewhere close by. Seth just had to find it. Along with his pride.

He'd hurt Devereaux's feelings without meaning to, but she'd given him no chance to explain. He wasn't a cheater, at least not in the typical sense. If anything, he was loyal to a ridiculous fault. Fact was that his heart hurt, both for the woman he could never hold again and for the one he'd let get away. For Katelynn and for Devereaux. What kind of two-timing loser was he?

Devereaux was right to be angry. In a way, he was a cheater, yet he wasn't at the same time. For years he'd idolized his fiancée. Put Katelynn on a pedestal. That was just the way he was made. A one-woman man to his core, he'd been ever faithful to the love of his life. Yet he'd known to his soul that something critically important was missing in his life during the long years after she'd died. It wasn't just her physical presence or the way her soft green eyes used to light up with love when she'd look his way. It wasn't that he'd never hear her breathy voice on the other end of the phone.

Nah. It was more than the fact that he wasn't just grieving. He was damned near mentally ill, and he knew it. If anything, he'd embraced grief as a lifelong friend instead of a challenge to overcome. Instead of grief counseling, he'd chosen mind-numbing alcohol to deaden the pain in his broken heart. It worked. He'd numbed his heart all right, but in choosing that course of action, he'd also pushed everyone away, including his parents. He'd withdrawn because, well, hell. Losing Katelynn hurt, and he never wanted to feel that kind of bad again.

But the feisty woman marching away from him was alive and vibrant. Maybe a little headstrong and foolish, but a flesh and blood woman with needs and wants. She'd made him feel something he hadn't felt in years. She needed him. He could tell, but what'd he do? Revert into a moron the moment things got too hot to handle. And Devereaux was hot. He could still taste her lips. If she'd let him, he wanted to taste a lot more.

Seth quickened his steps. A man shouldn't waste away, pining for a ghost he could never have, while the world went on without him, damn it. That was what he'd been doing. Pining. Dying a little more each day. Drinking alone and crying in his beer, wine, whiskey—whatever—like a pansy-assed fool. Being stupid and turning himself into a martyr.

For the first time, Seth weighed his loss against others and found himself wanting in the buck-up department. His best buddy Eric had lost his only child, a daughter. Had he quit living and giving back? Hell, no.

Seth's boss Alex had lost a young daughter, too. Kelsey, his pretty wife had lost both of her sons before she'd met Alex. Yet all three had managed to get on with their lives. They weren't drunks and losers. They were valiant, that was what they were. They were brave. Courageous in the face of incredible personal loss. In Kelsey's case, she'd overcome the brutal murder of her children and became the face behind the movement in the District that helped get street kids into warm shelters. Had she given up and wallowed in her beer? Another hell, no.

'*Stop being a damned crybaby, McCray.*' Alex Stewart's precise words had he been there. 'Course, he would've peppered that order with a few colorful expletives. Might even toss a chair out his window to emphasize his point. Seth knew it to his soul. The *poor me* shit had to stop.

But how did a man put what he'd thought was his one eternal love on hold long enough to make a meaningful course correction back to the real world? How did one renege on the everlasting vows made in the reverent wintery woods behind his parents' house on a still December night?

The moment he'd given Katelynn the diamond ring still called to Seth. It might sound crazy, but they'd loved each other since grade school. Even as a young man of only seventeen, he'd believed their love could transcend the last bitter, empty years of life when one spouse passed away before the other. That it was strong enough to reach through time and space, binding them to each other for eternity. All he'd known how to do was to honor Katelynn until his dying breath.

Until Devereaux showed up.

"I still love you," he told his dearly departed, even as he trailed after another woman he couldn't resist. Didn't that make him a total bonehead, the prize of his heart in one hand, while he chased after another? "I always will, Kate. I don't know how to do anything else. Only…" Dare he say it? "I'm lonely, sweetheart. I miss you every day, but I'm dying here without you. I can't live alone like this day after day. This isn't living, it's…." *It's Hell, one damned long, winding road into Hell.*

His gaze dropped to the weathered planks leading him onward and into temptation. "I'm worthless without you, and I hate feeling this way, like I'm cheating on you. I'm sorry if I let you down tonight, but…" *As Mom would say, rip it off like a Band-Aid. Get it out in the open. Spit it out.* "I have to move on."

Instead of ghostly cries of protest like Latoya would've shrilled, Seth's ears picked up the soft shuffle of heavy shoes on the dock ahead of him, punctuated by the quiet slap of bare feet. He quickened his steps in time to see some guy following Devereaux. Around two-fifty in weight, maybe five-nine in height, the guy ran a hand over the slicked black hair streaming down his neck and over his shoulders. Petting himself.

Seth caught the last of the guy's taunt. "…happen, Baby Doll. I get what I want, and now you're mine."

We'll see about that. "Devereaux! There you are," Seth called out, loud and clear. "Wait up!"

Already turned around and now facing both men, she looked like a deer caught in a hunter's crosshairs. Devereaux's gaze skated between Seth and the stranger between them. Her eyes were wide, and her chin was up.

She'd already canted her body to the side and braced her feet. Damn, the little thing's fists were clenched. She was frightened, but she meant to fight this creep.

Or she means to fight me.

Seth brooked no argument, just hurried past the intruder and straight to her side. She might not like him at the moment, but there was no way he'd let her face this jerk alone. Planting a hurried kiss to her temple, he wrapped one arm around her waist and flattened her to his hip and thigh, keeping a sharp eye on the intruder. "Thought we were going to your place, hon?" he asked her sincerely. "Told you I'd just be a minute. Why didn't you wait?"

Tension coiled in her body. The poor thing trembled like a reed in the wind, but he caught her sharp intake of breath. "Um, yeah," she said, following his lead. One sweaty, twitchy palm settled at the center of his chest as she turned into him, molding her body to his. "It's about time you caught up. Thought I'd lost you for a minute there."

"Not happening." Seth gave the stranger his chin. "Anything I can do for you, buddy?"

Dark, shrewd eyes scanned Seth from the dock up, but the guy was smart enough to keep his distance. He must only bully women and children. Smaller things that couldn't fight back.

"Nothing tonight, but thanks for the offer," he replied, his tone as smooth as twenty weight oil on a steaming pile of shit. "Baby Doll and I go way back. Just looking out for my talent."

"I'm not your talent," she corrected, swallowing hard enough that Seth could hear the gulp. "And stop with the Baby Doll crap, Sly. Take a hike. I've told you no, and I mean it. I won't work for you, not this week. Not next. Not ever." She ended with one short stamp of her bare foot.

Figures. Sly Valentine. The creep who thought he was tough because he owned a few bars. The guy muscling her to work—probably on her back—for him. So not happening.

Seth extended a hand to said douche bag but kept his tone low and sharp enough to cut nails. Devereaux had backup now. Valentine needed to understand that, here and now. "Name's Seth McCray, Valentine. Former Army Sergeant Seth McCray. I've heard about you. Good to finally meet the guy who's been looking out for *my Devereaux*." It felt damned good saying those two words. Saying it out loud made it seem real and right. *My Devereaux.*

Valentine offered a dark scowl instead of his hand.

Fine by me. Seth dropped the polite invitation to squeeze the shit out of the guy's fingers. A little power play between real men was standard operating procedure between the ranks. Never let it be said Seth McCray couldn't hold his own in a test of wills.

"Later," Valentine muttered, inclining his head to Devereaux like the gentleman he wasn't.

"Never," she spat at him, still trembling and her voice shaky. "Leave me alone, Sly. I mean it. I'm not working for you. You're a murderer."

The pig grunted. "That lizard bit me."

"Because you had no business in his cage. You killed him!"

Seth kept his splayed hand at the small of Devereaux's back, where it felt like it belonged. Not on her ass like he'd done before, but where she'd know he was a gentleman who respected women.

"Simply eliminating an obstacle," Sly rumbled, his gaze raking over Devereaux. "That's what I do. Trust me. You'll see."

"Back off," Seth growled, tracking Sly's every move with his eyes as well as his twitchy fingers. In a heartbeat, he could have his pistol up and on target. No doubt this punk had a blade hidden somewhere on his person. Sly was the kind of coward who stabbed people in the back.

The pig grunted again but kept on moving. Once certain that Valentine was gone, Seth buried his nose in the side of Devereaux's head and whispered, "Which way to your place?"

A quiet groan vibrated through her chest, the shivering one still pressed tight against him. "I can't do this," she told him, the edge in her voice set hard. "You're as bad as Sly. Go back to your island, Seth. Leave me alone."

That hurt. Before he gave his mouth license to speak, he blurted, "She's dead. My fiancée's been dead for five years, but I... I just..." Saying goodbye was harder than he'd expected. "I can't seem to let her go. In my head... I still love her, but I know it's time."

Devereaux eased out from where she'd settled under his chin to stare up at him. Her hands dropped to his hips. Sad blue eyes blinked at him. "She's... she's been dead for five years? But I thought you said... The way you talked back there..." Her brows collided and blink, blink, blink. "Five years?" she asked again, her tone incredibly—incredulous. "What are you, crazy?"

"Yeah. That's me." *Crazy. The biggest idiot on the East Coast. Maybe borderline insane. Maybe just a fool.* He didn't know which, his hands still gently holding onto her shivering shoulders.

Hell, everyone he worked with knew he'd been inconsolable since Katelynn died. For a long time, he'd been the guy no one wanted to work with, but he'd overcome so much since then. If Devereaux Shepherd was strong enough to take a chance on him, maybe—just maybe—he could let this impossible dream of honoring his vows with his fiancée, which, now that he thought about it, had been driving him to the brink of insanity for far too long, go. Maybe with Devereaux in his life, he could move on.

"It's just that, I'd loved her all my life. She was my girlfriend since kindergarten. When she died, I took it, umm, really hard." *The understatement of the year.*

At least Devereaux hadn't slapped him yet. Her fingers still fluttered over his chest even as angry as she was.

Seth kept explaining. "I didn't want to go on living, but then I killed that gangbanger girl in the bar in Chicago, and I—"

Suddenly, Devereaux was out of reach and he was holding an armful of air. "You did what?!"

Instead of retreating from this strong, beautiful pixie, Seth stepped toward her. "This is going to sound crazy, and I know I'm making a mess of explaining things, but yeah." He ran a hand over his head and ended scratching his brow. "Self-defense. Happened about a week after Katelynn died. I was in a bar with my buddies, drowning my sorrow. You know the drill. But then some chick, Latoya Franklin, showed up with a stolen gun and started shooting the place up. She took two shots at me and missed, but I… didn't. The police took my statement after it was over, but they didn't arrest me, and I was never charged. Latoya had a rep and a mile-long rap sheet. They knew her. Said I was a hero. That I saved her from killing anyone, maybe everyone in Harry's Bar that night."

Devereaux cocked her head as if trying to understand. "How exactly did she die?"

Oh, that. Seth swallowed hard. Latoya's death was nothing to be proud of. "Double tap. She never felt a thing."

Devereaux took a step into him, not yet touching him, but close. "Not her. I meant your fiancée. Katelynn."

Oh, damn. Her. His tongue ran one lap over his dry lips. "Car crash. On the freeway outside O'Hare. I had a couple weeks leave. She was on her way to the airport to m-marry me." His gaze dropped to Devereaux's pretty bare toes. "I loved her, but…"

And there he stopped, convinced he was the biggest loser of all losers. It was time to let Devereaux get on with her life. She didn't want someone like him in it. Didn't need the trouble.

"You know what?" he asked no one in particular as he looked over her shoulder to the channel that would lead him to open water. It'd be dawn soon. Might be time for a long, tiring swim. "I need a drink." *Maybe two.*

"No, Seth," she murmured, just before she launched herself into his arms. "What you need," she said as she kissed the hell out of him, "is this."

Dear Lord, please let this be real. Seth held on tight while she nipped at his lips, urging him back into this crazy thing called life with every stroke of her tongue and every bite of her teeth. For the first time in years, passion roared to a fever pitch in his veins. He allowed his tongue to tangle with hers as he tasted the fierce sweetness of her. A throbbing beat to protect and serve this audacious woman, to make love to her and never let her go, throbbed in his head.

Finally, she swallowed hard. Her fingertips tickling him with her nervousness. "You're something else, Seth McCray."

"I'm sorry," he said, and he meant it. "I loved Katelynn, and back there" —he nodded in the direction of Molly's Boathouse— "I wasn't sure which was worse, cheating on the woman I swore I'd love for all eternity, or watching you walk away. I honestly didn't know how much I've missed until you left me standing there like a jerk, but" —he licked his lips, striving to choose the right words at all times— "May I please walk you home, Devereaux Shepherd? I won't come in. I just need to know you'll be safe tonight."

She didn't answer, just leaned her soft body into his, even as her slender arms snaked around his neck. In exchange for the trust she'd given him, Seth let loose the quixotic burden he'd been carrying ever so carefully. Ever so valiantly. From sea to shining sea. For too damned long.

Katelynn was gone. It was time to let her go. With a shuddering sigh, Seth finally did just that. He bowed his nose to the top of Devereaux's head and, in his heart, he whispered, *'Goodbye Kate. I'll always love you, but I'm not dead and I'm sorry, but I have to live while I'm here.'*

Instant relief flooded the depths of his weary soul, releasing the wreck that had been his heart to the freedom of the night sky. *So, this is what the last step of grief feels like. Letting go. Moving on. Wanting to live again...*

"What am I going to do with you?" Devereaux murmured.

What could he say? The horndog in his pants certainly had very graphic ideas, but more than anything, Seth was a gentleman. He'd do right by this woman if she gave him the chance, but if she didn't? If this was just a stepping-stone to healing and better mental health? Well, he'd cross that bridge when he got to it. For now, he filled his lungs with the salt air and the uniquely feminine fragrance of the tiny fighter snuggled inside his arms.

His chin sank to the crown of her head. Seth closed his eyes. Letting go of Katelynn was hard but losing Devereaux seemed so much worse. Maybe even impossible. His fingers liked where they were in the middle of her back, and his nose craved the sweet fresh fragrance of her hair. It was easier to breathe with her in his arms. Life seemed—brighter. Worth living.

Yet tears stung his eyes. He swallowed hard as he said, "About that walk…"

Chapter Eight

They held hands the entire seven blocks to her apartment on Starfish Drive, a low rent district east of the city and away from tourist attractions. Seth seemed lost in his thoughts, which was good because Dev was thoroughly lost in hers. What kind of man hung onto the memories of a dead woman for five years?

She cast a furtive glance at said man. He'd lost his Katelynn around the same time she'd gotten pregnant with Scottie. That seemed to link them on some cosmic level where the universe maintained its balance, where lives were made, and spirits broken. To think that he'd lost the love of his life at the same time she'd received the priceless gift of her son…

Wow. Dev shook her head. The universe didn't work like that, did it? Take from one; give to another?

He kept looking behind and around them as if he suspected Sly might yet attack, but not once had Seth unlinked their joined fingers. He'd loosened his grip, letting her smaller fingers slide between his where they fit more comfortably. The man did have thicker digits. It was difficult to interlock hands with him, but he hadn't let her go. She liked that.

But really? No, really? Was this guy as crazy as he'd sounded back there? Was he for real? He still loved a dead woman? One who'd died five years ago? Okay, so she'd been his fiancée, and no doubt he'd truly loved her if he'd asked her to spend the rest of his life with him, but—Who. Did. That? Who mourned that long? Five years! What red-blooded male with an ounce of testosterone in his hot body—and Seth's handsome body was damned hot—could do such a thing? None she knew. Not even Cord, bless his rowdy, two-timing soul.

By the time she was home, Dev was certain of one thing. Seth McCray was a one-woman man who loved with his whole heart and soul. He was a rare and priceless wonder. And for now, he was all hers.

Finally beneath the trailing jasmine obscuring her front door like a fragrant privacy shield, her heart calmed. Inside this humble little bungalow of peace and hope, a little boy with bright blue eyes dreamed the dreams of the innocent while he waited for her to come home. Scottie was everything pure in Dev's life, and she meant him to believe in the goodness of others for as long as he could. Life was tough on fatherless children. She needed him to be little and innocent for as long as life allowed.

"This is me," she whispered to Seth. "Would you like to come in? For... for a cup of coffee or something?" *Maybe another kiss?*

He stepped in close, crowding her until her back was against the door. One hand settled at her waist, the other somewhere over her head as his forearm hit the doorframe. "I shouldn't. It's late, and honestly" —he drew in a shuddering breath— "if I come in, I may not leave."

Her head bobbed even as her thumb cocked over her shoulder at the door that led to her living room, a ratty second-hand couch, a card table, and three fold-up chairs. "Girlfriend. Trish. Remember? I'm pretty sure you'll be leaving."

A couple years older than Dev, Trish Crawford hailed from North Dakota. She and her husband of four years used to come south to the Keys every winter. When he passed away from a weak heart at twenty-six, she'd come south to stay. She said North Dakota held nothing but long, bleak winters, and she needed the sun. Because of his illness, they'd had no kids and she adored Scottie. If Dev could've picked a big sister, it would've been Trish.

Seth's brows arched, and her fingertips itched to trace those fine masculine curves and smooth away the question she saw there. "She lives with you?" he asked, his tone low and achingly tender.

"Next door, but she stays over when she watches Scottie for me." Dev would've looked to where Trish's bungalow butted against hers if she could have. She certainly should have. But Seth's head canted at the perfect come hither, kiss me angle. His gaze narrowed, and his mouth-watering lips were too close. Too tempting. Too warm.

Ah, hell. A whimper escaped. There was no way to resist this man. Dev lifted to the balls of her feet, tugged him into her face, and laid another one on him. His big body melted against hers, his hands cupping her jaw, and his thumbs soft and so sweet on her cheekbones. Heat rolled off his all-male body, and there in the Florida Keys on a hot summer night, everything inside her vibrated like a burning rattlesnake come to life, throwing enough sparks to ignite the world.

This guy was different than the others she'd allowed in her life. Gentle and warm, Seth's mouth covered hers, coaxing her to relax and enjoy instead of storming her defenses like a barbarian. He had scandalously delicious lips she didn't mind nibbling. Their tongues tangled eagerly, returning stroke for stroke. His air became her breath; the smoky taste of whiskey on his tongue, her new favorite flavor. She could've dined like this for hours and still been hungry for him.

When his teeth grazed the tip of her tongue at the same time his thumb skated over her nipple, then strummed it into a needy little knot, a bolt of pure molten pleasure lifted up from her core. Anticipation flooded her body with endorphins, hormones, and an outrageous burst of liquid lust. He played her like a delicate harp, plucking the string that connected her breasts to her heart to her core until… until… She nearly came in his hands. Right there at her front door. This guy was magic, and he truly knew how to entice and please a woman.

"Seth," she hissed, biting his bottom lip, and wanting so much more than just skin-on-skin. "Not here in the open. Oh, oh, okay then. Yesssssssss…"

There in the night, he gave her a full body press, his hips grinding against hers, his impressive cock heavy and hot against her belly, and his wide capable hands now tucked under her ass. Threading her fingers over his bristly hair, she drank him in, breathed him in, and handed over her heart, lock, stock, and barrel. Licking his lips and his chin, she relished the scrape of his one-day scruff on her lips and against her cheek.

Wanting that elusive 'more', her tongue trailed up the strong line of his jaw, and just that fast, her pleasure spiked to the stars. Like the winning Super Bowl touchdown, Dev tipped her head back and flew, the pleasure so exquisitely rare that she saw fireworks. Her toes curled with the sensual assault of her first, truly real orgasm ever. Fully dressed!

She unraveled in his skillful hands. The night exploded with wild, wonderfully wet fireworks that pinned her to the heavy wooden door like a butterfly, her heart revealed and hammering high in her throat. Like the lover she'd been searching for, Seth held onto her while her panting body settled back to Earth.

Unsettled at the power he seemed to hold over her, Dev lowered her head and swallowed hard. Panting, she burrowed under his chin. She hadn't realized he'd lifted her off the ground, but there she was, in the arms of one steaming hot guardian angel. Her nose pressed into the warm hollow of his neck, still drinking him into her soul and needing him more than she wanted to admit. This was a night of firsts, and he was definitely the best of them all. But man, he was strong. Her feet hadn't touched down since he'd kissed her.

The masculine scent of this gentle warrior reminded her of something she'd craved for too many years—home. Of security and strength, all the things she wanted for herself and for Scottie. Dev wanted a life that held more than a minimum wage job and danger at every turn. She wanted the heart of this amazing man with his timid, honorable mannerisms. The guy who, even now, held her off the ground as if he'd found a treasure he didn't want to lose. How incredibly sweet was that?

Trish needed to go home. Now.

"Not here," Dev whispered, her voice suddenly sounding as raw as the thrumming heart in her chest. Her track record sucked. Couldn't he please be a real man for a change? They were out there; she knew it. Her brother was a real man. Couldn't Seth stay the rest of the night for no other reason than he chose to stay with her? Not because they were each desperate for the other, but because she was his chosen one? His only one?

Breathing hard, his forehead sank to the top of her head, and Dev lifted her chin, searching for her reflection in his eyes. And there it was. Even in the dimness of her no-porch-light, one-step porch, a simmering intensity captured her looking up at him. But she also saw the vulnerability in Seth. Despite his rugged military vocation, this man truly believed in love.

"I like kissing you," he murmured, his tongue darting out to taste the tip of her nose. "A lot."

"I've never, umm, never come like that before," she told him truthfully, tears stinging her eyes and embarrassed at the echoing vulnerability he'd evoked in her. "Ever."

He was what she was. Alone in the world even though he wasn't, a loner holding onto hope in the face of insurmountable odds. Her own parents had rarely approved of her and they'd never laid eyes on Scottie, yet here he was on the doorstep to her whole world.

His chest rumbled with male satisfaction. "Good, but I don't want to cause trouble. If you'd rather I leave now that you're home—"

She shushed him with her whole mouth, whimpering as she clutched his head between her hands and swallowed his logical argument. This night and the emotions swirling in her heart had nothing to do with logic, and she wanted it gone. This was about the stars she'd just glimpsed inside the circle of his arms. This was about maybe—just maybe—having found the one soul out of millions who'd just made her feel complete and whole again.

"No, stay," she breathed. "Please stay."

Seth's answering groan as he set her on her feet was the best reply ever.

Chapter Nine

"You left your cell at home!" the Amazon warrior called Trish hissed the second Devereaux cleared the doorway with her hand still in Seth's. Tall, angular, and hopping mad, Trish stabbed a finger in Seth's direction. "Who's *this* guy? One of Sly's asshole buddies?"

"Shhhhh," Devereaux whispered as she tugged him into a sparsely decorated living room before she secured the front door with one deadbolt, two chain locks, and a padlock she slipped into an aluminum hasp. This feisty woman meant to keep her home safe, but those deterrents were paltry at best. "He's not with Sly. Trish, this is Seth McCray. He's George's nephew, and he walked me home. That's all. Seth, Trish Crawford, my neighbor and my best friend."

The compliment didn't slow Trish's wrath. Dressed in a gray T-shirt and jeans, the dishwater blonde had bushy brows and a nose like a honey badger, and all were bent out of shape. Seth offered his hand anyway, opting for courtesy instead of confrontation with this prickly friend of Devereaux's.

"Bullshit," Trish spat, her chin up, piss and vinegar in her eye, and her fingers clenched instead of accepting the friendly offer. "I'm not in the mood to meet your friend. Next time, take your damned phone with you, Dev. I've been trying to reach you for hours."

Seth lowered his hand to his side.

"Why?" Devereaux asked.

Trish lowered her voice, eyeballing Seth like he was Charles Manson instead of George's trustworthy nephew. "Cord called. He's bringing a boatful of…" If looks could kill, that lightning bolt of disgust she'd just shot Seth's way would've cooked him where he stood. "…of refugees," she finished lamely.

Seth zeroed in on her tells, the way she licked her lips. *Refugees, my ass.* The woman was lying. "What refugees?" he asked. "Are you bringing people in from Cuba?"

"None of your business," she shot back at him, her chin up. Turning on Devereaux, she spat, "If you'd keep your phone charged, he would've called you, and I wouldn't have worried myself sick."

"You know I can't always do that." Devereaux dropped Seth's hand. "It's an old phone, and barely holds a charge. When did he call?"

"Two hours ago. He needs you to be" —another evil glare slapped Seth upside his head— "you know where. Said he'd land at daybreak, might already be there. Damn it, you need to buy a new phone, one that works, before you take off again."

Devereaux shook her head, "Sun's not up yet. I've got time."

"Not if the sea's smooth and he made good time last night. God, Dev—"

"Trish," Devereaux said calmly, her tone brooking no more antagonism. "Scottie's asleep."

The honey badger's head bobbed at that gentle reminder that there was a child in the house. "Yeah, I let him stay up late. We had a good night. Popped popcorn and read stories. He wants me to read *'Old Yeller'* next time. Would you please take that crap off your bookshelf? You know I hate telling him no, but he's too young for that story."

Devereaux's shoulders scrunched even as she stepped to said bookshelf, a pressed wood creation comprised of three crowded shelves stacked to overflowing, a plethora of books upright and as many stacked horizontally on top of those. The woman had enough books on those shelves to fill another bookcase just as tall. A stack of dog-eared *National Geographic* magazines leaned against one side of the overburdened shelf. A long, narrow, floor-to-ceiling window concealed behind what appeared to be room-darkening drapes lined the other.

Retrieving her cell from the charger parked on the top shelf, she thumbed the keypad and lifted it to her ear, her bright eyes on Seth.

Whatever Cord was into, Seth had one of his feelings. His instincts kicked in and his sixth sense flared outward to detect the slightest ripple of danger in the cosmic web. That was the thing about being a trained sniper. Titled or not, ranked or not, Seth's instincts had automatically linked into the higher power that made him the kind of man he was today. Alex Stewart might've honed his hidden talents into a fine fighting machine, but the raw material began with Seth.

He took control of this two-woman show like the Ranger he was meant to be. "Show me Scottie's bedroom," he said to Trish, keeping the snap of command out of his tone, while he let Devereaux make her call in private.

When Trish balked, Devereaux lifted her chin from the cell and told her, "It's okay. He's here to help us, Trish. You can trust him."

Seth sent Devereaux a nod and a smile. Trust didn't come easily to this woman. He wouldn't let her down.

It still took a full minute of glares and stares before Trish nodded at the hallway to his right. The dim glow of a nightlight told Seth which one of the three bedrooms was Scottie's. First door on the left. Sure enough. The little guy slept face down in his pillow, his butt in the air, and his thumb in his mouth. Tow-headed like his mom. Cute. Make that adorable. Scottie snored, but the way he held that powder blue teddy bear under his arm, melted Seth's heart. The kid needed his mom to always be safe and sound. Seth intended to make certain that never changed.

"Backdoor?" he whispered to Trish since she stood behind him with her hands on her hips, her hackles still lifted.

Devereaux faced her bookshelf, her voice low and nearly imperceptible as she talked, he assumed, with her brother. Seth caught the tightness to her whispered question: "How many? How'd you manage that?" She groaned. "I thought something happened to you, Cord, it's been weeks." Then silence. Her chin dipped to her chest. She nodded at the floor and ended with, "Don't worry. I'll be there. You know I will. Keep everyone alive."

Turning, she caught Seth watching. "I, umm, have to leave for a while," Devereaux told him, her lips pressed tight and thin.

He took a step in her direction, then stopped when her bright blue eyes darkened, and that was the last straw. If these gals were running refugees out of Cuba, they were in over their heads. What the hell was Cord thinking? Using two women on a dangerous operation? *Not smart, man.*

"What's going on?" Seth asked. "Tell me now. I can help." Legal or not, he wouldn't let her fend for herself, not with Valentine prowling the streets and apparently keeping close enough tabs on her that he'd known she'd be on the pier tonight. Had he followed her to George's island? Tiny hairs bristled up the back of Seth's neck at that very real possibility. "Is Valentine in on this? Is that what he's holding over your head? You're running refugees up from Cuba, aren't you? Political prisoners? How's Valentine involved?"

Devereaux's gaze collided with Trish's, then volleyed back to Seth like a ball in a tennis match. He cocked his head waiting for one of them to speak. Crossing his arms over his chest, he spread his feet and settled in for the duration. "Well, ladies?"

"Not refugees," Devereaux said quietly, her eyes darting around her small room as if the walls had ears. "I don't know what Sly's doing besides running those tacky bars, but Cord makes a run to Cuba every time he gets a call from one of his contacts in Havana. Probably Miguel Rohos, he's the most honest of the four."

Trish snorted. "Only because Cord pays him by the head."

"True, but he has to take who he can, when the time's right," Devereaux murmured, an ocean of deep blue pleading in her eyes. "Seth, you have to understand. My brother rescues girls and women from the human traffickers. Havana's ripe for the taking and the streets are rampant with them. You know that. I have to go meet him. Something's not

right. I could hear it in his voice. You can come with me or—
"

"I'm going," he told her with certainty. "My boat or yours?"

Her eyes widened. "You've got a boat? Where?"

"Uncle George kept one somewhere near Molly's Boathouse. I guess it's still there, and knowing George, the keys are in the ignition or under the floor mat." Seth held out his hand to her, his palm open in invitation. "Coming with me?"

She scowled. "Why didn't you tell me that when we were in there?"

"What were you doing in the boathouse?" Trish barked.

"Nothing," Devereaux murmured, color blossoming up her neck and spilling over her cheeks. She ran a quick hand over her short locks, biting her lip and staring at his hand. "Trish, you'll stay here until I'm back, won't you?"

The Amazonian grunted like a man. "Don't I always? Go. Take this guy with you. Scottie and I will be okay, but be careful, Dev. I don't like stitching up little girls."

Little girls? This nightmare kept getting worse. Seth waggled his fingers, needing Devereaux to latch onto him. To trust him like he trusted her.

With one last sideways glance at Trish, Devereaux stepped into his arms and said, "Let's go then. Trish, we'll be back as soon as we can."

At her front door, she turned into him as she unlocked the deadbolt, and said, "Nothing you see tonight can be repeated, understood? You have no stake in this, so if you don't want to—"

With her still tucked under his arm, Seth commandeered the door, his hand on the padlock. Just because he could, he landed a soft spank on her backside. "I said I'm coming. Let's move."

At the last second, he froze. Every hair on his body had just lifted. His nostrils flared. He pressed one hand to the door over Devereaux's shoulder and snapped the deadbolt to the right, locking her in. His body had instinctively coiled for war, his hackles lifted up his spine, and his Pistol automatically in his grip. Someone was leaning against Devereaux's door. Not hard enough to break it down, but heavily enough the door shuddered.

Seth cocked his head, the moan from the other side of the wood unmistakably male. Valentine? Cord? "You own a gun?" he asked.

She shook her head.

"You and your girlfriend need to go into Scottie's room. Keep him safe."

Now armed with a nine-inch blade, Devereaux hip checked him. "Someone's at the kitchen door, too," she whispered.

"Get into Scottie's bedroom. Now! Cover him with a blanket and hide in the closet with him. Don't make a sound. Keep him safe."

Her head bobbed as she hurried down the hall, and once again, Seth cursed. America was no safer than the rest of the world, damn it.

Whoever stood on the other side of the door whined. Something scraped down the length of the door to the step. Seth stared at the wood, his senses acute, and every nerve in his system on high alert. One person he could handle. Taking a chance, he stepped away from the door to peer straight through the house, through the tiny kitchen to the rear exit. Like the front door, it had no window, not that he expected to see an intruder watching him. Still, it'd be good to see what or who or how many were out there.

He parted the drapes alongside the bookshelf, but darkness and vines obscured the view. Seth clenched his fist, biding his time, but ready to break loose if push came to shove.

Devereaux's cell vibrated from where she'd left it near the charger. Seth palmed it, read the caller ID, and blew out a breath. He thumbed the incoming call and hit accept without saying a word.

"Dev?" a man asked, his voice edged with pain. "Dev, what's wrong? Open up, damn it. I've got trouble."

"Cord Shepherd?"

That elicited an angry snarl. "Who the fuck's asking?"

"Name and USMC rank you held five years ago," Seth bit out. "Devereaux's safe, but you're not coming in until I'm sure who you are."

Fury laced Cord's terse reply. "Lance Corporal, you asshat. Who the fuck are *you*? I don't have time for this!"

"And I can't afford to be wrong," Seth replied. "Where were you stationed back then? Make it quick!"

"Twenty-Nine Palms in the middle of no-fuckin'-where," came through the door at Seth with a definite Devil Dog bite. "So help me, God, if you've hurt my sister or her son, I'll kill you with your own—"

Seth unlocked the door and jerked it inward and found himself face-to-face with one pissed-off former Marine. Cord's waterlogged pack fell to his feet. Seth just hadn't expected he'd have to look up at the guy. Son-of-a-bitch. Cord Shepherd was nothing like his sister. He was more Dwayne Johnson, the Rock, just without the cheesy flash of pearly whites. Big. Wide. Dark-haired and soaking wet, he was dressed all in black from his boots and cargo pants to his t-shirt. Heavily-muscled from the top of his jarhead to his boots, the guy ducked to clear the doorjamb.

"Welcome home," Seth snapped, pissed that this moron brought danger into Devereaux's home. "Who the hell's at the kitchen door? Your buddies? How many?"

Cord shoved Seth back a step on his way through the house. "Just one. Miguel. He's been shot, not like that's your business, asshole. Where's my sister?"

"Safe," Seth growled. "What've you gotten her into?" *You jackass.*

"Me? What have I gotten her into? That's rich," Cord tossed over his shoulder as he opened the rear door off the kitchen and stepped out of view. In seconds, he shouldered a sagging Hispanic male onto one of the molded plastic chairs around Devereaux's kitchen table. Bloody, watery footprints trailed with him.

"Trish! I know you're here. Get your first-aid kit and stop hiding! I need your ass out here. Now!" Contempt glared up from where Cord crouched on one knee by his buddy's side. "Neither of us would be in this mess if not for that crazy coot on Drunken Sailor Island. This is that bastard's fault, not that I blame him. What he's doing is a good thing, it's just damned dangerous."

Seth braced his forearms to both sides of the doorjamb, watching intently. "He's in charge of this rescue operation?"

Cord grunted. "If that's what you want to call it. Old guy's got friends from here to Timbuktu. If he's not jerking my chain, he sends others to get these women and children away from Montego. Wish I'd known I was rescuing so many this time."

"What kind of boat?"

Another grunt. "Who said I had a fuckin' boat, dickhead? What were you, Army? All we had was our CRRC. It only holds eight, least it did 'til it took a hit and nearly sank. Some of us had to swim."

"All the way from Havana?" That was what, a hundred miles?

Cord hissed, shaking his head as he stretched a muscular arm over one thick shoulder to scratch his back. "Varadero this time, not like it matters to you. We spent most of the time baling like hell or plugging holes we took before we lost everyone in the crossing."

Seth appreciated what Cord was doing. Rescuing women and children from sex slavers had become a full-time business for countries across the globe. Other former military members were heavily involved in operations just like this one. Even Alex Stewart funded a similar operation in Thailand. But who was the old coot behind Cord's operation? And what the hell did Cord have against Army? Departmental competition aside, everything out of Cord's mouth made Seth want to belt him. "Drunken Sailor Island? Where the hell's that?"

Reaching around his barrel chest, Cord dragged his fingernails across his side, still scratching like a dog with fleas. "One click off Molly's pier. Due south by southeast. You can't miss it. Fuckin' troublemaker."

That sounded a little too close to home. "You mean George McCray's place? He's behind this?" *Aw, shit.*

Cord's eyes came up sharp and deadly as his palm slapped the pistol on his hip. "Who the hell are you?"

"Cord, meet Seth McCray," Devereaux answered from the hallway. Entering the room, she ducked under Seth's arm and put her palm in the middle of his chest. He couldn't resist looking down on that pretty hand, claiming him in front of God and her brother, who might just be Satan. "Cord Shepherd, be nice to this guy. He's George's nephew, and he's here to help. George had a stroke. We may never see him again."

Cord tipped backward on his heels, his hand off his weapon, but his eyes as hard as obsidian and twice as sharp. His cheeks filled with air before he blew out a, "Thank fuck. Your damned uncle is out of his head. You do know that, don't you?"

Seth bit back his sarcasm. Uncle George wasn't the one running women and girls out of Cuba in the dead of night, was he? But what had George been doing? Organizing search networks? Saving girls and women caught up in the sex-slave trade while the rest of the family thought he was just an eccentric old fart, living on the edge of the United States?

Rushing in, Trish slammed an extra-large first-aid kit to the kitchen table. "Knifed or shot?" she asked, her fingers already peeling the injured guy's shirt off his shoulder to peer down at his chest. "Just his shoulder? Huh. Looks clean enough."

"Shot," Cord answered, still scratching. "One in the shoulder. Should be clean. He's been in the water most of the night."

"Get in the shower before you scratch yourself raw, Cord," Trish bit out. "You know the drill. Use plenty of hot water and slather that coconut cream you hate so much all over that handsome bod. Salt water's hell on skin, and if you've been swimming in it for hours...."

Miguel peered up at her, sweat streaming in his eyes and his thick, black hair drenched, though with blood or sweat, Seth couldn't be sure. For a Cuban, he was a ghostly shade of pale. "Thank you, Señorita," he whispered, grimacing through her rough handling as she stripped his shirt off with practiced ease. "May the Holy Mother bless you and your familia."

"That would be no one, tough guy," she grunted, tossing his dirty shirt to the floor. "So, save your prayers for someone who believes in all that crap and hold your ass still."

"Si," he said, grimacing again as she palmed the cuff of his shoulder, the pad of her thumb probing the bullet hole in the hollow beneath his collarbone. "Ow, ow, ow. I know you love me, Chica, but please, not so hard. And no kisses. People are watching."

Trish growled but kept on with her triage "You want me to remove this slug or not, tough guy?"

He nodded, no longer making eye contact. Miguel shook so hard that his teeth chattered. "Por favor. But maybe promise me a long, wet kiss once you are done, if it is not too much to hope for. Or a rubdown with some of that coconut cream, eh?"

Licking her lips, Trish leaned into his face. "Did I hear you right? You don't want anesthetic this time? Way to go, hero."

He moaned and slouched farther off the chair, his legs stiff and his eyes closed. "If that's what you choose. Love must hurt or it's not real, true?"

Trish huffed through her nostrils, but Seth caught the way she gentled her hand over Miguel's forehead as if checking for a fever.

"McCray's your uncle?" Cord's penetrating gaze flitted from Devereaux to Seth as if he knew something had gone on between them.

"One of several," Seth admitted.

"Figures. Get your gear, GI Joe. You're with me."

Not sure what Cord meant by that *'Figures'* comment, Seth nodded, his arm still around Devereaux. "Where to?"

"To get the women, dipshit!" Cord dumped a helluva lot of sarcasm into those five words. As he jerked the kitchen door open, he turned to Devereaux, his brows knit like two thunderclouds over the flashing lightning in his eyes. "Don't think this is over, Baby Sister. You and me are going to have words when I get back." To Seth he snapped, "What the fuck's keeping you! Are you coming or not?"

"Not until you shower, Cord," Trish nagged. "Now do as you're told and get your ass in the bathroom. You'll peel like a steamed tomato if you don't wash that salt off."

"Later," he snarled over his shoulder, the door slamming on his heels.

Seth gave Devereaux a quick hug goodbye and followed Cord out the door. *Uncle George, what were you thinking?*

Chapter Ten

The guys were gone a long time.

Trish bedded Miguel down on one of the mattresses in what was the guest bedroom. Looked like Dev's bedroom would be extra crowded by sunset with all these women if Family Services didn't show. Dev had placed a call to them after Cord and Seth left. By then she'd changed into her waitress uniform, dark blue slacks and a turquoise shirt that proudly declared *Conch Shack* in bright yellow lettering across her back, in case she didn't have time to change later. Things could get plenty harried when Cord retrieved more victims than anticipated.

While she waited for her company, Dev cleaned the kitchen and made stacks of peanut butter and strawberry jelly sandwiches. It was still early. Scottie hadn't gotten up out of bed yet, so she heated a stockpot full of chicken noodle soup for the hungry women and/or children soon to arrive. She never knew who or precisely how many Cord would return with. Just in case, she set the last of her fruity breakfast cereal on the table. Little kids would like that.

After arranging an array of paper bowls and plates, plastic utensils, napkins, and bottled water on her tiny kitchen table, she brewed a big pot of coffee. Sugar and cream packets came down from the shelf over the sink and joined the set-up. At last, she was as ready as she could be for visitors.

Scottie peeked into the hallway. "Again?" he whispered, his cute little brows lifted in childish curiosity.

Dev nodded. This wasn't his first rodeo. "Yes, honey, again. Want breakfast before everyone gets here?"

"Yes, please," he answered as he sidled up to his usual place at the table and pushed the stack of napkins out of his way.

Dev scrambled two eggs and made four pieces of toast, determined to enjoy her time with her son before Cord and Seth returned.

"You made a lot of sandwiches," Scottie said quietly, his eyes on the large covered plastic containers filled to the brim. "Uncle Cord must be bringing lots of ladies home this time."

"Yes, he is, so you need to eat before he returns."

"I can help," he whispered timidly.

"Of course you're helping," Dev exclaimed as she transferred the eggs to her best plastic plates and added buttered toast. "I'll need all the spare blankets from the closet in my bedroom. Could you get them for me when you're done eating?"

"Sure," he replied with enthusiasm, his fork already full of eggs. Nothing excited Scottie more than helping his mom. He didn't know the real reasons behind Uncle Cord's lady friends showing up at all hours of the day, and if Dev had her way, he'd never have to know. She'd only told him that Uncle Cord rescued women from some very bad men in the world, that those women needed someplace safe where they could rest and eat before they went onto their next destination, a nice clinic where professional services took over and made sure they went home.

Her humble bungalow was just one of many on the underground railway for these women, a no-kidding rest stop where they could get their bearings and prepare themselves for what lay in store. Physical examinations. Rape kits. Testing for STDs. Police reports. Those unpleasant necessary things.

"When you're done, brush your teeth," she reminded Scottie.

"Yes, Mom," he mumbled around a mouthful of toast.

Seth couldn't believe his eyes. He and Cord had returned to Drunken Sailor Island in Uncle George's much larger pontoon boat. Painted Navy gray, the watercraft could hold two-dozen people, plus supplies. But Uncle George hadn't bought this island a hundred miles north of Cuba just for the view.

"You look like him," Cord said as Seth cut the motor and idled toward the dock he and Devereaux had left only hours earlier. "Only problem is you're Army."

Determined to get along with Devereaux's brother, Seth let the dig slide. "How'd you get involved with my uncle?"

"Old bastard called me the day after I left the Corps. Don't ask me how he knew. Said my service to my country wasn't over yet. Said he needed men like me, that America needed men like me." Cord spit over the side. "Usual bullshit. Once a Marine, always a Marine."

Like that answered anything. Seth rolled his annoyance with Cord out of his neck. "Talk to me, Shepherd. How long have you been intercepting the human trafficking out of Cuba?"

"Now you're interested?" Cord seemed to have a mile-wide chip on his shoulder.

"Now that I'm involved, yes. How do you know my uncle?"

"Already told you. He's a Marine, I'm a Marine. Figure it out." Cord waved toward shore, and holy shit didn't begin to explain the view. Seth lifted his hand to block the morning sun piercing the edge of the cloudless horizon like a laser pointer. Nine women of varying ages sat huddled beneath the closest palm tree on his island. Two little blonde girls. A deflated CRRC - Combat Rubber Raiding Craft.

"You rescued all these women?" Seth asked, willing to cut Cord some slack in light of the awesome job he'd done rescuing so many women in a damaged raft.

"It's what I do," the big guy bit out as over the side he went. Instead of waiting for Seth to pull alongside the dock, he hit the surf and swam the rest of the way.

Seth maneuvered quickly and securely. Once alongside the dock, he tied the boat fore and aft to steady it for the anxious passengers on the beach. The women swarmed Cord, then dragged him into the shade, pointing toward Seth, their voices raised with distress. He waved to dispel their anxiety while Cord spoke to them. The man spoke Cuban. Good to know.

Only the smallest of the refugees advanced, the two little girls. They couldn't have been more than eight or nine. Had to be sisters the way they clung to each other.

"Are you hungry?" he asked, needing to get these fair complexioned girls out of the sun before they burned, and out of sight before this rescue went sideways. One never knew who was out there watching, or what drones were flying high overhead, snapping pictures and listening in.

The girls shook their heads in unison, like the twins on some horror show he vaguely remembered. Big brown eyes stared at him. Of course they weren't hungry. They didn't trust him enough to accept food from him, a stranger, and why should they? Whoever had kidnapped them had probably used a similar line to lure them away from their parents. *Candy, little girl?*

Seth folded his frame to the dock and sat Indian-style. He had all day. He could wait.

"McCray!" Cord bellowed from beneath the trees. "Get your fat ass over here!"

Again with the insults. Seth winked at the girls as he lifted to his feet, then skirted around them, keeping his distance so as not to frighten them. He'd barely cleared the closest sister when the softest whisper reached him, "Are you gonna take us home to our mommy, Mister?"

Riiiiiiiiip went his rugged almost-Army Ranger heart, which, come to think of it, wasn't so rugged after all. Seth took a knee, but kept a respectable distance. Trust was a delicate thing, and he wouldn't hurry it. The next step was up to them, but they looked so small against the world, and so scared. He clasped his palms over his raised kneecap. "I am," he said, blinking hard. "I'll take you anywhere you want to go. Just not back to Cuba."

"Home," the other sister mumbled around the dripping wet thumb in her mouth. "We wanna go home."

"Are you girls twins?" he asked, though it seemed obvious.

"Ah-huh," the first girl replied. "I'm Emma. This is Maddie. We're sisters."

"I see that. Where does your mommy live?"

"In a big white house," Maddie said, again around her thumb. "She lives there with my daddy and… and…" Her mouth opened wide. "We wanna go home!"

Emma edged closer to Seth while Maddie's wails turned to hiccups. "Please, Mister. We got lost, but we didn't do nothin' wrong, and Mommy doesn't know where we are, and we just wanna go home really, really badly."

That did it. Seth swiped a hand over his eyes with one hand, while he gestured to the boat with his other. "Then climb aboard, ladies. I'm taking you to your mom and dad. Do you know your phone number? Would you like to call them?" He pulled his satphone up from his pocket. A smart man never went anywhere without one, not in this day and age.

That did the trick. Maddie's little body hit him first, then Emma's, and Seth found himself flat on his back on the dock, holding both girls and crying with them. He misdialed the first time and got a disconnect because he couldn't see straight. The second time, a woman answered with a quiet, "Hello?"

"Excuse me, ma'am, but are you missing your daughters, Emma and Maddie?"

She shrieked. "My babies! My girls! Thayne! Thayne!"

Seth held the phone from his ear, then tried again, but a man spoke now. "Who are you and what do you want? I'm not rich, but I can come up with—"

Seth cut him off before the poor man broke his heart. "Former United States Army Sergeant Seth McCray, at your service, sir, and I don't want anything. Hell, no. I'm not the guy who did this to you and your family, but I do have your daughters. They want to come home, sir, and to be honest, I'm new at this, but your girls are safe and… You have my word, sir. I'll keep them safe until you and your wife can get here," he ground out, his voice gone hoarse and tight.

"Where…?" Emma and Maddie's father could hardly talk as well. "Where are you? Please. Tell me."

"Florida Keys, sir. Drunken Sailor's Island, but we'll be on the mainland in a couple hours." Seth passed his phone number to the distraught father while Emma and Maddie's mother sobbed in the background.

"Tell them I'm on my way," their father said. "Yes, honey. I'll ask. Are they h-hurt? God, where have they been all this time? It's been months."

Seth ran an appraising eye over the kids hugged up against him, clinging to him as if their lives depended on him. What an incredibly powerful feeling. Wide-eyed and finely boned, they reminded him of Devereaux.

Cord bellowed again, but the cocky Marine could wait his turn. Seth had his arms full of two little pixies who needed him more. "I can't say for sure if they're hurt or not, sir. They look physically well to me, but I'm no doctor. Right now, they appear to be tired, maybe hungry. They were located in Cuba, and I imagine they're on their way to the Florida State authorities this morning. They'll probably be in touch with you soon, and you might not hear from me again, but—"

"Th-th-thank you," the poor man broke down, sobbing wretchedly. "God bless and keep you and… Thank you so damned much, Seth McCray. I don't know you, but I owe you everything."

Emma's and Maddie's mom must've grabbed the phone. "Can I talk to them?" she asked, her voice shrill and panicked. "Are they with you? P-please? Let me talk to my girls."

"You bet, ma'am," Seth said as he held the phone to Emma's ear. "Your mommy wants to talk to you."

Emma took the phone. Rested it to her ear. Blinked. "Mommy?" Then tears. Then sobs. By the time she was done, Emma had hold of Maddie's shoulders, and both girls were shuddering emotional wrecks. Maddie took her turn with the phone but could hardly say a word. She squeezed both eyes tight and just nodded at the sound of her mother's voice, and that was okay. Seth knew how much power mother's and father's voices held.

After a few more words with the girls' father, who Seth now knew was Thayne Ward of Charlotte, South Carolina, Seth signed off. That explained the slight southern twist to the girls' words.

He lay there staring at the burgeoning blue morning sky overhead and breathing hard while they settled into his arms like they were meant to be there. Maddie hiccupped once her sobs subsided. Emma burrowed under his chin and fingered his collar. What a good, good day.

Cord finally stomped over to the dock, but once he saw the girls, his expression mellowed. "You got them to talk? Well done, McCray. I was afraid… Well, let's just say they've been through enough."

Seth nodded. He understood 'enough'. "What's next? The authorities? The hospital? Where do we go from here?"

"Back to Dev's place. She'll feed them, then Family Services takes over. They'll make sure they get the medical attention they need. They'll contact the families."

Chagrined, Seth revealed the satphone in his palm. "I might've already done that."

A genuine grin cracked Cord's ugly face. "Good on you. But next time, hold off on that, okay?"

Next time?

Chapter Eleven

Dev had barely inhaled her breakfast when her heavy-footed brother sounded at the kitchen door. Scottie stuffed his last bite into his already full mouth and asked, "Should I go to my room now?"

"No, but let's get out of Uncle Cord's way. Come stand with me. Once everybody's inside, you can run get the blankets."

"Yes, Mom," he said, his tone serious as Cord dragged a blonde woman barely able to walk into the kitchen.

"How's my main man?" he asked Scottie as he took her into the front room. Seven more young women trailed past Dev, all Caucasian, some limping, some helping another, but every last one of them deathly quiet and sticking close to Cord. The last, a teenager with straggly red hair that hung to her butt in dirty tangles, closed the door quietly behind her and turned to face Dev. "Umm, hi," she said in a tiny voice.

This was where Dev shined. "Hi," she said quietly, one hand extended, the other clamped onto Scottie's shoulder. "I'm Devereaux Shepherd and this is my home, but you can call me Dev. All my friends do. Can I get you something to eat? A drink?" *A hug, you poor, poor thing?*

Frightened green eyes shimmered at her. "Yes, please," she whispered, her gaze darting past Dev to the group huddled in the other room. "I'm Rhonda Malevich, and I'm from Brooklyn, and I… and I…"

This was the moment most rescued women realized they were finally out of Montego's clutches and fell apart. Rhonda was no different. When tears brimmed to overflowing, Dev set Scottie to her side and held out both arms. Rhonda sucked in a sob and ran into Dev, burying her face in her neck and whining, "I want to go home… Please… I just want to go h-home. I want my mom and my dad and… pleassssssssssse."

Scottie whined as well, his little hand gripping the corner of Dev's shirt. Sad people always made him cry.

Dev held the girl as tightly as she dared. It wasn't much, and Dev always wished she could do more, but right now and for Rhonda, being held was everything. Some of the victims of this awful industry were too traumatized to tolerate touch once they were finally rescued, but Rhonda seemed to crave it.

Dev smoothed one hand over the girl's wet head and murmured, "I'll bet you haven't eaten anything worthwhile in days. Let's get some soup and a sandwich or two into your stomach, and you'll see. You'll start to feel better. Who are your friends in there?"

Rhonda sniffed. "The big guy's Cord, but Seth's the one I like. He's not here yet. He was behind us a bit with the little girls. He's sure handsome, huh?"

A smile tweaked her lips as Dev peered over Rhonda's head to Cord in the other room. Of course this poor shivering teenager assumed she'd meant the guys. Rhonda would probably crush on both of her saviors for a long time after this night, and that was fine by Dev. She knew what it meant to be rescued, and how beloved that single rescuer would always be. That handsome, bossy, arrogant jarhead in there, the big guy kneeling over the blonde on the couch and running the back of his hand over her forehead, was her favorite crush. What little sister didn't love her big brother, the one who'd rescued her from the same life these women had been headed for, with all her heart and soul?

As for Seth? Speak of the devil. He'd just angled his big wide body through the kitchen door, his arms full of two little girls with big brown eyes, both clinging to his neck like sad little orangutans. He nodded at Dev, but said to her son, "Hi there, big guy. You must be Scottie. Good to meet you."

The twinkle in Seth's eye had been diminished by what he'd probably seen on this rescue, but this was the first time Dev noticed that the tint of those eyes matched the clear, warm color of whiskey on ice. Startlingly clear. Like well water that ran deep and true.

Dev clutched Scottie's shoulders, bringing him in front of her before she forgot herself and tripped into Seth. "Scottie, this is my friend, Seth McCray. George McCray is his uncle, and he's here to help us. He'll be staying a while."

Scottie's head came up. "You know George? He and Gru's my best friends."

Dev winced as her gaze connected with Seth's over the top of her son's head. She still had to explain George's stroke and now Gru's death to her son, though she'd never divulge the gruesome details.

Seth must've noticed. "Why don't you and me play ball when this is over? You do own a baseball and mitt, don't you?"

"Course I do," Scottie crowed. Tipping his head to the side, he peered up at Dev. "Can I, Mom? Is it okay if I catch some flies with Seth?" He was proud of the baseball phrase he'd learned watching the World Series.

She tousled his soft, blond hair. "With Seth, yes, but keep inside the backyard. Maybe I'll come out and play, too."

That did the trick. A grin split his cute little face, and off Scottie went to get those important blankets. Dev thanked Seth with her eyes as she went to assist her houseguests.

Seth took a seat on the floor and leaned against one end of the couch, still holding the little girls who looked like they had no intention of letting him go. His eyes kept track of her as she came and went. Just knowing that he watched, gave Dev an added bounce to her step.

The women were quiet, all seated on the floor or the fold-up chairs that Dev had bought, one by one, when she could afford it, from the Bargain Basement over on Palm Street. Scottie ran back and forth, dragging more blankets and helping Dev distribute them. One woman faced the corner and sobbed quietly. A couple whispered *thank you* and *gracias*, but most just stared and waited.

Cord looked uptight. Worried. He hadn't left the blonde's side.

Trish finally showed up with her first-aid kit and promptly knelt with him. "She needs a doctor, Cord. I can only do so much."

"Then call your friend," he bit out. "But no hospital. Not yet."

More words Dev couldn't hear were exchanged, until Cord lifted to his feet and walked away, but something was up. This woman was different. Who was she and why did Cord look so—guarded? The man glowed like a nuclear reactor about to implode.

Dev honestly didn't have time to worry about that, so she filed it away for later. For now, she had a room full of people to feed, more sandwiches to make, and all before she left for work. Seth shot her a handsome wink as she headed for her kitchen. What a way to start the day.

Seth had to give Devereaux and her brother credit. They seemed to know what they were doing and how to comfort a house full of strangers. Even Scottie ran, first to get more blankets, then waiting on *'the ladies'*—as he called them— retrieving bottles of water or *one more sandwich, por favor*. Not once had he whined or complained that he'd rather go outside and play.

The poor women were hungry, and more than a couple showed definite signs of hysteria and traumatic stress. Seth understood those things, so once the twins fell asleep on the blanket he'd arranged on the floor for them, he went quietly from woman to woman, being careful not to touch them and keeping his voice low. Making no sudden moves. Just asking if they were warm enough, or if they needed one of the generic OTC medications Devereaux had on hand. Over and over, he assured each woman that he'd gladly get whatever they needed. All they had to do was ask. He was there to serve.

Another man with a large black bag and a backpack slung over his shoulder showed up within the hour. A doctor. The stethoscope dangling around his neck gave him away. Cord hustled him off to where he'd moved the blonde with a terse, "Right this way."

Done with her cursory examination of the other women, Trish followed Cord down the hall. It was nearly two hours later when he escorted his doctor friend to Devereaux's front door with a muttered, "I'll be in touch."

"See that you are," the doctor told him. "This damage is serious."

When the kind people from Family Services arrived just after noon, the little girls were still sound asleep. Cora Blair led the way, her sidekick, a tall, mousy woman with *Harry Potter* spectacles, on her six. Both women took over with ease, and for that Seth was glad. Most likely, he'd never see these poor women again, but knowing they would be in capable hands helped.

He'd watched Devereaux interact with them, and everything she did, she'd done with extreme gentleness. In fact, she seemed perfect for this task, much like the respectful flight attendant he remembered from years ago. Not once had she mentioned how hard she'd worked to make all the sandwiches that disappeared like candy when the women arrived. No sir. She just kept making more sandwiches, emptying her cupboards, and serving her house full of sad strangers.

Her generous nature tugged his heartstrings. Devereaux might have a mountain of problems nipping at her heels, and for certain she lived on a shoestring, yet here she was, a smile on her face while these women ate her out of house and home.

"Ladies," Cora called out. She and her assistant stood ready at the door. "The bus is waiting. Shall we go?"

Wearily, the women lifted to their feet and followed her. But saying goodbye to two sleepy girls? Damned hard. Seth had promised their father he'd personally take care of them, but that wasn't possible, neither was it encouraged. He knelt on the floor. Both girls snuggled into him like they had nothing more to worry about, and of course, his arms circled them just like he'd done on his uncle's dock. Emma blinked those pretty eyes up at him, and his heart got stuck in his throat.

"Your daddy's got my phone number," he told her to soften the pain in his chest, "and once you get home, you call me anytime you want. Day or night. I'll always be there for you girls."

Her bottom lip stuck out. Maddie buried her face in his shirt, hiccupping and scared again. He was sad too, but for them, not himself. While they'd been kidnapped, and heaven knew what else, he'd been stuck in a never-ending pity party, lost between booze and depression. Well, no more.

He lifted those little angels with him as he got to his feet. "You be brave, Emma and Maddie Ward, because you're soldiers now, just like me. You're going home to your mommy and daddy, and once you hug and kiss them and cry all over them, you tell them that you're stronger than those bad guys that took you. Tell your parents that you're the winner because you're alive and you're free. Can you do that for me?"

Emma's head bobbed against his neck, and hell. Seth knew he was probably talking over their heads, but he needed to instill a sense of victory in these little waifs before he gave them up. They *were* strong. They *would* be okay. They just had to be smarter than him and keep on keeping on. They had to believe in themselves.

Out of the blue, Maddie circled his neck and squeezed. "You're gonna be okay, too," she whispered. "I'll tell Mommy and Daddy what you said."

Out of the mouths of babes. Seth gave the girls one last heartfelt hug, and just in time, Miss Spectacles stepped up and relieved him of Emma, while Cora Blair secured Maddie under her arm. The girls didn't take their eyes off him until they were out the door and safely sequestered in the rear of the van with another social worker.

Struggling with yet another loss, Seth followed along with Devereaux and Scottie. They paused at the walk just short of the curb where the Family Services bus parked, its doors opened wide to receive its passengers. He couldn't see the twins, and that was just as well. They didn't need another emotional farewell any more than he did.

Rhonda Malevich gave Devereaux a tiny wave when she set foot on the lowest step. Then they were gone in a puff of diesel fumes. All except for the woman Cord had secreted in one of Devereaux's bedrooms.

"What's up with your brother?" Seth asked as he escorted Devereaux back inside.

"Uncle Cord's got another girlfriend," Scottie drawled.

"Hush, Scottie. That's not nice," Devereaux scolded.

"So, who is she and why's she still here?" Seth had to know.

Devereaux shrugged. "That's what I'm going to find out."

Chapter Twelve

After securing the plethora of locks at her front door, Devereaux headed straight for her bedroom, hers if Seth guessed right.

"Wanna help me pick up?" Scottie asked, his bright blue eyes alive with expectation.

"Sure," Seth told him easily. Why not? Devereaux had to leave for work soon. It was the least he could do.

Scottie ran to the kitchen and returned with a black garbage bag. He draped one edge of it over the back of a fold-up chair and commenced gathering plastic bottles, plates, and other debris. The bag was nearly stuffed full when he looked at Seth and exclaimed, "I almost forgot!" before he bolted out the kitchen door.

Fear pumped an overdose of adrenaline straight into Seth's heart. He cleared the kitchen on a dead run to the corner of Devereaux's fenced-in yard, but he was too late. A large wire cage filled the corner and inside that cage, an amazing habitat of strategically placed logs, a cut-off piece of garden hose, a tiny waterfall that dropped to a careful arrangement of smooth stones. In the nearest corner, a large flat rock caught the afternoon sunlight.

But no iguana.

Scottie stood there sobbing, his chest heaving. The pool of dried black blood just outside the habitat stopped Seth cold. This was where Gru had lived and died. And now Scottie knew. Shit.

He turned on Seth, his blue eyes brimmed and blinking. "My lizard's gone. Look." He pointed to the blood. "He's hurt, and he needs me and you gotta help me find him."

Seth looked at Scottie. Scottie looked at Seth. Words were utterly useless. Seth dropped to one knee and said, "I'm sorry. I'm so sorry, Scottie. He's… Gru's not hurting anymore," was all Seth could think to say.

"But I can help him," the boy cried. "Hurry. Come with me. Help me look! We gotta find him before he crawls out to the street. He might get runned over."

"No, Scottie. He won't get to the street. Gru's…" *Damn, how to say this?* "…dead, son."

"But why? Was he sick? Is he at the vet? Mama took him to see Dr. Lawrence one time when he got a tummy ache."

Seth held out his hands to Devereaux's son. "Come here, little guy."

"But I took real good care of him," Scottie whimpered, rubbing his nose into Seth's shirt. "And we used to play hide and seek, only he wasn't very good at finding me." A man-sized shudder racked his body. "And now I got no one to play with when Mom's working, and I'm sad, Mr. Seth. I'm really, really sad."

Ah, shit. Seth scooped the boy up and turned his back on the tragic scene. Devereaux hadn't had time to hide the evidence, but this wasn't her fault. She'd been busy caring for the women. Sly Valentine was the problem, and he had a war coming his way, the bastard.

Devereaux burst through the kitchen door then, her hand to her mouth. When Seth shook his head, she flung herself around him and the boy. "Scottie, baby. I'm sorry. Gru died and…" Her words got stuck in her throat, and suddenly, Seth was holding a woman and her son while they cried against him.

Lowering his butt to the single step outside her screen door, he settled in for the storm. While Scottie sobbed, Devereaux seemed to need her hands on her son as if she could erase what had happened to their beloved pet. Over and over, she stroked her fingers through his sweaty head until Seth caught her hand and brought it to his lips. "Enough," he whispered. "This is hard but let him be a man. Your son's tougher than you think."

She lifted her teary face to him. "But I'm not."

Seth kissed her forehead. "Oh, yes you are, Devereaux Shepherd. You are the epitome of your last name. You're the fiercest shepherdess I've ever seen in my life and trust me. I've been to Afghanistan. I've seen a few shepherdesses who had no problem nailing a jackal with a few well-placed stones if it came near their flock."

She stilled, her arms around her son and Scottie's head against her breasts now. Dipping her lips to Scottie's hair, she kissed him, but the nervous hands had ceased their frantic petting.

Scottie lifted his chin and looked Seth in the eye. "I love my Mom," he told him.

I'm starting to love her, too, Seth thought, but he said, "That's because you're a good man, Scottie Shepherd, and good men take care of our women, don't we? We love them with all our hearts."

The boy's head bobbed. "And we bring her coffee in the morning when she's sad and we put lots of cream and sugar in it just like she likes it, huh?"

I'd certainly like the opportunity. Seth cocked his head at this little charmer. Already Scottie had been taught to think of others. "And sometimes we clean up the place when she's too tired at the end of the day."

Still shivering, Scottie swallowed and nodded. "Yeah, cuz my mom's a good mom and I hafta take care of her, cuz Uncle Cord can't always be here." Another sniff and he swiped a brave fist under his nose.

"You think your mom needs one of those cups of coffee now?" Seth asked, content to hold these two as long as he could.

"Ah-huh," Scottie murmured, his lips pinched into a pout. "And then I gotta find Gru and make sure he's okay, cuz he's bleeding."

Oh shit. Devereaux whimpered and burrowed her face into Seth's neck, and that was okay. He knew what to do. Setting her on the step at his side, he shifted Scottie to one thigh where he could tell him the bad news. "Gru's not hiding, Scottie. He had an accident late yesterday and he died. Do you know what that means?"

Scottie's sad blue eyes flooded again. "Uh-huh."

But he didn't. Not really. "It means he's up in heaven with some of my friends."

"He is?"

Seth nodded as wisely as an old soldier could. The concept of death was easier to explain when cushioned with stories of friends who'd gone on before, men who'd honestly loved, brothers who'd fought their damnedest to keep you alive, a loving fiancée, and, oh yes, the eternally annoying Latoya Franklin, God bless her wayward heart.

Somehow, the image of his bossy nemesis dealing with an iguana in heaven brought a smile to Seth's heart. He'd lay nine-to-one odds that Latoya would squeal, turn tail, and run for her ghostly life, never to haunt him again. Tipping Scottie's chin up with his finger, Seth told him what every soldier tells another. "Good lizards never die, Scottie. They just fade away."

The little tyke glanced around the yard. "You mean he's hiding?"

Seth pointed that same finger skyward. "In heaven. Gru's hiding in heaven." That seemed to do the trick. With a grunt, Seth lifted to his feet and swung the boy up high on his shoulder, where he landed with a subdued giggle. Better days were coming. They just weren't here yet.

Devereaux shot him a coy smile as she swiped a finger under her teary eye. "That was very kind and thoughtful. Thank you, Seth."

He shrugged her praise off and said, "Come on, Mama. Let's get you that cup of coffee."

Chapter Thirteen

Dev kept Scottie on her lap. The house was quiet. Seth and Cord were in her backyard, cleaning out Gru's habitat. She had less than a half hour before work, but the Conch Shack was a straight shot from her place if traffic complied. If not... Well, she'd been late before.

Cord had wanted to run right out and buy Scottie another iguana to replace Gru, but Dev told him no. Life shouldn't work that way. Death was hard, but to trade one life for another as if livings things were replaceable wasn't the lesson she wanted Scottie to learn. So she rocked him and let him be a sad little boy a while longer. Another pet would come along, and she'd take it in then. Just not now.

For a four-year-old, he'd seen too much, and today was no different than many others she'd put him through. Things had to change, yet the thought of what those poor women and girls had endured in Roland Montego's prison always kept Dev in the game. She'd been in their place. She knew how awful Montego was to the girls and women he favored. Turning her back on them wasn't an option.

Until this excursion into Cuba, things had gone smoothly. Cord handled the infils, as he called them. Miguel handled the exfils, which meant he stayed with the CRRC while Cord and his buddies infiltrated Roland Montego's lair and returned with as many victims as they could. She'd never gone with Cord on his forays, just supplied a resting place for the women when he returned. This was the first time gunplay had been involved, which meant Roland Montego had known Cord and his men were coming. The thought of all she could've lost slayed Dev. Hence Scottie wasn't going anywhere without her.

But now she wondered. Where were the other former Marines who usually traveled with Cord? Why hadn't they accompanied him to Dev's house? Where were Stevie "Wonder" James, Ryland "Sonic" DeLorenzo, and Cleveland "Rabbit" Miller? Not that they always came home with him, but what was Cord thinking, keeping one of those women? The blonde should've gone with Family Services where she'd be properly cared for, her injuries documented, and her family notified. The nerve.

"I want Gru," Scottie whined, his ear pressed to Dev's heart.

"Me too," she told him honestly. "Remember when Goldie died?"

"Ah-huh," Scottie sniffled. "You think Gru's in heaven with her?"

"I'm sure of it. All animals go to heaven, especially iguanas. So do goldfish." Only mankind had to work his ass off to gain entrance. Which was fair. He was the sinner.

Goldie was Scottie's first pet. She hadn't lasted long once Scottie decided she needed the entire can of fish food for breakfast. Instead of flushing her, Dev had held a simple funeral before she and Scottie buried Goldie beneath the Gumbo Limbo tree straddling Trish and her backyards.

"Will I get to see him and Goldie again?"

"Yes," she told him wistfully. *But not until you've lived a very, very long time.*

"I like Mr. Seth," Scottie mumbled through a tremendous yawn. "I tired, Mama."

Thankful that little boys were easily distracted, Dev pressed her nose to her son's head, breathing his scent into her soul. She still used baby shampoo on his fine, straight hair, and the smell never failed to remind her how blessed she was, and how that one night's indiscretion had resulted in the greatest treasure in her life. "Me, too. Let's go read a quick story before I leave for work."

"'Kay," he murmured as he pushed off her lap, automatically headed for his bedroom and his bookshelf. "But not Peter Rabbit again. That one's for babies."

Dev adored the way her four-year-old said 'babies' with so much scorn, as if he were so much older and wiser.

"Not *'Old Yeller'* either." She couldn't bear another tearjerker so soon after losing Gru.

Scottie sniffed. "Then how about the dinosaur one?"

Ah, yes. The colorful tale of a smiling cartoon tyrannosaurus rex eating his way through the smaller herbivores in his jungle to get to the scary stegosaurus always made for a lovely bedtime story. This little guy definitely had his Uncle Cord's blood running in his veins. But at least the dinosaur story didn't deal with the real-life scenario of losing a beloved pet.

So if Scottie wanted it… "You got it."

Once they settled against the pillows on his bed, Dev kept her voice low. Out of the blue some four years earlier, Cord had insisted on room darkening curtains for every window in the bungalow except the kitchen. The kid-friendly version at

Scottie's single window maintained just enough light for him to see the pages—and to lull a tired little man to sleep. He drifted off before she finished the third page.

With the guys still hard at work in her backyard, Devereaux eased away from Scottie and tiptoed to her visitor's room. She had ten minutes. She'd no sooner cracked the door when—

"I'm awake," her visitor said. "Please turn the light on so I can see you."

Dev flicked the switch at her left. The blond in her bed sat propped at the gold padded headboard with all of Dev's pillows at her back. Pale, with bruised cheeks and a swollen lip, she stared at Dev through melted chocolate drop eyes so large they almost made her look regal. Chin up. Eyes forward. An urge to curtsey—or something—sprang to Dev's mind. *Yeah, right. Not in my house and most definitely, not in my bedroom.*

"I'm Devereaux Shepherd. How are you feeling?"

"I'm Lianna Khadeem, and right now, I'm good. I'm afraid I may not look like it, but this is nothing. I'll survive."

Dev cocked her head. She'd expected a sassy California name, or at least one from somewhere equally as—blonde. "You're Arabic?"

That earned her a curt nod and a huff, as if Dev should've known better than to ask. The traumatized women Cord rescued were often so tightly wired by the time they arrived on Dev's doorstep that they fought even the kindest treatment. Dev let it go, but the poor woman's thickly wrapped hands didn't look like nothing had happened. "You're hurt. What did Montego do to you?"

Lianna lifted both hands, her gaze harsh before it softened, and her eyes met Dev's. "They'll heal. How are those little girls, Emma and Maddie? Are they" —her throat muscles constricted— "alive?"

Some victims were in full-blown denial by the time they arrived at Dev's front door, and Dev got that, but Lianna had not only artfully avoided answering the question, she'd changed subjects as well. Montego was a known sadist with a penchant for BDSM straight out of Hell's playbook. Dev very much wanted to unwrap those hands to see what he'd done to Lianna.

"Family Services has custody of Emma and Maddie until their father arrives in Florida. They'll be home where they belong soon."

Lianna's head tipped back against the headboard. Trembling, she blew out a deep sigh and whispered, "Praise Allah." Both eyes closed. Her lower lip quivered. Her breasts heaved as if holding back a flood. "They… they were so scared, and everything frightened them. They wouldn't speak, they wouldn't even look at me, and I was afraid…" Her throat worked a mighty swallow before she whispered, "I was afraid he'd already d-d-destroyed their souls."

So… The twins were the important ones, not Lianna. Interesting.

"We need to end Montego once and for all," Dev said to soothe Lianna's nerves.

"Not him!" Lianna snapped, her dark eyes flashing.

Dev stopped trying to breach the wall around her guest. She waited, knowing that deep down, Lianna needed to talk. She needed a woman's shoulder to cry on. Dev dropped her gaze to the old-fashioned chenille bedspread pulled around

Lianna. The room chilled as the silence grew. Dev's ten minutes to be on her way to work was long gone.

The breakthrough began with a tiny cry emanating from deep within Lianna. A hitch of breath betrayed her next. Then her bulky hands, clasped so tight she had to be hurting herself, gave her away. After another noisy gulp, she said, "I am a princess in my country. A woman of noble birth. I did not know…" A strangled sob wound out of her. "I did not know men could be so cruel."

At last. Dev had never had royalty in her shabby home before. Unsure of proper protocol, but certain this shuddering woman needed a woman's touch right here and now, she asked, "May I approach, Your Majesty?"

She got a stiff upper lip and a curt nod for that. So be it. Dev knew how to be humble. Slowly extending her arms, palms upward, she moved to the edge of the mattress at her guest's side.

Lianna fell against her, sobbing. "He… he… he…"

Dev rocked, biding her time. Things like despair and pain, heartache and hysteria, kept no schedule, and this woman seemed on the verge of all that and more. Taller than Dev, Lianna buried her face in the crook of Dev's neck and shoulder. She was a soft armful, model-worthy, her breasts high and full, her legs long, and her waist trim. She was every man's dream. Everything Dev wasn't.

But all too soon, Lianna stiffened as if she'd remembered she was in the arms of a commoner. Dev didn't slide away, just kept a gentle hold of the distraught woman's wrist as Lianna eased against the headboard once more. Now wasn't the time to interrogate her, and Dev wouldn't have known what to ask anyway. Which was why Lianna should've gone with the kindly Family Services people. This was their mission. Cord and she only handled infils, exfils, and the first rest stop on the way home for these tormented women.

"My father signed the marriage contract when I turned three," Lianna whispered. "I remember the day he told me. We were in the date fields. Fruit hung heavy from the trees. The air beneath the fronds was thick with the honeyed scent of the ripe fruit. I thought he'd taken me there because he loved me. Instead…" Her gaze fluttered to her bandaged fingers. "He'd sold me to a prince, whose wealthy father wanted his son to marry a respectable girl. My father owns the entire Quari'im Peninsula. It is a land rich with orchards and fields and industry. My betrothal was not for me, it was for him. Signing that contract gave him the sole rights to the Saudi shipping lanes in the Persian Gulf. With Dubai and Bahrain to the south, it is a location of great power and wealth. The sad truth is that I always knew my betrothed. We played together as children. He was so handsome then, so tender and kind. As a young man and a prince, he traveled the world. I knew he'd made a reputation for himself, that he'd changed, but…"

Dev knew when to keep her mouth shut.

Lianna lifted her wrist, effectively easing out of Dev's hold. "I never knew he was capable of this."

The bedroom door slammed open. "Who the fuck did this to you?" Cord demanded from the doorway.

Lianna paled. "M-my husband. Basheer Bagani."

Cord cast a baleful glare Dev's way. "You got a minute?"

Appalled at what she'd heard, Dev followed Cord into the hall. He shut the door tightly behind her, then fast stepped her into the kitchen and stabbed an index finger at the backyard. "Get rid of him now."

"Who? Seth?"

"Yes, Soldier Boy needs to go, the sooner, the better."

Enough! "Seth is no boy, Cord. He helped you today. It seems to me you could be a little kinder and besides, why should I?"

Cord's cell interrupted, buzzing in his pocket. His brows clashed over the blade of his nose as he tugged it up. His lips thinned. He lifted the phone to his ear as he told her, "Because this is bigger than both of us, Dev. I can't risk this getting out."

"But Cord—"

"Need to know, Dev. This is an eyes-only op, and Soldier Boy's got no need to know. Now get him the fuck out of here. Just do it!"

Chapter Fourteen

Seth untangled Devereaux's garden hose and wound it in even loops before he hung it over the curved hanger on the wooden post beside the now clean iguana habitat. He'd washed the blood away, while Cord had raked the loose gravel inside the cage and around the neatly framed wooden border surrounding it. Devereaux had done a bang-up job building a home for Gru.

Ensconced beneath a huge flowering tree, Gru should've lived to be a hundred—or however old iguanas lived, in this clever, multi-level playground. It was a shame to leave it vacant, yet Devereaux was right when she'd told Cord very clearly, "Don't you dare go out and buy Scottie another iguana just because you can't stand to see him sad. This isn't about you. It's about a little boy who's learning that life isn't fair, and how no one gets a participation trophy. I said no."

Shutting the door, the top corner of the habitat didn't fit quite right. It took less than a twist of Seth's thumbnail to tighten the screw on the upper hinge. There. That'd hold until he located a screwdriver and tightened it properly.

"You're still here," Devereaux said behind him.

"Where else would I be?" Man, she was pretty, standing on her back step with one hand on her hip, the other on the open screen door. He couldn't help the grin that cracked his face as he took stock of her waitress outfit, navy blue and turquoise. His favorite colors. "Need someone to walk you to work?" He cocked a thumb at his chest. Damn, she was pretty. "I happen to know a guy."

She looked past him to the habitat. "You didn't have to do that," she said like she was annoyed. Or something. She hadn't yet smiled, not even a little.

He lifted both shoulders. "'S no big deal. Cleaning up the yard gave me a chance to work with Cord. Your brother's a real Devil Dog to his soul, isn't he?"

"Yeah, umm… about that. I'm not going to work. I, umm, called in and took the night off." Devereaux told him, her chin still up and her eyes clear, but—wrong. There was no light in those deep blues. She looked downright unhappy.

Seth took a step forward but stopped when her hands came up, when she said "I can't do this."

"Do what?"

"This. Whatever's going on between us. I don't… I don't have time for more drama in my life. I've got a kid and a job and more… and people depend on me to be there for them." Her gaze dropped to her feet. "I can't."

That made no sense. He'd brought no drama to the Shepherds' doorstep, and calling Scottie a *kid* seemed out of character for Devereaux.

"So…" And there she stalled. Not making eye contact.

Seth swallowed past the dry knot in his throat. He got the drift. So this is how it ends. That was what she meant to say. *It's been nice, but don't let the door hit you on the ass on the way out. So long. Goodbye. And all that crap.*

"Guess I'd better be going then," he said when he could speak.

She nodded but didn't take a single step toward him. Not even one. She meant this to be a no contact goodbye. Somehow, he'd gone from being the hero of the day to nothing more than hired help you could fire without regret. Not that he'd expected anything for helping retrieve those women and girls, but another kiss from Devereaux's sweet lips would've been—

"Bye," she whispered.

Yeah. Not happening. No kiss. No hint of what he'd done to piss her off, either. Just the cold shoulder and another bucket full of unmet expectations.

Seth gave her what she wanted. Swallowing his pride, he walked away. Then he ran. A couple blocks down the street, he decided he'd had enough being everyone's patsy. For a moment out there on Uncle George's dock, he'd contributed to Cord's rescue operation. Those little girls had needed him. He'd done a good thing today, and he'd do it again.

Cord had said *next time*, damn it, like Seth's sticking around might be a good thing. Yet he'd also given off the vibe that he didn't need an Army guy on his six. Obviously, Devereaux didn't either.

Fine.

Seth settled into an even run that ate up the miles to the dock. Instead of revving up the pontoon boat and taking off like a madman, he jumped in and idled it to a different location across the bay, out of sight. He emptied his pockets into a waterproof ziplock bag and secured the boat, covering it with the heavy canvas tarp to keep out the leaves and sun. Once he'd winched the cable on that tarp good and tight, when he was certain the watercraft would be safe, he tucked the ziplock bag into a larger, waterproof bag with an over the shoulder handle. The handle went around his neck. It'd still drag, but Seth was past that. He'd cared enough for one day.

The water jolted when he dived off the dock. He'd expected it to be as warm as it looked. Not that temperature mattered. Life sucked sometimes, and he needed a drink. One click was nothing to swim.

By the time he reached the north side of his uncle's few acres of ocean front property, he'd lost his anger and every last good intention. His arms ached, his hamstrings, too. The sun had set, painting a brilliant lemonade glow in the western sky. A clear purpling midnight blue commenced in the east. Night would soon fall dark and deep.

He stood there panting and dripping, marveling at how the atmosphere distorted a simple sunset into a truly spectacular light show at the end of what had begun as a good day, but ended being crap. How it melted those pinks and blossoming orange against the gathering night. How that perfect blue hue reminded him of—

Nope. Not going there.

Seth took a deep breath and left that stupid thought behind, too. What he wanted didn't come in pretty colors, and it wasn't sweet. Jack-fuckin'-Daniels was calling his name.

Tugging the bag off his neck, he rubbed at the welt around his neck that his foolishness had cost. Small price to pay when a man needs to be somewhere—anywhere—but on Molly's dock. The air inside Uncle George's two-room shack was stale when Seth unlocked the place and shoved inside. *Must be why George never invested in locks. This place needs to breathe.*

He emptied the bag, secured his weapon for another long night, set the satphone on the nightstand where it belonged for now and forever, then told his old friend Jack, "Hello, there." Didn't grab a glass or ice. Didn't need them, just grabbed onto the neck of *Old No. 7,* and he was good to go.

Devereaux was spot on when she'd said Gru would've liked the view. Seth liked looking south to Cuba, too. There wasn't any sense sitting on the north beach, was there? Not where every light blinking would remind him of a tow-headed pixie and her impish son. The taste of her lips. The glow in her eyes. No one smiled like Devereaux when she was happy, and for sure no woman had ever gotten to Seth as easily or as quickly as she had.

Still. Not. Going. There.

Dragging out of his wet clothes, Seth tossed his shirt and shorts to the sand and settled in for another night alone on the beach. The first gulp burned all the way down to his gut. The second gulp went down easier. The third, quick and smooth.

There was still enough light in the sky and on the ocean to see everything. The night was young. Hell, Latoya Franklin might show up and wouldn't that be terrific? *Other guys ended up with a girl, but not me. I ended up with a ghost. Yeah. Fuckin' good times.*

Seth upended the fifth and took another long swallow. Then another. Whiskey used to sit in his gut like a chunk of molten lava, and eventually, it made him upchuck. Not anymore. He'd had practice. Now it made him numb, and he liked that in a bottle. A bottle of forgetfulness, that's what Jack Daniels was. Dizzy. Blessed. Forgetfulness.

But he should've seen it coming. Karma, that was what this day was all about, a bitch slap for cheating on Katelynn and failing to be all that he could be. That was the real problem. Loneliness had become an integral thread in the fabric of his life. He'd tied his future to Katelynn and secured it with knots so tight, they couldn't be broken. One night of lust did not an eternal covenant make, and what he'd honestly thought he'd felt for Devereaux hadn't been real. Couldn't have been or he wouldn't be sitting here all by himself, would he?

How did a man simply forget the woman he loved, the one whose smile turned him inside out when he'd been a younger man? The one who skipped their prom after he'd broken his leg in a skiing accident the previous winter? Even now, Katelynn's memory remained eerily vivid.

Staring at the swell of the ocean and the never-ending march of breakers as they curled into themselves and rolled ashore, he could still feel the soft curls of her honey-blonde hair between his fingertips. The satiny warmth of her skin against his cheek. The heaven of her lush lips on his mouth and the scent of rose petal. The soft sweet lilt of joy in her laughter. The way she struggled to pronounce 'perpendicular' because of her stuttering issues.

Blowing out a gut full of regret, Seth yearned for a way to change what had happened. If he could do things over, he wouldn't have been so all fired up and eager to get home to Katelynn that last leave. He wouldn't have told her his arrival date. That way, she wouldn't have been on the freeway that day. She wouldn't have been in that lacy white dress and she wouldn't have gotten in the way of that drunk driver. She'd still be alive, and they'd be happy, and...

Shit! Seth kicked both heels into the sand, so damned weary of the never-ending what-ifs rattling around in his head. The truth was that life wasn't fair. He got that. Bad things happened, and when they did, they left good people with holes in their hearts and sorrow in their souls. Time, the Almighty Healer, was supposed to make everything right in the long run. Things were supposed to work out and life was supposed to get better. Well, bully for that son-of-a-bitch. All Seth had gotten from Time was one disappointment after another.

It was past time to go home. Uncle George's place would be fine. If he never came back, Seth would return long enough to put the island on the market and be done with it. He'd sell the pontoon boat, and he'd discount everything to put this wasted day behind him. Like he'd been doing since he'd lost Katelynn, he'd keep moving on.

With another deep breath, Seth stuck that half-empty jug in the sand to his right and let his head drop back on his shoulders. More and more stars winked on in the inky darkness overhead, just like those lights off his north shore were winking on right about now. Devereaux would probably be putting Scottie to bed about now. She'd tuck him in. She'd kiss him. He might blow her a goodnight kiss like little boys did. Then he'd stall and ask for a drink of water. Maybe ask her to read him a story. Not Walt Disney's *"Old Yeller"* though. Nope. Unfortunately, that story was off limits for the sweet little guy.

Aw, shit. I'm doing it again.

Seth settled back on his elbows, determined to erase the sight and taste of Devereaux Shepherd from his memory. He stretched both feet toward Cuba. With another stinkin' long night ahead of him, he had nothing to look forward to but his usual midnight visit from the 'gangsta' girl who'd tried to kill him.

Yeah. Life's a bitch and then you die. Don't I wish?

It shouldn't have turned out like this. He'd worked hard to get to where he was today. The long days of depression were far behind him—mostly. He'd conquered depression and PTSD, and by hell, every day was a damned good day. Mostly. He lived a life of control now, and until his uncle's stroke, Seth had avoided taking much downtime. By hell, a man alone doesn't need a yearly vacation in sunny Florida. Adventure was *not* his middle name.

Yet over and over, that was where he'd ended up, in life-or-death situations where by the grace of God, his fast thinking, and the Army's muscle training had kept him and others alive.

"God," he groaned to the darkening sky. "There's got to be something better than this."

A pelican arrowed into the water offshore hunting another meal. The waves rolled in. The tide went out. God never answered a prayer. Why would He answer this one? Life fuckin' went on and on… and on… and it was time for another drink.

Too bad Jack was already half gone. That made Seth legally drunk on the beach. Ha! He'd need a designated driver if he wanted to go anywhere. That deserved another snort. Might just deserve another drink, too. Seth McCray wasn't going anywhere. Hadn't been for years. He'd been stuck. Mired to that single day in his life that changed his world.

Shit. Everyone knew that.

Katelynn seemed closer tonight for some ungodly reason, but Seth didn't want to talk with her. Or to her. Since she'd gone away, not once had she sent him a message of her undying love from the other side. Not once. *Can you believe that?* He'd stayed true and faithful to her memory—well, almost—for years, but had she looked down from her heavenly perch even once? Had she sent him a dream or the smallest hint of her undying love? Uh-uh, no she most certainly had not. If she had, he'd have known it, wouldn't he?

So why'd the hairs on the back of his neck stand up like a ghost was hovering over him tonight, leering at him. Watching. Warily, Seth twisted his neck and glanced at the island behind him. The palm trees swayed like an army of drunken sailors at his six, but there was no ghost. Not even Latoya.

That made him laugh. "An army of drunken sailors," he told the waves crashing offshore. "Get it? Army? Sailors? Aw, never mind."

His fingers came unbidden to his scarred brow, the back of his nails rubbing over the lines that some bastard a world away had carved into him before Seth killed him. Masters. That was his name. Another Marine. Another asshole. Like Cord. The world was full of them and every last one of them packed a ton of shit they had no trouble dealing out to anyone unlucky enough to cross their paths.

Something or someone rustled behind Seth. He looked over his shoulder one last time, which was getting mighty difficult, his equilibrium being what it was. Palm trees. Sand. Uncle George's shack. Yeah. Not a whole lot of anything going on there.

Settling his back to the warm, soft Florida sand for another lonely night, Seth reached for the neck of that cozy brown bottle before he closed his eyes. The sun would wake him up come morning. Until then... blah, blah, blah.

Wait. What was I talking about?

He startled awake, his heart racing and his head still spinning. Someone was on his beach. He might be drunk, but he'd heard—it. Them. There was that noise again, the slow rasp of sand. A muffled hiss. Couldn't be Latoya, not out here.

Seth glanced down the length of his arm to where his friend still sat in the sand. But Jack didn't look so friendly anymore, and the sand had turned cold and damp. Yeah. Time to crawl into bed and sleep off another fuckin' great day.

That annoying sound again!

Seth lifted to his elbows. A definite scratching noise came to him from the trees. A rat? A parrot? *Guess I'll have to check it out. Might be another desperate woman burying her lizard. Only this time, there'll be no kissing. Ah-uh. Absolutely none and never again. Not going there, no sirree.*

Rolling over to his hands and knees, Seth instantly regretted the vertigo that came with motion. The sand might not be moving, but his head and stomach sure were. Make that spinning. He spit, angry with himself for stooping to this level. He was better than this.

On a good day…

Yet whatever was making all that noise out there needed investigating. Deranged woman or not, this was his island. He couldn't let Uncle George down. Wouldn't think of it.

But Seth couldn't exactly stand either, so he crawled on his hands and knees toward that… that sound. By the time he made it into the shadows, he was a very sick man. Drinking on an empty stomach was never smart. Morning would not be fun.

This time, the scratching sounded closer, which was a good thing. He hadn't crawled all this way for nothing. Seth blinked to his left. Then he started digging. The sand had moved. He knew it. He only scooped a few big handfuls when—*Lordy, Lordy!*

Seth tugged a wiggling, hissing Gru out of his shallow grave and instantly received the whip of an angry iguana's tail across his cheek. "Whoa, boy," Seth soothed as he placed the big fellow's belly to the sand but kept his fingers around Gru's very muscled neck. Flick, flick went an extremely long tongue. Two beady black eyes blinked sand out of them then stared up at Seth. Who in their right mind could love this ugly guy?

Devereaux Shepherd, that's who.

"You okay?" Seth asked his new friend. "Need a drink? Of water?"

Flick, flick went Gru's tongue. Still covered with a coat of fine sand, his neck wrinkled when his scaly head rotated toward the ocean. Then…

"Oh, no, you don't," Seth called out as the lizard took off running. For a critter fresh out of the grave, Gru had no trouble hot-footing it straight for the water. Pushing up to his feet, Seth beat the lizard to the beach by, well, not much. But he did catch a writhing, clawing Gru by his hind leg before he made it into the open water.

"You're not going anywhere, big guy," Seth told Gru as they set a new azimuth. Uncle George wouldn't mind an iguana inside his shack for one night. Okay, make that two. One to make sure Gru would live. Another to make sure Seth did.

Chapter Fifteen

Dev stood at her open kitchen door, looking out. The night seemed especially dark. Especially empty. Exhausted after the drama of the day, Scottie was fast asleep in his room. Cord had yet to explain himself. He'd been on and off his cell most of the evening, talking with his guys. Stevie "Wonder" James had been by, but hadn't stayed long, just enough to tell Cord that this—whatever *this* was—was bigger than the two of them. That they'd really stepped in a pile of shit this time.

How well Dev knew. She'd Googled the Khadeem name and came up against the intimidating profile of a very wealthy, very powerful Mideastern family. Not only did Lianna's father, Farraq Khadeem, own the entire peninsula that extended into the Persian Gulf, he also owned one of the world's richest oil conglomerates. With three sons by his first wife, and five sons by his second, Lianna's mother, the man dabbled in investments that had doubled his wealth over the last two months. Two months! He seemed to have everything, but obviously, that wasn't enough, or he wouldn't have given his only daughter to a known pedophile and a serial rapist, would he?

In every news photo of him that Dev located, Farraq Khadeem looked every bit the part of an arrogant man. His nostrils flared as if he challenged all reporters and photographers, both Saudi and foreign. He interrupted interviews, and he sneered when he spoke, as if everyone were beneath him. His face seemed ever wrinkled with permanent disgust, making his hawkish nose more pronounced.

The white, flowing robes he wore lent the usual mystique that other leaders in that part of the world exhibited, but Khadeem's dark eyes never smiled. There was no illusion of graciousness to anything he said or did. The man even walked like an apex predator as if people everywhere had better get out of his way.

His wives' faces had never been photographed, and the women were not seen in public. His daughter, Lianna, was the only one who'd accompanied him on diplomatic visits. Even then, walking briskly with her at his side, he rarely glanced her way. If anything, it was as if he was the important one. Not her.

In every aspect, he portrayed a powerful man—at least, a man who thought he was powerful—yet not a one of his tall, dark, and handsome sons were ever seen with him. Instead, one very blonde woman, whom Dev learned, would one day inherit his kingdom, always accompanied Khadeem.

Dev couldn't locate anything on the two women Farraq had married, but Lianna's mother had to be of European descent. There was no record of a wedding anywhere Dev looked, yet it seemed obvious. As dark as Khadeem's skin and hair were, as dark-skinned as his sons were, there had to have been a white woman—somewhere—in Khadeem's past.

Dev had also Googled Basheer Bagani. Though not directly related to the reigning kingdom of Saudi Arabia, there was enough royal blood in his line to merit the title he flashed around the world. Ugly rumors and accusations surfed the swells of his shadowy wake. It seemed playboy Basheer particularly liked the energy of high-roller cities. Las Vegas, Nevada. Atlantic City, New Jersey. Monte Carlo, Monaco. Macau, China. He enjoyed being seen and photographed with call girls, showgirls, and supermodels, their ages unimportant. While he flaunted his illicit contacts, police reports abounded, yet the Teflon-coated snake had avoided indictments in several countries, the latest in Ireland.

The puzzle remained. How had Lianna, a woman of seemingly protected, noble birth, ended up in the basement prison of a depraved human trafficker? *Perish the thought.*

Chills raced up Dev's spine at what she herself had lived through in that dark, dank place. There'd been no lights when she'd come to that night, on what had smelled and felt like a concrete basement floor. She'd never seen the actual structure of her prison after she'd been jostled off the streets of Havana and shoved into a nearby rusted-out van by two random guys, not after they'd pulled a burlap bag over her head. Then one of those big, brave men had knocked her out.

Why they'd taken Gru along with her became apparent when she came to, and someone struck a match to the kerosene lantern hanging on a chain from the ceiling of the squalid room. Gru had been crammed into a wire cage dangling from the same ceiling. Over a bed of coals.

She'd screamed and wished she'd left her handsome pet home. They'd laughed. Then things got ugly. Instead of torturing Gru like Dev thought, they'd left him to hiss and cook, while they'd dragged another screaming woman out of her cell and bent her over the metal rail at one end of the rounded room. Dev had watched as the men took turns with the poor woman. While Gru squealed and grunted in pain, she'd watched in morbid fascination at what would surely happen next—to her.

By sheer coincidence, Ryland "Sonic" DeLorenzo had been on the same Havana street that day. He'd seen Dev's broad daylight abduction, then tracked the men who'd kidnapped her. In hours, Cord had shown up in all his big brotherly glory, armed to the teeth, and glowing with nuclear rage. How Montego's dirty little secret still stood after the barrage of hellfire he'd let loose in that cramped Cuban basement prison remained a mystery. Cord meant to kill anything that moved that night, and Dev was okay with it. All she'd wanted was to be safe at home.

While Cord had grabbed Montego's rape victim on their dash to freedom, Dev grabbed Gru's cage and ran like Cord told her to—like Hell was on her heels. She never looked behind her, just ran all the way to the beach, over sand and stone, until she leapt into that lifesaving boat where Miguel waited. Her feet were cut and bleeding by then, but Gru was safe and wet rubber had never smelled as sweet as it did that night.

But poor Lianna was different. She *had* been tortured. She couldn't have walked, much less run, which meant someone carried her out of Montego's lair. Dev wondered which of Cord's guys had that honor. But how exactly had they known she was there? Had anyone? The order to rescue these women hadn't come from Uncle George this time. Then who?

"Get it done," Cord growled into his phone. "You should've been straight with me from the get-go, damn it, Rabbit."

Dev stepped out into the night, missing Gru. Missing Seth. But not needing Cord's steady angst in her ear. He'd been adamant to the point of hostility that she lose *Soldier Boy*—his tag for Seth—once and for all. Cord said he'd tell her what was going on as soon as he heard from Cleve "Rabbit" Miller, one of his guys. But Cord was on the phone with Cleve now, and getting angrier by the minute.

Lowering to the single concrete step off her kitchen, Dev left her brother's foul mood behind. She had bigger, more mundane problems. Rent. All of her dreams sat behind her in the little bungalow that wasn't really hers, but needed paint. The rent came due in three days. She'd never been late before, but she worried now. And food. She'd given everything in her cupboards away this morning. The refrigerator was bare. Breakfast would be dry cereal because she had no more milk. No coffee. No juice. Scottie had eaten dry cereal before, but damn it. Dry cereal was a fun treat when it was his idea, but when it was the only thing to eat? This was no life for a child.

A match struck to Dev's right, and Trish's face came out of nowhere. "Soldier boy go home?" she asked, blowing a puff of cigarette smoke upward. Cigarette smokers always did that, as if they could ever send second-hand smoke high enough to not hurt the people around them. Trish didn't smoke often. *She must be upset.*

"He won't be back," Dev said simply. "How's Miguel?"

Trish didn't need to know how Seth's departure had hurt or the look of betrayal in his soft brown eyes when Dev let him down. But Cord had been so fierce, insisting there were things going on that *Soldier Boy* had no business knowing. That one more operator was a definite no-go. But seriously, all Seth had done since he'd shown up was help. He hadn't pried, just followed Cord's orders and put up with his shitty attitude and his bad language.

"Skippy's fine," Trish replied, her gaze on the billowing fumes she'd just spewed at heaven. "One fragment splintered off his collarbone into his pec. Stupid man refused painkillers."

"You like him."

Trish grunted. "Maybe." Another puff of leftover nicotine hit the night air. Another lie along with it.

"Maybe, nothing." Dev arched her back, tired of being tired. "I see the way you look at him. He's different and you know it."

Another puff and another indifferent, "Maybe."

Dev turned to look at her friend. "I think you and he would make a good couple. He's obviously smitten with you, though I'm not certain why. You're so hard on him. You're mean. Even when he's wounded and flirting with you, you still put him down."

Trish's shoulders lifted. "It's a gift."

"You call him Skippy?"

By then Trish had taken a seat next to Dev. "I call him a lot of things. The guy's a jerk."

"All guys are jerks," Dev answered, not sure if she meant Miguel or Cord at that precise moment. For sure not Seth. The only mistake he'd made as far as Dev knew had been hanging onto the memory of his dead fiancée too long. Even that wasn't so bad. It spoke of dedication and honor. Of a good man's broken heart. A man who loved that deeply was a rare find indeed. And because of that ornery Marine blustering on the phone in the house behind her, she'd told Seth to get lost. It didn't seem a fair trade.

"You're sure quiet."

Dev didn't dare look at Trish. "Yeah, well, it's been a long day. Aldrich wasn't happy filling my shift on short notice."

"He give you any shit?"

"He said there'd better not be a next time. You ever feel like you're burning the candle at both ends, while you're running out of wax in the middle? That nothing you do is good enough? That everyone wants a piece of you until there are no pieces left?"

"Yeah. When I lost Evan."

"I'm sorry. I shouldn't have said anything. It's not my..." What else could Dev say? Losing the husband you loved, watching him waste away day after day because his heart had never been strong, was infinitely worse than losing a minimum wage job pushing crab cakes. "Please forgive me. It's not my place to tell you how to feel about Miguel. I had no right to complain."

Trish's warm hand landed on Dev's wrist. "'S okay, Devereaux. You meant nothing by it, and I'm glad you think Miguel's got his eye on me. For so long I've dreamed..." She sent another puff into the night. "Let's just say that it takes a while, you know? Part of me's still stuck in the past with Evan. When I wake up in the morning, I expect to see him beside me like when he was healthy. He used to roll over in bed and grin at me, his hair tousled and his eyes bright, and you know. He'd get frisky. We'd make love, fall back to sleep and start all over again."

Man, how would that be, to have loved someone so perfectly, even for a day? Dev honestly didn't know. The only one who'd ever truly had her back was Cord. *And Seth…*

Trish swallowed hard enough that Dev heard it in the quiet night. "Never thought I'd be the one to be left behind, not like I was. Not after all we went through together. Always, right up 'til the end, I knew he'd get better. I just knew." She stabbed the cigarette butt into the side of the step. "But I was wrong. It's hard to trust yourself once you've been wrong like that. Don't think I could handle another…" She let her heartache trail away.

"Seth was engaged," Dev whispered, not sure she wanted to share her feelings about him with Trish.

Right on cue, Trish grunted. "Was or is?" she asked, her tone sharp with sarcasm.

She could be a hard woman. She said what she meant, usually with a take no prisoners attitude, a hearty *'what's it to you, wise guy?'* and plenty of venom. An early death hadn't just taken her husband. It had left her traumatized and angry. In a way, she was just like the women Dev had served and waited on today. Trish was in recovery.

"Was. His fiancée, Katelynn, died five years ago. In a car crash. He, umm, still loves her."

"Like I said, jerk."

"You're probably right." Dev refused to argue. When Trish turned pensive like she was tonight, nothing anyone said got through to her. Which was probably best, since Seth wouldn't be back, not after the way Dev had hurt him. There was nothing to argue about.

Trish blew another plume up to heaven. "You love him?"

Stupid question. "Who me?" Dev scoffed. "I just met him last night, so that answer would be not only no, but hell—"

"Yep. You love him."

"I do not." Dev eyed her friendly, prickly bestie. "How can you even ask that after what I've been through with James?"

"Because you're better than me, Dev. You give your heart away to everyone you meet. You do. James was a fool not to have seen what he could've had with you and Scottie, but Seth…" Trish lifted another cancer stick to her lips, covered her mouth as she sparked another match and blew the first fragrant puff away from Dev. "Uncle George's nephew couldn't take his eyes off you today. Trust me. I was watching. It was easy to see he thought you hung the moon."

Oh, that was rich, wasn't it? "You are the pot calling the kettle black, girlfriend," Dev chided. "Did you hear me when I said we'd just met? As in midnight, last night? And what about Miguel watching you this morning? As much pain as he was in, that man flirted with you like it was his one and only chance to make you smile. That kind of attention is something you can absolutely count on, yet you ignore it like it's nothing. What's in that thing you're smoking? Hash?"

Another smoke signal went skyward with a melancholy, "I wish."

An empty kind of silence enveloped the yard, where once a lumbering iguana had made his home. Where once a little boy had delighted in his lizard friend's forays into the shrubs and up the trees. Dev attempted to salvage the night. "You're not alone, Trish. You've got friends."

"No, I don't. Don't need them. Don't want them. Only one I like is you."

That raised Dev's brows up to her hairline. "Me?"

Trish dropped the barely smoked cigarette to the packed dirt between her sandaled feet and ground it out with her heel. "Yeah, you. You're… safe. I don't have to brush my hair in the morning if I don't want to, don't have to dress up to impress you. I'm okay the way I am. I'm…" She licked her bottom lip. "…enough. You never judge. You just love people. Yeah, it gets you into trouble sometimes, but that's who you are. You're… nice."

"In case you haven't noticed, nice people finish last. Look around. I'm not exactly living on the edge, unless it's the edge of poverty."

"Which proves my point." With an unladylike grunt, Trish pushed to her feet. "You don't have to live like this, but you choose to because you know what it's like to be where every last one of those women and girls you fed and hugged today were before they came to your place. You know what it's like to be in their shoes. You might not be smart, but you are nice."

Dev waved her off. "Enough with the compliments. I get it. I'm nice and dumb. I just can't…" She looked up into the dark sky, thinking of a man with seriously sexy eyes, seeing the hurt in them, the—something else—she hadn't yet defined. It wasn't regret lurking in Seth's dark eyes, as much as… acceptance? Exactly. That was what had shadowed his eyes, as if long ago—possibly five long years ago—Seth had accepted the single most traumatic loss of his life. As if he'd fully expected her to turn away because everyone else had. As if he knew he deserved nothing but the ghost of the one woman who hadn't left, the woman he still loved.

Her fingers lifted to her throat at the thought of him out there and alone on his uncle's island. All she'd given Seth to remember her by was the body of a dead iguana. "I'm not nice," she whispered to her friend. "I'm a bitch."

That earned her a snort. "That'd be the day," Trish bit out as she turned to make her way to her bungalow. "I'm the bitch, remember. You're Goody Two Shoes." She loved getting in the last word. Dev didn't have to wait long.

"Call if either Miguel or that mystery woman run fevers. And don't let Cord screw this thing with you and Seth up like he's done with the rest of your life. You're not one of his soldiers, so stop acting like one. You're a mother and you owe your son more than you owe that bully you call a brother. Seems like you're the one who needs to be rescued."

"Who, me?" Dev could barely make out her friend's face in the shadows. "Who do I need to be rescued from? Besides Sly?"

Another grunt came from the gate that separated her tiny backyard and Trish's. "I meant Cord, Devereaux. Answer me this if you're so smart. If Seth's been faithful to a dead woman all this time, how long do you think he'll be faithful to you?"

Chapter Sixteen

Right on time, morning broke like it had a schedule to keep. Seth groaned as one retina-searing ray of startling bright sunlight pierced the billowing sheers at his right and set his room—and the inside of his cranium—ablaze. Jack Daniels was not a good friend.

It took Seth a minute to weave his way into the bathroom and sit without falling down. There was no way he could aim straight this morning. He didn't even try, just sat there like a woman and let the three bottled waters and one helluva lot of Jack Daniels leak out of him.

Then he remembered. He had a new friend, probably because that new friend had just lumbered up to the bathroom doorway, his lizard claws shattering the silence in the quiet shack like nail guns. Clickety. Clackety. Click. Click. Click.

"Ouch, damn it. Shhh." Seth winced at the reptile sprawled there with his chin up in all his iridescent emerald green glory. Wow. In the light of day, the lizard was a looker, even if you could only open one eye to see him.

"You… you're kind of handsome, you know that?" Seth whispered to the scaly gentleman. "No wonder Devereaux likes you."

Pivoting as if he abhorred the praise, Gru scurried away in a flash of green, his head raised high and those dastardly toenails punctuating every board in his path with another sharp rat-a-tat-tat-tat.

"Do you have to be so loud?" Seth called out after him, instantly regretting the volume. Both eyes rolled back in his head. His brows lifted. For a second, he contemplated what people would say if they found him nude and dead on his throne. Not. A. Pretty. Sight.

Groaning now, because a helluva good night spent feeling sorry for yourself didn't feel so good just because the sun came up, Seth finished his business, eased to his feet, and faced one ugly SOB in the mirror.

"Way to go, McCray," he whispered extra quietly. "You know better, yet you do stupid stuff like this." Ah, well. Today was a brand-new day, and for once, Latoya hadn't come calling during the night. He'd slept straight through, and what was up with that? Even drunk, Seth hadn't had a single, complete night's sleep until…

Leaning around the bathroom door, he asked, "Gru? You still out there?" For having been murdered, this lizard had a lot of get-up and go. "Oh, there you are. Under the bed. You must need to rest, too."

Seth let the creature do his thing, which had better not lead to any cleaning up of messy reptilian bodily functions, not today. Most definitely not after guzzling half a fifth of Jack. Just the thought of what he'd done to his body sent a nauseous wave rolling around Seth's stomach. Yeah. The day after a good drunk never felt as good as the night tying it on.

Slowly, he shuffled to bed. He had some sleep to catch up on, but Gru was alive. Wouldn't Devereaux and Scottie be surprised?

"You what?" Dev nearly shrieked, she'd whispered so loudly. If not for Scottie still being asleep in his room, she would've screeched. What was Cord thinking?

He came back at her with, "What else could I do? Leave her there? You don't know half of what we were up against or what she went through."

At the moment, they stood near her front door, as far away from Scottie's room as they could stand. It was early morning, too early to be fighting, yet there they were. They'd both grabbed a shower, yet neither of them had had any sleep. Cord wore his standard: black jeans, black t-shirt, and work boots. She'd opted for denim summer shorts and a red tank top. But the humidity was already stifling. She'd have to turn her air conditioners on if this kept up.

Trish had returned during the night to check on Miguel and Lianna. Both were sleeping comfortably, but Seth was still gone, and the more Dev thought about what Trish had said, the more she resented all that Cord expected of her. Trish was right. Dev was Scottie's mother first, not Cord's.

"She's a princess," Dev reminded her high and mighty brother. "You can't keep her here. The State Department will have your neck over this. Mine, too. We could go to jail! Scottie's had a tough enough life without losing his mother. Did you ever stop and think that he could be taken away from me? That I could lose him? Damn it, Cord. You should've handed that woman over with everyone else."

The veins in Cord's temples bulged, whether in anger or frustration, Dev was past caring. Still, they were in this together. Cannibalizing each other over something they could no longer change wouldn't help. But shit. A real Arabian princess now rested in Dev's bedroom, sleeping on her bed while the Shepherds' house of cards collapsed.

Reaching for every last shred of her inner calm, Dev lowered her voice and tried again. "You know how much I love you and what you do, Cord. Honest. I'm proud to serve at your side. What you're doing is a good thing, and more people like you should be fighting this plague of human trafficking. You've changed my life—hell, you *saved* my life," she emphasized. "You love Scottie as if he's yours and I can't complain, but I need to understand. Tell me why we had no choice. Why does Lianna Khadeem have to stay here?"

Cord's jaw clenched tight and his lips pursed like they did before he blew his cool. His shoulders twitched and rolled like the giant draft horses did when annoyed by flies. He hadn't always had a temper, but with every deployment he'd been away on, it had escalated. He didn't often snap at her or Scottie, but she'd witnessed his men take an unnecessary butt reaming when he blew.

Taking a deep breath, Dev faced her brother. He might not like it, but he had some explaining to do.

One dark brow spiked imperiously, but at last he said, "We need to keep her off the grid, that's why. Now drop it."

Not good enough. "No, Cord. This is my son's life we're talking about. He's my first responsibility, not you or the women you save. Tell me now. All of it."

The man swelled with the rage. "She doesn't want to go back, Dev. That's why, now let it go. We have to keep her safe, so stop fighting me on this."

Still not good enough. "Why was a princess in Montego's basement jail to begin with?"

Cord sent her another controlled roll of flashing black eyes. "Her husband, that mother-fuckin'—"

Dev put one hand up to stop the tirade before it began. "Not in my home, Cord. Keep your voice down. Scottie's four. He doesn't need to cuss like a man before he starts pre-school."

Another deep breath. Another shoulder roll. And Cord spilled. "Remember Twila Judge?"

Dev nodded. "The Hollywood starlet. Yeah. I remember her. Sort of. Wasn't she the gal who disappeared—?"

"She didn't just disappear, Dev. The authorities found her in a shallow grave outside New Delhi after a photo shoot, where, by the way, she was last seen with Bagani. Her fingers were missing and..." Cord swiped a hand over his hair. "Other parts were missing, too. Bagani takes souvenirs."

Oh. My. Hell. "Is that why...? Are Lianna's fingers...?"

Cord shook his head. "No. She was just... She's just..."

Please don't say raped. Dev caved and went to her big, brave brother before he could answer. She'd never seen him so pale or so undone. "She's been tortured, Cord, I know that. Who did it? Bagani? Is he in league with Montego? Is that how she ended up with those other women?"

Cord's chest heaved, stretching his unembellished t-shirt into a solid wall of muscle. "That's what we don't know yet. Right now, Wonder and Sonic are back in Varadero. Rabbit's working as discreetly as possible behind the scenes to get diplomatic immunity for Lianna. He knows people, but this..." Cord's throat muscles seemed not up to the task of swallowing. He turned his head to the side as if he needed to spit. Dev surely did.

"This mess has the potential to put the United States in the middle of another Mideastern war, Dev. Farraq Khadeem's a powerful, greedy man and his reach is worldwide. When he discovers that a Saudi Prince handed his only daughter over to human traffickers, and that those men reduced her to a sex slave…" There went Cord's hand again, his biceps bulging as he made another pass over his head. "When he finds out that we rescued her, that she's in the States and has requested I seek asylum on her behalf…"

"He'll be mad," Dev stated what Cord didn't seem able to equivocate. "So? Let him be mad. He's the one who sold her in the first place, didn't he? Where was his righteous indignation then?" *Men!*

She didn't want to seem heartless, but surely the elder Khadeem had known what he was getting in the trade. Bagani wasn't the king of Saudi Arabia. He wasn't even a close relative. There was no direct blood connection between him and the ruling power. He was nothing more than the product of an in-law who'd married royalty generations back. What had Lianna's father really needed from Bagani's father that he'd bartered his only daughter away?

"That's not the real problem, Sis. The real problem is the peace treaty Ambassador Miller had been hammering out between the Saudis and Khadeem. This marriage was intended to join those two families once and for all. For the last sixteen years, there's been an uneasy peace in that part of the world, only now…"

Dev cocked her head, pissed at what men in that particular part of the world did with and to their women.

"There'll be another war, is that what you're trying to tell me? Oh, my hell, I am so freakin' surprised. Another war in the Mideast, what a shocker. Like we haven't heard that before. Khadeem sold his only daughter when she was a three-year-old, Cord. For Christ's sake, pull your head out of your ass. If there's to be another war, it's on his head. Not hers."

Cord turned deathly still. "Understood, Baby Sister, but you've never been to war, have you? You've never seen what I've seen, and you sure as hell have never had to do what I've done. So back your self-righteous shit up and think for a damned second. Who gets to clean up behind Bagani and Khadeem when this shit blows sky high? And it will, trust me. It sure as hell won't be Soldier Boy." He stabbed a thumb into his chest. "Hell, no. They might've been first into Iraq back in ninety-one, but it'll be Marines like me who hit that desert this time around. *Marines*. You feel me? *My* brothers and *my* sisters!"

Dev took a step away from Cord, never more aware than at that moment, that her brother, her hero, the guy she'd always believed could do anything, had suffered greatly during his time served. Yet he'd never let it show. Never talked about it. He'd just kept on keeping on. Stepping up for one more deployment. One more push back against the evil in the world. Always fighting the good fight. Which had now come to her front door.

"How did you know Lianna was there?" she asked quietly, needing to defuse the tension before Cord punched her wall or something. "Or did you already know? Was finding her there with those other women just a coincidence or did you have prior knowledge?"

"I knew," he blew out on a sigh. "I have a man inside Montego's organization. George McCray hired him. That's how we know when to go in and when to lay low. He feeds us the numbers, how many women, how many guards on shift, and when the women are the least guarded. He tells us when they might be moved, only now..."

Shit. Dev hung her head, overwhelmed and underpaid, overworked and underappreciated. "Let me guess. You have to go back to Varadero for him. You can't leave him behind. Do you even know his name?"

"Julio Juarez."

That name meant nothing to Dev. "He's not one of your guys?"

Cord shook his head. "No, he's a fool who works undercover. Used to be a SEAL, I think. Not sure who he works for now. Nobody knows."

Dev swallowed hard. The United States had been going to war to bolster other countries' economies and borders or to right their wrongs, for so, so long. In the name of freedom, Marines, soldiers, airmen, and SEALS had become the world's police force, ever ready to fight for the cause of capitalistic greed in the name of democracy. Why now? Why again? It didn't seem fair that honorable young men like Cord should feel obligated to put their lives on the line over and over again.

Standing here in front of her was the reason Dev did what she did. Because of her brother. Yes, she truly cared about every last woman and child he'd saved, but they never would've made it to her house without Cord's and his men's dogged persistence and their bone-headed courage. She herself wouldn't be standing there arguing with him if he'd been anyone else. It all came down to the brother she loved and that crazy, hard-as-nails USMC heart beating in his chest.

"What do you need me to do?" she asked on a breath of resignation.

Chapter Seventeen

An iguana's an interesting creature. At nearly five feet long from snout to the tip of his whip-like tail, Gru had to weigh near twenty, maybe twenty-five pounds. And he could run. The old boy proved it last night. Yet the rasp of his scaly belly across Seth's wooden floor lent a comfortable feeling of—something—to Uncle George's sparse, utilitarian shack on the beach. It had been nice to not wake up alone for a change. Gru's nails needed to be clipped though, which was why Seth rummaged through his shaving kit. He'd had a nail clipper in there somewhere.

For now, Gru held stock still with his head up and his eyes closed, on a stretch of the sunlight dappled floor just inside the shack. Seth wasn't brave enough to let the big guy roam the beach for fear he'd sprint for open water like he had last night.

Seth had been Googling proper diet and iguana care since he'd showered and eaten his own meager breakfast of a banana, toast, along with a glass of orange juice with four aspirin. Dressed in a clean pair of dark tan boat shorts and a plain white undershirt for the day, he'd put Jack back in the cupboard, where the troublemaker belonged. Seth's queasy stomach couldn't yet handle the thought of bacon and eggs for breakfast.

"Found it," Seth told Gru, palming the clipper.

No comment. Not even a blink. The lizard wasn't coy so much as he probably knew Seth was leery of the mighty whip Gru dragged behind him. His tail *was* a monumental weapon, but Seth was just thankful he hadn't grabbed onto it last night when Gru made his mad dash for the ocean. He hadn't known it then, but iguana's tails broke—as in right off their bodies—if someone grabbed them just right. While Gru would've eventually regenerated his tail, surprising Devereaux with her living, but tailless iguana, wasn't what Seth had planned.

Opting to take his chances, Seth folded his long legs and sat alongside his reptilian friend. Pocketing the clipper for now, he opted for discretion and reached for Gru's breakfast on the counter. Because of all he'd read, Seth now knew iguanas were vegetarians. He'd mixed a generous portion of fresh greens in a plastic container, mostly parsley and the bok choy he'd intended for a stir-fry, then added a couple slices of green pepper, an eighth of the banana from his breakfast, and a sliver of watermelon. To make sure the wound that Devereaux was so certain Gru had suffered—enough to bury him certain—wasn't infected, Seth needed to examine this pretty fellow. But to do that, Gru needed a diversion.

Extending the slice of apple, a nice crisp Jonathan, Seth tapped his free hand to the floor to get Gru's attention. One lizard eye flicked open. Rotated in its socket. Then closed.

That is so cool.

Gru turned his head, then quick as a blink, the apple was on the floor under his dewlap, and breakfast was served.

Seth eased the rest of his peace offering alongside the apple. While Gru crunched and indulged, Seth meant to test the limits of their fledgling friendship and hopefully, not get tail-whipped for being too up close and personal. After Seth treated whatever wounds he found, he'd clip those clattering nails, too.

Very gingerly, Seth tipped Gru's front leg up and peered at the lizard's belly. Gru was a handsome boy, a lovely shade of green from the tip of his tail to his shoulders, where the green gave way to silvery freckles, which Seth now knew were called tuberculate scales. The larger silver discs at the sides of his puffy neck, just below the holes in his head, which passed for ears, were subtympanic shields. Although their iridescent sheen enhanced Gru's already spectacular hue, they could swell if he needed to look any more intimidating than he already did. But that spiky row of spines running along Gru's back and under his very fine dewlap? Damned impressive.

Thin brownish-gold stripes circled his belly but faded halfway up his sides. Wider, darker stripes circled his tail, which was fairly thick until the last six or eight inches of its lethal charm. The flap of lizard skin dangling under his chin, his dewlap, faded from emerald green to silver, then back again to green. This fellow was nothing short of a mini-dinosaur, and Seth understood why Devereaux loved Gru. He might not say a lot, but he was still good company.

Five long toes on each rear foot, along with a rake of mighty fine claws, gave him running power and speed. His skin, er, umm, his scales, were tough, and Seth suspected, waterproof, as fast as he'd headed for the ocean. Jowls hugged his shoulders like fluffy pillows. When he blinked, his irises fluctuated between gold-ish orange to orange-ish brown. Gru also had what was called a parietal eye in the middle of his forehead. *A third eye! How cool is that?*

So, yeah. Seth was very careful in how he handled his all-seeing, albeit hungry, friend. While Gru munched, Seth slipped both hands over the gentle beast's shoulders. So far, so good. Running his palms along Gru's sides, Seth located no bloody patches. No missing spines. Just lots of smooth, chilly scales, and the fine sand from his grave.

On his knees now, Seth bent over the reptile, needing to understand how Devereaux could've misinterpreted what she'd seen. She'd specifically said Gru had screamed and her clothes had been streaked in blood, but… was that blood his?

"So, Lazarus, how'd you survive a knife attack?" Seth asked, but then he saw it. Ouch. A two-inch wound lay hidden within the recesses of all those leathery folds, just under Gru's left armpit. Yeah. That had to hurt. *Damn that son-of-a-bitch, Sly.*

Easing away from his prehistoric buddy and making no sudden moves, Seth rolled to his feet to retrieve a tube of Neosporin, a bucket of warm water, and his own personal supply of Betadine. Then patiently, he cleansed and doctored his first injured iguana.

While he worked, Gru kept crunching and eating. Interestingly, he made no sounds other than the occasional swish of his tail on the wooden floor. Not once had he screamed, and he didn't growl. Hadn't made so much as a peep or a squeak despite Seth's handling of a wound that would've made a grown man beg for a local. Gru would need to see a lizard doctor within the next day if Seth's home doctoring didn't work, and if that wound showed signs of infection. But for now, the prehistoric baby dragon was just hungry.

"There," Seth sighed, the deed done and his buddy oblivious to the fact that he'd returned from the dead, well, the grave anyway. "Feel better?"

Never had he suspected he'd be sitting on the floor in Uncle George's shack talking to a lizard, but he was. Gru was a handsome boy. Strong, Resilient. Clever in his own way, too.

When a sharp crack of thunder shattered the morning calm, Seth jumped as the ground vibrated from a nearby lightning strike. "Damn, where'd that come from?"

Pushing to his feet, he glanced out the window. The daily storm that usually graced Florida with intermittent showers had come up quickly. The ocean had traded its blue for molten gray. Dark clouds now scudded northward, obscuring the sun, while traces of white lightning flitted from black cloud to black cloud. Whitecaps studded the rolling breakers as the wind kicked up, sending dried palm leaves shuffling across the beach. Even the gulls and brown pelicans offshore seemed suspended in mid-air like two-winged kites.

"You stay here and finish your breakfast," Seth told the reptile. "I'm going to duck outside and grab a bucket of sand for, umm, a lizard box for you to, you know, pee in. I won't be long."

Lightning flashed and thunder rolled as if warning Seth to make it quick. Just as he opened the door, the first of the rain hit. He ducked into the weather and ran to the small utility shed east of the Uncle George's shack. Quick, he could do.

Then he was going back to bed.

The more Dev learned about the situation brewing in the Mideast, the more she knew she had to reach out to Seth McCray. Cord wouldn't like it, but by the time she returned with Seth, her brother might very well be headed for Cuba to find his buddies and save that missing Julio guy. She couldn't let Cord make that journey alone. Seth would help; she knew he would. That was all he'd done since she'd met him, plus, he had the boat and the equipment to make the hundred-mile round trip safely. She had only to ask. He might be angry at first, but she could work with that. He'd come around and he'd come back with her. She knew he would.

Covertly, she called Trish, who came right over to watch Scottie. "What's he supposed to eat?" she asked at Dev's open refrigerator. "There's not much in here, but… how old is this cheese? Is there a zombie apocalypse coming that I don't know about or are you culturing penicillin for the black market?"

Dev cringed all the way to her toes. "I know it's pretty empty. Can I borrow a cup of milk, two-percent if you've got it? I'll pay you back once I can get to the store."

Trish's sharp eyes met Dev's over the second-hand Kelvinator's half door. "I'll do you one better. I need a few things at the drugstore. Scottie and I'll stop for a burger on the way, then I'll keep him at my place until you return. I've got plenty of his toys and a couple blankets over there. I know what he likes to eat. He'll be okay."

"Thanks, Trish. You're a lifesaver," Dev murmured as she kept an ear out for Cord. He'd been with Lianna for a while, and Dev needed to be gone before he nixed her plan to bring Seth to the rescue.

Trish eyed the lanyard Dev had just slipped over her head. "Where are you going?"

"To get Seth," was all Dev offered. The less Trish knew about who Lianna was, the better.

Trish huffed as if she'd scented a lie in the air. "What are you not telling me?"

"You don't want to know," Dev said hurriedly. She had to get out of there before Cord caught her and before Scottie woke. "Tell Cord I had an errand to run, will you? That's all. Don't say a word about where I've gone. He won't like it, but I… never mind. This is something I have to do."

"Go. Get your man," Trish said as Dev headed into yet another rainy Florida day.

Dev scowled. "He's not my man." *I just hope Seth's still there by the time I get to him.*

Worried, she set a steady pace to the dock. Her boat would be wet with rain, but you either learned to love the quick thundershowers that rattled through Florida on a daily basis, or you stayed indoors like an old woman afraid to melt, until they passed. Dev had never been one for backing down, not even from Mother Nature. That might not be her wisest attribute, but it had served her well over the years. Besides, the slicker she kept onboard would keep her warm once she hit open sea.

Jogging the rest of the way, she dodged puddles, branches and fallen palm fronds while lightning crackled overhead. The air was full of electricity. The last hurricane had devastated the Keys, Key West in particular, but this was no hurricane. Just a good, noisy thunderstorm. Just Mother

Nature doing her thing and reminding the world who was boss.

Once away from the bay and finally on open water, Dev donned her bright yellow rain slicker. She ignored the small craft warnings on her radio while she aimed for Drunken Sailor Island and the man who could help. Her small boat crested whitecap after whitecap, making the usually short trip worrisome and long. But it gave her time to think. It was interesting that, for all Sly Valentine's bluff and bluster, he hadn't accosted her on her way to Molly's today. Guess he was one of those namby-pamby crybabies who didn't like to get his feet wet.

It took a bit of wrangling alongside Uncle George's dock before her boat was steady enough to tie off a bowline. But where was the famous McCray pontoon boat she'd heard so much about from the women? Uncle George's island had but one dock. Where could Seth be if he wasn't here? Had he already left?

I'm too late. Scared for the damage she'd done dried up every speck of saliva in Dev's throat. There was no light in Uncle George's shack. No sign Seth had returned.

Climbing onto the dock, she sheltered her eyes against the driving rain coming down in sheets. Casting her gaze out across the wild gray ocean to the south, she struggled against the wind and weather for a glimpse of any watercraft out there riding the waves. Hard knots climbed up her throat, choking her even as the wind whipped her hair and the blowing sand stung her eyes. She'd come all this way for nothing. Worse, she'd hurt the man she'd begun to care about, the first decent guy to come along in years. She'd sent Seth packing as if he'd been the loser, when the real loser was her. Again.

A pinch started inside her heart and quickly expanded, making it hard to breathe. The corners of her rain slicker slapped against her thighs as if punishing her for throwing herself at Seth, then driving him away. Toying with him. Hurting him.

"Where are you, Seth?" she cried. "Come back. Please. I'm so sorry."

Chapter Eighteen

Whistling into the wind and rain, Seth rounded the corner of his shack with a bucket full of clean sand and the tattered piece of an old rug he'd found in his uncle's shed. The sand was for Gru's indoor lizard outhouse. The rug was for his bed, if he slept on a bed. Come to think of it, Seth wasn't quite sure lizards did that, but Gru had to sleep somewhere, and since there were no trees inside the shack… You get the drift.

But it was interesting what else he found in that locked shed. One side of the cramped twelve-by-twelve wooden building was stacked to the ceiling with wooden crates of ammunition, all makes and calibers, as well as a couple open crates of military-grade weapons, all sealed with a layer of good old cosmoline. M-16 assault rifles, Rugers, various other pistols, and—*Damn, Heckler and Koch VP Tacticals, sweet*! Uncle George stored an equally impressive array of noisemakers, aka flashbangs, as well as rocket-propelled grenades. Seth had no doubt there were a couple grenade launchers stashed in there, he just hadn't found them yet.

And, oh yeah, an inflatable Zodiac—a Combat Rubber Reconnaissance Craft, equipped with a bilge pump and all. This one-of-a-kind specialty wasn't as large as the one Cord used, but what the hell? Seth hadn't known Uncle George had even been in the Corps, much less brave enough, downright gutsy enough, to take on human traffickers inside their own country. Uncle George wasn't just a crotchety old man. He was a damned genius!

Despite the pouring rain, this was a good, good day. Make that—great! The same blood that pumped through Uncle George's heart pumped a wellspring of positivity into Seth's. He had a plan that included two of his very favorite people, Devereaux and Scottie. Until then, all he had to do was keep Gru happy, healthy and—

A flash of yellow waterside caught Seth's eye. A woman stood there on the dock, facing the ocean, her hands stuck deep into the pockets of her bright yellow rain slicker. A diminutive, barelegged, barefooted woman with attitude.

"Devereaux!" Seth called out, but the wind tossed his voice back at him.

Gru's lizard box could wait. Setting the supplies on the step, Seth jogged the distance. He didn't slow until she stamped one delicate foot to the weathered dock and screamed into the wind, "I can't do this anymore! It's... it's too hard!"

What now?

"I made a mistake already! I was wrong! Why can't you ever, ever cut me some slack? I work hard every day and sometimes all night! But all I get from you is more work and more grief! You're picking on me! Scottie doesn't deserve what you're doing to him. Neither do I. Stop it, God! Just stop it!"

That gave Seth pause. *What mistake? Me? Should I turn away and mind my own business?* But she sounded so sad.

Swallowing hard, he cupped a palm to her heaving shoulder and asked, "Devereaux, what's—?"

SMACK! One second, he was standing, the next he was flat on his butt. Seth stayed where he'd fallen, astounded out of his wits and blinking to clear the ringing in his head.

"Seth? Oh, Seth!" she cried as she knelt between his knees. "It's you! I'm so sorry. Are you okay?"

"Umm, yeah," he said, gingerly rotating his jaw to make sure he hadn't lost a tooth. Her fingertips fluttered over his cheeks while he sat there seeing a couple stars, but damn. She'd just nailed him a good one and it hurt. "You hit me."

"I know, and I'm sorry, but I thought you were Sly, and…" Her rapid-fire apology dissolved into a whimper even as she climbed over his hips. "I'm sorry for the way I treated you yesterday, and I'm sorry I sent you away, and… and…"

And man, she was adorable. Seth forgot the punch. It didn't really hurt anyway. With her nearly straddling him, yesterday became ancient history in a hurry. Cupping her rain-drenched jaw between his hands, he tugged her forward until she had no choice but to wrap her long legs around him. "It's good to see you, Devereaux. I missed you."

She blinked big blue eyes at him, the rain coming harder now, drilling into his forehead and cheeks. "R-r-really?"

"Yes," he murmured before he tugged her in close and personal, and kissed the lips she kept biting. The wind blew over them. Lightning sizzled around them, and any second now—

CRACK! Right on cue, a deafening boom answered the sizzle. Yet Seth couldn't tear his mouth from the woman French-kissing the life out of his tonsils, nor could he move his palms from where they'd settled on the rounded globes of the tempting ass beneath her yellow slicker. He could only lay there and soak in every last kiss and murmur, while Mother Nature—and a few tears—trickled over his face. Aw, damn. Devereaux was crying.

This was what he'd been waiting for, this passionate woman who loved with her whole heart, and who threw every last bit of her soul into all she did. But when another flash of lightning struck close enough that he smelled ozone, it was time to move.

"Come with me," Seth urged as he lifted to his feet and took hold of her hand. "There's someone I want you to meet." He gave her no time to ask questions as they ran for cover. Easing the door open, so he didn't bump Gru, Seth ushered her into his dark little shack, which had gotten darker with the storm.

The lizard was nowhere in sight, but that didn't stop Devereaux from looking around. "There's no one here. Who'd you want me to meet?"

Seth held a stern finger to his lips. "Shhh. He might be asleep. He needs to rest and—"

"Uncle George? He came back? How could he? Where is he?"

"No, not George, but…"

Gru scurried out from under the bed then, puffed to twice his size, hissing, and snapping his tail like Zorro did his bullwhip.

"Holy hell," Seth gasped at the powerful display of reptilian wrath. "I love this guy!"

Devereaux sank to her knees. "Gru! But how? But, but, but…"

"But I guess Sly didn't kill Gru after all. Must've knocked him out, is all I can figure." Seth joined the happy reunion, content to sit by Devereaux wherever she landed.

"But Sly stabbed him. I know he did. I saw the blood."

"Yeah, about that…" Seth scratched his itchy brow as his chest filled with that intoxicating, *everything's-right-with-my-world* sensation. "Did you happen to notice if Sly's hands were bandaged when we ran into him on the dock that night? I think most of what you saw was *his* blood, not this little dragon's. Gru's got a good-sized slice under his arm. I cleaned it and smeared antiseptic on it, but I've been reading up on iguanas. They don't bleed all that much. All that blood on your hands and clothes must've been Sly's. It's just possible he got more than he bargained for when he tangled with Gru."

"No, I… I didn't notice. I was too scared and…" A hiccup choked her reply. "But Gru was dead. I was so sure. He wasn't moving, and he wasn't breathing, and… oh man! I buried him alive!"

Devereaux reached for her baby, but Gru hadn't relaxed those beautiful pointy spines on his back yet. Uh-uh. Hissing, he lunged as if he meant to bite her fingertips, not moving forward, but just enough to be scary. Posturing his handsome, scaly body, and going for no-kidding intimidation—just like any guy who'd been buried alive by the woman he adored—Gru's throat swelled, and with it, the puffy discs on his cheeks all but glowed with opalescent defiance.

"Has he ever bitten you?" Seth had to ask before things got further out of hand. Gru looked that pissed.

Devereaux shook her head, raindrops spraying his face when she tossed her silvery-white locks. "Never. It was love at first sight. Honest. Here, baby. Come to Mama," she crooned, her fingers extended again as she coaxed her scaly 'baby' to let her approach.

Which Gru did. It took him a couple minutes, but finally, the ridge of spines up his tail and back relaxed. He seemed to deflate, especially when she curled her index finger under his chin and scratched. Damned if that tiny dinosaur didn't close both eyes and smile. The corners of his lizard lips curved up. Seth was sure they did. Obviously, Devereaux was as irresistible to male iguanas as she was to him.

Shoving up from the floor, Seth grabbed a dry t-shirt from the end of his bed and shrugged into it. From the bathroom cupboard, he snagged a couple bath towels and handed them to Devereaux.

"Thanks," she said as she wrapped one around her shoulders and the other in a turban over her head while still holding Gru. Uncle George had installed an electric heater beneath the kitchen cabinet. Seth set it on low, and then rejoined the happy family in the middle of his floor.

He kept his distance this time, though, his elbows on his knees and his hands clasped between them. Women were highly sensitive, emotional creatures. He wasn't about to assume Devereaux wanted anything more than that first impetuous kiss she'd blessed him with on shore. She hadn't come out here in the middle of a treacherous storm for no reason. She wanted something. It'd be nice if that something were him, but yeah. Seth knew better than to jump to that crazy conclusion again. He held back, and he held on.

Gru wasn't the cuddly type, yet damned if he wasn't snuggling on Devereaux's lap while she stroked the floppy dewlap under his chin and rocked him like a kid. The funny guy basked—yes, basked—in her arms. His eyes closed, and his chin lifted the way it did when he'd been soaking up the early morning sun. The sappy sight was enough to make a hot-blooded man jealous of a cold-blooded reptile.

At that uneasy realization, Seth scrambled to his feet and retrieved the supplies he'd left outside at the front door. The sand in the bucket was good and wet, and the rug wasn't much better. They stayed where they were, while he came up with the only other option. *Looks like Gru's sleeping under my bed tonight.*

Leaning his hip to the kitchen counter, Seth crossed his arms over his chest. The one thing every soldier did best was to hurry up and wait. It happened on good days, bad days, and in between, *I'm-so-bored-out-of-my-mind* days. That was Army life for you. Hurry up and wait, then get ready to do it again tomorrow.

So he waited. After soothing her baby a few moments longer, Devereaux lifted her gaze. The prettiest topaz-blue gaze rested on Seth. Except for her blonde hair, the black towel she'd draped over her head gave her the Mideastern appearance of a much younger girl. An innocent girl. With the way she chewed the inside of her cheek, there was hope in the look she sent him. Her hair was tousled and wet. The apples of her cheeks glowed red. Her eyes seemed bluer. Darker.

"Thank you for what you've done for Gru, Seth," she said very quietly. "I don't deserve it, not after the way I treated you."

"Yeah, well…" he mumbled, suddenly ashamed how he'd wallowed in yet another pity party of his own making last night. "He's the one who scratched his way out of his grave. I just intercepted him before he hit the beach and took off."

Devereaux closed her eyes, her lashes spiked and wet. This courageous woman had some hefty problems of her own, yet she hadn't resorted to feeling sorry for herself. If anything, she gave back a hundredfold. Scottie had no idea how much his mother sacrificed for him, but the cute little guy definitely knew he was loved, and that was most important. And look at that charming Gru. He'd returned from the dead, and by hell. He. Was. Smiling.

"How about a cup of coffee?" Seth asked as he set his long legs to doing something useful, like walking over to Uncle George's compact fridge for a dozen eggs, then whipping up a couple omelets to go along with that coffee. Devereaux needed the distraction of breakfast as much as he did. His stomach had set to growling, which reminded him. The generator out back needed more fuel, but he'd left the pontoon boat docked on the mainland. *Not smart, McCray.*

Easing out from under Gru, Devereaux lifted to her bare feet. "Seth."

He turned, and damn. There were no words for the beauty standing in the middle of his uncle's shack, and Seth couldn't have uttered them if there were. A beat of silence stretched between them. His brain turned to mush, just before an intense bolt of desire traveled the short distance, from her sultry blue eyes to his, like sniper fire.

"Yes?" he replied, his voice gone rough with desire. The storm crashed outside. Lightning still flashed, and thunder still cracked like Thor's hammer. Rain poured down in wicked, noisy torrents, but Seth could've stood and stared at Devereaux forever. The light in her eyes was back, and he was falling.

She took one step to him. No smile breached her pretty pink lips, but those blues brimmed with an ocean of regret and repentance. Aw, hell. He was no hardass, just a weak, lonely man seeking his own repentance for dealing with the crap life had thrown at him. They weren't so different.

Closing the distance, Seth tugged her willing warm body against him and prayed for another chance to be part of her life. For a kiss. Hell, he'd settle for a crumb if it came from her hand. What he got was a luscious armful of Devereaux Shepherd.

Chapter Nineteen

At last. Dev launched herself, crashing into Seth's powerful chest, and not willing to settle for less this time around. He wrapped her legs around his hips, while his hands mapped the feel of her skin from the crook of her knees to the curve of her ass. His fingers kneaded her derrière when they finally settled, while she clung to his neck and took extra special care of his mouth.

Fire burned between them. Red-hot flames that licked up her spine and her belly, then nipped at her breasts, hardening both tips into diamonds against his chest muscles. *So, so good.* She arched, pushing for more of that incredible, out of control sensation he'd started, the lust building between them like a flash fire she relished with every wild beat of her pulse.

A groan lifted up his throat, filling her mouth as her tongue tangled with his, stroking and dancing, tasting and craving. Seth. All she wanted was Seth in her mouth and in her body. In her soul.

"Bed," he mumbled, returning lick for lick and groan for groan.

"Yes," she hissed, her core weeping for the hardening length now grinding against the inseam of her rain-drenched shorts.

She had no idea where Gru was at the moment, but Seth must have known. He was thoughtful and careful like that. When he released her to stand on her own two feet, she stood at his bedside. But the look on his face…

There was heat in those whiskey brown eyes, a scorching ferocity that snapped between them. It was lust. It was fire. It was flame. His. Hers. Electricity lifted the hairs on the back of her neck. Was he primed to attack—or was she?

Careful not to break eye contact, she let the towels drop to the floor. He stretched one arm over his back and his shirt landed with them. His eyes had gone dark and bright at the same time, like a panther on the prowl, gauging her every move. But the sight of that muscled wall… The tension in those very athletic shoulders… The sheer size and width of this guy… *Focus!*

Dev hadn't dressed for the storm. Floridians spent most of their lives in shorts and swimming attire. It took mere seconds to lose the tiny t-shirt and shorts she'd put on earlier. By then, he stood before her in only boxers with one magnificent hard-on.

An unexpected groan rumbled up from her belly. This guy was all man, a real man, plain and simple. A massively gentle man with muscles to spare and every last one of them was primed for action, one in particular.

Like the palm trees in the wind, she bent with the hurricane called Seth, brushing the rigid tips of her breasts to his pecs and moaning when those tender buds tightened even more. Her entire body ached with a desire so intense, there was only one remedy. Him. Now.

Because he hadn't yet moved, she lifted a knee to the edge of the bed and ran her hand over the mussed sheets, clearing them out of her way. "Want to talk?" she asked coyly.

A hungry man's gaze stared back at her, but Seth shook his head. He wanted her, that was very obvious, yet he stood at the foot of the bed, flexing his fingers.

She patted the mattress beside her in case he was undecided. "Sit with me?"

Another headshake, and "Why are you here?" he asked, his voice still thick with lust and his chest heaving. "I need to know."

Oh, that.

Damn. Why *was* she here, and nearly naked at that? Just to use Seth again? Just to rely on his inherent honor and goodness for her own purpose? To take and take and take? Sure seemed like it.

Dev tugged the sheet up to her chin, needing the cover. No matter what she said or did next, her reasons for being here had not always been pure. Initially, she'd come because Cord needed Seth's help, and like a fool, she'd put Cord's need above everything and everyone else. Again.

But somewhere between Key West and Drunken Sailor Island, somewhere between the 'more' that Cord always demanded of her, and what Trish advised, Dev's heart had stood up to be heard. Until these last days, her life had been all about Scottie and making a decent life for him. She'd been Cord's willing baby sister after he'd appeared on her doorstep with his latest need to serve America. Man, she loved the guy, and she'd jumped into his mission with both eyes open to save what women and children they could. She thought she'd known what she was getting into. Helping women and girls escape human trafficking was a noble cause, but somewhere between that noble need to serve and the reality of holding onto a minimum wage job, mothering Scottie, and striving to be all she could be, Dev had lost—Dev.

Cord had no idea how much he asked of her and Scottie, or how much it took out of her, financially and emotionally. Yes, she was strapped for cash and walking a fine line with her boss, but every person Cord had rescued had also taken a thread from the fabric of her soul. Knowing precisely what they'd suffered at the hands of human traffickers tore at Dev, but knowing that there were so many more out there in the world whom she hadn't been able to help, made sleep a hard commodity to come by. Not to mention she worried day and night for Scottie's safety. Sly thought he'd killed Gru. What would he do next time, break and enter? Threaten Scottie? Worse?

It had to change, and for the first time in years, Dev realized she had needs too, needs that didn't just tend towards childcare and brotherly love. This was about filling her cup for a change, grabbing that damned gold ring with her name engraved on it, just hers. She'd been running on empty for years, and she was hungry. Her candle wasn't just burning at both ends. Hell no. It had long since melted into a wickless, worthless puddle of wax.

Did she love her brother? Absolutely. Was she an undercover operative like his buddies? Never and neither did she want to be. Did she adore Scottie? Undeniably. And Seth? Was she ready to climb into bed with him because of Cord's imminent return to Cuba, or because she truly cared about Seth?

"I, ah, I…" Her lashes fell. There was no taking anything back. Cord did need Seth's help, but Cord had nothing to do with why she'd tossed her clothes to the floor. "I'll be honest," she said, meeting Seth's unwavering stare. "Yes, I came here to ask you to help my brother."

Seth blinked once. His gaze shifted from passionate to indifferent to somewhere over her left shoulder.

Dev tugged the sheet tighter under her chin, wishing she weren't such a spontaneous idiot. "But that's only because I knew I could depend on you even if you were, umm, are— angry with me. You're a good man, Seth. You're strong and you're noble. You're courageous and you're true." *And I'm still Chatty Cathy.* "But I had time to think on the way out here." She swallowed her pride. "I'm... I'm tired of what I've become. I'm tired of giving everything I own away every time Cord shows up with another boatload of desperate women and girls. I love what I do, but I want more than empty cupboards in my house and in my heart at the end of the day." She dashed the blur of unwanted tears off her lashes. "There has to be something besides work in this crazy life of mine, and I..." Big sigh. "I want that something to be you."

His head canted ever so slightly as his gaze reconnected. Trembling with the audacity of her words, Dev only lifted her chin higher. Somewhere out there on the ocean, in the gale between Key West and Drunken Sailor Island, she'd found her heart's desire, and he'd better stop standing there and looking at her like she was crazy, or... or... had she read this all wrong?

Embarrassment enflamed her cheeks. Maybe that was precisely what he was thinking, that she was just some crazy chick with a kid and an iguana and a death wish.

"Never mind," she bit out. "I know what this must look like, so think what you want. Yeah, I'm easy and I'm fast. And I'm stupid. Don't forget stupid." *Shit, I am so stoo-pid!*

She shoved his covers away, not caring that she was half-naked and making a fool of herself. Stupid people did that! It was past time to go and he needed to get out of her way. "Listen, I had no right to come here, not after what I said last night, and—"

And Seth was in her face, his mouth a heady suction on her lips. He ravaged her mouth, biting the bottom lip gently, tugging at it for her to let him in. Opening her mouth for him, she eased onto the pillow, breathing hard and ready to give him whatever he wanted.

His fingers moved greedily from her neck to her shoulders, then one hand slipped down to cup her breast. Palming the weight of it, he kissed a moist, hot trail to the valley between her satin encased breasts.

Breathing hard, Seth buried his face there, his breath scalding her sensitive skin. Dev pressed her nose into his short hair, breathing in the salt and rain they'd run through. He hadn't moved, and she couldn't make him, his wide shoulders expanding and contracting with every breath as he lay there. Just breathing. Just holding. Urgently on fire for the timid warrior in her arms, she lifted her hips in case he had any second thoughts.

While she waited, she used her time wisely, smoothing her fingers over his shoulder blades and up the back of his neck, rubbing her fingertips into his scalp and over his ears. Memorizing the jut of his jaw and the press of his thighs between her knees. Mapping warm male flesh that quivered at her touch like the withers of a giant draft horse in the sun. Kissing what she could reach of his forehead.

"I'm not into casual sex," he growled to her breasts, the rumble a delicious vibration against her naked skin. "I don't cut and run. If we do this…" Another rumbly growl. "It means I'm staying."

"Yes, yes, stay," she agreed, her eyes closed as she absorbed the heat coming off this man.

That seemed to do the trick. With expert slowness, Seth tugged her bra straps off her shoulders and eased the cups down to her belly. He tipped his upper body just enough for the heated lust in those whiskey browns to scorch a path over her bare skin. Never well-endowed, Dev thrilled at the male satisfaction simmering as his hooded gaze licked at each nipple, then down her centerline to her navel. And below.

"Wait, damn it," he growled as if she'd pushed him too far, when she'd barely started pushing him at all. Stretching that glorious male body, Seth opened his nightstand drawer and produced a foil-encased condom.

"You don't need that," she informed him. "I'm covered."

Still fingering the condom, he canted his head. "By?"

And wasn't that intent light in Seth's eyes just too sweet for words? He cared. He honestly cared! He knew what he was doing with her—to her—and he cared enough to act responsibly beforehand, something What's-His-Name had never considered, not before or after their one hook up. Wow. The difference that one little word made.

"The three-month shot," she breathed. "Depo-Provera. I made that mistake once, not making it again."

"You didn't want Scottie?" he asked, his voice filled with incredulity.

"I didn't then, but I do now," she explained. "That ended up being the best mistake of my life, but next time, I want to do things right with the right guy."

One sexy brow spiked. "Am I doing things" —the hottest gaze stroked over her bare flesh on its way to the scrap of lace between her legs— "right?"

"Yes," she squeaked, her heart climbing up her throat, squeezing her voice box. *And you are so much the right guy.*

"Well, okay then." Bending over her, Seth drew her nipple into the hot cavern of his mouth and suckled, drawing the bowstring between her breasts and her core so damned tight that she arched into his hips as if he'd pulled her there. If he kept this up, she'd be finished before they started. She'd come like she had on her front porch step, in his hand.

While he devoured her breasts, his fingers slipped down her belly to her panties, easing them out of his way and spreading fire everywhere they touched. She bucked against his fingers, needing him to burn with her. Moaning his name and mewling for more. The calluses of a working man's fingers and thumb scraped over her tenderest flesh, while his mouth laved her nipples with tender precision.

"Seth," she hissed into the top of his head. She'd wanted him to come with her, but that wasn't happening, not as fast as this slingshot into the stars was taking her. If he didn't hurry…

"Yes," she growled, grinding into his hands, wanting more of him. All of him.

Seth obliged, stripping her bare, even as his body joined hers with one firm thrust of his hips.

The heated connection burned as they flew. Soared. Rocketed. All that and more, this joining so fierce that it brought tears to Dev's eyes. Thrumming with the exquisite pleasure this man's body had brought hers, she swallowed hard, wondering at the sudden tsunami of tender emotions cresting in her heart. *Why him? Why now?*

She'd known Seth McCray less than a day, which didn't equate to knowing him at all. She had no idea of his likes or dislikes, when his birthday was or how long he planned to stay when he'd said he was staying. What did that mean to a man in the throes of passion and lust? Probably not what she'd thought it meant. Which meant... trouble.

Staying power was a hard commodity amongst men. They came and they went, and in between coming and going, they told just enough lies to shatter a girl's heart when they'd finally had enough of her and left. Even Cord, whom she'd adored her entire life, had never stayed with one woman long enough to bring her around, much less introduce her to Dev. Yet here Seth was, another man. A very different man, giving her his passion and what surely felt like a piece of his heart.

Squeezing her eyes tightly shut, she stifled a sob, holding onto him, so he wouldn't see the hot mess she'd turned into.

Seth pressed a steamy kiss to her eyebrow, then another onto her sweaty forehead, his lips so damned tender and impossibly sweet. "What's wrong, Devereaux?"

She couldn't speak, didn't dare. There was nothing wrong, just very, very right—if she'd interpreted his words correctly. For the first time in years, Dev felt as if someone might truly have her back. It was just possible she didn't have to fight the world alone anymore.

Chapter Twenty

Seth trailed his fingertip over Devereaux's lush lips, now swollen and red from his mouth and his whiskers. She hadn't answered, so he let it go. Sometimes, the heart was just too tender to express itself with mere words.

He'd ended up leaning on his knees between her legs, still sheathed in her deliciously warm body, and not finished making love with her by a long shot. One elbow rested on the pillow above her shoulder, while his other hand cupped her backside, never wanting to let her go. This was a first for him. While he'd never shared sex with Katelynn, he'd hooked up now and then after her death, but never skin to skin. The delightful sensation of being intimately bare inside Devereaux made this intimate act somehow sacred and holy. Rare.

Male satisfaction washed up his spine as aftershocks surged through her core and rippled along his length. This woman was fire and ice, one moment telling him she didn't need him, the next, throwing herself with wild abandon into his care, and he was fairly certain, giving her heart away, too. She didn't seem to know how to do things half-assed, not this girl. She loved deeply, and she gave freely, but as much as he loved that quality in Devereaux, Seth could also see how depleted her emotional stores were. She gave too much, too quickly, and it was killing her zest for life.

Not with him, of course, but with everyone else, she needed a buffer before there was nothing left for her to give Scottie.

"Mmmmmm," she purred beneath him, the soft, wet heaven of her mouth a heady balm to his weary soul. He'd been alone and adrift for so long. Dropping his lips to hers, Seth closed his eyes and let his heart believe that she was that one-in-a-million, once-in-a-lifetime woman. That lightning did strike twice. That he could—please, God—be lucky enough to know how to please her and to keep her.

Licking her bottom lip one last time, he eased to his knees enough that he could see where her body joined with his. Warm and willing, her hands on his biceps, she arched into him and whined, "Don't go. Not yet. Please. I need—"

"More?" He grinned at that utterly feminine request. "Yes, ma'am," he whispered as he began a tender version of what they'd just done. Slow and easy, he eased himself into the best task he'd set his mind to in a long while.

Devereaux cooperated every slippery inch of the way. When he licked her lips, she kissed him like he'd never been kissed before. When he thrust, she bowed her body, arching up off the bed and into him. This woman knew what she wanted and let him know with her lips, fingertips, even her toes, that were now smoothing up the sides of his thighs as her body blossomed for him. Devereaux had no low or medium speed. She was reckless, and everything she did was full speed ahead, and *yes, yes—Yes!*

A ferocious need to possess and protect her stormed Seth's finer senses, driving his body deeper into hers, while his teeth and lips marked her neck and breasts. Love bites. Raspberries. Claiming her body, and hopefully, her heart. He'd never felt this depth of passion or lust, not with Katelynn or any of those very forgettable one-night stands. This thing with Devereaux was no one-time coming together, no easy hook-up with blithe regrets and goodbyes come morning.

Seth was into this woman to win her.

Her screaming second orgasm drove him toward the finish line. Then, as if filled with the same need to claim him, her fingernails scratched down his shoulder blades and over his back. Marking him. Ah, the glorious pain of ownership. Those welts would physically heal, damn it, but the coinciding marks on his heart, true or not, would last far longer. If anything, he was as bad as this woman. Hoping too soon. Expecting too much too quickly. Giving the damn farm away after one glorious day of the tenderest lovemaking he'd ever known.

She complied as if she'd read his mind. Devereaux arched, thrusting her hips off the mattress as he pounded into her. Giving all, even as he took all. Release hit him hard, a fiery surge up his spine that ended with a husky growl of, "Devereaux! God, Devereaux…"

Then…

Pure. Bliss.

A rumbling groan of sublime pleasure vibrated through every spent sinew and throbbing vein until Seth collapsed into her arms, breathing hard with his nose nestled in the crook of her neck. The sweet musky scent of her sex intoxicated him all over again. Raindrops and sunshine—that was Devereaux to her core.

"Mhmmm," she purred, her body gone soft and warm beneath him like melted maple syrup on piping hot French toast, his favorite. Angel soft fingertips fluttered up his back and down again, settling on his hips, which he hadn't realized until this moment, were ticklish as hell. "You're something else, Seth McCray."

"No, I'm not," he replied. *Not compared to you. You're the saint. I'm the sinner.*

"Oh, yes you are." Her voice pitched low and sultry. Smoky. "You just made me see stars. I might've even touched heaven. I've never done anything like it before."

His lips quirked with masculine pride. "Then you've been with the wrong guy." *Thank you, Jesus.*

"I have," she admitted on a sigh.

Rolling to his feet, Seth eased to the floor, then walked to the bathroom for a cloth to clean his lady. *My lady.* Two simple words that had changed many a man's life, and just possibly his.

"Mhmmm," Devereaux murmured from the bed. "I'm loving the view. Hurry back. I want to see the flip side."

"I've seen your flip side," he flirted over his shoulder, pleased to his toes that she seemed to see beyond the scars to the real him.

At her side again, he took special care of her, then discarded the cloth in his hamper before he climbed into bed. Tugging her tempting body against his chest, he drew the sheet up to cover them both. They spooned, her back to his chest, his fingers intertwined with hers under her chin. Life had a funny way of making him believe this could last.

"You're still a redhead," he said because he'd sure as hell noticed. "So why the bleached blonde look? I almost didn't recognize you that night."

Her shoulders scrunched as she giggled. "Because I needed to make some drastic changes in my life. I'd just survived having a baby on my own. My mom and dad didn't want me hanging around. It was time to make changes, so I got up one morning, cut my hair, and turned into a platinum blonde. Then I packed up my baby and my bags, and here we are."

"Your parents didn't want you around?" Seth couldn't imagine the day his mom and dad didn't call or text him. Even as remote as he'd become, as withdrawn after Katelynn's passing, they still touched base with him nearly every week. If not them, one of his uncles or his mother's sister, his Aunt Sheena.

"My turn. You actually inked mom in that tattoo of yours?" Devereaux asked as her fingers traced the vines inked into a heart on his left bicep.

Oh that. "Mom had a cancer scare. Melanoma," he admitted without an ounce of embarrassment. "I was overseas when I got the word, but she didn't want me coming home until I had to, so I did the next best thing. I got inked and put her in my heart. 'S no big deal."

"But there are two hearts on that meaty muscle," she teased. "The other's still empty. Is the other one reserved for your dad?"

"Katelynn," he said honestly. Devereaux might as well know everything. "I was going to have her pretty face inked there, when I got home, only..." And there he stopped, the memory of the woman he'd lost still too tender to merely chat about.

Devereaux turned in his arms to face him, her head resting on the double hearts on that bicep. "I know how much you loved her. That had to be the worst day of your life. I'm sorry, Seth."

He pressed his lips to her forehead. "One of many. No worries. I'll survive."

She snuggled under his chin then, her ear to his breastbone, and her fingertips smoothing up his bicep to his shoulder. Massaging a comforting circle of warmth as if she knew how much that simple gesture meant to a loser like him. He'd never been lucky in love. He might not be now, but... *a man can dream.*

"You can still put Katelynn there, Seth. You should. You loved her."

If the depth of understanding and genuine kindness in that simple suggestion didn't slay him, nothing could. "I've thought about it," he admitted, his throat gone dry, "but it seemed... wrong, you know, if I ever married, to have another woman's face permanently inked into my skin."

Wide blue eyes peered up at him. She had a habit of biting her bottom lip when she was thinking, and man, he was falling deeper into the ocean called Devereaux.

"But a smart woman who truly loved you would understand that you had a life before," she told him, tugging that lip between her teeth and worrying it. "I've seen plenty of guys and gals with tats on their arms, chests, and calves honoring their fallen friends. Why's this any different? A love like you had with Katelynn should live on forever, even if it's just in a picture. True love's rare, Seth. Think about it. You can still add that memorial to her. I know a couple good tattoo parlors in town. Jordie's would do you and Katelynn proud."

Me and Katelynn? Hearing that spoken out loud sounded—wrong, as if Katelynn and Seth were someone else. Another couple. Another time. As if they'd had their chance and missed it. Going back in time to recreate a history that wasn't meant to be, seemed counterfeit. Fake.

"Really? You wouldn't be jealous of another woman's face on my arm?"

The corners of Devereaux's lips curved into a hesitant smile. She knew as well as he did what his question implied. Only girlfriends and wives had the right to be jealous. Which was she?

Her lashes fell as her palm moved to his chest, warming him with her heat. "Not at all, Seth. It's what warriors do. They remember their friends. They never forget the people who mattered the most to them. I think it helps them get on with their lives." Her voice had gone breathy, and he could see her pulse quickening in the hollow of her neck.

"You'd come with me?" he asked as his fingers splayed over her shoulder blades, holding onto the one pure thing in his life. "I mean, if I ever decided to get that ink? You'd be there with me, wouldn't you?"

Devereaux looked up at him, her lashes wet. "Yes, Seth. I'd go anywhere with you."

He kissed her hard and he kissed her long, so thankful for that willing answer. She seemed like a gift he didn't deserve but would—God willing—spend the rest of his life nurturing and pleasing. Time went by so quickly, and he of all people, knew the cost of complacency, of taking those final few seconds and minutes of life for granted. Each second was a treasure, an opportunity to work and live, to sweat, bleed, but mostly—to look up at the stars and to play and to love.

His lips burned to tell her, to whisper that one binding word, but it was too soon. Way too soon. But he thought it, even as he kissed her with every beat of his heart. *I think I love you, Devereaux. I do.*

Breathlessly, they ended the kiss. Indebted to this charming pixie with the strength of a lion in his arms, Seth pressed for information. "So tell me about Scottie's father," he asked quietly. *Who is the jerk?*

She didn't hesitate. "James Brand, one of the copilots I worked with. He's rich and entitled. I was just one of many."

"He pays child support?"

"No way. That would mean he has parental rights, and trust me, he's the last person Scottie and I need in our lives."

Seth waited. There was more to the story. She just needed to want to share it with him.

She tucked their joined fingers under her chin. "He told me to get an abortion when I chased him down and told him, so yeah. Brand has no rights to Scottie, and he never will. My son deserves a real man in his life, not some worm with a god complex."

"Scottie's a good kid," Seth agreed. "He's smart. I can tell. One of these days, we need to read *'Old Yeller'* to him. I don't think he'll be as upset by it as you think."

"Maybe," she murmured, her voice heavy with sleep. "He keeps asking, probably because of the big, fluffy golden lab on the book cover. They're such a happy-go-lucky breed. Maybe I should get him a dog, something to snuggle."

"Labs are almost as smart as Gru," Seth said, tongue in cheek. "But *'Old Yeller'* is a story about a boy becoming a man. Scottie might not understand that, but he's already quite the little man. You've done well with him. Who's watching him now? Cord?"

"No, Trish has him for the day, at least until I get home. Cord's too… busy."

"We can leave whenever you're ready," Seth offered as he breathed in the scent of his woman.

"I don't want to. Not yet," she purred, wiggling her backside against his belly, arousing the simmering fire still coursing through his veins. "I don't get many days off. This is nice, being here with you."

"It is," he agreed, holding onto every last second with her. "It was Cord's idea, wasn't it? He told you to dust me off."

"Ah huh." A big sigh. "Something's going on he doesn't want you involved with."

"And that would be?"

Gradually the story came out. Princess Lianna Khadeem. Basheer Bagani. Roland Montego.

"No kidding? How long's Cord worked for my uncle?"

"Nearly two years," Devereaux answered, her voice growing drowsier and drowsier. She couldn't have gotten much sleep last night. Yet there was more to the story. Seth knew it, or she wouldn't have ventured out into a storm that, even now, whipped at the walls of his shack like a soaking wet demon dog shaking a bone.

Ducking beneath the sheet, Seth pressed a kiss to the nape of her slender neck. "Sleep tight," he whispered. "I'll be here when you wake. Then I want the rest of the story."

Chapter Twenty-One

Devereaux stretched in her sleep, surrounded by warmth and the delicious scent of the man she was falling in love with.

Too soon, her inner diva nagged. Jiminy Cricket would've been proud of this annoying troll of a conscience.

Better than too late, Dev nagged right back.

There was a time she'd second guessed every decision, but she'd learned to go with her gut these last five years, instead of her guilt for never being good enough. Because of her failure with James, she'd avoided men like the plague and she'd lived like a nun. Well, no more. Decent men didn't come along often. If Seth was as good as he seemed—and she knew he was—she intended to spend as much time with him as possible. Every second, if she had her way. Maybe forever.

Gru stretched alongside the bed like a yard statue, his spiny back to her and his beautiful hide a puzzle of emerald greens mingled with limes and hunter greens. Guilt for having buried him alive brought Dev to her feet. Wrapping the bed sheet toga style around herself, she knelt beside Gru.

"I am sorry I buried you," she told her lizardly bestie. "I really thought you were dead. I mean, you were bleeding, and you were colder than usual, and..." She dropped to the floor on her knees, stroking Gru's magnificent spines with her fingertips, her head canted at the way his emerald skin wrinkled when he breathed. "I should've taken better care of you, Gru. I wouldn't blame you if you bit me, but I hope you don't."

"I sure will," Seth said from the bathroom door, refreshed and with his hair still wet, a towel tied off at his hips. "Bite you."

Be still my heart. Dev licked her lips at the sight of the Grecian god in her life. And that chest. It could've been carved out of marble for the flat planes of muscles stretched over his pecs and the rigid valley between them. Muscles rolled down his belly, punctuated with one long exclamation point of fine hairs that ended—*there*. Beneath his towel. If there was a sexier man in the world, Dev didn't know him.

"I called your brother."

Well, damn. "Way to burst a girl's libido," Dev muttered as she dropped the sheet and stood to face Seth, her body completely bare and her nipples hardened at just the sight of him. Any talk about Cord could wait.

Seth's gaze hooded as the tip of his tongue slipped over his bottom lip. She liked that tongue. He'd done amazing things to her with that tongue. One step. Then another. Finally, Dev stopped at his feet to look up at him. *My, my, my, what a handsome man he is, all muscle, brains, and—and mine.*

The black in his eyes swallowed the brown, and Seth was caught. He couldn't look away any more than she could. She lifted to her toes to kiss those wet lips but ended on her back in his bed. Seth's towel was gone, and her heart beat a crazy thrum throughout her entire body. His knee settled between her legs as his palms captured her head, holding her still as he plundered her mouth with long, wet strokes.

Passion ignited between them, and Dev gave herself up to the pleasure of the flame. Tenderly. Slowly. Seth worshipped her body. From her lips to her breasts. From her nipples to her belly button. All the way down, then up again until he settled his hips between her legs for the—love. A random thought surfaced that Katelynn's death had happened for a reason, that this was where Seth had always been meant to be. Not up north in chilly Illinois, but down south in tropical Florida. Not settled down with *her*, but with—*me*.

"Thank you," Dev whispered to the unseen angel in his life who'd unwittingly stepped aside, enabling Seth to be here on this beach at this particular time.

"I haven't done anything yet," he whispered, his voice a ragged rasp against her cheek as he entered her body with one slippery thrust.

"But you will," she told him, her eyes closed but her tender heart opened wide and exposed to all possibilities in the universe. She'd known enough bad times in her life; it was time for the good. If Seth was the guardian angel he seemed to be, Dev meant to hang onto him as long as she could.

But first—he took her to the stars. Again, and again…

And again.

'Brrrrr-riiiingggggg!' Groggily, Seth scrambled to answer his satphone before the ringing woke his sleeping beauty. She'd been so tired, and man, he loved waking up to her warm body in his bed.

Calls from Virginia were alarming any time of day. Had to be his boss. It started up with another *'Brrrrr,'* before Seth thumbed accept. "Yes, boss," he murmured as he ducked into the bathroom and quietly shut the door behind him.

"How's your uncle?" Alex Stewart asked without preliminary chitchat.

"He's holding his own. Sleeping most of the time. Dad wants to move him home with him and Mom in Illinois, but not until he's stable. How's everyone on The TEAM?" The TEAM, aka Alex's less than brilliant brand, had nonetheless achieved, and now set, brilliantly high standards in the covert world of privately contracted surveillance. Established on a wing and a curse, after his life took an unexpected hit, forcing Alex to forsake his USMC dreams, The TEAM's reputation for integrity and just plain getting the hard jobs done excelled above all others. Alex had a knack for hiring the best, though there'd been a couple bad apples over the years. Seth blessed his lucky stars he wasn't one of them, at least, not any longer.

"Busy," came back, terse and tired, over the line. Alex thrived on caffeine and stress, though Seth suspected the stress might catch up with his taciturn boss one of these days.

"Might help if you'd get away from the office a couple days. Boss. You're always welcome here."

"Can't. Cassidy Dancer's in trouble," Alex growled as he cut to the chase. "Eric Reynolds and she have been inside Cuba for three weeks working with FAST. Just heard from Commander Delaney. Dumbass led his team straight into an ambush. Eric's in bad shape, but Cassidy's missing and wounded, assumed taken."

'Or dead' hung between Virginia and Florida like an unwanted specter of things to come. The need to run and

assist his fellow agent prickled up Seth's spine. Cassidy and Eric worked out of the Seattle office. Both top-notch snipers, they must've been on a damned serious mission if they'd been embedded with FAST. USMC's premier *Fleet Anti-Terrorism Security Team,* was one of the best highly-trained and hard-hitting, dedicated counter-terrorism units in the US arsenal.

"Why Cuba?"

"Human trafficking," Alex snapped, like Seth should've already known. He did, he just hadn't expected Alex to be involved in the same business Cord was.

"You wouldn't happen to know former Lance Corporal Cord Shepherd?" He had to ask. After all, *'once a Marine, always a Marine,' right?*

"Should I?" Alex snapped again.

This was going nowhere. "Where do you need me to be?" Seth asked, his feet already pointed toward the door.

"Dancer and Reynolds encountered a team of foreign mercenaries in an abandoned prison on Isla de la Juventud, thirty miles south of the western end of Cuba. They contacted FAST for back up. A team deployed within hours, but FAST only sent six operators. They should've sent a hundred. That was what Cassidy and Eric were up against—a damned battery."

Battery was USMC jargon for an entire company of Marines, a hundred plus men and women.

"So they weren't embedded. Okay, that's different. What kind of mercenaries?"

"Saudi," Alex bit out. "Eric relayed as much as he could before they were overrun. FAST already had intel from their CI in Riyadh that the Cuban government allowed Khadeem's men free rein in the country. Princess Lianna Khadeem's been abducted." *Oh, shit. Alex knows about the princess.* "Her father's an important friend of Saudi royalty. Khadeem's demanding blood on a rock. He's claiming US intervention, that we're behind it all."

"Send me, Boss," Seth replied without hesitation. Cassidy Dancer was a damned good agent and a woman in need. She would *not* die in Cuba. "I can get into Cuba before anyone else, but there's something you need to know." He swallowed hard. "I know where Princess Lianna is."

"You WHAT!?" The thunderbolt hurled from TEAM headquarters to Florida was a megaton more explosive than anything Mother Nature was throwing down on Drunken Sailor Island.

Gritting his teeth, Seth repeated, "I know where Princess Lianna is, Boss. She's safe. Cord Shepherd brought her ashore yesterday with a group of women he rescued from Roland Montego, the bastard running a human trafficking ring out of Varadero, Cuba. I've seen her. She's been roughed up, but she's alive and…" *And shit. I've just outed Cord and Devereaux, the very thing I promised I'd never do.*

The "Son-of-a-bitch!" that bellowed from one mad-as-hell former Marine stung Seth's eardrum like a pissed off hornet. "How'd Montego get her?"

Seth shrugged, not exactly sure of the details, so he told Alex what he knew. In for a penny, in for a pound, right? "Her husband, Basheer Bagani, sold or gave her to Roland Montego. I don't know which because I haven't had the chance to question her after Cord rescued her along with eight other women and two little girls."

That caught Alex's attention. "Two children? How old?"

"Twins. Eight, maybe nine?" Seth had no idea, but that sounded about right.

But that piece of intel had to be ripping a new hole in Alex's heart. He'd lost his only daughter to a car accident years ago, but anything—anything—that had to do with rescuing endangered children had his name stenciled in big, black CAPS all over it.

Seth proceeded carefully. "Boss, I fail to see how Cord rescuing those women lays any blame on the United States. He did a good thing, and he's doing it on a shoestring and a prayer, with just a handful of men, his sister, and without a single dollar of federal aid. American citizen or not, Khadeem ought to reward him for rescuing his daughter."

Something crashed at Alex's end. Might've been another window. He was known to throw things when stress pegged what little good humor he'd started his day with.

"I'm only saying this once," Alex finally replied, his tone as steady as the weather in the eye of a hurricane. "We're on friendly relations with Saudi Arabia, not the damned sheik of the Quari'im Peninsula. Farraq Khadeem is balls deep in ISIL, the Taliban, you name it. If there's a terrorist cell out to kill Americans, he's funding them and they're working out of his ports. For years he's wanted the method and means to pick a fight with the United States. Looks like your buddy just gave it to him."

"No, Boss," Seth maintained, "he didn't. Cord Shepherd did a good thing. He's part of a network my uncle pulled together. How Khadeem can spin this into anything more than what it is—saving his daughter's life—is a lie. Unless..." Seth sucked in a gasp of enlightenment. "Holy shit, Boss. Khadeem's behind this. He knew, may have even orchestrated, what happened to Lianna. That was why he handpicked Basheer Bagani. Out of all the eligible Saudi princes, he married her off to a known pervert and rapist. Khadeem had to know Bagani was in tight with Montego, that—"

"Not hardly. Not in that part of the world. Those two were probably betrothed when they were kids."

"But surely once he became aware of Bagani's crimes, a father would—"

"The bastard!" For the savvy businessman that Alex absolutely was, he could be one mean son-of-a-bitch when backed into a corner. "Montego's a flaming sadist. He doesn't just sell women and children, he panders to the sickest clientele and..." *BANG!* Another loud crash sounded at Alex's end.

"I can be ready in an hour, two, tops," Seth assured his flaming mad boss. "What was Cassidy's last known location? Do you know?"

"Your uncle?" Alex bit out.

Oh, that. Talk about the shit hitting the fan all at once. "Yes, sir. I just discovered Uncle George was a former Marine like you. Not even sure my dad knows. Did you know him?" *No, of course not. George is a Vietnam era vet. You're Desert Storm. Dumb question.* Seth drew in a deep breath and kept going. "He's been networking with other Marines for years, infiltrating and rescuing as many as he can. It's been crazy here the last couple days, and—"

"Don't ever call me, sir, *Agent McCray.*"

Oh, shit, yeah. Seth knew better than to do that, too. Hell, everyone on the East Coast knew better. Alex respected military officers; he just didn't like most of them. "Yes, Boss, but you need to know I can get into Cuba today, may even have access to a couple hard-assed Marines." *Like you.*

"Stay," Alex hissed. "I can't proceed without State Department concurrence, not after the intel you just shared. Shit!"

Exactly. Seth kept his opinion of the State Department to himself. Most federal partners built their empires around their rapacious need for an ever-growing piece of the federal budget pie, as well as an inherent policy of CYA, covering their asses. Hence the layers and layers of federal bureaucracy that could stop this rescue before it started.

That the State Department had even come to Alex for an assist inside a foreign government usually meant one thing: they wanted a dirty job done, but they also wanted deniable plausibility in case things went bad. In other words, they'd never admit they'd funded a private contractor to do what they couldn't do legally. Cassidy Dancer and Eric Reynolds were collateral damage, two civilians the Feds would turn their backs on in a heartbeat when or if shit hit the fan.

Guess the State Department had no idea who they'd signed on with when they'd hired The TEAM. Even twelve hundred miles away, Seth could hear Alex's mental gears grinding out possible scenarios to get his agents back, probably thinking, *'Screw anyone who gets in my way'* at the same time.

Alex would only follow federal protocol for so long, but the man wasn't hard-wired to give a shit when his men's lives were on the line. Hell, one time he'd called in every last Navy favor ever owed to bring Adam Torrey home from some deserted island in the middle of the Pacific. With an aircraft carrier, no less.

The skeleton of a damned fast emergency infiltration plan fast-tracked through Seth's mind as well. Cassidy didn't have time to waste on bureaucratic bullshit, but Seth had a boat and the means to get into Cuba and retrieve her. He had access to the same former Marines his uncle had relied on. Supplies, ammunition, tactical gear, all that. ETA sixty minutes and counting—if he could tactfully—the word of the day—get Alex off the line.

Seth cleared his throat, summoning the most effective argument, when a mighty, "Fuck!" lanced his eardrum at the same precise instant that a thunderclap struck the beach, its too-close-for-comfort detonation rattling the shack's floorboards and window panes.

Good enough. Seth grabbed the opportunity and thumbed 'end', disconnecting the call. Alex would be flaming mad, but Seth had a woman to rescue, and he was the only agent close enough to get the job done. By hell, if a sixty-year-old former Marine like Uncle George could do it, so could his US Army nephew.

Still in the bathroom, Seth faced southward. Damned if he wasn't looking at himself in the mirror, but that wasn't who he saw. Instead, he saw a cocky blonde female agent with a perpetual suntan and the brownest eyes. Cassidy Dancer was no slouch in the covert world. If anything, she worked harder than most men to prove herself every single day. And she needed him now.

Cuba lay beyond the walls of Uncle George's humble little shack, and somewhere on that tropical island, Cassidy was being held prisoner because of the calculated gamble of a known despot who'd likely traded his daughter to start a war. Khadeem already had boots on the ground just one hundred miles off United States' shores. The Keys were accessible and as vulnerable from that foreign insertion as Cuba was to what Seth had in mind.

There was no other choice. Seth speed-dialed Eric Reynolds.

"Seth!" Eric hissed when he answered. "Shit, man, where are you?"

"Headed your way, buddy, and bringing Hell with me. What's your GPS?"

"Thank fuck!" Eric breathed as he rattled off his coordinates, the tremor in his tone belying his panic. "I lost her, Seth. I had them in my sights, but there were so many, and… shit. This is my fault. If she dies—"

"Not happening, Reynolds!" Seth bit out, the roles reversed as he offered support to the man responsible for nurturing him through so many stinking hard times that Seth had lost count.

It felt good to be on the giving end for a change, especially with Eric. Once a Navy Corpsman, he'd traded in his medical kit for a sniper rifle, but a natural born medic never lost his need to serve his fellow warriors, even the broken kind. Eric was one of those enigmas in life, a medic at heart but with the eye and the aim of a fully qualified scout sniper. Guess he thought if he killed enough assholes, one less US soldier would die. Yeah, that was Eric, half-angel of Mercy, half-angel of Death, and the man Seth owed his current peace of mind to.

"When?" Eric asked, his voice raw with emotion. He was also a new father of triplets. He needed to be on his way home as much as Cassidy.

Seth mentally double-checked Eric's coordinates against his to-do list. Could he be packed and ready in time? Was travel into Cuba even possible? *Hell, yeah.* "Three, four hours at the most," he promised.

"Damn, in this storm? You sure?"

"Bad weather's the best time to invade, don't you know? When no one expects you?"

That merited a weary chuckle. "Man, you're crazy, but yeah. Pull a George Washington on these bastards. I'll be waiting."

"Are you still with the guys from FAST?" Seth needed to know.

"Lost two of them in the ambush, but yeah. This isn't Benghazi. Reinforcements are definitely on their way."

That was good to know. "How many?"

"The whole damned company from Guantanamo."

That gave Seth pause. The Corps followed the rule of three: three men to a fire team, three fire teams to a rifle squad, three rifle squads to a platoon, and three rifle platoons to a company. That put the number of Marines coming to Eric's aid at a good one-hundred-twenty, maybe more once you counted all team, squad, platoon, and company leaders. "Jesus, Eric, you don't need me with that kind of support."

"Yes, I do. Come," Eric pleaded. "It's not enough. Trust me, Seth. I need every man standing. You should see these guys. They're Arabic, every last one of them, and they're trained killers."

"But Eric, the Marines of FAST are better trained."

"But they're not enough, buddy. I need every last gun in this fight or we'll lose Cassidy and..." A shudder raced through the line between Eric to Seth. "She's hurt, Seth. I know she's been hit, and she's a woman, and… Shit. I've got to get to her."

Eric's anguish for this captured teammate radiated within the chambers of Seth's heart. Cassidy was one of the few non-military members on The TEAM. This might've been her first time in combat. Yes, she was one of those types who thought she could fight the world alone, but she was still a woman, and tough guys like Eric and Seth had grown up with an inherent chivalry woven into the deepest threads of their all-male American souls. A man's primary job on Earth was to protect and serve his women and children. End. Of. Story.

Seth relayed what he knew, including where Lianna Khadeem was and who was keeping her safe. He ended the conversation with, "Watch for me, Eric. I'm bringing the heat." *I only hope I'm bringing enough.*

Turning off his satphone, he popped the battery free of its compartment. Alex would be flaming mad, but he wasn't here, was he?

Swallowing hard, Seth opened the bathroom door and prepared to confess what he'd done. Devereaux might be angry, but she knew the rules. A man never left his buddies behind. Even now, two of Cord's guys had already reinserted into Cuba to rescue that Julio fellow. Yeah. She'd understand.

Chapter Twenty-Two

"No, I don't understand! You told your boss everything? How could you betray me like that?"

Seth's palms came up to placate Dev, but the steadfast glint in his eyes hadn't wavered since he'd told her he'd spoken with Alex Somebody-Or-Other in Somewhere, Virginia. He'd said sorry a couple times, but sorry didn't change the fact that someone else now knew where Princess Lianna was—had been—safely hidden. What if that bigmouth talked to another bigmouth, and word got out to the wrong people? Cord would be so, so angry, and he'd blame her and...

"I'm not asking again," Seth said firmly. "I need Cord's help, so please, what number can I reach him on?"

Dev paused, then flounced out of bed and tugged into her shorts and shirt, knowing that Seth's heated gaze tracked every move of her naked body as she slid into her clothes.

"Humph," she snorted. He'd turned into as bossy a man as Cord. Still… Seth's reason was sound, just like every last one of Cord's. These two guys were cut out of the same, know-it-all piece of cloth.

Reluctantly, Dev told Seth how to contact her brother, then crossed her arms over her breasts and waited while he replaced his satphone's battery and made the call. *This ought to be good.*

Her bra was nowhere to be found. Just when she needed to be tough, her girly parts jiggled under her too thin t-shirt. The room had gotten chilly and holding her arms as tight as she was only squeezed her nipples together until they were pointing at Seth. Of course, he noticed. His gaze hadn't strayed for one second from her chest, not even when his voiced rose with a snappy, "Because I don't leave a man down, that's why, Shepherd!"

Or a woman in this case, Cassidy Dancer, one of Seth's agent buddies. Why'd Cord only have men on his team? Not that it mattered, but still, a female tough enough to work with a guy like Seth, huh? Dev wanted to meet this Agent Cassidy Dancer.

Cocking her head, Dev studied the new dimension to the man she was pretty certain she was falling in love with. Seth had changed since he'd spoken with his boss. His back seemed straighter, more erect—or something. He carried himself differently, with confidence and power, as if he knew perfectly well where he was going and what he'd do when he got there. Even the blade of his nose seemed—sharper. Put a uniform on that rugged man's body, and he'd be Cord all over again, on his way to fight the world—or die trying.

She settled onto the corner of the bed nearest Seth, not going to argue with a good man just doing what he knew how to do. But Cord was still Cord. She could hear him yelling over the line, something about *'cowards who run at the first sign of trouble'*, about being *'spread too thin across too many fronts.'* As usual, complaining and throwing acronyms until

Dev had no idea what he was talking about. Cord could be such an ass.

"Trust me, I know," Seth replied evenly, "but FAST is involved. A hundred or so guys just like you are on their way to rendezvous with my guy. Are you coming with me or not?"

That grabbed Dev's heart and her attention. A hundred men? Seth wasn't just marching off to save a buddy. He was marching off to war. More telling was when the conversation turned from a yelling match into Seth relaying more practical intel like, "Ammo, already have lots of it. Bring what you can, but yes, I've got enough weapons to arm a small army. I've got you covered there, too. Uh-huh, sure, there's a raft, but it's smaller, six men tops. Bring enough staples to last a couple days. Okay. My boats tied up across from Molly's. Key's under the floor mat beneath the wheel. Sure. The pontoon's water supply ought to last until we get back. Camelbaks? Sure. I'd prefer the smaller version. Water's heavy. Thanks, Cord."

Whatever Cord said next, sent Seth's hand scraping over his head to the back of his neck as he disconnected. His handsome face twisted with a grimace that could only mean Cord was still being himself—a jackass. Seth stared at his phone before he popped the battery out and pocketed it.

"I'm on your side, Seth," Dev told him quietly. "I know you have to leave, and I understand why you did what you had to do. It just surprised me, that's all."

"Yeah, well, sometimes there are bigger things at stake than pride." His right shoulder lifted, no doubt because of the pain in his neck called Cord Shepherd.

"What'd my brother tell you?"

With a big huff, Seth expelled his long-suffering patience. "The usual. That I'm a dickhead. A loser. I'm sure you've heard it all before."

She nodded. Cord was a tough nut to explain—and live with. Tender with Scottie one moment but puffed up with toughest-guy-on-the-block bravado the next, he never relaxed enough to enjoy life. "He believes in himself, Seth," Dev said quietly. "He has to, or he'd never be able to do what he does."

"Understood, Devereaux, but a man's got to unwind between deployments or he's a danger to his team."

"But he thinks he is the team," she offered for lack of understanding how Cord's hard head worked.

"And that kind of attitude will get a man or his buddies killed in a firefight, Devereaux. I'm not trying to scare you, but Cord *will* work with me on this, or I'll bench his ass and go it alone."

Whoa. *Who* is *this guy to think he can bench a behemoth like Cord?* Something had definitely changed inside Seth. The gentleman was still there, but the persona of a wickedly dangerous—and sexy-as-hell—badass now radiated from deep within those whiskey-brown eyes. Seth had a mission, and every fiber of his being was tuned to accomplish his task.

"You left your boat at Molly's?" She had to ask. "You swam all the way out here? Why, Seth?"

His gaze lifted, snaring hers, and she knew why. Like a fool, she'd listened to her bossy brother and in doing so, she'd hurt Seth.

"Yeah," he admitted, his head cocked as if he thought he needed to defend himself. "I've been known to do a dumb thing, now and then." His chin came up. Yes, this man wasn't going to apologize for anything.

Easing off the bed, Dev took a step into him. "Is drinking all by yourself one of those dumb things?" She hadn't forgotten the taste of the first kiss they'd shared, but how sad. Seth had beaten himself up with a long, hard swim, then drowned his sorrows last night, all because of her.

He had the grace to blink and nod. Yet he said, "I do," without hesitation. "Once in a while, yeah. I drink too much."

"Last night? Did you get drunk last night? Because of me?"

Seth cocked his head the other way as if he might ask, *'What do you care?'* Instead he said, "I quit the drugs and cutting, but a drink now and then…" His right hand took a swipe at his forehead. "Never mind. It's not your problem."

Oh, yes, it is. Dev closed the distance, needing to put her hands on this lonely man. She'd hurt him enough that he'd needed to deaden the pain in his heart. That was why he'd been drinking last night. It wasn't something she was proud of, but he had to know that she'd never do anything like that again. From now on, Seth came first. Scottie and Seth. They both came first.

Snaking her arms around his waist, Dev pressed her ear to his heart, content with the steady beat. "I am the stupidest woman alive," she told him. "Don't ever drink alone again, Seth. Promise?"

His hands settled on her waist, but no answer rumbled from his throat. And that was fine. Her request had sounded as if she'd always be there for him. He might not be ready to believe that just yet, and she didn't blame him. Actions spoke louder than words. She had to prove she meant what she said. And she would.

"When will Cord be here?" Dev asked, changing the subject.

"As soon as he contacts his guys in Cuba. Wonder and Sonic?"

"Stevie 'Wonder' James, Ryland 'Sonic' DeLorenzo, and Cleveland 'Rabbit' Miller," Dev translated as she took a step back to gauge the look in Seth's eyes. There was no anger there, just a tender, sad shadow she longed to erase. "Those are the guys Cord works with most often, but I think Rabbit's working a different angle. I don't think he's in Cuba."

"You're right. Cleveland Miller's in Washington D.C., negotiating with his father, Ambassador Miller, who's been fighting an uphill battle for years now to get Khadeem and the Saudis to come together in peace," Seth said, his chin up again. "Khadeem's not only pissed off the US of A with this stunt in Cuba, he might just have bitten the royal hand that feeds him. The King of Saudi might cover his ass because Khadeem's another Arab, but once the king discovers what he's done to his only daughter..."

Seth shook his head. "The Saudis treasure their families, Dev. Things could turn ugly damned fast. The Persian Gulf's a strategic asset the United States can't afford to lose, but now—"

"Rabbit's dad's an ambassador?" Dev interrupted. "Really? Does Cord know?"

Both Seth's shoulders lifted. "I don't know. Ask him when he gets here, but for now, I've got packing and stacking to do."

By then, the thunder had ceased, and the rain was lessening. Instead of pounding, it had reduced to a chilly drizzle. Dev shrugged into her wet rain slicker to give Seth a hand. In no time, the dock was piled high with heavy ammo boxes and assorted, plastic wrapped weaponry from Uncle George's shed.

"I had no idea your uncle was behind this," Dev told Seth.

"Don't feel bad, neither did I."

"You need a jacket."

"Nah. I'm fine," he insisted, his hair gone curly wet, but his jaw was firmly set. He'd been careful not to bump her in passing while they'd transferred the gear, but he'd be leaving soon. Dev wanted him in her arms where she could taste his handsome body one last time.

Sure enough. The second she thought that, an outboard motor buzzed over the waves to the west. Had to be Cord clearing the western edge of Drunken Sailor Island, flying to the rescue in Uncle George's pontoon.

Standing on the dock, Seth glanced from the pontoon boat to the stacked supplies as if calculating their weight against what the boat could carry.

"Seth," she said, her heart up high in her throat. The day that began so incredibly fine was slipping away, and there was nothing Dev could do to hold onto it.

Her single word brought his head up and she was in his arms. "I'm here, baby," he whispered as if he'd known what she'd needed all along.

"But you're leaving." *And I'm staying.*

"Shhh. I know. I know."

No, you don't. Not yet, because I haven't told you what I need you to know before you leave. Dev buried her face in his chest, inhaling the unique scent of his skin, while her fingers roved around his waist. Clutching his back, she pulled herself into the warmth and strength of his body. Paradise. She'd found paradise, and she was losing it all in the same day.

Dev bit her lip. Cord had taught her well. Saying goodbye would be as hard, maybe harder, on Seth than for her. Instead of baring her heart and breaking his in the process, she murmured, "Please be safe out there," instead of screaming, *'I don't want you to go!'*

"I will," he promised, his breath warm at the top of her wet head, the hood of her slicker long ago tossed back when she'd carried box after box, helping Seth, readying him to—leave.

The words she didn't dare whisper burned her throat and eyes. What if this were their last moment together? What if he never knew how much he meant to her before he left? What if—he didn't come back?

Brushing her cheek against his chest, she stifled a sob, her throat squeezed tight and her heart breaking. Of all the men in the world, she'd fallen in love with one of the few, the brave, and the proud. There were damned few of men like Seth out there. She would know.

Tenderly, he cupped her chin in one palm, his other hand skimming over her head, his fingers threading the strands and chunks of her wet hair as he held on tight. Slowly, his mouth descended on hers, and he kissed her with so much passion, it brought tears to her eyes. It was as if he poured every last piece of his heart into hers... as if he knew something she didn't... as if he were saying goodbye.

And Dev broke. "No," she cried into his lips. "You're coming back to me, I know you are. I... I love you, Seth McCray. I know it's too soon, but I don't care anymore. I love you, damn it. You are coming back to me. I know it because you have to. You just have to."

They stood there trembling together in the chilly cold, his nose pressed to the top of her forehead, one arm around her shoulders, the other around her waist, holding onto her as if his life depended on hers. Breathing each other's air. Sheltering each other against what, Dev didn't know, nor did she care. He was her refuge and her strength. Her world. And this was too hard. She needed him! Only him! Here with her and Scottie, not lost in some scary part of Cuba where anything could go wrong.

Biting her bottom lip to control her panic, Dev clung to him, memorizing everything. The scrape of his whiskers on her skin. The scent of soap drifting up from the hollow of his neck. The way he held her as if he'd never let her go.

That he hadn't returned her impulsively spoken sentiment meant nothing. Men were slower thinkers than women. It took them longer to get in touch with their feelings. Everyone knew that, but not once did she doubt the tenderness she found within his steady hold. Seth loved her, which was why he had to leave. He wouldn't be the man she wanted in her life without the blazing streak of honor running through his soul like a wellspring of strength and courage to others in need. That was Seth to his true, blue core, and because Cassidy Dancer needed what only he and men like him offered, Dev would let him go. Any. Minute. Now.

'Please, God, bring him home safely to me,' she prayed.

Long after the pontoon sidled up to the dock and Cord cut the motor, Seth stood there holding her. Rocking as if Time stood still. If only Cord's big mouth would. "Sis!" he snapped as one big boot hit the dock like an exclamation point to the order she'd better obey.

'*Not now,*' she thought, still tucked under Seth's chin and wrapped up tight in his arms. '*Maybe never again.*' From now on, Cord would have to learn to wait.

"Sis! Enough already. Break loose of Soldier Boy and give me a hand."

"No," she whispered. "I'm staying." *Right here where I belong. For as long as I can.*

Seth's big warm hand splayed into the curve of her back, pulling her in tight for one last kiss. It was everything, and more. Her soul absorbed the essence of his taste as their tongues tangled. Her nose drew the spicy, soapy scent of his skin into her heart. This was the man she wanted in the rest of her life.

Too soon, Seth relinquished his hold, and whispered, "This isn't goodbye, Devereaux. I will be back. You can count on it."

Blinking like a total sap, she met his gaze. The hard, determined man was gone, replaced by her tender lover, and that lover was blinking as fast as her.

"I'll be waiting," she promised.

"Aw, for shit's sake, you two idiots—!"

And Dev lost it. "Will you shut up?" she told her loud-mouthed brother without breaking eye contact with Seth. "Just… just hush, Cord. I'm… I'm busy."

Seth's fingers tangled into her short locks before they dipped down to caress her cheek. "It's getting dark. Will you be safe getting to Molly's all by yourself?"

"Sure," she said, wishing this moment would never end. "I've done it plenty of times. Just need to run the bilge pump before I get underway."

"But how will you transport Gru?"

She shrugged that one off. "Same way I brought him out here when I thought he was dead—in a bag. He won't like it, but he'll be okay once he's in his habitat again. He'll forgive me. You'll see." *Because you are coming back to me, aren't you?*

"You're something else, Devereaux," Seth murmured before he landed one small kiss on the end of her nose. "Tell Scottie I'll read *'Old Yeller'* to him when I return, if it's okay with you. I don't plan to be gone long."

"I will," she told him obediently. "That'll make Scottie happy."

Seth surely said all the right words to make Dev believe he was different than the others. That he meant what he said. Stepping aside while the guys finished loading, she kept her mouth shut and the pain in her heart to herself. There was no sense making things more difficult for Seth. He had a job to do, and she wouldn't stand in his way.

The white-capped waves, now gray in the lessening fury of the storm, had settled into calmer swells that lifted the pontoon, rubbing it against the dock. The wind had ceased, and Mother Nature was calm again. Most of the black clouds had already scudded farther west, where they'd drop the rest of their rain in the Gulf of Mexico or maybe far off Texas.

Finally, Seth secured all stray boxes and bags on deck with bungee cords, then covered everything with a gray tarp. To another boater, the pontoon boat looked loaded with supplies instead of weapons and ammo.

Predictably, Cord commandeered the wheel and expertly engaged the pontoon's motor without a single sputter. Uncle George had chosen well. This sturdy watercraft would get Seth and Cord into Cuba safely.

With a heavy heart, Dev waited. At last ready to go, Seth glanced over his shoulder and winked up at her. She blew him a kiss, and that was that. He turned his face to the open sea, his nostrils flared and his chin up. Cord waved in that overly confident way that he had, and they were gone.

Dev turned to the shack, rubbing her biceps to chase away the chill and the blues of once more being left behind. But damn, Uncle George's boat had better be just as good at bringing her guys home as it was at taking them away.

Chapter Twenty-Three

The bumpy ride to Isla de la Juventud at night jarred Seth's nerves as much as Cord's terse silence. He could still smell Devereaux on his fingers. His tongue still roamed his mouth, greedily searching out every last taste of her skin like an alcoholic laps up the last drop of Everclear. He hadn't dared turn around once the pontoon started south. He never would've left her if he had.

It wasn't until the pontoon boat skirted the western most tip of the Island of Cuba and headed southwest to Isla de la Juventud that Cord broke loose on him. "You do know I'll kill you if you hurt my sister, don't you, McCray?"

"You do know I don't give a shit what you think?" Seth shot back, sick to death of Cord's bullshit. "Seems like you don't mind putting her in danger any time you show up. At least I haven't done that."

Cord turned from the wheel to face him then, his brows narrowed. "She's not in danger."

Seth took a step into Cord's space. He hadn't minded when the cocky shit took over the wheel like he thought he owned Uncle George's boat, but enough was enough. "Then tell me, who rents the house she lives in? Who pays the bills?"

"She does," Cord spat, his face twisted with venom. "She works hard, you asshat, so don't go making yourself comfortable in her bed or in her life. Trust me, she doesn't need the grief." His thumbed the center of that big chest of his. "I take care of her and—"

"Bullshit! You're the one putting her and her son at risk. Climb down off your self-serving hero worship for a change and think. If it's her house, why are you dragging your business into it every time you need her help? Did you happen to notice her cupboards are bare after waiting on your rescues yesterday, or did you go shopping on her behalf when you woke up this morning and discovered she hadn't come back? What's left for her to feed her son tomorrow morning or the next day? Is she supposed to hop on over to the local IGA in the middle of the night for milk and Cheerios before Scottie wakes up?"

"She's. Fine." Cord clipped out two very definite bullets that Seth didn't waste time dodging. "I'll make it up to her when I get back."

By that time the men were nose to nose. Seth didn't want to fight Devereaux's brother, so he sucked in a breath of patience, and stepped off. If only Cord had. Mistaking Seth's reluctance for retreat, his fingers fisted. The minute he cocked that big arm and his bicep flexed, Seth landed a fast as lightning sucker-punch to his broad nose.

Cord dropped to his knees with a mighty, "Shit!" Scrambling to his feet, he charged, knocking Seth against the mountain of supplies aft, his arms around Seth's chest. "I said, stay the fuck away from my sister, or I'll—"

"Or you'll what?" Seth asked as he powder-kegged Cord, boxing both of his ears with his fists, hopefully, not shattering his eardrums.

Cord was a bull of a man, but down he went again. He wheezed, his eyes watering plenty. "Where'd you learn to fight like that?"

"From a Marine," Seth growled, wiping the sweat from his brow. *Thank you, Zack Lennox!*

Cord stayed on his hands and knees on the floor of the boat shaking his head and spitting. "Shit, man, you're good."

"Guess all those workouts with Zack Lennox paid off then," Seth growled at Cord, not trusting this blowhard for a moment. Marines fought dirty, and they never gave up. If you were dumb enough to believe them when they said they did, then you were dumb enough, and not likely to remember what happened by the time you woke the next day. If you woke up.

Seth kept his distance and his footing, ready to strike the cocky son-of-a-bitch again if he had to.

"I give," Cord grumbled, his hand extended but his lying eyes on the floor.

"Then drag your sorry ass to your feet and let's get this night over with," Seth ordered, not falling for that old I-need-a-hand-up ruse. Oh, hell no.

Cord peered up at Seth then, his nose bloodied and his forehead dripping with sweat and humidity. "You're all right, McCray."

"And you're an ass," Seth hissed. "Now back the hell off, cuz I swear, the next time you hit me'll be your fuckin' last." Zack Lennox hint: *'Never back down to a Devil Dog, not until you've whupped his ass enough that he respects you.'*

Cord dragged to his feet, wiping the blood off his chin and lips. "Damn, you got some fight in you after all."

"And another thing, I'm not staying clear of Devereaux," Seth told him just to be clear.

Cord cocked his big square head, his eyes as black and fierce as the night. "Then you'd better be good to her, McCray."

"I will," Seth snapped, but then added, "I know you're her brother, and I know you love her, but she needs out of this business of saving your ass every time you turn around, Cord. Give her a break. She's Scottie's mother, not yours."

Cord's head snapped up at that. "You think I don't know that, wise ass?"

"Not the way you take her for granted, you don't. For hell's sake, Shepherd, move the fuck out of her house and grow up."

The muscles on Cord's bulging shoulders flexed, and for a split second, Seth thought he'd charge like the bull-headed idiot he was. But then Cord huffed. His mouth twisted into a grimace as if he'd tasted something sour and couldn't spit it out. "Damn it, that's what I'm doing, aren't I? You might be right, McCray. Well, I never..." He ran a hand over his bulging head, though the muscle housed in there wasn't well used. "You might just be right."

"I am," Seth told him. "Devereaux's running on fumes and a prayer. Can't you see that? She's so quick to help you, but that means she's always putting herself last. Tell me, who buys the supplies after your guests eat her out of house and home? Do you think all that cereal and bread in her cupboards just shows up like she's got a Cheerios fairy?"

"Dev's smart. She saves coupons and she shops bargains," Cord answered, but Seth had done what he'd meant to do. He'd given Cord a few things to think about, and if Cord were half the man Seth knew he was, the big guy would do right by his sister. "Jesus Christ. I do need a bigger place. One with more beds. Better beds. Dev's crappy little apartment's always so crowded and messy."

And that pissed Seth off. "Then clean it!" ripped out of him before he knew what he'd said.

"You're right. Guess Wonder and Sonic could—"

"Not your guys. You." Seth poked a finger into Cord's chest, surprised that all that muscle really did feel like a brick shithouse. Not that it stopped him. "Devereaux's also quick to clean up after your mess. It's time you opened your eyes and your wallet and put her first for a change."

The first hint of moonlight broke through the cloudy sky, shining off Cord's wide shoulders. "That's not as easy as it sounds, McCray. There's never enough money, but you're right. I have been using Dev. Haven't meant to, just grabbed onto the first thing that worked for me, and Dev's always been there, and..." His voice trailed away as the whine of an approaching outboard motor sounded portside.

Seth squinted into the darkness. Like the pontoon boat, the incoming watercraft displayed no running lights. "How far are we from Isla de la Juventud?"

"Less than one click," Cord replied, his voice hushed. "Grab a weapon, McCray. Let's see if you're as good with a rifle as you are with your big mouth."

Seth dropped to one knee, one of Uncle George's VP Tactical pistols already snug in his palm. His Glock still rested in the back holster of his pants, but he'd always wanted one of these nine-millimeter babies. Now he had a box full of them. Their threaded barrels lasted longer and the polygonal bore on their barrels made for increased muzzle velocity, a straight-up damned good weapon to have in a firefight. But Jesus H. Christ, how'd Uncle George procure these weapons? It made a man wonder what else the old guy was into; if maybe he hadn't dabbled in arms dealing as well as fighting human trafficking.

"Shit, they've seen us," Cord growled. "Keep your head down, McCray. They're speeding up. We're going to crash!"

Chapter Twenty-Four

Dev slipped her trusty boat alongside Molly's dock just after midnight. If she timed it right, she'd have time to swing by the twenty-four-seven market on Sea Turtle Drive for a half-gallon of milk and a bag of *Krispy Kreme Donuts* on her walk home. Scottie loved the sweet glazed confections, and she couldn't blame him. Sugar and fat were her best bad habits, too.

After making certain her boat was secure, Dev shrugged out of her slicker and stowed it under the pilot's seat, where it would keep until she went out in the boat again. It never hurt to be prepared. Tucking the keys and most of the lanyard into her shirt, she cradled the burlap bag with Gru wiggling and hissing inside, then set a quick pace for those donuts and home.

Seth loved her; she'd seen it in his eyes before he and Cord had taken off for Cuba. Like no man yet in her life—and Cord didn't count—Seth would come back to her. She was sure. Thinking about those strong arms of his around her, and the way he'd smelled when she'd first kissed him, of whiskey, the color of his eyes, put a bounce in her step. Life was going to be good again. She knew that, too.

Until she rounded the corner, where Molly's wooden dock joined with the city's concrete sidewalk. Sly Valentine stood leaning under the streetlight there, his arms crossed over his chest, and… *Lookee there. His right hand's sporting a bright, white gauze bandage. Poor asshole must've hurt himself trying to kill an iguana.*

"Knew you'd be back 'bout now," he said, pushing his dark glasses down his nose with his index finger, though why he needed those sunglasses at night was worrisome. Dev had always assumed he was a dealer, but did he use, too?

Tugging the burlap bag under her chin, Dev stuck her chin at Sly even as the hairs on the back of her neck lifted. "Gru's alive, you ass. You didn't kill him like you thought you did, so let me pass." If she could only suppress the nervous quaver in her voice, she'd sound a lot tougher.

"Just here to walk you home, Baby Doll," he drawled. Dressed in black denim pants, a black t-shirt, and a denim jacket, he'd tied his hair in a queue, but Sly still looked the same. Slick. Twisted. Guilty.

Dev edged around him with poor Gru struggling against his confinement. "Stop it. I don't have time for this, and you know it. I have to get home."

"But Baby Do—"

"I said stop!" she hissed. Sly had never laid a hand on her, but the velvet insinuation in his voice creeped her out, especially now, in the dead of night when most people were home and traffic was light. Despite continually setting him straight, he'd always acted as if he'd owned her. Dev's heart kicked into overdrive as Gru wiggled again, as if he sensed the jerk who'd tried to kill him stood nearby. "I have to get some milk on the way home," she blurted, frightened now and ready to run.

Gallantly, Sly bowed and gestured her forward. "Be my guest. It's late. I'll escort you to… where? Figarino's good enough for you?"

"Y-yes," she muttered. "That's where I was g-going anyway."

Shrugging out of his jacket, he swept it over her shoulders before she knew what he'd done. "Nights get chilly this time of year, especially after the storm we just had." He tugged the collar up her neck and situated the shoulders over hers, so it wouldn't slip. "Don't want you catching cold."

Dev cringed, the weight and smell of that denim, cigarette smoke and sweat unbearable. Wrapped up in Sly was the last place she wanted to be.

"Don't," she growled, fear driving her now. Figarino's was two blocks away, her safe little bungalow another three after that. "I'll… I'll be fine on my own and tomorrow, I'll return your jacket. Now, take off and leave me alone."

"'S no problem," he murmured, his voice husky and deeper than usual.

Shivers skittered up Dev's spine. There was no way out of this creepy walk home. She set her eyes on the sidewalk and started walking as quickly as she could. Better to get this over with fast. Maybe she'd be safe once she got into Figarino's. Maybe one of Key West's police officers would be there for his nightly caffeine and a *Krispy Kreme*. Maybe she could accidentally on purpose bump into him, spill that coffee, and convince him that she had a stalker on her six. *'Please, yes,'* she prayed.

Sly's heavy hand cupped her shoulder. "Where's the guy who's been hanging around you?"

"He'll catch up any moment," she lied, casting a quick glance over her shoulder. *I wish!*

Sly chuckled, more of a growl than a laugh. "Well, good," he purred, drawing out the good. "I'd like another chance at him. What'd you say his name was?"

"Seth, Seth McCray. He's George McCray's—"

"Shit. That explains a lot." Sly's palm gripped her shoulder tight, forcing her feet to stop moving. "Where is he? I know he wasn't on that thing you call a boat. He's gone after the prince, hasn't he?"

She forced a laugh, though it sounded more as if she was choking. "P-prince? Wh-what are you talking about?"

"Knock it off!" Sly ripped the bag from her arms and flung Gru aside. "You ought to get out more. Play poker with the big boys. You can't bluff worth shit."

Her poor baby had landed with a thump in the rain-filled gutter. "No!" she cried, reaching for the iguana. "Not again! I can't, I won't lose him again!"

"And I can't afford to lose you," Sly growled as he jerked her off her feet, his arm around her waist. "You know too much, Dev, now shut the fuck up!"

"I'm not going anywhere with you! No!" she screamed, kicked and bucked, fighting for her life. Scottie and Gru needed her. Seth and Cord, too. She couldn't let this happen. Whatever Sly had planned, she had to fight until—

A black limousine with its headlights turned off pulled to the curb, its windows dark, narrowly missing where Gru struggled to get out of the bag.

"Stop, Sly! At least let me let Gru out. He'll die in that bag." Beads of rain dripped over her panicked reflection in the shiny gloss coat of the limo, now parked directly in front of her.

"Shut up," Sly growled, one hand at her throat, "or this'll get worse."

"Get your slimy hands off!" One warning was all she gave him as she tipped her head back and let out the loudest scream she could muster. Then another! She turned her mouth and lungs into an air raid siren—

"Looks like you have your hands full," another male with a definite Mideastern accent called out from the vehicle.

Dev stopped screaming then, hoping against hope that this guy would help her, and buying time for one of those Key West officers to drive by, catch Sly in the act, and arrest the creep.

The olive-skinned stranger lifted to his feet from the backseat of the limousine. Of course, he had money and a chauffeur. "Put her down, Mr. Valentine. Please. Introduce me."

A shiver rattled up her spine. This man might look handsome and his black eyes might sparkle, but there was something sinister to him. *Oh. My. Hell. He's Lianna's husband, the man who'd tortured her fingers, that Bagani fellow.* Dev still burned to know exactly what had happened to Lianna. Now, she just might find out.

Dressed in an immaculate, gray linen suit, white shirt, and black tie, Prince Bagani stood there on the sidewalk, fiddling with what looked to be pure gold cufflinks at his wrists. Tall, slender, and a definite man of the world, he flashed straight white teeth beneath a perfectly trimmed mustache. It wasn't as heartbreaking a smile as Seth's, when he'd finally smiled, but it was a smile. Kind of smirky. Kind of suave. Kind of—not.

This guy's eyes were dark, rimmed with either kohl liner or the thickest, blackest lashes she'd ever seen. Man, he had debonair down to a fine art, the way he'd enunciated his request in perfect King's English. But he was no Englishman, not if the seal engraved in lovely Arabic script on the gold ring on his finger meant what Dev suspected.

As if he'd read her mind, Bagani swept one arm to his waist and performed a small bow just as Sly muttered, "Your Highness, Prince Basheer Bagani, meet Devereaux Shepherd, the girl I've been telling you about. Dev, the Prince who's going to make you wish you'd been smart and worked for me."

Prince Bagani tilted his head. The corners of his lips curled with the most evil smile. Even his mustache seemed delighted to see her.

Dev screamed into the chilly dark night. But this time, no one came to her rescue.

"Eric!" Seth called out to his good friend just as Eric maneuvered his wide rubber skiff alongside the pontoon boat. "Knew it had to be you out here in the dark."

"Thank God!" Eric called out. "You made good time. Didn't think you could do it, not this fast, but damn, it's sure good to see you."

"Yeah, well, it finally stopped raining." Seth glanced over his shoulder at the long dark stretch between Cuba to Key

West, between him and Devereaux. "Came as soon as I could. Eric, Cord Shepherd." Seth nodded to the belligerent guy with his pistol still trained on Eric. "He's here to help. Cord, meet former Navy Corpsman and USMC scout sniper, Eric Reynolds, but you can call him 'Sir', so put your weapon down."

"Ha!" Eric chuckled as he turned to the two men with him. "That'll be the day anyone sirs me. Seth McCray, meet my good buddies, and two of America's finest, Sergeant Wilson "Ace" Allen and Corporal Johnny "Tex" Ritter."

Sergeant Allen growled, "Make it quick," but neither man made a move to come aboard.

"You talked with Alex lately?" Eric asked.

Seth crinkled his nose at that. "Not since I hung up on him. Right now, he thinks my phone's fried, or I wouldn't be here with you."

Cord leaned over the boat railing and reached for Eric's hand to pull him aboard. "Semper Fi. 'Bout damned time we got a couple more Marines to stand with us. You ready to fight, brother?"

Eric landed on both feet, but lengthened his grip on Cord's forearm until the two were eye to eye and fist to elbow. "You ready to die?" he gritted out. "Because I'm here to tell you, there isn't a better man to have beside you in a firefight than former Army Sergeant Seth McCray, you feel me?"

What was it with all that posturing, staring, and squeezing the shit out of each other's dirty mitts that Devil Dogs always seemed to do? "Guys, enough already," Seth barked, more amused than exasperated. "You're both mean as shit, now what's the plan, Eric? How do we get Cassidy back, and where is she? Do you know?"

Eric released Cord's hand first, no doubt because Cord's big head was harder than Eric's, and it'd take another minute or so before his synapses fired strong enough to relay Seth's question from Cord's big brain all the way down his arm to his hairy fingers.

Eric turned to face Seth, the laugh lines at the corners of his eyes a different kind of sunshine on a night so dark. Wearing his usual cargo pants with its pockets probably all stuffed with first-aid supplies along with the essentials, like ammo, the man was a sight for sore eyes. "All I know is where we think they took her, to the other side of the island. You guys came in on the west side, but there's a small navy tucked into one of the bays on the east side.

"How many ships?"

"One frigate, two patrol cruisers, a few smaller boats to get supplies ship to shore. Visibility's pretty much nil at night, so it'll be rough going. Once we get there, the beaches are coarse black volcanic sand, and in some places, it's sharp as hell, so be aware of that. You bring any extra gloves? I lost mine in the ambush."

Seth whipped open the tarp, pulled up a box of leather gloves, and tossed that to Eric.

"Thanks," he growled as he ripped the end of the box open, jerked out a couple pairs and pushed his long slender fingers into the first one that fit. "You have no idea what that sand'll do to your skin."

"I've got *Vaseline* if you need it," Seth offered.

But Eric shook his head. "No, thanks. FAST is due anytime now. We need to get you guys ashore and this rig stashed."

"What about a Cuban navy. They even got one?"

Eric shook his head. "No worries. Cuba ranks seventy-fifth in the world for military firepower. Their total naval assets number a dozen patrol craft, which they mostly use to keep their people from skipping the island." His gaze swept the pontoon boat from bow to stern. "Let me guess, Uncle George left this to you."

"That's a story for another time," Seth muttered as he secured the bowline of Eric's raft and prepared to tow. "Let's go get Cassidy."

Chapter Twenty-Five

They put her in the trunk! The trunk! How stupid did Sly and his prince-buddy think she was? Dev found out soon enough. There was no glow-in-the-dark escape latch—anywhere—and no other cord, toggle switch or hidden button that she could find in the dark. Maybe they weren't so stupid after all.

She couldn't very well escape through the backseat, so she hadn't even tried, not with his royal highness, Bagani's ass planted there. Probably Sly's fat ass, too. Damn it! American-made cars were supposed to come with a trunk safety release, weren't they? This limo was American-made, wasn't it? *Guess not.*

But there had to be some kind of trunk release cable that opened this coffin on wheels from inside the car, something the chauffeur could trigger from his seat or the steering wheel. Dev searched on her hands and knees while the vehicle took her farther from home.

If there were a release cable, she couldn't find it, and time was running out. She hadn't come across so much as a tire iron or tire-changing kit, either. Too soon she'd be lost to Scottie forever, and that just plain wasn't happening!

Angry now, she focused on what had to be the brake light wires. *Ha! You are so screwed, Sly, you and your asshole highness!*

It took a few minutes, but Dev persevered, her trembling fingertips tender and raw by the time she shoved those taillight housings out of their metal frames and into the night. But dangling taillights weren't enough.

Going for broke, she jerked the wires free, then peered through the hole she'd created. It was plenty dark out there. No headlights behind her. It looked like the limo was on the Overseas Highway, the southernmost leg of U.S. Highway 1, that ran the length of the Keys. Not good. She had to get to Gru before he got run over, and she was not—absolutely, was not!—leaving Scottie to wonder for the rest of his life what happened to his mom. Uh-uh, no way.

This crazy plan might not work, but Dev also knew there were plenty of law enforcement cruisers along this stretch of road. There was still hope. Back she went searching for a tool, anything, to pry the trunk lid and *'get the fuck out of there'*, as Cord would say. The carpet, though nice and soft, still had edges, which she promptly ripped to the side, until… Ah ha! A flat compartment lid lay beneath that carpet.

I am almost out of here!

Excitement ramped up her already frantic breathing, but this was her last chance. Fumbling in the dark, she found her weapon of last resort. A sleek mini crowbar that fit her hands perfectly. All she needed was for one car, just one alert driver on this stretch of highway and she'd be free!

Sweating in the cramped quarters, she knelt alongside the rear edge of the trunk lid, stuck the flat edge of the crowbar between the car frame and the lid, and… *ARGH! What the hell? Is the damned thing welded together?*

With her heart racing now with her fingers slick with sweat, she stabbed the tool into the thinnest space between lid and frame, and tried again, throwing her weight into it this time. It had to work, damn it! She had no other options. She grunted. Cursed like one of USMC's finest, until…

At last—*thank you, God!*—the lid popped just enough to let in a welcome burst of chilly night air. But there was no traffic behind her and no headlights, not that Dev cared. The limo wasn't speeding, and she wasn't hanging around.

Wow. Talk about scary. With all fours balanced at the edge of the trunk, she led with one hand placed below the trunk on the shiny chrome bumper. Then a knee. Then it was go-time. Curling her body into itself, she ducked her head between both arms and…

Oomph and Damn! Wow, that hurts! The concrete pavement was a painfully hard wall with no give and no mercy. It peeled the skin off her left bicep and thigh on contact. She bounced, rolled, and okay, yeah, she squealed and cried out, too. Who wouldn't?

But best yet, the spring latch on that fancy trunk lid had snapped it closed behind her. Lying there on the warm concrete with her head on her arm, she watched Sly and Bagani's fancy ride carry them away from her. Hopefully, they wouldn't realize she was gone until they got to wherever they were going. Good riddance.

"Hell, yeah!" she squeaked out as much enthusiasm for her brave accomplishment as she could.

Still infused with that mighty burst of adrenaline, she crawled her trembling body off the highway, but wow. She was now in the middle of nowhere, and it was dark out here, wherever she was. Scary dark. Okay, and yes, she was more hurt than she thought she'd be. Jumping out of a moving vehicle might get her out of an untenable situation, but it definitely had its downside.

During one of those less than graceful bounces, her forehead had met the highway. Hard. She'd thought she'd cracked her skull. But she was free, and for now, that was what counted more than anything. A few scrapes she could live with. Not those creeps in the limo.

Dev lifted to her hands and knees and crept farther from the highway and into the brush, weeds, and sand to make certain Sly and Bagani couldn't find her. She was so grateful the limo hadn't been on one of those miles long bridges that connected Miami to the Keys. But holy hell, every last limb, muscle, and joint hurt like a son-of-a-bitch. Even her fingertips. Blood dripped from the lip she'd bitten, another unexpected cost of freedom. Spitting into the sand between her palms, she pushed through the scratchy weeds and brush and kept on going.

Another thought intruded. There were other scary things along this stretch of road. Florida panthers. Alligators. Maybe even a few endangered Key deer, those tiny white-tailed deer that people hardly ever spotted anymore.

Dev was so tired, she couldn't move another inch. Her mind wandered. *Key deer aren't scary,* she scolded herself. *Cord and Seth aren't, either.*

Now that she was free and alone, the impulse to fight or flee had left her high and dry. Her energy had fled with it. There under the scrub brush and seagrass, she curled onto her side and pulled her tender scraped knees into her chest, shivering, trying to keep warm. If she were lucky, there wouldn't be a nest of fire ants nearby. She could catch a few Zs.

But if she were really lucky, some kind person would come along, not that anyone could find her, as far as she'd crawled into the brush. It was hard to see the road from here, but miracles still happened, didn't they?

Damn it, Trish was right. I should've bought a new phone.

Infils rarely encountered enemy or hostile fire due to the days, sometimes weeks spent in thorough pre-planning, practiced rehearsals, and as many what-if scenarios as an Army squad could come up with to preclude the surprise factor.

Unfortunately, Seth and his team of Marines hadn't had that kind of time. Even now, they skirted the southern curve of Isla de la Juventud, counting on the stillness of the midnight hour to recover their missing agent, and, as Cord kept saying, to get some payback for the two FAST lives lost.

Running silent and dark, the pontoon was the perfect ghost for this particular job. She left no wake, and her motor, now throttled down on approach, was more of a whisper on the wind than a rumble. Uncle George had made some adjustments. Pipes from the engine vented the exhaust below water, leaving nothing but a wake of bubbles instead of sound.

Eric had chosen to remain on board with Seth and Cord, while his FAST counterparts, the sullen Sergeant Allen and Corporal Ritter kept to the skiff. Allen's gloved fist flexed tight on the tiller. The guy had yet to offer more than a grunt, even when Cord voiced his enthusiasm for "two more Devil Dogs in the fight. That makes four. No way we can lose! Hoo-rah!"

It seemed even among Marines, Cord had the uncanny knack of alienating everyone.

"Tell me about the island," Seth told Eric. "What are we walking into?"

"It's a sad place," Eric said as he nodded toward shore. "The island itself is the largest in the Canarreos Archipelago, which stretches south of Cuba. It's as narrow and as long as the Florida Keys. To the north, between Cuba and Isla de la Juventud is the Gulf of Batabano. To the east, the Gulf of Cazones, and to the west…" Eric pointed behind the boat, "the Los Indios Channel. You're looking at the southern side now. It used to be covered in pine forests, but between the continual logging and all the hurricanes these last few years, the lumber industry's taken some hard hits. Hell, everyone on the island's struggling. There's still logging equipment and plenty of men during the day on this side though, so watch out for that."

Taking a deep breath, he continued. "Americans used to own parts of the island before Castro came to power and nationalized everything. The Cubans who still live here call it the Isle of Lost Dreams. It's seen pirates, Spanish conquistadors, American capitalists out for a quick buck, and Castro's guerillas. You name it, they all came, raped the land, enslaved the people, and left."

"Sounds like you're our resident expert for the night," Seth said.

"Not me. Those guys have been here longer." Eric glanced at the skiff following silently in their wake. "Just so you know…" His voice lowered. "The guys from FAST are not here for Cassidy or us. Their mission is to engage the Saudi Army before it's entrenched on America's doorstep. These guys are combat-trained and we're in their way. Their orders are clear. This is one of those undeclared wars, Seth, and we're right in the middle of it."

"Been there, done that," Cord growled from where he still stood at the wheel. He nodded for Seth and Eric to step forward, his voice just as low as Eric's. "The way I see it, guys, we're expendable, and those guys know it." He cast one quick glance at the men in the skiff. "Why do you think they didn't come aboard? The first chance they get, they're out of here."

"Not FAST," Seth argued.

"Yes, FAST," Cord hissed. "Trust me on this. They have a mission to complete and they won't let a couple contractors like you get in their way. My guys are already on this island—"

Seth cut him off. "Stevie "Wonder" James, Ryland "Sonic" DeLorenzo, and some guy named Julio," he told Eric. "Have they caught up with Julio yet?" he asked Cord.

"Yeah, they've got him," Cord assured, still keeping an eye on his buddies in the skiff as, without a word or a wave, the skiff cut loose, its motor engaged, and a rooster tail churned in its wake as they took off for the island. "What'd I tell you? Those guys don't need us, and they don't want us."

Seth turned to Eric. "How many men are we looking at? How many Saudis are we up against?"

Eric ran his fingers through his dark hair. "I'd say two hundred, maybe three. They hit us hard. Cassidy and I were tracking Roland Montego, the man responsible for—"

Seth held a hand up. "I know exactly what he's responsible for. Cord here's been hustling women and children out of Montego's clutches on a regular basis."

Damned if Cord's chest didn't swell with those words.

"Anyway…" Eric hissed. "We weren't expecting an attack, and there were so many of them. Before I knew it, they had us against the sea, and we were fighting for our lives. If it hadn't been for some jarhead with a bazooka, we'd all be dead." He ran his hand over his head again, Eric's tell when his emotions ran high. "I saw her fall, Seth. I saw her go down, and yeah, she was still kicking and fighting plenty. You know Cassidy, but there were too many. So, so many…"

"Where is she?" Seth asked.

"In the prison," Cord bit out before Eric could respond.

"In what prison?"

"Not in prison," Cord repeated. "In *the* prison. You know which one I mean, don't you, Reynolds?"

"Yeah, I know," Eric breathed. "They handed her over to Montego, the son-of-a-bitch. I know because I followed those bastards. God, he's a pig, Seth. He had his men take her to the Presidio Modelo, Seth. Cuba's infamous Model Prison."

Seth put his hand to Eric's shoulder. The guy was taking the loss of Cassidy hard. "Tell me about the place. Don't leave anything out."

"Shit," Eric hissed. "Where to start."

Seth found it odd that their roles had been reversed, that he was the one providing emotional support for one of the toughest men on The TEAM. "The beginning works for me," he said calmly.

Eric nodded as he started again. "Built between 1926 and 1928, it's a broken down Panopticon, the supposedly perfect prison where all the cells line the inside walls of a couple wide circular, concrete towers, five or six stories high. The circular cellblocks were constructed around much smaller guard towers, observation posts, so the dictator at the time didn't need many guards to track the up to twenty-five hundred prisoners housed inside. No man unlucky enough to end up there, ever knew when or if he was being watched or targeted for elimination. There was no humane treatment for prisoners in that place, much less privacy. Back before the Cuban Missile Crisis in 1962, Fidel Castro had the floors drilled and packed with dynamite to blow the place in case of rebel takeover. The prison's a rundown museum and a national monument now, but the dynamite holes are still there."

"Cassidy's in a rundown museum?" Seth asked.

Cord's head bobbed. "The basements beneath that prison are beehives of dislocated cells, McCray. Castro kept political prisoners secluded there, where he could do what he wanted. I've been inside the place before to collect a few women. Montego keeps moving his lair, so yeah. Your girl could very well be detained in one of those cells, and nobody would ever know what he's doing to her."

The thought of any woman in Montego's cells was disturbing. "Where is this shithole?" Seth asked.

"Not far from here, in Chacón, Nueva Gerona," Eric replied.

"Let me guess, that's on the other side of the island?" Seth asked.

Both Eric and Cord nodded. "I already told you that's where she was. See why I needed you here, Seth?" Eric asked. "I knew I couldn't depend on FAST, not after two of their men were killed when Cassidy was taken."

Well, shit. Seth turned into the breeze, facing the darkness of the island now passing on his left. "Then we'd better get moving. While FAST engages the Saudis, we'll skirt the east side of this island, and hopefully, locate and rescue Cassidy."

Cord's meaty palm slapped his shoulder blade, jarring Seth. "Good plan, McCray. Let the Marines do the dirty work while we save the lady. I like how you think."

Seth shrugged Cord's unwelcome camaraderie off. "I'm not *letting the Marines* do anything, Cord. In case you didn't notice, they're the ones who aren't here now, are they? No! Without one damned word, your USMC buddies took off and left us behind, so quit with the noble, *'let the Marines do the dirty work,'* jarhead bullshit. The way I see it, we're on our own, and we're walking straight into a warzone without sufficient backup or recourse. Now shut the fuck up and get this boat as close to that defunct museum as you can. I want Cassidy out of there by dawn. Understood?"

Oddly, Cord inclined his head. "Sure thing. Sit tight. We're moving." He turned to the wheel, and Uncle George's pontoon boat, as unlikely a combat vessel as it was, kicked over the waves and into the wind.

Only Eric wasn't smiling. Neither was Seth. Once FAST engaged the enemy, all hell would break loose. Cassidy was running out of time.

Chapter Twenty-Six

The ants march in,
The ants march out,
The ants play pinochle on your snout...

Dev smiled at the silly childhood chant spinning round and round in her aching head, even as she brushed a trail of touchy, feely insects off her bare arms. Sly's jacket, smelly as it was, would surely come in handy about now, but she'd left it behind when she'd forsaken the dubious comfort of the limo's trunk.

Finally, enough was enough. She rolled to her back and stared at the stars overhead, brushing more crawly critters off her face and out of her hair. This was the thing about the Keys. On a clear night, there was little to no bright city lights to obstruct a person's view of the universe. You could almost see forever.

But forever was c-c-cold. Carefully, her hands eased up over her biceps for the warmth of her own touch. Dev cringed when one palm rubbed the shredded skin on her left bicep. Freedom definitely came at a hefty price. Now all she had to do was find a way into town. Before dawn would be nice, but at least before whatever was chewing on her ass ate her alive.

Gingerly, she tipped up and onto her butt, another sore part of her anatomy. She wasn't just bruised, she was battered, her arms, thighs, and kneecaps covered with burning patches of road rash that stretched too tight over her shivering muscles. But she was alive, and she knew where she was. Mostly.

Okay then. Let's roll out.

Soon. Very soon…

For now, it was enough to be able to sit without throwing up. Man, she was one dizzy woman, and the stars weren't just in the skies. Dropping her head to her knees, she avoided the tenderest skin, needing something to hold her shaking head before she lost her cookies. She just might have a concussion, but like her brother always said, a man can heal later. Guess a woman could, too.

Swallowing her fear of the night's worst predators once they caught her scent, she climbed to her feet, with nothing but the flimsy bush at her side to help keep her balance. Not happening. Quicker than quick, she sank to her butt before she fell down. She wasn't going anywhere. Not yet.

"You know what?" she asked herself. "You'll feel better after a little nap. Rest now, then when the sun comes up, try again."

Good idea…

At least Cord knew the Cuban Islands well enough to maneuver the pontoon boat past murky, alligator infested Lanier Swamp and then the American cemetery at the northeast corner of the island. This half was fairly bare of trees and more civilized, with a population of over fifty-nine thousand residents, modern looking city buildings, and paved highways, all of which Seth intended to avoid.

The city of Nueva Gerona itself lay west of the Presidio Modelo ruins, aka the *'national monument'*, but damn. The ferry to the Cuban mainland had just landed as Cord pulled in close to shore. Not many people offloaded, but scores of cars and trucks were lined up to leave, their headlights on and their brake lights flashing in the pre-dawn darkness.

"Heads on swivels, guys," Seth cautioned as he placed one hand to the railing and jumped into the surf off Isla de la Juventud. Volcanic black sand stretched for miles in either direction, but he only had eyes for the easy climb straight ahead and up that grassy knoll. He'd purposely directed Cord to pull the pontoon into this secluded stretch of beach south of Playa Colombo. It meant for a longer hump to get to the prison, but it avoided the public dock and the road that led directly to the Presidio Modelo. Seth didn't need witnesses to what was without a doubt, an unauthorized United States incursion into a foreign country.

While Cord maneuvered the boat, he and Eric suited up with tactical vests, holsters, knives in sheaths, and a couple gear bags loaded with extra pistols, magazines, ammo, water bottles, any and everything to ensure this mission's success.

Seth stopped Cord before the big guy jumped in with him. "No, Shepherd. You stay with the boat. Keep it out of sight and safe," he ordered as he slapped the plastic-encased two-way radio in the chest pocket of his tactical vest. "Channel twelve. Wait for my signal, then get here as quick as you can. We'll be moving fast. You may need to lay down suppressive fire 'fore we board. But if Cassidy's hurt...." Well, Seth just plain didn't want to think about that scenario.

A wounded male was hard enough on his heart, but a wounded woman…

Thank God, Eric was here. He'd know what to do if and when.

Cord's upper lip lifted like he wanted to buck the order, but once Eric bailed overboard and joined Seth in the water there was no choice. Someone had to man the getaway boat. "Fine. Will do," Cord bit out. "But make it quick, guys. Sun gets damned hot this time of year."

Seth turned his back on the most belligerent Marine he'd ever met. One thing he'd learned early in the Army was that a real tough guy didn't have to open his mouth to prove it. He didn't need to brag, argue, or minimize other soldiers, either. He. Just. Was.

All a real man had to do was keep on keeping on, through the best and worst of times. That was what and who had made America great, the quiet tough guys behind the scenes. The common farmer sweating in the cornfields in Nebraska. The uneducated family man in the dirty, dangerous coal mines of West Virginia. The bone-weary fishermen risking their lives and health off Alaska in crabbing boats on the Bering Sea.

America's greatness didn't come from the twisted halls of Washington, D.C. Oh, hell no. It came from the Heartland, from the very soul of the silent, but deadly, American majority. God bless 'em.

"You got anything in case she's bleeding?" Seth asked out of the corner of his mouth as he splashed to shore alongside Eric. "Any *QuikClot*?"

"In my side pocket with my satphone." Eric tapped two fingers to his chest pocket. "Everything I need's right here. If I go down, you can still save her. The green hypo will slow blood loss; the red's a painkiller. Four cc's ought to do it. Cassidy's no heavyweight. Also got a plastic tourniquet."

"You're not going down," Seth growled, his eyes on the sloping hill ahead. "Does Alex know what we're doing?"

Eric's head shifted from side to side with a definite negative. "No need to call him. It'd only piss him off and we're not in trouble yet. Figured I'd wait to see how this goes down."

That was Alex for you. The man wasn't one of those micro-managers out to second-guess the expert men and women he'd hired. Hell, no. Obsessive Compulsive, yes, but when Alex gave an order, he expected you to obey, file a report when the mission was accomplished, and wait for his next call to arms.

The need to confide in Eric persisted with every step Seth took. If things went bad—if he was the one who fell today—he wanted someone to tell Devereaux that he'd died loving her. Thinking about her. Yet to talk about that now…

Yeah. No. Not happening. Sharing feelings only conjured bad mojo. Seth kept his big mouth shut as he and Eric left the surf behind and climbed the scrubby hill ahead. Daylight would break soon, and they had to hurry, but what a sight. Seth dropped to his belly alongside Eric in the tall grasses just as they'd cleared the top.

A cluster of several massive, rounded buildings sat against the dark emerald backdrop of the Caballos and Casas hills to the southwest. The birds of morning called and cawed from the far-off trees beyond the *national monument.*

"I wasn't expecting this many buildings," Seth admitted hoarsely. There were five that he could see, all of them broad and imposing, with an array of smaller buildings to the north and another to the south of the prison blocks. To securely breach and check every last one of them would take days. "What'd Cord say? She might be in a honeycomb of basement cells? Where's that and how do we get into it?"

"Let's check." Rolling to his back, Eric rang up their man boat-side. "Can you give me a definite place to start looking?"

Cord's voice came through loud and clear in the early morning hush. "See the squat building in the center, the one with the wrap around portico, or whatever you call it? That's the main interrogation building. It's full of offices and shit. Montego keeps a couple locked rooms below. Enter through the south door on the first level, take a right and walk about a hundred steps. I promise, it'll lead you straight to the basement, but the door'll be locked. Either of you wise guys think to pack any C4 in those fancy bags?"

Eric looked at Seth, his thumb over his mic. "Damn, he's abrasive. Think I should let him go on thinking he's smart, cuz I'm here to tell you, he's not."

Seth nodded. "Hell, no, tell him. Might shut him up for a second."

"Hey, Asshole," Eric drawled. "You ever heard of dimethyl ether?" Aka: industrial strength freeze-spray.

"Shit, you've got some of that? You got extra?"

Eric clicked off without further explanation. "Let's just go. I can't take this guy's ego."

Which wasn't like Eric. He was one of the few who got along with every one of The TEAM members, be they jarhead, grunt, or sailor. But Eric's nerves were stretched tight and Seth didn't blame him, not with another agent's life on the line.

Silently, they crossed the grassland between them and the complex. Eric led the way forward, twenty feet or so, while Seth covered his six. Once he caught up to where Eric crouched waiting, Seth tapped his shoulder, then assumed point and went forward another twenty feet, while Eric covered him. And so on until they reached the rounded porch of the center building.

But what an eerie sensation, all those dark, shadowed prison cells staring down on Seth. More than once, he caught himself looking up to see if anyone was watching from those vacant windows, not that he could've seen them. Every last hole in the rounded walls was dark and black. The whole place felt dead. Seth glanced upward again, certain that he and Eric were not alone.

Finally at the south door on the first level, he signed Eric to hold. All it took was one booby-trapped doorknob and this mission would be over. Dropping to one knee, Seth removed the LED flashlight from his gear belt, and illuminated the doorframe, jamb, and the transom over the door. Everything looked right, yet Seth wasn't convinced.

Out came his miniature flex neck spy cam, a two-foot necked baby small enough to slide under doors and see around corners. Designed with an LED focused beam, it'd have no trouble pinpointing the source of Seth's anxiety.

"You okay?" Eric asked, his gloved hand resting on Seth's back.

There was a time when Eric did that regularly, a time when the touch of a brother soothed Seth, but Seth was a different man now. He nodded at the steady support, slid the snake beneath the door, and whispered, "Classic booby trap,

Reynolds. A single grenade and a twelve-inch wire. Montego's waiting for us."

Smoothly, he retreated the snake, wound its neck around his fingers, and tucked it away for another day and another door. "We need a different way in."

Eric huffed at Seth's left. "I didn't see any other exterior doors or low-to-the-ground windows, did you? So, where's the basement?"

Licking his lips, Seth looked past Eric to the way they'd come. "Not in this building, but I'll bet they're all linked. Get Cord on the line. Maybe he knows something we don't."

Seconds later, Cord anted up with, "Already told you. Weren't you listening? There's a regular beehive below ground. If you can't get in through that building, backtrack to the cellblock due east. No one'll be in there, but at the rear of the main hall, you'll see two rusted steel doors behind a long metal railing. Those doors might be how Montego comes and goes. He and his men are too lazy to set and reset traps every time they exit."

Cord made sense, so Seth and Eric followed his opinion. Soon, they found themselves standing in the broken-down doorway of one of the prison's massive cellblocks. The sky had barely lightened with the coming dawn, but there was enough light to see the rows upon rows of empty cells lining the hollowed interior wall of the cylindrical structure. The place was built like an enormous silo, straight up, with a wide, wooden slatted roof. A single tower, maybe three stories tall, stood in the center like a lighthouse, only with gun turrets at the highest ledge, their rifle slots now vacant, and the metal coated in rust.

A man had only to inhale one lungful to know the massive shadowy fingers climbing up the walls were layers of black mold.

"You've got to be kidding me," Seth rasped as he craned his neck to take in the view. Talk about a desolate way to languish. Each cell contained one window facing out, while metal bars comprised the entire wall facing inward. Iron rails lined each level. And gloom. There was no privacy anywhere.

The need to run and grab Cassidy, so she wouldn't spend one more minute in this awful place suffused Seth's very steady nature. But it was Eric who said, "Now. We've got to find her and get her out of here, right damned now."

Apparently he'd seen enough, too.

Seth gulped. "Then let's do this."

Chapter Twenty-Seven

In her dream, Dev was safe and sound. She was warm, not too warm, but just right warm. That alone should've alarmed her. The sudden softness beneath her head should've told her something was wrong. Maybe the scent of body odor in her nose, but instead she breathed deeply.

Her heavy limbs refused her brain's halfhearted command to get up and move, to find out where she was or if she should run. Her limbs seemed locked into this incredibly, so, so soft mattress—or cloud. It could very well be a cloud as light as her head felt resting on it. She might just have died, and this place might be heaven.

Okay then. Problem solved. With a concentrated "Oomph," she rolled to her side and fell back to sleep.

As Seth expected, the double metal doors creaked the moment Eric shouldered them aside and disappeared into the maw of black shadows beyond. The stiletto beam from his LED flashlight directed Seth to veer right, his own beam focused on the concrete floor.

Eric led the way, and Seth understood the survivor's guilt that drove his friend's need to be the first one in. A good man never left his buddies behind, but knowing that the other person was injured and suffering, that his buddy was a woman this time, ate at the hearts of most male warriors. Just because a guy bucked up and strapped on enough armor plating to protect his chest and gut didn't mean any of that crap protected his heart or his soul. Hence the Stateside epidemic of PTSD and suicides from warriors returning home. This 'job' could suck the soul out of the strongest person. Times that by a million when a man's innate instinct failed to protect the 'weaker' sex during an op gone sideways.

After traversing a maze of corridors, Eric stopped, his arm up and his fist clenched, the signal to cease and desist. Seth stopped in his tracks and cocked his head, listening for whatever Eric had heard. The far-off bang as if a hammer had just hit a nail, then a groan, came back to Seth. He strained to understand what he'd heard. Another bang. Another groan, this one rapped higher as if—

"They're crucifying her!" Eric spat.

Or someone. Seth steeled his heart. He'd seen retaliation shit like this before. Beheadings. Crucifixions. Scalpings. All done to shock the boys and girls from America. Damned brutal shit worked.

Taking one step forward, he put one hand on Eric's broad shoulder. "Steady. We do this right and we're out of here in minutes. She's on her way home with us. Understood?"

Eric's head bobbed, but Seth caught the glistening sweat pouring down his buddy's face. Might've been tears.

"Lights out," Seth ordered as he stepped around Eric and assumed point. Crouched low, he kept his rifle tucked under his chin, its sights set to engage anything that moved ahead. After taking several steps, he glanced over his shoulder. Eric had gone scary silent, and Seth needed to know he was still there.

The pitch-black darkness gave way to the amber glow of propane lanterns hung from metal hooks protruding from the concrete walls of a rectangular room, its walls lined with jail cells, bars and all. Within each cell, more shadows, but Seth could sense the suffocating presence of more people than just the three at the center of the room between the rows of cells.

Two men and a woman, only she'd been forced to kneel on some kind of a kneeler like the ones Seth had seen within sacristies of Christian churches. Her arms were tied behind her back, and she was crying and moaning. Instead of a cushion, the kneeler consisted of a metal grate, the kind with serrated treads and a toe-kick like you'd see at construction worksites. The kind meant to scrape shit, dirt, and thorns from the tread of a workingman's steel-toed boots, not to press kneecaps and tender flesh onto.

Shit. That thing wasn't a kneeler. It was a rape stand, intended for degradation and depravation of the worst kind. They hadn't nailed the woman to it, but swinging one helluva big hammer, nailing the chains around the kneeler into the ground. Laughing. Jerking at the kneeler. Testing it as if they needed to make sure it wouldn't move. Terrorizing her.

Seth knew what would happen next. Without thinking, he took one pissed off step into that stinking room, counted his adversaries: six sweaty men, all with eyes wide-open. They hadn't seen him coming, well that was good-god-damned fine by Seth. His index finger squeezed and—

Holy shit, Reynolds!

Before Seth got a round off, gunfire exploded to his left, all but deafening him. Eric wasn't quiet anymore, not with the gleam of fire and brimstone in his dark eyes. Not with the rapid-fire *Br-r-r-r-t-t-t-t* of the most excellent weapon ever created, spitting death and vengeance from his righteous fist. It made a man proud to have an avenging angel of this caliber on his six, so Seth stood back, held his palms over his ears, and let Eric have at it.

"Kill 'em all," he whispered, quietly urging Eric on. "Send those fuckin' bastards to hell where they belong."

At last, Eric ceased firing. He stood there heaving, his jaw jutted forward, his body shaking, and his teeth bared. Seth's ears were still ringing, but it was then that the people in those individual cells stepped forward. One by one, nine women came out from the shadows, all of them gaunt, their bodies and clothes streaked with sweat and grime. All of them wide-eyed with shock and fear.

And Seth said proudly what he'd said in other foreign countries so many times before. "I'm an American soldier and you're going home."

One woman choked, her hand fisted to her mouth. Another stretched both of her arms through the bars. It never got better than that, seeing the pure, unadulterated relief in people's eyes, when they realized they were in the company of guys and gals who would actually die protecting them.

Eric stepped around Seth and asked, "Cassidy Dancer? We're looking for our friend. Do any of you know where Cassidy Dancer is? Is she here?"

A tall blonde with straggly hair pointed wordlessly to what appeared to be an empty cell across from hers. That Cassidy wasn't standing like the other women was telling.

"No," Eric cried out as he ran to the bars. "Shit, Seth, she's here and she's—"

"Not going anywhere," a gravelly voice from out of nowhere snarled.

Seth shifted his sights on the barrel-chested, dark-haired man who'd just stepped around the wooden crates stacked in the far corner. *Shit. Roland Montego.* He must have had a bolt-hole hidden there.

"Wrong, asshole," Seth spat. "She goes with us, just like the rest of these women."

"I think not," Montego said as he tossed his chin at Seth, then jerked a frail little waif of a boy from behind the crates to stand in front of him. Blond. Eyes brimming. The boy could've been an older version of Scottie.

Seth swallowed the real fear that this mission now relied one hundred percent on a messed-up man like him. Nonetheless, like the true Army Ranger he'd never been, he taunted Montego. "You think I can't make a headshot from here, jerk-off?"

The Cuban lowlife sneered a truly ugly smile, his crooked teeth dark, and his black eyes filled with malice. "You think I sell these women and children to *my* people?" he asked, spitting to the side. "Not so, gringo. It is not Cubans who come to me for dirty sex with dirty women, willing little girls, and tight little boys like this one here." He shook the frightened boy's shoulder. "It is rich American men like you who pay me for drugs and guns, whores and babies. I am simply another capitalist" —Montego rolled his lying eyes as his voice pitched higher— "like you. Now go, before I cut this precious boy's throat. He is somebody's baby, no? Somebody's only son, perhaps? Or is this why you came here to me? You know what I have to offer, si? You have heard great things about me and all I can offer you. You just want a dead body with a warm hole to satisfy your—"

"Shut the fuck up!" Eric bellowed, Cassidy forgotten for the moment and his rifle barrel snapped on target. "You say one more fuckin' word and I'll blow you to Hell!"

Montego tipped his head and laughed, and when he did, the boy's head jerked back. Seth saw it then, the glint of wire circling the poor kid's neck. Montego held a garrote that could behead this little guy in the space of a heartbeat.

Not happening.

Seth didn't waste a breath second-guessing his will or his better judgment. Just as it had in that dark Chicago bar a million nightmares ago, his heart led the way. His muscle training took over. His fingers flexed and—He. Just. Fired.

One to the forehead.

Another dead center through Montego's sweaty neck, right below his flabby, double chin.

With a sickening whoosh, blood and brain matter hit the wall behind him, and Seth was glad. *Damn it, yes!* He rejoiced in the best shot he'd ever made and the innocent life he'd saved and he'd do it again.

When Montego's body crumbled to the floor behind the kid, the wire loosened and fell with him. The kid's eyes went wide. His jaw dropped, but he stood there with his mouth open, frozen, and afraid to move. Afraid to breathe. Until Seth shouldered his rifle, dropped to one knee, opened his arm, and said, "Come here, little guy. I'm taking you home."

The poor kid hit Seth's chest like a tiny freight train, sobbing and shaking, his thin shoulders heaving as he burrowed his runny nose and sweaty face into Seth's shirt like he wanted to hide and never come out again.

"Shush," Seth whispered to his frantic new buddy. "I've got you. You're safe and you're going home now, but I need your help."

"N-n-no," the little guy cried, and that was okay. Seth had cried plenty in the past, too. He, of all warriors, understood how scary and big the world could be. But there wasn't enough time to smother one child with security, when so many others stood patiently waiting their turn at salvation from the hellhole Montego had dragged them into.

"What's your name, buddy?"

"Ch-Chris-toph-errrr…" the boy whined, his breaths coming fast, short, and so damned hard. It was a miracle he could speak the way he trembled.

"Well, Chris, can you help me unlock these cells, so these nice ladies can go home to their little boys, too?" Seth asked, even as his much bigger palm remained flattened over the kid's shuddering shoulder blades to calm him.

"He's got a key," the brave tyke murmured more into Seth's shirt than at Seth.

"Great. That's terrific information. Do you know where he keeps it?"

"In his p-pocket, mister. His pants pocket. Right side. Just where my dad keeps his car keys."

Eric pounced on Montego's still twitching body and quickly divested the creep of a ring of keys. In minutes, all the women were freed, including the poor thing at the rape stand, and Eric was on his knees beside his fallen TEAM agent.

Still dressed in her trademark khaki shorts and the black TEAM polo—thank God!—Cassidy lay on her side, her knees bent, and her arms sprawled at her sides. Seth didn't think he could stand it if her clothes had been torn or stained or—worse.

Eric said nothing as his hands moved methodically down her sides, over her chest and stomach, diagnosing and triaging, before he jerked his blowout bag up from one of his many pockets. By all appearances, she hadn't been molested, but she had been severely beaten. One side of her face was mottled black and bloody. Dried blood caked around her nose and mouth. Her lovely golden locks were wet with sweat and smeared dirt, probably more blood.

Seth watched Eric work on Cassidy from where he knelt with Christopher. He hadn't moved any closer. The boy didn't need to see all Eric might have to do to the woman.

"Is he a doctor?" Chris asked.

"You bet. One of the best."

"What's your name?"

"Seth McCray, former Army," Seth added loud enough so all could hear and know just how qualified he was to rescue them, that they were in safe hands.

Chris's fingers knotted Seth's shirt into two tight balls, his voice reduced to a timid whisper as he peered over his shoulder at Cassidy's cell. "Who's she?"

"That lady is Cassidy Dancer, and she's one of my best friends," Seth admitted, his heart stuck in his throat. Cassidy had only been married a year or two. She was a real spitfire if Seth had ever met one. She had to be okay. It'd kill her husband, Jude Cannon, and his daughter, Judith, if Cassidy were to die from her injuries. She and Jude hadn't had enough time together yet. Their love story couldn't end here, not like this.

Instantly, Seth's mind jumped from Cuba to a quiet little bungalow on Starfish Drive, where a ferocious, white-haired pixie waited on his return. He hadn't had enough time with Devereaux, either, and he wanted more. He wondered if she'd had to wrestle Gru into that bag she'd intended to carry him home in. That would've been a sight to see.

"She gonna be okay?"

"I sure hope so," Seth answered Christopher honestly. "Do you know what happened to her?" *My God, what have you been forced to endure while you've been here?*

"He… he hit her cuz she had a knife in her boot and she kicked him with it, so he hit her, and he kept hitting her until she fell down, and then I had ta stop watching cuz he was scaring me, and she wasn't fighting anymore. She didn't even cry no more, but… but I cried when he'd hit me like that." Chris sucked in a deep breath as tears streamed down his pale cheeks.

Seth tipped back, cupping the kid's jaw and for the first time, he saw the dark bruises under Chris's chin and on his throat. "That ass—I mean, that man—hit you? He punched you?"

Chris's head bobbed, and his eyes brimmed. "He… he slapped me here…" Chris reached for the back of his head. "And he punched me here…" One little hand fell to his stomach before he quickly secured it inside Seth's shirt. "And I'm glad you killed him because he was a very mean man and I wish you could kill him again and" —a gut-wrenching hiccup lurched out of Chris— "again." His tirade ended in a pitiful whine.

God, this little man was breaking Seth's heart. He pulled the boy under his chin and kissed his forehead, wishing he could make Chris forget the Hell he'd been through. But that was what counselors and moms and dads were for, to soften the memory, because no one ever forgot crap like this. Like Alex Stewart said, they just learned how to pack it away and carry it for the rest of their lives.

Still, Seth had to know. "Was that all he did to you?"

Chris's head bobbed, and Seth hoped he was being honest, but again, there was nothing Seth could do to change what had happened or what might still be happening inside this sweet little guy's heart, mind, and soul. Some scars healed, but some wounds festered until, in the end, bastards like Montego won. Hell, Latoya Franklin still paid him nightly visits, and on the rare bad day, she brought two innocent fuzzy lambs with her. Wasn't that one helluva mind fuck?

Seth and his partner sat there and rocked while they waited on Eric. But with every ragged breath, the hollow at the base of the boy's neck sucked in as if he wasn't getting enough air, and that was worrisome. This kid was sick.

"Take it easy," Seth murmured, inhaling to show Chris how to calm himself. "Take a deep breath and let it out slow. Nice and easy, there you go."

Even as he watched Cassidy, Seth kept the steady contact between his much larger hand and the boy's shivering back. Chris was running a fever. Seth was almost sure of it. "How old are you, Chris?"

"Seven and a half," said every American kid ever. That half-year meant a heckuva lot when you were seven.

"You're in what, third grade?"

Chris held up two fingers. "Only second, but I'm gonna graduate this spring, and then I'll be a third grader, and I might get to be in Mr. Cousin's class. He's a good guy, and he used ta be a Marine, and I might get to go on a field trip with him to a shooting range if'n it's okay with my mom and dad." A long deep breath followed that tremendous amount of information.

But Seth only half-heard the child's rambling. Cassidy hadn't stirred yet, and all the women had now clustered around her open cell door, their own pains forgotten as they held onto each other and watched Eric treating her. One rocked another. One woman sobbed and cried, while yet another kept praying the *'Hail, Mary,'* over and over.

But it was the grim light in Eric's eyes and the curt shake of his head that was worrisome. Cassidy had yet to respond to any of his expert ministrations, even the smelling salts. When he peeled one of her eyelids back and shone his LED flashlight into her eyes, he bit his bottom lip and shook his head. Not good.

Seth lifted Chris with him as he shoved to his feet.

"Don't!" Chris squealed, his fingers digging into Seth as he scrambled to attach himself to Seth's ribs. "Don't let me go, mister! I don't wanna get lost no more!"

"Shhh," Seth soothed the frightened child, rubbing a hand over his head, cupping him against his body. "Trust me, I'm not letting you go, Chris. You hear me? But you need to hang on tight to my neck when I start to move, so we can get out of here, okay?" He adjusted the boy's body until Chris straddled his left hip, clear of the rifle slung over Seth's right. "There. That's better, isn't it?"

"Ah-huh," Chris breathed, his poor heart pounding under Seth's arm like an entire brass band. His fingernails dug into Seth's neck, a small price to pay to keep this kid calm. But they had to get the hell out of this viper pit, right now. Cassidy was running out of time.

Seth opened a channel and hissed into his two-way, praying Cord had his ears on. "Man down, damn it! We're coming in hot. Cover us!"

Chapter Twenty-Eight

She didn't know where she was, only that someone moved silently around her. Whoever her caretaker was, he or she kept the room that Dev lay in dark, and the noise level nearly non-existent. The temperature was near perfect, but her poor head was still filled with shadows. Given the way her brain throbbed each time she tried to open her eyes, Dev didn't—couldn't—fight what was happening around her. Not that she needed to, but still… Something kept telling her to try.

"You've got a concussion, Angelique" a gravelly voice murmured at her right. Not Seth. Not Cord. Definitely not Sly. And somehow, knowing that much, that it wasn't Sly who'd come for her was—enough. For now.

"Name's Devereaux," she said as she ran the tip of her tongue over her dry bottom lip.

Instantly, she was rewarded with a cool, moist sponge bathing her face, then the tip of a straw pressed to her lips. Breathing hard, she latched on and sucked down a swallow of what tasted like coconut water. *Oh, so good.* Sipping another long draw, the refreshment eased down her parched throat like a sweet taste of heaven.

By the time she lost traction on the straw, she'd forgotten what she'd wanted to ask. Something about… something… someone…

"Rest easy, Angelique," the same husky voice, still from her right, whispered.

Dev wanted to turn to that guy and set him straight. She wanted to open her eyes and know who'd dared or cared enough to rescue a complete stranger from the roadside, even if he had her mixed up with someone else. She wanted to know what he looked like, if he was a priest or a doctor or just a guy with a good heart.

Not happening. She had just enough energy left to murmur, "Ah-huh," before her energy gave out and she drifted to sleep.

"You heard me. We've got nine women who can walk, a seven-and-a-half-year old boy who's ready to fight, and we've got Cassidy, but she's in bad shape. Stand by for rapid evac, I don't care who's on your ass!"

"Copy that," Cord replied like the true professional he could be—calmly and without one smart-assed dig for a change. "Be aware that FAST has just engaged the enemy to the south of us. We've got mortar shells pounding the south beach, panicked civilians everywhere, and dozens of black-uniformed bastards flaunting spiffy red berets with some Arabic shit on 'em. The quicker you get out of there, the better for all concerned."

"Copy that," Seth bit out with Chris still bouncing on his hip and nine frightened women crowding his six as he hot-footed it back the way they'd come. For now, Chris helped by aiming Seth's flashlight straight ahead. Eric followed the harried procession, carrying Cassidy, while another woman scurried at his side with his flashlight.

Eric hadn't detected any broken bones during his quick exam, but Cassidy had yet to regain consciousness, and Seth was worried. Concussions left unattended were brain killers. He'd suffered two while playing football in high school until his father put his foot down the last time, and said, "Enough!"

"You might have to walk if we run into any bad guys," Seth warned Chris.

"Oh, okay." The boy hadn't let up his stranglehold since he'd scrambled into Seth's arms. "Are you gonna shoot 'em?"

"Only if they shoot first. We're getting out of here by boat, so when we hit the shore, and I tell you to run, you head straight into the water, and don't look back. My good buddy Cord'll pull you aboard, and once you're there, you stay with him, okay?"

"'Kay," Chris murmured against Seth's neck. "I like you."

Seth grunted at that out of the blue compliment. He'd reached the end of the line, but when he pressed one shoulder to the metal doors, they didn't budge. He hadn't noticed until now what he wished he'd seen on his way through these doors. There were no doorknobs or handles on this side, not even a hole or fitting where one would've been. Shit. They were trapped.

Crouching low, he set Chris's feet to the ground and told him, "I need you to be brave, tough guy. Stand back with my buddy and the ladies, while I get us out of here."

"Okay," Chris said, still aiming the light at the closed doors.

Seth sent a glare at Eric. "They're locked. What do you think? Grenade or a hundred rounds?"

"Fire in the hole," Eric answered, motioning for Chris to join him. "Come on, everyone. We're going around the corner where we'll be safe. Send a message to those bastards, Seth. Light 'em up."

Good answer. Seth waited until Chris and everyone else had retreated safely out of sight and beyond the blast zone. But shit, he was sick and tired of Montego's rat bastard buddies. Approaching the door again, he splayed both palms over the rusted metal, wishing he had x-ray vision. Crouching, he ran his fingers along the threshold. Damn. There was no space for his flex neck spy cam. He and everyone with him really were trapped. Like rats.

Like hell.

The doors were rusty, and every door had hinges. Carefully, Seth retrieved one of the two aerosol cans of freeze-spray from his gear bag. After he donned a pair of leather gloves and a pair of *photochromic* safety glasses, he applied a good dose of the spray to both sides of the doorframe. Then he backed off from ground zero, crouched against the nearest wall, and curled both arms over his face and head in case the hinges exploded.

Metal, especially compromised metal, cracked under pressure, and this doorjamb was crackling plenty. This particular blend of freeze-spray contained not only dimethyl ether, but also propane, making it downright lethal in the right hands. Doctors used a much weaker version of it to treat warts and cancer cells, but the military grade version was blow-your-hands-off wicked. And Seth wanted to blow whoever was waiting for him on the other side of these doors, straight to hell.

In very few seconds, the distinctive popping sounds coming from the distressed metal hinges told Seth it was go-time. In one fluid motion, the spray can went back into his bag. His assault rifle slid over his shoulder and into his arms like a pet dragon, ready to breathe fire and mayhem.

The women in the dark hall behind him were quiet, and they were his last thought. He was doing this for them and Scottie. For every other battered woman in harm's way. For Devereaux. For Lianna and Christopher and Cassidy. Seth pushed off the balls of his feet and charged into the centerline of those doors. Throwing his weight into it, he lead with his left shoulder while he aimed to kill anything that got in his way.

He was NOT blinded by the light that hit him square in the face once those doors burst off their hinges, though. Uh-uh. The safety glasses he'd snapped on had instantly compensated for the sudden shift from dark to bright, shielding his retinas from the sunlight now streaming through the dilapidated roof on the other side of those doors. The clear-as-day vision allowed him to accurately see the seven men in gray uniforms, all with rifles raised and ready to fire at him. Not Americans. Not Cubans. But every last one of them was decked out in red berets with some piece of shit Arabic symbol front and center over their black brows.

The Saudis seemed surprised. Some dropped their mouths as if they'd never seen a pissed off American soldier before. Toby Keith's rowdy chorus, *"How do you like me now?"* rang out like a rebel cry in Seth's head as he hit the dirt running.

Sliding like Babe Ruth into home base, he laid down a healthy round of rapid-fire, rotating his rifle from left to right as, still on his butt, he breached his enemy's perimeter.

The Saudis were damned slow to respond, no doubt because he'd gotten in too close and too personal, way too fast. Nearly at the nearest guy's knees before the bastard aimed and fired, the prison ground turned into an old west shooting gallery with the Saudis at Seth's right, firing into their own guys on his left. They'd panicked. They were killing each other, firing wildly like a bunch of idiots.

Someone got off a lucky shot that actually ripped high into Seth's shoulder like a hornet, but by the time he looked back to see how many, if any, of those badasses were left, the game was over.

Eric was the only one standing, the AR in his hands smoking almost as much as he was. "You're an idiot!" he hissed as he stalked toward Seth, his jaw set hard and his brows clenched like one dark thundercloud over two blazing mad eyes. "You could've been killed, you dumb shit!"

Seth nodded as he shoved up off his knees, the hammering in his chest making it hard to breathe. "Well, yeah, but I knew what I was doing. They didn't," he said as he nodded to the losing team, on his way back to Eric.

One Saudi soldier clutched his pant leg as Seth passed by. Begrudgingly, Seth dropped to one knee beside the guy and asked, "You got something you want to say, asshole?"

After a drawn-out gurgling groan, the poor guy spat a river of blood along with, "Who… who are you?"

Seth cocked his head. He'd expected some terrorist rhetoric, *'death to the infidels',* or some bullshit rant about

'Allah's will', not a frightened question in broken English. "Me? I'm nobody, but who the hell are you?"

"Rashid..." the guy whispered, wheezing through the multiple bullet holes in his chest.

Seth took a second look at the man he'd bested. Shit, Rashid was no more than a kid, maybe eighteen. Maybe younger. Swallowing hard, Seth glanced over his wounded shoulder at the others sprawled around him. None of them were geared up. They wore no tactical vests. No body armor. Nothing to shield them from the killing effects of modern-day warfare. But they were all dying. It didn't make sense. This Saudi army was nothing more than a bunch of kids with guns?

God, not again. "How old are you?" Seth had to know.

Rashid held up three bloody fingers. "Fif... teen."

Holy shit. "Why are you guys in Cuba?" Seth asked more gently, needing to understand what the hell was going on. "Why'd you ambush me, Rashid? Why'd you take our female agent prisoner?"

"Must... save..." Wheeze. Spit. Groan. "Princess... Lianna..." With those final words, Rashid expired on a hiss.

Thoughtfully, Seth closed the younger man's eyes before he looked up at Eric, who still surveyed the carnage, ever watchful. Ever faithful. Ever covering Seth's six like a brother. But that was what military training did to a man. It turned him into a skilled, professional warrior. A guard dog. A killer. Something these kids obviously were not.

Shit. I've killed a child, children. Again.

Rattled to his soul, Seth told Eric, "I don't get it. Khadeem sent kids to save the daughter he betrayed, but he sent them without sufficient protection or training. Look at them. None of them are soldiers. They're not wearing bulletproof... anything. Not even a vest or body armor." Exasperated with himself as much as the psycho on the other side of the world, Seth said, "Khadeem sent these—these children—to die for a cause he knew wasn't true."

Eric's shoulders lifted as if he didn't care, but Seth knew better. Eric's love for his fellow man knew no bounds, but he also prioritized that love. His brothers and sisters always came first. "Like Alex says, once a bastard, always a bastard. Seems to me Khadeem wanted what you'd call plausible deniability. If his own people, his army, thought America was behind Princess Lianna's disappearance, then why aren't they Stateside blowing up airports and churches and... shit. Why are they here?"

"Apparently because..." Seth's head jerked up. "Shit, Eric. Khadeem knew he could never get his men into America. He didn't send them to retrieve Lianna. That's not what this is about. He sent them here to die. Don't you see? Two wrongs don't make a right, but Jesus H. Christ! What he's done to his daughter and these boys will start a war with America. He told his army to come save his daughter, but that's what he really wants—war. We've got to get to FAST. Now! They've got to stop fighting before they do exactly what Khadeem expects. It's not even a fair fight. Those Marines will kill every last one of these poor dumb kids, and then—"

"And then we'll be at war with Saudi Arabia, every country that backs them, including Russia, and—"

"And shit!" Seth hissed, on his feet now and pissed at the treacherous snake behind this evil plan. "Khadeem's one sick bastard, Eric. We're not fighting Saudi Arabia, though I have no doubt that's what Khadeem hopes to achieve. No, these aren't the king's soldiers. These are the sons of Khadeem's tribesmen."

Jerking his satphone out of his pocket, Seth stuffed the battery into its slot and did what he should've done a day ago. He called home.

"Stewart," Alex bit out.

Without any preliminaries, Seth stated emphatically, "Boss, I need you to call your highest-ranking USMC buddy and tell him to direct FAST to cease and desist all military action on Isla de la Juventud. Right damned now, Boss! FAST needs to stop killing, because—these kids are not Saudis! Understood? They're untrained teenagers. We called this all wrong. Khadeem sent unskilled young men without protection, and … Shit! Just fuckin' disengage before we get sucked into another war!"

The line went dead, and Seth wasn't sure if Alex hung up on him or what. Seth had never spoken to his boss like that. His thumb hit redial, and once again he got his boss, but all he heard was the one-sided conversation of one angry son-of-a-bitch telling another, "You heard me, General Pratt. I've got boots inside Cuba, and my guy's telling me… Yes, I trust my man! He's the best man I've got! Now, sir! Call your FAST commander right damned now and end this mess before it blows up in our face. This battle is not, I repeat, *not* what we think it is!"

The best man I've got? Me? Holy shit. Alex had just done precisely what Seth asked—and more. Instantly. No questions asked. For some crazy, inexplicable reason, tears stung the rims of Seth's eyeballs. He brushed them away, but holy shit. Alex—listened.

Seth's phone clicked and rattled a couple times before Alex came on the line and snarled, "What now?"

"Thanks," was all Seth could manage, but it came out so quiet, he wasn't sure Alex heard him.

The huffing and heavy breathing coming over the line told Seth his boss was one fired up badass, but Alex finally calmed enough to say, "Well done, Seth. Tell Eric I'm sending reinforcements. We'll be watching for him. Have you located Cassidy yet?"

"Yes, Boss. We've got her. We were in the middle of exfil when we encountered a group of seven, umm, shit. Kids..." *Whom I killed.* "She's unconscious right now, Boss, but there's a boat waiting offshore for us. Eric'll get her there. Should be home before sunset if all goes well."

"I'll have a team and an ambulance standing by to receive, just tell me where and when."

"Copy that," Seth said meekly, wishing Alex would get off the line before he caught on.

But Alex had an uncanny knack for reaching across a thousand miles and touching a guy, either with venom or with something much more powerful. And that was what Seth was afraid of, that—other weapon, the concise scalpel Alex wielded like a surgeon.

"Let it go, son," Alex said, his voice gentled and soft. Downright kind.

Seth bowed his head like a kid and swallowed hard. The sting of Alex's venom he could've handled, not—this.

"You had no way to know who you were facing, not as quickly as things spun up down there. Let it go and don't carry these ghosts with you, too. Those kids were armed, young, and scared. On adrenaline alone, they would've killed Eric, Cassidy, and everyone with you."

Seth nodded, though his boss couldn't see him, but yeah. In his head Seth knew he should let the deaths of these innocents go. Those kids would've killed him, no questions asked. They might've bragged around the campfire tonight about the dumbass American they'd shot, about what a fool he'd been to charge into the middle of them like he did. They might've told each other all the lies and crap boys forced to become men told each other at the end of the day. But try telling Seth's heart that. In the end, those *men* he'd killed were somebody's little kids.

Damned if Eric didn't make everything worse when his big hand landed firm and brotherly between Seth's shoulder blades like it had so many times in the past. "You're a good and decent man, Seth," he said quietly. "I'm damned proud to work with you."

Shrugging yet another nightmare off, Seth turned to the other man in his life whom he respected more than most. "The press will be all over this if the Marines massacre Khadeem's men. You know that, don't you? They'll spin this to their own political agenda, and whatever we do here today will be the only thing that'll make or break their lies."

Eric nodded. Usually a positive guy, he'd grown more and more grim, almost morose, the longer this rescue mission took. "I've got to get Cassidy to the boat. The women and the boy, too. They can't wait, and they need off this island."

"Christopher. His name's Christopher, Eric." That seemed more important now than ever.

Eric tugged a plastic wrapped blow-out kit up from one of his many pockets and handed it over. "You're wounded,

Seth. Take a minute to patch yourself up before it gets infected."

Seth stuffed the kit into his rear pocket. "Will you be okay?" He had to know.

Eric gave him one curt nod before he turned to where Chris and the women now huddled around Cassidy at the shattered doorway.

"You go with Eric from now on," Seth told the brave little soldier still pointing his flashlight at Seth. "He'll get you home to your mom and dad, to your teacher, Mr. Cousins. He'll make sure you go on that field trip, too." *He'll make sure you grow up to be a better man than most.*

Chris nodded. Eric crouched to lift Cassidy up into his arms, and that was how Seth left them. Behind.

Chapter Twenty-Nine

Dev opened her eyes to a brand-new day, her head finally clear of murk and shadows. Her stomach growled, and she desperately needed another sip of that delicious coconut water, but she wasn't entirely sure it hadn't all been part of a dream.

Lifting to her elbows, she surveyed the tidy but cramped quarters she found herself in. This was the heaven she'd imagined? Ah-uh. Looked more like a cheap hotel room complete with a hint of gray on the ceiling from painted-over mold. Not what she expected at all. Where was the priest, doctor, or the guy with a good heart who'd rescued her?

It was dark. The curtains were drawn tight and the only light in the place glimmered from beneath the bathroom door. Lying under a sheet on a lumpy mattress, Dev smoothed one hand down her thigh. Thank God, her shorts and shirt were still where they belonged.

"You're safe. Are you hungry?" her benefactor asked, still keeping to the farthest shadows of the room. She knew he wasn't Sly or that rat bastard Bagani by the definite Spanish accent, not like that made Dev feel much better. This place wasn't a hospital where an injured woman found alongside the road should've been taken, and any guy who lurked in the corner like a vampire was no Good Samaritan out to do a good deed. Definitely not a priest.

"Where am I?" she asked quietly. *And who the hell are you?*

A grunt came back to her. That he hadn't answered her simple question was alarming enough, but instead of whimpering, Dev swallowed her fear and firmly projected her intentions. "I'm leaving."

Adding credence to that statement, she tossed the bed cover aside, set both feet to a matted carpet and said, "Thank you for helping me. I appreciate all you've done. Really, I do, but I'm going now." *And you can't stop me.*

"You're not going anywhere." His tone shifted from feigned kindness to grim, yet still he wasn't brave enough to face her. The coward. What was that all about?

Dev stood, instantly gauging the running distance to the door. She could make it. Opening the door would cost her precious seconds. It might be locked, but all she needed was enough time to scream for help.

"Sit," he snapped.

Pissed that he thought he could threaten her, she turned on him. "I said I'm leaving and—"

And damn he was fast, one moment hidden, the next looming over her on the mattress where he'd shoved her like a bear with a kitten, his knees on both sides of her hips and his breath in her face. The rank odor of sweat mixed with beer stifled her as long, golden-red hair draped off his shoulders and fell onto her cheeks and into her opened mouth.

Huffing, she blew the oily stands away and sealed her lips, her heart jackhammering up so high in her throat, surely he could hear it. Yet he said nothing, just studied her with an intensity so fierce she could feel the desperation in it.

"I am not most men," he growled. Whatever that meant.

'No, you're an ass,' she thought but asked, "Who… who are you then? A kidnapper?"

"Joachim," he said as his nose dipped into the crook of her neck and he nuzzled her like the dog he was. "Just Joachim. That's all you need to know."

First names only, how cliché? *God, give me strength,* she prayed as she stared at the mottled ceiling. "H-how'd you find me?"

"I'm never far from the man I serve," he muttered, his breath as rank as a dog's.

"And that would be?" She hated to ask.

He just grunted, the scrape from the scruff on his ugly face on her tender skin unbearable.

"M-my name is Devereaux Shepherd," she breathed, hating the hitch in her voice as much as the heat rolling off his body. But the more this creep knew about her, the better her chances of surviving whatever he had in mind, right? That was what other survivors all said. "B-but m-my friends call me—"

"Angelique," he hissed, his breath warm and thick as he tongued a line up her neck to her ear. "From now on, you will be Angelique. It will be my pet name for you, and no one else shall call you that but me. Only me."

This fruitcake was seriously off his rocker.

"Angelique and Joachim will go down in history as the most famous lovers of all time, even more famous than Bonnie and Clyde."

Okay, that came way out of left field. What was this guy, c-c-crazy? "No, Joachim, I'm Devereaux Shepherd, and I have a little boy waiting for me at home, and he needs me, and I—"

Joachim reared back, his dark blue eyes bright with anger as the rest of his hard body shifted against her belly. "You are not a virgin?"

Dev would've lied if it would've gotten her away from the steel rod in his pants poking her belly, but she'd already blown that option. Shaking her head, she determined to undermine whatever lies he'd been told. "No, Joachim, I'm a single mom with a minimum wage job and right now, my rent's overdue. If you don't let me go home soon, my four-year-old son will be scared, and I'll lose my home." *Really soon!* "Who told you I was a virgin? Sly Valentine?"

His nostrils flared as his eyes scrolled over her face, over her chin, and down her neck to her non-existent cleavage. "Santa Madre de Dios. Four-years-old, eh?"

Dev nodded, hoping that light in his eyes meant enlightenment instead of—that. Gooseflesh shivered up the back of her neck and over her shoulders. "Yes, and I'm in a committed relationship now. Want my fiancée's name and number?"

Joachim rolled one shoulder as if he were weighing his options. The tip of his tongue ran one lap around his lips before his teeth snared his bottom lip. "But I paid for a virgin," he murmured as he ran a hand over his hair, pulling it over one shoulder. "That dirtbag lied to me."

Yeah, had to be Sly, but what the hell made him think he could sell her? The ass! This was lower than low. Feverishly grasping at straws, Dev nodded to get Joachim off of her and out the door. "Who… who lied to you? Sly? Was it him?"

"Yes, my friend, Sylvester," he replied, his tone filled with amazement as if he couldn't believe Sly would ever lie. *Give me a break.* That was what Sly did best, which explained a lot.

Dev said the first thing that came to her mind. "He's not the most honest man." Talk about an understatement. "Sly sold me to you? How much did you give him?"

Instead of answering, Joachim leaned over the side of the bed, reaching for something beneath it. Unexpectedly, he grabbed her wrist, and—

Snap. Just when she thought things couldn't get any worse, they did. A metal cuff now graced her wrist. She swallowed hard as Joachim lifted to his knees and climbed off the bed.

"Stay," he bit out. "In a little while, I will deal with that liar, and when I come back, I will deal with you. Now I'll ask you one last time, Angelique. Are you hungry?"

Dev shook her head, afraid to meet his eyes. "No. I just want to go home."

That earned her a snort. "Not happening. I paid good money for you, and you will serve until I'm through with you."

When pigs fly…

Chapter Thirty

With his mission clear, Seth humped south by southeast, away from the Presidio Modelo, over grasslands, through forests and swamps, and onto the edge of the marshy inlet where Khadeem's camp of hundreds now lay in smoking ruins. Damn. The Marines had been as lethal and as quick as a scythe the way they'd mowed through the enemy's encampment and laid everything low.

Rows of ragged young men now sat cross-legged on the ground with their wrists cuffed and their hands behind their heads, while scores of fully-armed, geared-up Marines patrolled the lines, fore and aft. As if any of these frightened kids knew how to escape. There wasn't a fancy red beret in sight, and all their gray uniforms were muddied, bloodied, or both.

"TEAM Agent Seth McCray!" Seth called out loud and clear as he breached the USMC perimeter. Now wasn't the time to get shot. "Coming in!"

Immediately, he found himself pushed to his knees and a dozen rifle barrels in his face. His wounded shoulder reminded him it didn't like rough handling just as Corporal Johnny "Tex" Ritter pushed his way around his men. Just in time, too, as some jarhead's thick knee had just speared Seth's kidneys.

"That's him," Ritter said quickly, peering past Seth into the trees and swamp behind him. "He was with Reynolds. They're here to locate their missing agent. Cassidy Dancer. You're former Army Seth McCray, right?"

"Yes," Seth replied, his hands behind his head as he waited for the gun barrels in his face to stand down.

"Where's your friend? Your boat?" the surly sergeant in charge asked as he leaned over and stared into Seth's face. The guy was squared-jawed with the mandatory high and tight haircut of a professional 'lifer'. Ritter had taken a step back, but he was another story. Intelligent eyes scrolled from his sergeant to Seth, yet he stood there and said nothing.

"He should be off the island by now. I left him at the Presidio Modelo after we encountered and engaged a group of Khadeem's men."

"You kill 'em?" the sergeant asked, the corner of his lip lifted in a sneer.

"Yes, sir, I did," Seth replied quickly. *And I'll never forgive myself.* Marines didn't understand anything less than the cold, hard truth, so he kept how he felt about what he'd done close to his chest for now.

"Good," the sergeant spat. "On your feet and report, McCray. Why the fuck are you here in Cuba in the middle of a top-secret operation no one's supposed to know about, huh?"

"Because this alleged war is a set-up, sir," Seth replied as he shoved off the ground, his eyes forward and his spine ramrod stiff. This sergeant expected protocol, and by God, he was going to get it. "I've also uncovered intelligence that these men are not Saudi Nationals, sir. They're just kids Khadeem sent to die, so he could start a war with the United

States. Khadeem wants the Marine Corps to massacre these young men, sir. That's his real plan. He wants you to look bad. He started this mess rolling when he sold his daughter to Prince Basheer Bagani, who in turn, traded her to Roland Montego, for what price, we don't yet know. Then Khadeem garnered support in his country by lying to his people. He told them that America had kidnapped their princess, that we'd concealed her here in Cuba. He threw this army together and sent a bunch of kids to retrieve her, knowing full well that the USMC Company stationed at Naval Station Guantanamo, you, sir, would intercede swiftly and lethally."

"And we did. It's what we do. And then he planned to scream massacre and foul play, is that what you believe's happening?" The sergeant leaned in closer, the brim of his sweaty cap nearly against Seth's forehead and his hot breath in Seth's face. Man, he was built like a bulldog. Square jaw. Square head. Flat stubby nose that might've been broken a time or two. Or twelve. "You got proof?"

"I do, sir. You already know none of these men were wearing body armor. They're cannon fodder, nothing more. You're a career warrior. You know these kids are greener than snot, that they're not trained soldiers. You know just how dumb they are."

"I do, huh? Hmmm...." The sergeant ran a gloved hand under his chin and down his throat, flicking the sweat and grime of battle away with a snap of his wrist. "You're right. None of the men we've questioned so far hasn't turned to crap and cried like a baby. They fight like shit, and that explains why we now have two hundred and thirty-one assholes in custody. Jesus Christ, I didn't come here to round up a bunch of prisoners of war!"

"Sir, if I may ask, how many" —Seth coughed at his next word— "casualties?"

"A dozen or so. Theirs, not ours," the sergeant snapped, his chin up as he stared down his nose at Seth. "Christ, we couldn't just mow them down. At first, we thought we were being overrun. Lost two damned good men, but when my men arrived and started laying down fire, the bastards' first line caved. They turned and ran like a pack of sissies. You mean to tell me we were killing" —his head cocked to the side— "children?"

Wow. How to tell a hardcore Devil Dog who'd been sent to Cuba on the President's errand that, yes, he and his men had killed a dozen young men—children—who'd had no business taking on the Corps like they had. Most of them no doubt thought they were in for a treat, coming to a tropical island. But that wasn't what the hardnosed man breathing down Seth's neck wanted to hear.

Instead of the blunt, straightforward approach, instead of saying that yes, US Marines had murdered children—like America's press no doubt would—Seth opted for, "I can't say for sure, sir, but I do know the seven I killed at the Presidio Modelo were definitely unskilled kids. I questioned one before he died. All he knew was that he was there to save their princess. But you and I both know Princess Lianna isn't in Cuba any longer." Seth paused, not so sure what this hard-assed Marine knew. "Khadeem's army might've had rifles, but they aren't trained for combat, nor did they know how to defend themselves against one Army soldier."

"And that'd be you, huh? They went down easy, is that what you're telling me?"

"They didn't have a clue," Seth admitted, this line of questioning growing harder by the minute. The look on poor Rashid's face when he died would haunt him forever.

"Well, then... if a guy like you killed seven of them..." The sergeant paused, looked down the rows of prisoners, then singled one of the dark-haired men out and barked at Corporal Ritter. "Him. Take him to Major Delaney's tent, and you," he said to Seth. "Come with me."

Gladly. Seth rolled one shoulder and stepped forward, only to find himself escorted between four Marines, their weapons trained on him and nowhere to go but with them. No matter. This was about stopping a war, not proving who had a bigger dick.

Shortly, Seth found himself standing at a desk opposite USMC Major Delaney, a stern, prematurely gray-haired man with smile lines etched at the corners of his bright blue eyes. "So, you're the man who stopped the war?" he said as he lifted to his feet and extended one arm across the desk.

Since the sergeant had already concluded introductions, Seth accepted the handshake. "Sure hope so, sir."

Wide-eyed and drenched in sweat, the unfortunate young man from Saudi waited under armed guard at the doorway, his gaze darting from left to right as if he'd expected something much worse in the tent than what he was seeing.

"Sit." Delaney gestured Seth toward the plastic, folding chair in front of the desk. "Can I get you a drink?"

"Thank you, sir, yes," Seth replied. He hadn't spared time to drink or eat during his mad dash to prevent the killing of more innocents. Imagine his surprise when Delaney poured two fingers of Scotch into a glass tumbler and passed it over.

Seth took one hard swallow, felt the burn all the way down to his gut, and set the glass on the desk with a decided, "I don't suppose you could spare a bottle of water?"

Delaney chuckled, gestured at the armed Marines hovering in the background and told them, "For hell's sake, can't you see the man's thirsty? Get a couple bottles and bring a chair for that youngster. At least make him comfortable."

Bowing respectfully, the young man murmured a quiet, "Shukran."

Someone shoved another chair through the entrance of the tent and in came a harried Corporal Ritter. After a few words in Arabic, the prisoner accepted the already opened bottled water Ritter offered him between his manacled hands, tilted his head back, and swallowed.

The sight of his neck muscles working as he quickly drained that bottle dry tore at Seth's heart. This was just a thirsty kid, too far away from home and damned scared. His black, curly hair glistened with sweat. He probably didn't understand a word of English, and he sure as hell didn't want to be in Cuba anymore. Hell, this might even be his first time away from home.

Three more bottles appeared out of nowhere, and Seth emptied the first with one long gulp. "It's a long run from Nueva Gerona."

"You're injured," Delaney noticed.

"No, sir, I'm fine. It's just a scratch."

Delaney spiked a brow, his blue eyes twinkling. "You mean to tell me one of them got off a lucky shot?"

"Something like that."

The man in charge grinned. "You've got the makings of a damned fine Marine, Agent McCray. You ever consider switching to the right team?"

Seth shook his head, suppressing his own grin. "No, sir. I've already found the right TEAM. I'm sure you've heard of Alex Stewart."

"So you work for him," Delaney said, nodding as the amber liquor swirled in his glass. Just then, the *thwack-thwack-thwack* of heavy air transport beat the sides of the tent. Delaney held his silence, a smile teasing the corners of his mouth. Once the noise abated to a steady thrum, which meant those choppers had landed and were staying awhile, Delaney said, "Stewart's our poster boy for what to do right after you leave the Corps. How is that bastard, as big a shithead as ever?"

Seth could've laughed out loud at Delaney's spot-on description of his boss. Marines. Love 'em or hate 'em, they did make the world go round. "You know him?"

"Never had the chance to work with Alex, but I know of him. He's a legend, but how's he to work for? I hear he's a born leader."

"He is a good man," Seth said thoughtfully. "Hard as a son-of-a-bitch, but rock solid when you need him. Wouldn't work for anyone else, present company included, sir."

Delaney took the hit with grace. He downed what was left of his Scotch and turned to business. "You're right," he said, sticking his chin at the prisoner. "These kids aren't trained and they're not soldiers. Half of them don't even know how to reload the weapons they're armed with. We figure most are camel drivers, farmers, or school-aged kids."

To the prisoner, he asked, "What's your name, son? Who's your father? Your mother? How old are you?"

Timidly, the boy's shoulders lifted. His dark eyes widened as he looked to Corporal Ritter for interpretation. After a lengthy back and forth conversation in Arabic, the boy replied, "Husam al Din."

"His name means *sword of faith*, sir," Ritter inserted before he spoke again to the boy in his language. Turning again to Delaney, Ritter said, "Husam's mother was killed by a roadside bomb when she went to her sister's wedding in Syria last spring. He hasn't seen his father in years, not since the night the *honorable Khadeem* sent him to prison. His words, not mine, sir."

"Christ, the man's probably dead by now," Delaney growled. "Khadeem's not known to be lenient with his enemies. When was that?"

Ritter passed the question along, and Husam's lashes fell. He swallowed hard and shook his head, mumbling as his gaze hit the floor. Poor kid looked lost.

Corporal Ritter cleared his throat and explained, "Eleven years ago. Khadeem's men took his father when Husam was just five. They came into his village one night, rounded up, and imprisoned all adult males. Now Husam works the camel market to keep his three younger sisters fed and clothed. They have no other family."

"Shit! This kid's only sixteen?" Delaney growled. He glared at Seth and said, "See? This shit right here's why we're stuck in the Mideast, caught between assholes who murder their own people in the dark of night, then turn around come morning and praise Allah all the damned long day. Bastards, every last one of them." His fingers thrummed the desktop until he asked, "What'd Khadeem promise Husam if he joined his army?"

Gently, Ritter leaned forward and relayed the question, his palm on the poor kid's quaking shoulder. Seth held his breath until at last, Ritter turned to Delaney and said, "Three goats, an acre of land, and a small house. Most likely a shack. That's a small fortune for these people, but he also promised that his three sisters will never see the inside of prison like his father did."

"It takes a big brave man to threaten a kid," Delaney hissed. "Damn Khadeem."

Wasn't that the truth? Seth let out a breath, sick at heart for his part in the crimes perpetrated against these kids. "I killed seven of them," he said, pretty certain that Eric hadn't killed a one, that he hadn't joined the fight quick enough back at the Presidio Modelo to have done anything more than show up when the damage was done.

"What's your point?" Delaney asked, his brow spiked. "These boys might be kids, but they were armed. Trust me, I get your drift, but shit happens in war, McCray. I'm sick about the ones my men killed, too, but we didn't send them here, and we sure as hell didn't put weapons in their hands so they could kill us. But because of you and that ballsy boss of yours jerking my commander's chain, I've got… what? Three hundred prisoners of war who are going to live?" He turned to the aide standing off to his side. "Is that count still right?"

"Three hundred thirty-one alive, sir. Thirteen dead, twenty counting the men Agent McCray said he shot."

"Son-of-a-bitch. Khadeem sent three-hundred fifty-one children to fight a man's war, the coward." Delaney minced no words. "Then I say job well done, McCray. If you need a ride home, we're transporting all prisoners to Guantanamo today. That's why the choppers. The CIA wants these guys and the CIA can have them. If you hurry, you can ride out with the first group, then hitch the first available ride to the mainland."

Seth nodded even as Ritter led Husam outside, no doubt to sit and wait with his men until it was his turn to face the consequences at GITMO. Damned shame, but what could Seth do to help the kid? He was already carrying a butt load of guilt. Standing, he extended his hand. "Thank you, Major Delaney. It's been an honor to meet you, sir."

Delaney's grip was callused and firm. "Keep in touch, McCray, and tell that ornery boss of yours to look me up the next time he's in GITMO. I'll keep the lights on for him."

That made Seth grin. "I'm not sure he'll ever be *in* GITMO, but I'll tell him. Thanks again."

Corporal Ritter ducked into the tent in time to escort Seth to the helicopter. On the way, Seth asked, "So, what happens next? Interrogation? Waterboarding? Exactly what will the CIA do to these kids?"

Ritter sucked in a deep breath before his cheeks hollowed as he blew it out. "They'll all be interviewed, sir, but waterboarding's a thing of the past. When we get kids like these, and trust me, we see a lot just like them, we work hard to either repatriate them, when possible, or they go into a version of the WPP once they're interrogated and we've properly vetted them."

"The Witness Protection Program? Honest?" That surprised Seth.

Ritter nodded. "I'm a Marine, sir, I'm always honest. If we can secure Husam's sisters without drawing Khadeem's attention, his entire family could be offered protection. I've seen it happen, but sometimes, these guys are so fed up with the state of affairs in their countries, they seek asylum instead of entering the WPP. Because of their unique status, Immigration tends to go easier on them."

"What unique status? Why them instead of other refugees?"

Ritter's shoulders lifted. "It's complicated, and to be honest, I don't know all the answers. But you have to understand, Khadeem's holding something over each one of these men, err, boy's heads. They owe a debt they could only pay by fighting his war and by dying. Because of you and what we know now, that's changed. Once word gets out that Khadeem's ruse failed and these boys are still alive, he'll unleash his death squads to exact retribution on their families, only the world will never hear one word about it."

"How do you know that?"

Ritter grunted. "Because I know how the press works. They pick and choose what sad stories they want to tell Americans. Trust me. No one's interested in what happens in the Mideast anymore. America's sick of hearing the same old bylines about IEDs, ISIS, and terrorists. They've moved on. Just wish we could."

"Shit," Seth hissed under his breath, his fingers already digging his satphone from his pocket. "I need to make a call. You wouldn't happen to know the name of Husam's town, er, village, would you?"

"Yes, sir, I do. Abu Dat. It's off the beaten road in the middle of nowhere, due west of Ras Al-Khair."

Wherever that was. "You've been there?"

Ritter shook his head, but Seth was pretty sure the corporal had said more than he'd let on during those less than rapid-fire questions and answers with Husam. Seth thumbed the preset key for Alex. The phone never rang.

"Been waiting for you," Alex said, a weary hint of patience in his tone.

"I hate to ask, Boss, but one of Khadeem's men, Husam al Din, actually, he's a sixteen-year-old prisoner of war now. Anyway, he left three sisters behind in a little village called Abu Dat. It's due west of Ras Al-Khair on the Persian Gulf, and—"

Ritter interrupted with, "Tell him Ras Al-Khair is sixty miles north of Jubail. That will help him triangulate."

Seth shot Ritter an appraising nod. "Did you catch that, Boss?"

"What are you asking me to do now?"

Seth drew in a deep breath before he said, "I'm asking you to send someone to rescue those little girls before Khadeem finds out that every one of the boys he sent to Cuba surrendered to FAST today. Khadeem's entire army is comprised of teenage boys, Boss. The only reason they're here is because he's threatened their families, and as soon as word gets out that they're still alive, Khadeem's death squads will hit the streets, er, villages, and there'll be nothing left for these kids to go home to."

Alex didn't say one word, but Seth could hear him breathing over the line. Right about now, he'd be squeezing the bridge of his nose between two fingers, his eyes would be closed, and that razor-sharp brain of his would be ripping through solutions, scenarios, and strategies with the concise precision of a Ginsu knife. A steady migraine would be pounding inside his skull, and he'd be one tired SOB, because—

Oh shit. Seth squeezed the bridge of his nose, too. Too late he'd realized—*it's Saturday. That's why Alex is at the office? Because of me. Damn. I've asked too much this time.*

"What else?" Alex asked, not a hint of sarcasm coloring the question.

Seth didn't dare ask if Alex planned to rescue Husam's sisters, so instead he asked, "Have you heard from Eric yet?"

"Yes. Adam and Maverick intercepted your uncle's pontoon off the Keys. As soon as he lands, we'll move everyone to safe quarters and treat Cassidy. Anything else?"

"How is she?"

"She's awake and pissed. Eric's had to sedate her to keep her from jumping ship to go back after the rest of Montego's men. She said there's more women and more kids, that she's not leaving them behind."

That sounded just like Cassidy. "Thanks, Boss," Seth said quietly.

Until this exact moment, he'd never considered the entire cost, nor the weight of all that Alex shouldered so The TEAM could accomplish what they did on a daily basis. The endless infils into and the exfils out of hostile countries. The worries. The near hits and misses. The fear of answering his phone one day only to hear those two awful words: *Man. Down.*

Alex carried the weight of the world, yet he was always first in the office every morning, and the last out at night. The man seemed propelled through life with more energy, more willpower, and more guts than anyone Seth had ever known. Well, except for Uncle George, the mystery man in Seth's family, whom he was going to have a serious chat with once George woke up.

"Are you okay, Boss?" he had to ask.

"I will be once your ass is back on US soil. You got an ETA yet?"

That sounded more like the tough guy Seth knew and—loved. "I'm headed for GITMO now. I'll be on the next flight out of there—"

"Tomorrow morning," Ritter interrupted with a definite nod. "Delaney left orders for a one-way ticket to the Keys, departing at oh five hundred hours."

"I'll be home first thing in the morning," Seth relayed.

"Don't miss that damned flight," Alex ordered.

"Copy that," Seth said, ending the connection. "You're all right, Tex," he told Ritter. "You're all right."

Ritter shot him a cocky grin. "I'm more than all right, Agent McCray. I'm a Marine."

Chapter Thirty-One

Dev waited until Joachim finally left. By then it was dark. He'd paced the cramped motel room like a trapped panther, which told her he was hiding from someone. Not like she didn't already know he was some kind of criminal. Any guy who manacled a woman to his bed was a dirtbag, and she had no intention of hanging around until he returned.

He hadn't touched her since that one and only encounter, but… *the nerve!* Shivers raced up her bare arms at the thought of his greasy hair in her eyes and mouth, and at the way he'd pinned her to his bed. As soon as she got out of this cuff, she was gone!

Rolling to her feet, she took quick stock of her precarious situation. Metal cuffs. Metal bed frame. Metal headboard. All seemingly inescapable and attached to each other, which meant she wouldn't get far since she couldn't drag the bed through the door. No matter. There had to be another way out of this mess.

She'd already tried to slip out of the cuffs, but that hadn't worked. Spying the phone across the room on the battered, shabby credenza, she traced the cord visually from the receiver to the wall connection above the baseboard. It certainly looked authentic from where she stood. Useable.

All righty then.

On her feet now, she shoved the mattress off the frame with both feet since she had limited mobility, and her arm only stretched so far. But damn. Who in their right mind bolts a bed to the floor and the headboard to the wall? This baby wasn't going anywhere.

Which told her precisely what kind of a motel this was, didn't it? The kind with hourly rates, bed bugs, and ugly, greasy blond, two-legged rats. The kind where cheaply made headboards banging into walls could make a lot of noise unless everything was bolted down.

Swallowing hard now, she stretched for the phone, but it might as well have been on the moon. Desperate, she glanced upward. Every motel room had a handy, dandy spigot on the ceiling in case of fire, didn't it? Not. This motel wasn't up to code, and she was running out of options and time. Joachim would be back soon. Sly maybe, too.

Hurry, Dev. You can do it. Hurry!

Stubbornly, Dev stamped one bare foot and declared, "I will not be turned into a nameless statistic, not by Sly, and not by Joachim. There has to be a way out of here."

Standing there in the empty room, still shackled to a bed frame that had to be from the turn of the century—hadn't these people ever heard of *Memory Foam*?—she broke out in a sweat. "I can't die like this," she told the silence as her heart started pounding an anxious beat. "I've got a son to live for. A man who actually loves me, I know he does. I've got a life!"

Her nagging conscience piped up with: *And look what you've done with it. You're still worried about James, you've been sold by Sly, and now you're trapped in a motel room, by a man who thinks he got a bad deal when he got you.*

I know, I know. Think, Dev. Think.

He'll be back soon. Hurry!

Okay then. If this was the end, she meant to let the whole world know. Dev opened her mouth and screamed. For minutes upon minutes, she yelled for help, screamed, "Fire!" and just plain bellowed her heart out.

For nothing.

After giving her all without even a single knock at the door or a friendly, *'hello, are you in there?'* she dropped to her knees on the matted, grungy carpet, out of breath and running out of time.

Guess this wasn't the kind of motel where considerate people intervened in other people's business, either. No, she had to end up in a motel where murderers shot slasher films, while some unwilling victim earned several minutes of fame the hard way, by getting her throat cut. This was where good girls turned into hookers, and where hookers died hard lonely deaths when they pissed off their pimps.

Her time was running out. No one knew where she was, but here she would die. Maybe. Joachim would be back soon. Maybe he'd bring Sly and that creep, Prince Bagani.

Oh, God, not him. What else can I do?

There seemed nothing left to do, but… cry.

Seth made good time after he hit GITMO. The facility itself was a bastion of gray against the green Cuban landscape, but instead of waiting for a chopper in the morning, another already sat on the tarmac to take him to Florida. Before he knew it, he was in the air and on his way to the land of the free. Nothing felt better.

His heart turned toward Devereaux and her ragged little bungalow on Starfish Drive as the camouflaged bird flew low over the waves between Cuba and home. America always looked grand after a hard operation, and this one had been tougher than most. Seth still didn't know whether Alex would help Husam and his sisters or not. What had seemed a simple request only hours earlier now seemed an impossible dream.

Alex didn't just send his TEAM off without vetting his intentions through proper federal channels, and when he did, it was usually because he'd signed a contract to support whatever federal entity needed his help. He wasn't running a charity, but a topnotch business known the world over for getting the hard jobs done right. He followed his own strict protocol, and because he did, he'd garnered trust throughout the world. He had allies in Afghanistan, Liberia, even inside Russia and China.

For the most part, Alex followed the order of law. Yet there were a few times, he'd stormed the beaches to get one of his men or women back, politics be damned. Seth hoped this might be one of those rare times. Otherwise, poor Husam, his sisters, and his brothers-at-arms didn't have a prayer. Khadeem's death squads would squash their families, and Corporal Ritter was right. Because of the political quagmire America's supposedly free press had turned into, very little of the world's real news ever hit American palates.

By the time the chopper's skids touched down at the United States Coast Guard Station at Islamorada, Florida, instead of on Drunken Sailor Island, which Seth would've preferred, night had fallen. But he didn't argue with the location. Home was home, and he knew how to drive. Within the hour, he'd rented a Chevy truck from a twenty-four-seven rental agency and was on his way west.

Traffic on Overseas Highway US Route 1 was light but steady. His shoulder still ached, but the quick patch job he'd done on himself once he'd left Eric behind at the prison must've been enough. The bullet hadn't struck him full on anyway. He'd only been grazed, and the wound wasn't feverish, just sore. He'd live.

The night was warm and the breeze off the Atlantic filled his nose with the scents of wind, sand, and salt. All the truck's windows were open, and for the first time in years, life was on its way to being good again. Make that great. He had a woman in that life again, and she made all the difference. How well he knew that man wasn't meant to live alone—or with ghosts.

He'd been coasting on *'good enough'* for too long. The moment he'd taken Devereaux in his arms and made love with her, his life had changed for the better. Colors were brighter. The air smelled sweeter. Even his heart pumped differently, as if it had a reason to keep him alive, as if his veins pumped more oxygen now. As if the ghosts of his past had finally let loose the stranglehold they'd had on him and his heart.

His chest expanded with every breath of—life. Damn, it was good to be headed back to Devereaux's home. Just one smile from those pretty blue eyes, and he was a goner. She had a way of making him feel better about himself, and it wasn't just because of the incredibly hot sex they'd shared. No. Though that was definitely one of the things he loved about her, there was more going on between them, and he knew it.

Despite her economic situation, Devereaux had an eternally optimistic take on life that seemed to sweep others along in her wake. Of all the people in the world, she had a right to be bitter, and he wouldn't blame her if she were. Most single moms worked their asses off just to end up living on the fringe of poverty, and because of her pig-headed brother, Devereaux wasn't far from being homeless. Yet she gave and gave until her kitchen cupboards were literally bare.

Well, no more. Seth intended to remedy at least that much. There had to be an all-night grocery store, at least a 7-11 open between here and her house, where he could stock up on a few necessities for breakfast. Seth's shoulders lifted like a little kid hiding a gift behind his back for his best girlfriend. Wouldn't Devereaux be surprised to see him on her doorstep with his arms full of groceries in the middle of the night?

That 7-11 had better have a box or two of donuts. Everyone loved donuts. And a rose. Didn't all convenience stores keep a bin full of silk roses near the checkout stand for sappy guys like him? Seth hoped so.

Memories of kissing Devereaux's warm, lush lips warmed his blood. It was time to tell her. Hmmm. Yes. Tonight was the night.

Chapter Thirty-Two

Dev lifted her head at the sound of heavy footsteps outside her door. Joachim had been gone for hours and the room was a mess. He might as well know she wouldn't go easy, not with him, Sly, or whatever rat bastard he was bringing with him.

Still manacled to the cursed bed frame, she stood and planted her feet, posturing for one or two good kicks to the big guy's nuts. Damn him and damn all dirtbags like him who thought they could abuse women and get away with it. A woman shouldn't have to be so scared that she couldn't think. Her heart shouldn't be pounding like a freight train so hard she could barely breathe. Her stomach shouldn't feel so ready to crawl up her throat.

But Dev was all those things and more. The doorknob twisted, but just as a hairy knuckled hand reached in, feeling the wall for the light switch, she barreled into the door and crushed that arm between the door and frame. *There! Take that!*

Shaking like a leaf, she knew she'd lost the element of surprise, but fear had won out over common sense. She'd panicked and given herself away, and now Joachim was pissed. Well, so was she.

"You bitch!" Joachim bellowed as he cleared the door and slammed it behind him. Once again, he hit the switch and glared at what she'd done to the place. "You fucked up my room!"

'Yeah, well, you're next,' she thought, shifting her weight on the balls of her feet, ready to go down swinging, but scared to death. Cord always told her to fight back. Well, today was that day. Or night. Or whatever. She honestly didn't know what time or day it was.

"You ass," she hissed, her tone as lethal as she could make it. "Unlock these cuffs and let me go."

The idiot had the nerve to roll his eyes like some drama queen. "What part of *'I paid for you'* did you not understand, woman?" he bit out as he took a menacing step toward her. "You're mine and you're going nowhere but where I tell you to go, and if you mess up my room like this again, I will beat the shit out of you."

Damn, he was big, and he flexed those massive fingers like he wanted to choke her. Dressed in dirty jeans, a tie-dyed black-and-white Ron Jon t-shirt that looked like one big bird dropping, Joachim's size alone intimidated Dev. He was wider than Cord, but not fit in any way. Over-weight, slack-jawed, and unkempt, the stench of body odor rolled off him in waves, along with the distinct stink of tooth decay, alcohol, and cigarettes on his breath.

Dev flexed her fingers, too. Yes, she was way out-matched, but it was time for some payback. "I'm leaving," she told him. "Unlock these cuffs and let me go."

"Sit your ass down," he ordered, stabbing one long finger at the floor.

"Let me go," she ordered, though she hadn't intended the shrill tone in her demand. But damn, he had big, mean, capable-of-breaking-her-neck hands, and her false bravado would only get her so far. "I have a son, Joachim. I need to go home now, before my friend calls the police. I should've been home hours ago…" *Maybe days.* "So, let me go before she files a missing persons report with the police, and they come looking for me. I won't say a word. I won't tell anyone what you've done."

Joachim cocked his head at that. "What *I've* done? Who do you think you are? Some kind of princess from Arabia I should bow down to?"

Damn, he knows about Lianna. What else does he know?

Her heart stalled, and Dev's tongue took a futile swipe over her dry lips. "Please," she murmured, her resolve crumbling as she took a step backward. "Please let me go, Joachim. I'm no one important. You don't want me. I'm not one of your pretty, party girls. I've had a baby and my boobs sag and my belly's got stretch marks all over it and… Please. No one will ever pay even a dollar in ransom money for my return, if that's what you're after."

His chin came up at that plea, and those big hands settled on his hips. "You've got me all wrong, Angelique. I didn't buy you for ransom money. Oh, no, baby, you're my first investment in a scheme that's gonna make me rich. Just wait and see. I've got big plans for you. You might not be a virgin, but you're still grade-A, prime flesh on the hoof."

What a creepy thing to say. It made her sound like a cut of beef.

"No," she spat. "No, I won't, and if you make me, I'll fight everyone you force on me, and I'll hurt you every chance I get. I'll scream and I'll—"

She only heard the pop inside her head when that big hand of his lashed out and knocked her to her knees. Dev fell, her jaw surely crushed, it screamed so loud inside her head with startling, blinding pain that radiated through her skull and down into the tendons of her throat. Tears came unbidden to her eyes to drip down her nose and onto the ugly, dirty carpet beneath her fingers. The room spun, and she could barely breathe, much less fight back.

All she saw was the dusty rounded tips of Joachim's work boots right before he clenched a handful of her hair and jerked her head far enough from the floor that she had no choice but to look up at him. "Do you see me now, princess?" he hissed, spitting into her face.

Dev nodded, sure he meant to kill her right there, at his feet.

"Now you listen and listen good," he breathed. "I'm only going to say this once, and it's important, si? Sylvester tells me you love your kid. His name is Scottie, is that right?"

"Ah-huh," Dev whimpered, her head bobbing as tears streamed down her cheeks.

Joachim's nostrils flared, and for a moment, he looked like Satan come to life. Dark. Cold. Intensely evil. "There, that wasn't so hard now, was it? It pays to be a good girl, Angelique," he said, his voice turned as slick as oil. "Now you understand who is the boss of you, and that is me and nobody else. If you love your kid like you say you do, you'll do as you're told, because Sly knows where you live, and if you think he enjoyed gutting that puny lizard of yours, imagine how much fun he'll have playing with your blue-eyed, blond little boy."

Oh, God. Scottie. Sly has Scottie!

"No," Dev cried. "Not my son. L-l-leave him alone!"

That earned her another head jerk, only this time Joachim lifted her off the floor by her neck. "Say it, Angelique! Say your name!"

"Ang… Angelique," she whimpered.

He shook her like a rug. "And who am I? Say it!"

"Joachim…"

His hands slid to her neck. "No! Not Joachim! I am the boss of you, never Joachim! Say it!"

"You…" She could barely speak, he clutched her so hard. "You're the b-b-boss of me."

He shook her like a dog with a bone, an ugly light in his eye as if he'd won and she'd lost. "Yes, I am! And you will wise up and act like a good girl from now on, and you will do as I tell you. Me, only me! I am your master, and if you do everything I tell you to do, Scottie lives. If you don't…"

"Okay. Yes. Just… yes." Dev closed her eyes, kissing the last of her dreams goodbye even as she nodded and lied to the beast that held her in his dirty hands.

"Yes, what?" he growled as he lifted her up into his face.

She gave him what he wanted. "Yes, you are the boss of me, m-m-master."

Dev wanted to throw up. No one was the boss of her. No one had the right! But for Scottie, she'd do anything, even—this.

Chapter Thirty-Three

Seth made good time, but the only store open this late was a joint called Figarino's. He'd Google mapped it on his way, secretly thrilled when he discovered it was only a couple blocks past Starfish Drive where Devereaux lived and Molly's dock. Fate was definitely smiling at him tonight.

After cruising the shelves at Figarino's, Seth had enough breakfast food and snacks in his arms to last Devereaux and Scottie the rest of the week. He'd also selected a bag of healthy vegetables for Gru. That bad little guy wouldn't have anything to eat either, and by hell, a man takes care of his whole family, even the four-legged kids. And didn't that word—family—feel good just to think it? To say it? Damned straight.

Invigorated by the upcoming surprise Devereaux had in store for her, Seth grabbed a bottle of wine from the rack at the counter at the last moment, a Moscato from a local winery called, of all things, *Virgin Beaches*. Sex certainly sold everything in this crazy mixed-up land that he loved.

Methodically, and oh, so slowly, the clerk rang him up, chatting as many graveyard shift employees were prone to do. Seth kept his comments brief, needing to be gone and back in Devereaux's arms.

In the morning, he'd reconnect with Eric, hopefully Cassidy, too. He'd check in with Alex again, maybe ask for another week off. Hell, he'd contact Corporal Ritter as well, just to stay in touch with news about Husam and his men. They might be considered men in their country, but they were just teenagers to Seth. They needed someone to care what happened to them. If he had time, he might even find a home for those boxes of shoes he'd brought with him. Yeah. It was definitely good to be alive.

Out the door he went with his groceries, whistling. It sounded good in the fresh night air. It sounded positive. Like Devereaux. He could already picture the surprise in her sleepy blue eyes when she opened her door after unlocking all those silly, ineffectual locks that he was going to replace—tomorrow—right after breakfast. Maybe she'd be in her pajamas. Maybe she would've been sleeping on the couch waiting for him to return. She'd smile and give him that *'are you crazy?'* look that he was starting to love. Because, yeah, he was crazy. For her. Crazy in love.

Offloading the groceries onto the passenger side seat, Seth rounded the truck to make his getaway. The headlights of a speeding car blinded him at the same time something in the gutter across the street caught his eye. Seth dodged in front of the car, needing to get to the burlap bag that moved like something was trapped in it. He dropped to one knee at the curb, loosened the knotted string at the lip of the bag, just enough to know for sure...

No. It couldn't be.

But it was. What was Devereaux's iguana doing out here without her? His head snapped up as the speeding vehicle screeched to a stop alongside his truck.

"Hey, Soldier Boy. You seen my sister?" Cord bellowed from the open driver's window.

"No, but she's in trouble," Seth growled, on his feet now and the bag with Gru cradled in his arms. "I just found her iguana in the gutter."

"Damn it! I finally get home and all hell's breaking loose. Get in, dumbass. We need to find her!"

"What do you mean, all hell?"

Cord's lip curled as if he didn't like to explain himself. "I left the princess with Trish and Scottie. Figured they'd be fine there until I got back."

"You left two women and a little boy alone? Where's your guys?" Seth couldn't believe what he was hearing. "Are you telling me Scottie's gone? Lianna and Trish are missing, too?"

Cord glared. "I'm telling you I don't know where they are. Trish isn't home, and someone tore her place apart. Dev's too. My guys are still in Cuba. Now get your ass moving, McCray!"

"I'm right behind you," Seth shouted over his shoulder as he headed for his rental. "Where are we going?"

"Beers-n-Babes," Cord called out as he punched it and smoked the tires on what Seth had just noticed was a damned straight 1970 Chevy Chevelle. Blue metal-flake paint job. Rear chrome pipes and its meaty tires smoking rubber. Holy shit. Cord drove a restored vehicle like that? Then why the hell was Devereaux living hand to mouth and working overtime?

Quickly, Seth climbed into his truck and followed, headed for Key West while his brain pinged over what he thought he knew. Everything led back to the human trafficking that Cord and Devereaux were involved in. That was all that made sense. Somehow Sly Valentine was involved in Montego's illicit business, though Seth hadn't any evidence to prove that. Just his gut, and his gut was eating him alive.

Before long, Cord slammed to a stop outside a dingy beer joint with neon flashing beer mugs taking up the entire two front windows. Parked cars crammed the dirt lot to the south of the bar, while more lined the street. Two longhaired young women in too much make-up, tiny mini-skirts that barely covered their asses, halter-tops, and stiletto sandals, laughed as they crossed the street from the parking lot and ducked inside.

"Stay here," Seth told Gru as he patted the poor lizard through the burlap. He hadn't yet had time to inspect Gru for injuries. First things first.

Cord was already inside Beers-n-Babes by the time Seth entered, but unlike Cord, who'd probably been inside the place before, Seth took time to size up the establishment. Everyone in it was rocking to the talented band in the far-left corner, but there was a definite grunge vibe to the place. Maybe because of the bright, flashing purple neon *GIRLS NIGHT ~ FREE BEER!* over the massive black bar on the far side of the dancers. Could be due to the bare-breasted pole-dancers spotlighted in black metal cages at the ends of the bar. Or the barmaids, all strutting their stuff in tiny black satin shorts, skimpy black camisoles, and six-inch heels.

So, this is where Sly wanted Devereaux to work. Doing what? Lap dancing? *Oh, hell no.*

Peanut shells littered the hardwood floor, and the aromatic scent of beer, hard liquor, and pot suffused the night air. Seth's nostrils flared at that other scent on the draft—the sweet cloying stink of chloroform. He'd expected the rancid stench of vomit in a place this dark, not the number one choice in anesthetics for kidnappers the world over.

Dressed in jeans, a black shirt, and a leather bomber jacket, Cord cut an arrogant swath through the crowded dance floor, while heavy rock music thumped a monstrous bass and overhead strobe lights flashed from all corners of the ceiling. Young girls filled most of the floor, some of them dancing with other girls, their arms up and their tummies exposed as they moved sensually to the throbbing beat. Some mixed it up with other couples. But as far as Seth was concerned, all these girls were too damned young to be shaking their fannies at a beer joint this time of night.

Still playing catch up to Cord's Mr. Macho, Seth's sharp eyes quartered the room, taking in the dozen or so men lurking in the shadows and behind the bar, all of them in black suits and wearing dark glasses, like they'd just stepped out of a bad remake of *The Godfather*. That was the first clue something wasn't right with Beers-n-Babes.

The second clue? The wires connecting their earpieces to whatever radios were tucked inside their black button-up shirts. They weren't black operators, though, not these guys. But they were communicating with each other. Signaling each other.

It's called a lack of situational awareness when an angry guy strutted into a lion's den like he owned the place, the way Cord had just done. Man, he was an arrogant mother. Despite the gun on his hip, Cord had better watch his step.

Seth palmed his pistol, nose to the floor. Things were about to go bad, and Cord needed a retreat if that cocky swagger of his meant what Seth suspected it did. Trouble.

Up six feet ahead of him, Cord stopped when a slender man dressed in a black suit confronted him. Pleated trousers. Black dress shirt. Black tie. Shiny, black dress shoes. The works. The man's palms came up. His head cocked as if he hadn't heard Cord right.

Cord rolled one shoulder, his elbow cocked, his fists clenched, and… sure enough. Two thugs from the shadows headed in Cord's direction. Another stepped out from behind the bar. They had to have seen his weapon, but if any of these tough guys thought they had any chance of intercepting Cord before Seth got to him, they were dead-assed wrong.

He quickened his pace, his six senses expanding with every step forward, filtering through the noise and the laser light show to understand what was really going on here. On his right, one buff, black shadow cradled a limp woman who looked more like a teenage girl in his arms. She might've had too much to drink. She might've just passed out, but Seth's hackles lifted when the guy caught him watching. His chin came up, and he turned his back on the dance floor, blocking Seth's view as another guy closed in tight behind him.

Just then Cord's voice lifted above the din. "Now! I want Sly's ass on the floor, right damned now!"

Seth was forced to turn away from what sure as hell felt and looked like a kidnapping in progress to defend Devereaux's brother. Seth had closed in on Cord mere seconds before the shadows tracking Cord did. Instinctively, he clutched Cord's wide shoulder to let him know he had his six, and that something was dead damned wrong. Outmanned and most likely outgunned, they needed to leave. Now.

The man in the suit's upper lip lifted into a snarl as he said, "I'm very sorry, but Mr. Valentine isn't here, Mr. Shepherd. He's taken the night off like I told you. Family business, I believe he said when he called."

A muscular blonde woman with a very masculine buzzcut came up behind the guy in the suit. The angle of her jaw and the cold in her black eyes made the guy look like the Welcome Wagon in comparison. "What seems to be the trouble, Jenkins?" she clipped.

Jenkins gestured to the gyrating dancers on the floor. "Same shit, different day, Giselle. Some guy wants his Baby Doll back, but as you can see, no chick in here wants to go home with—"

Cord's fists were instantly around Jenkins' neck, and Jenkins was up against the bar, dislodging several of Sly's patrons from their bar stools. Not that they seemed to care. All three quickly grabbed their drinks and relocated to somewhere else. "She's not your Baby Doll, you maggot! She's my sister! Dev Shepherd! Have you seen her tonight?"

Stepping forward, Seth laid a restraining hand on Cord's forearm as he kept an eye on the security team tracking them. "They're not going to tell you even if she was, Cord. Come on. I know where she is."

The hulking shadows at Seth's rear materialized into several bouncers blocking his retreat. He let them stand there. For all of thirty seconds.

Then he turned his back to Cord's back, and Seth stared the nearest tough guy down. An African American, the man was bulked up and massive. He damned near made two of

Seth. The sleeves of his dress suit stretched tight as he folded his arms and looked down his wide, flared nose at Seth.

"You've got two seconds to step aside," Seth warned, his feet already spread, his stance shifted for combat.

"Or what?" The guy grunted like a grizzly bear about to eat a snack.

Without blinking, Seth's weapon snapped up and on target. "I said back off!" he gritted out, tracking every last asshole shadow he could make out in the bar as he edged toward the exit sign.

A tiny red laser dot danced now over *Stretch Armstrong's* forehead until it settled on his impressive chest where the equally impressive power of Seth's pistol now focused. Time was officially up, and Seth could go to jail for pointing a gun at an unarmed man. But he seriously doubted that was the case here at Beers-n-Babes, and Stretch needed to understand one thing. Seth never pulled his weapon unless he meant to use it.

About time, Cord moved with him, and Seth hoped he had that pistol of his up as well. One fool against a dozen or more wolves wasn't good odds.

"This isn't over," Cord bellowed over the noise.

"Shut the hell up," Seth hissed, his eyes still wide and his nostrils flared as he ensured no firepower waited beyond the bar to smoke them once they cleared the entrance. He didn't have time to track Jenkins' or Giselle's whereabouts, but if they were as smart as they thought they were, they'd stay out of this.

At last, Cord climbed into his car and slammed both fists into the plastic dash, splintering it. "Where is she? You said you know, and so help me God, you'd better!"

"I'll tell you what I know. She's not in there," Seth yelled right back at him, "and those guys were going to kill you. How can you help Devereaux if you're dead?"

"That's all? You said you knew where she is, so where is she?" Cord jerked his door open, and just that fast, Seth kicked it shut. "Keep your ass in that car and listen. She's not here and neither is Sly. What does that tell you?"

"That they're lying!" Cord's left eye twitched.

"Prove it!" Seth bellowed. "Go in there and prove it. If he's got her, why would Sly bring her to his club? Think, Cord. This is where he baits women and traps them. Where he drugs them. If he's got Devereaux, he's already moved her."

Cord's face turned ashen, the taut cords in his neck fighting him as he tried to swallow. "He's got her somewhere else. But wh-where?"

Unexpectedly, Seth faced a belligerent Marine who appeared to be falling apart. "That, I'm not sure. Where's Sly live? Do you know?" Honestly, there was no way to know where Devereaux was at this point, but risking a brawl at Sly's bar wouldn't prove anything and it wouldn't get her back. They had to start somewhere. Why not Sly's?

Cord nodded, blinking and his mind going a mile a minute. "Get in."

"No. I'll take my ride. You lead."

Seth barely had time to scramble back to his rented truck before Cord laid rubber, his Chevelle fishtailing like a shark out of water as it careened down the street.

"That's right, you idiot," Seth muttered as he revved the truck and thumb dialed Alex. "Attract a cop, go to jail, and be no damned help to Devereaux just when she needs you most."

"Stewart."

"Sorry, Boss, but I've got a problem I can't handle at the moment. There's a kidnapping going down at a joint called Beers-n-Babes in Key West, southwest corner of the island. Sly Valentine owns the place, but he's got a ton of muscle working tonight, and I'm certain I saw one of his men handling an unconscious woman. She looked to be around five-five, maybe a hundred twenty pounds, long blonde hair, and, oh yeah, a tramp stamp, three blue butterflies, on the small of her back. You think maybe you could send in one of the guys or the police or… or something?" Seth cringed even as he asked yet another favor of his boss.

"Anything else?"

"Nope, that'll do it," Seth said as blithely as he could. Anything else and Alex would start asking questions, like *'what's so important that you can't handle a simple call like this?'* "Gotta go. Bye."

Still cringing, Seth cut Alex off before his boss caught on. He stuffed the satphone in his pocket, then followed Cord as the guy took a sharp right and raced east for a couple blocks before he turned north in a cloud of smoky white.

Seth stuck close to Cord's bumper, wishing he knew where Sly lived so he could head Cord off at the pass. The man was volatile, and Seth understood. He was just as upset over Devereaux's situation, but going off half-cocked wouldn't help her, Trish, Scottie, or Lianna. Now was the time to transform all that USMC bravado into something worthwhile instead of just one pissed-off jarhead with anger management issues.

At last, Cord dumped the clutch and the Chevelle shuddered to a stop alongside what looked like a prestigious gated-community. He'd just rounded his front bumper when Seth jumped the curb and cut him off.

"Hold up," he called out as, once again, he stroked Gru through the burlap to quiet him before leaving him behind and locking the rental. "By now, Sly's got to know we're coming. Jenkins and the dominatrix back at the bar would've called him. We can't just climb over the fence and barge in. If he's got Devereaux, he'll hurt her. If she's not there, he'll be laying for us. Settle down. Let's do this once and do it right."

Cord drew in a deep breath. "Yeah, you're right."

"Are we good?" Seth asked, purposefully restraining his sarcasm. *Of course, I'm right, you moron.*

"Yeah. Good. Real good," Cord said, rubbing his hands like he was cold or something. More likely, he was just wired to the gills and needed to punch something.

Seth scanned the eight-foot-high brick wall between him and the plush townhouses inside. Elegant palms lined the opposite side of that wall, as well as halogen security lights on twenty-foot posts. "How much does this guy bring down? Do you know?"

"No, but it's got to be a bundle. He's always driving a new Corvette or Porsche. Last year he showed up one time with a Lamborghini, but that didn't last. The next day, he was back with another silver Corvette. Newer model."

"So what's he into? Drugs? Human trafficking? Gun running?"

Cord's head hadn't stopped bobbing since Seth started asking. "All that and more."

"Does he work with Montego?"

"I wouldn't be surprised." Cord's gaze shifted from one end of the wall to the other as he took a knee. Pointing to the far end, he said, "Sly lives that way, at the end of the cul-de-sac there. His home's two levels, white brick with an open lanai on the upper level facing east, and a four-car garage. Three palm trees stand between him and the far wall, but he's got dogs, two Rottweilers. His property's fenced, but if they're loose, we're screwed."

Seth nodded, "And?"

Cord had settled down enough to be trustworthy. "And a Cuban maid, but I doubt she's working tonight. I say we breach the wall, case the place, then make our move once we're sure the dogs are inside."

Sounded good. "Then what?" Seth wanted to know the whole plan, not merely enough of it to get him and Cord killed.

"Then..." Cord sucked in a deep breath and exhaled slowly. "Hell, I don't know. We improvise. It all depends on those dogs."

"What? Do you plan to kill the dogs once we get inside?" There had to be a better way.

Cord's sharp eyes scrolled over Seth's face. "If I have to. I can't lose her, damn it. She and Scottie are all I've got. After our parents did what they did... God. I've got to get her out of there."

Seth settled a firm hand on Cord's shoulder. "What did your parents do?"

"They kicked her out when she got pregnant, said they never wanted to see her again." And Cord was pissed all over again. "Dad said a lot of other mean shit to her, too. He's the local minister, but he humiliated her. It wasn't like she was living at home with them anyway. She had a good job and her own place, but it broke her heart the way they shunned her.

Mom wouldn't answer her calls, and damn it, with a baby coming, Dev needed someone at her side."

He turned from Seth and stared at the wall beside him. "I couldn't stand the thought of her living alone while she was expecting, so I brought her down here, closer to me."

"That's why you left the Corps, wasn't it?" Seth asked as he kept one eye on their surroundings. "To help your sister."

Cord's upper lip lifted. "What else could I do? Leave her to the wolves in this world? Not likely."

And yet, if Sly were involved in Montego's filthy business as Seth suspected, Cord had unwittingly exposed Devereaux to the very wolves he'd meant to protect her from. "You ever think about retiring from saving the world, maybe letting someone else do it for a change?"

Cord nodded. "You have no idea. But it's hard to turn your back on people in need, you know?"

"I do," Seth murmured. He had that hard-wired, need to save the world, god-complex, too.

"You love her, don't you?"

What could Seth say but, "Yes, I do."

"Sure wish you were an accountant. She deserves better than falling for guys like me."

Seth gave as good as he got. "You're right, which is why she's got me. I'm Army; you're just a jarhead. Let's roll."

Chapter Thirty-Four

She hadn't noticed the bag Joachim dropped when she'd surprised him by crushing his arm in the door. Not that she could've hurt him. His arms were thick, just like his head and his neck. But Joachim had brought 'presents' for his *Angelique*—Dev's new name. Which was why she now sat in the tub up to her neck in fragrant bubbles that stunk like roses. She didn't want to wear the trashy get-up he'd told her to put on after her bath.

"And be sure you scrub your lady bits until you glow, or I will," he'd told her before he'd closed the scummy bathroom door behind her, his brows waggling as if he thought flirting would make her like him.

Not. Happening.

There were no windows in this rundown bathroom, only peeling plaster over the tub and mildew in the corners. Bowing her head, Dev faced her toes. "You have no choice," she told herself, "so buck up and get it over with. It's just sex, that's all. Think of it as a bodily function, like throwing up and peeing. Other women do it, and some of them make damned good money doing it."

'But I don't want to do it,' her heart cried. *'Rape is* not *sex. It's ugly, violent assault.'*

"But you will do it. You'll grit your teeth, and you'll endure it to the end, and because of you *doing it*, Scottie gets to live, so shut the fuck up and get on with it." Tears stung her eyes. "Man, Dev, you've been through lots of crap before. You can do this. Get through this one bad night and try to escape again tomorrow. He's got to go to sleep sometime."

If only her tough act convinced her poor aching heart. But all Dev thought about was the bright blue eyes of the little man she loved whenever she'd come home after a long, hard day. Scottie had never failed to light up her world. He was always so happy to see her, and man that little guy could talk a mile a minute when he wanted to. Not that Dev would ever tell him to hush, or that she was too tired to listen like her mother used to do with her. Or that her feet hurt, and she needed peace and quiet, blah, blah, blah. There was no day on God's green Earth that Dev had ever been too tired for Scottie.

And Seth. What would he say once he found out that she'd willingly, more or less, whored herself out, even though she'd done it to save Scottie's life? If she ever saw him again, would Seth still get that dreamy look in his brown eyes when he saw her? Would he gather her up in his arms and run away from this place with her? Would he ever kiss her again? Would he want to?

"No," she murmured as her throat tightened with panic. Her first date—her john—was due any moment. Joachim wanted her fresh from the tub when, whoever that slimy rat bastard was, showed. Her stomach churned at the prospect of any man climbing over her, breathing on her, touching her, doing—that.

Joachim's sharp rap at the door startled her out of her well-deserved pity party. "It is time, Angelique. Your gentleman caller is here, and everything is ready. Prepare yourself and come out." He made it sound like he was announcing the next contestant in a beauty contest.

'I don't want to,' her heart reminded her even as she lifted out of the grimy bathtub and dried herself. Then—eww—she slid into the mesh bra, as in metal wire mesh, that Joachim had bought for her, and snapped the front clasp, also metal, also extra creepy.

Whoever this john was, he had to be the biggest perv to want the woman he hired for the night decked out in metal. Even though it was finely knitted, thin gauge wire, the silvery color made Dev look like Milla Jovovich out of Bruce Willis's *"Fifth Element."* Panties made of the same mesh came next. Where had Joachim come up with a costume like this?

He knocked harder. "Angelique! Come out of that tub before I drag you out!"

So much for gentlemanly pretense or showmanship. Or her make-up. Apparently, good looks weren't required for this—whatever happened next.

Trembling, she turned the doorknob and stepped into the bedroom. *Oh, hell no!* Dev spun on her heel, NOT going willingly into the night. Not ever!

That was why the wire mesh get-up. This night had nothing to do with sex. It was him. Prince Bagani. A car battery now sat on the nightstand under the lamp like it belonged there. He meant to torture her! And he was grinning!

"If he doesn't show in ten more minutes, I'm going in," Seth told Cord as he scrubbed one hand over the back of his neck, sure he was being watched. Just like at the Presidio Modelo, when he felt like all those blank empty windows in those deserted cellblock towers were staring down at him, he knew damned well someone else was out there. Watching his every move.

"Agreed," Cord bit out, his left boot tapping nervously away like no black ops guy ever did. They'd planned to observe Sly's place for thirty minutes before breaching both front and back doors at the same time, but the longer they'd waited, the more convinced Seth became that Devereaux didn't have that kind of time.

Still, they'd had no sign if Sly was home or not, nor what waited inside once they breached the doors. The dogs hadn't barked, not that that meant anything. Well-trained guard dogs didn't always bark before they attacked. No lights were on inside the two-level split, and every door and window was locked up tight as a drum. Seth had already run a perimeter check, studied all ways in and out, and come up with nothing. Getting over the security fence and into the gated community had been easy. Waiting was not.

"Aw, hell," Seth bit out. "Take the rear entrance and be quick about it. Let's do this."

For once, Cord did what he was told. Crouched over as he ran, Seth closed the distance on the front way in, sidling up to the door in case Sly waited to ambush them. Filled to the hilt with angst now, Seth crashed his right shoulder into the door. The pain from the bullet hole in the same shoulder he could handle, but he couldn't handle one more second of not knowing where Devereaux was.

As quickly as the door swung wide, Seth rolled to his knees, both arms raised, and his weapon aimed. Other than a clock ticking somewhere nearby, there was no sound in the place until Cord barged in through the back way and bellowed, "Clear!"

"Clear," Seth echoed. "No dogs either." That alone didn't set well with him. If Sly had guard dogs, who were they guarding and where?

The hairs on the back of his neck lifted. That feeling of being watched persisted. Yet he'd encountered no sign of Sly or his men anywhere since he'd left the bar. Seth brushed it off as a leftover symptom from his severe bout of PTSD. Civilians thought it went away after a guy or gal came home, or when they left the military, but Seth knew different. Hypervigilance. Flashbacks. Insomnia. Suicidal thoughts. All the things that had made his life hell after he'd lost Katelynn. Interesting, though. He hadn't thought of her since he'd made love with Devereaux. He might just be getting better.

Seth brushed that thought away, too.

Working quickly now, he advanced through each darkened room, until he met up with Cord in the hallway between the kitchen and the front room. With each step, his eyes had grown accustomed to working in the dim light.

"There's no one here," Cord bit out, his tone full of accusation.

"Then sue me," Seth snarled, sick to death of Cord's whining. "There are no dogs here, either. So where are they?

Stop griping and let's rip this place apart until we find something that will lead us to Devereaux."

"That's your plan?" Cord hissed. "Start looking? For *something*? In case you haven't noticed, this is a son-of-a-bitchin' big place and—"

"And I don't have time for this!" Seth snapped. "Maybe coming here wasn't the smartest idea, but what other options were there? If you've got a better idea, stop bitching and tell me!"

Not waiting for an answer, Seth turned his back on Cord and marched to the credenza at the side of the entryway. He didn't have the time or patience to argue, so he rifled through the drawers, then scanned the entertainment center and the end tables before he headed into the kitchen. Sly hadn't struck him as being a meticulous kind of guy. He had to have left something behind. A clue. Just one. Anything that would give Sly's and Devereaux's whereabouts away.

"Does he have a boat? A plane?" That'd be good to know.

"Just the cars I told you about," Cord answered. He'd finally stopped complaining and followed Seth's lead, rummaging through a hall closet, pulling things out and leaving a trail.

"The cars, yes. Good thinking." Seth turned for the kitchen door to Sly's adjoining garage. Didn't it figure? He'd no more than twisted the knob than a ferocious growl emanated from the other side. "Found the dogs."

"I heard," Cord said at Seth's elbow. "Here. Let me."

Gladly. Seth stepped aside as Cord opened the door and called out, "Bacon!"

Great. Now both Rottweilers were waiting for fresh meat. "Brilliant! That's your plan? Incite them to come running? Ring their dinner bell?"

"Just wanted to make sure I had their attention." Easing the door open, Cord peered through the crack. "I don't know if this will work, but here goes." He started to open the door wider.

Oh, hell no. Seth slammed it shut with his palm before Cord could stick that big square head into those Rottie's mouths. "I have a better idea." Man, how he wanted to add 'dumbass' to that statement. But he didn't. Instead, he depressed the garage door opener on the switch beside the doorframe.

"Good thinking!" Cord hissed as the dogs took off while Seth closed the doors.

There was so much more that Seth wanted to say, but he just nodded, and while Sly's dogs pitched a nasty barking fit outside of the now secured garage, Seth and Cord went on inside. Apparently Sly treasured his cars enough to guard them when he was gone. That said a lot about the guy. Since he wasn't home, it also said he'd left with someone else.

Four vehicles occupied the four bays: a brand new silver Corvette, a yellow Ford Mustang from the '60s, a current model black limousine, which was a damned interesting vehicle for a guy like Sly to own, and lastly, a shiny black, brand new Hummer H2 on steroids, with plenty of chrome piping to almost—almost—make it look like an authentic military vehicle. Not.

"Where's Sly tonight if all his wheels are here? Who's he run with? He got a driver?"

"He's probably on foot. Key West isn't that large."

"Yeah, but…" Seth knew the geography of this particular island. Area: five-and-a-quarter square miles. Length from east to west: four miles. Width: a mile. Elevation: a whopping eighteen feet above sea level. "I can't see Sly hoofing it to work and back, not with his ego."

Still… All vehicles were shiny except the limo. He went to that automobile and jerked the driver's side door open. Sand on the floor mat. Soda can in the drink holder. Seth climbed inside, searching for something more. He found nothing but a crushed candy wrapper on the front passenger seat. Okay, so whoever'd driven the limo last was a slob.

Popping the button to trigger the trunk lid, Seth scrambled to his feet. Devereaux had to have been in this car. He couldn't explain it, he just knew it. Sly'd threatened her plenty in the past, and the guy was a Class-A jerk. He's said he wanted her to work for him or else. What if that 'or else' had to do with the kidnapping Seth was certain he'd witnessed at the bar.

Thank God, Cord had climbed into the rear passenger area, doing something constructive for a change. The moment Seth lifted the trunk lid, his heart jerked. There lay a leather jacket, Sly's by the size of it, shoved way back inside the trunk. Not folded carefully where a decent man might leave it, but crunched into a wad in the farthest corner. Certain he'd found the clue he'd needed, Seth leaned in for a better look. The carpet had been torn away from the spare tire compartment, and holy hell, one of the taillight housings was loose.

"Cord! She was here. Look at this."

"Son-of-a-bitch," Cord hissed while Seth all but climbed into the trunk, his fingers splayed over the carpet. Something had to be here. The tiniest bit of evidence could point to Devereaux. *God, please. Just—something.*

He came up with nothing but a bump on his head when he climbed out.

"What now?" Cord bit out. "We've already committed a B&E. Might as well go all the way."

Damn. Seth had been so sure they'd find something to help locate Devereaux. Bowing his head to his chest, he scraped a fingernail over his brow and the long ago reminder of another hopeless situation he hadn't thought he'd survive. But he had, thanks to Hunter Christian, another teammate.

For all Seth knew, Sly might have her out at sea on a boat by now—or worse. Did Sly even know Montego was dead? Was this part of Sly's plan to takeover the bastard's human trafficking business? Or, judging by what went down at the bar, was Sly already balls deep in the trade? Who exactly worked for who?

"Let's assume Sly's working with Montego, that he's a supplier," Seth said as the scar under his brow itched. "He's certainly got the means. How would Sly get women he kidnaps into Cuba? He'd need a boat for that."

"Or a chopper, something that could get in and out without attracting a lot of attention. Shit, McCray. How would I know?"

And they were back at square one. Seth's heart clenched as a physical pain lanced through it at the very real possibility of what Devereaux might be going through while they farted around doing nothing at all. Anger swelled and he slammed the trunk lid out of sheer frustration. Then slammed it again when the damned thing popped back up, asking for more. The lid wouldn't shut, so he hit it again and again, until—

A tiny slip of paper fluttered from inside the trunk, just enough of a glimmer that it registered at the corner of his eye. Slapping the trunk wide open this time, Seth ducked under the lid and latched onto the paper. "You got a flashlight on you?"

"You bet." Cord produced a slim LED penlight out of nowhere and aimed it at the gas receipt between Seth's fingers. *Exxon* in East Rockland Key. Forty dollars cash sale. Date stamped zero-dark-thirty yesterday morning.

"Where the hell's East Rockland Key?"

"Due east of here, past Naval Air Station Key West, but I know that service station. It's on the north side of the highway, out in the middle of nowhere."

Seth cocked his head at Cord. "Why would Sly be there in a limo in the dead of night?"

Cord shrugged. "There's a helluva lot of swamp and brush north of the highway. If Dev's there, we'll never find her."

Seth's eyes scrolled from the limo and back to Devereaux's brother. "Want to bet?"

Chapter Thirty-Five

Prince Bagani liked to talk. A lot. Too bad Dev didn't like to listen. Yet listen she did, since she had no choice, and every word out of his lying mouth meant one more second of life without pain.

And now she knew precisely who Joachim served. It had taken every last bit of her fury and her strength before he'd managed to get her out of the bathroom. By then, the shower curtain was shredded and the mirror over the sink shattered. She'd clawed his face, arms, and neck until he bled. She'd kicked his privates and cursed him to hell for what he was doing to her.

But the ass was bigger and meaner. Once he'd gotten a handful of her hair and punched her tender jaw again, she'd gone down for the count.

She lay cuffed on her back to the bed on black plastic sheeting, the kind that normal people covered their furniture with when they painted or stored it. When they wanted to protect it. But Bagani was far from a normal human being, and he had no intention of protecting her.

Dev had never felt more exposed or more afraid in her life. She now knew what the plastic was for—her dead body. He'd laid the proof of his deadly intentions on the bed alongside her shivering bare legs. His tools, he'd called them.

Scalpels. Delicate surgical hammers. A speculum. Battery cables. Needle-nosed pliers. Something shiny and wicked that looked like a long crochet hook. Something else that resembled an eyeball-sized melon-baller.

God, get me out of here!

"I met a pretty woman on an island once," he said, gazing past her to a spot on the opposite wall as if reminiscing. "She was almost as pretty as you, but the difference between you and her is that she was and remains the only woman smart enough to escape my, ahem, charms."

Devereaux stared at the ceiling while Joachim sat waiting in a chair at the foot of the bed, either as a spectator or Bagani's assistant in crime, she still wasn't sure. Once Bagani stopped monologuing, she'd find out, but for now, Dev sent her prayers heavenward, just not to the fire and brimstone God of her parents.

They'd told her this would happen, that women who'd kept the children they bore out of wedlock were doomed for hell and damnation. That God would never grant a person like her mercy, and that Satan would catch up with her one day. *Just wait and see, young lady. Like it or not, you'll get your comeuppance because that's what sinners like you deserve.* Suffering. Burning in hell. Stuff like that.

She could almost hear her father's final curse when he'd bellowed like some fiery *Old Testament* prophet, "Begone! Never darken my doorstep with your shadow or the product of your illicit sexual affairs again! You are dead to us. Dead. Get thee hence!"

Yeah, right, Dad. Scottie's no product, you asshole. He's a sweet, innocent baby boy, and you and Mom could've loved

*him. But no, you self-righteous prick. You're the one who
threw your only grandson and me away. You're the sinner.*

A tear welled at the corner of her eye. She'd never
believed in the cruel God her parents yammered on and on
about, yet here she was, about to get an almighty
comeuppance from their god of wrath and hate. But that
wasn't right, and she knew it. Her parents were misguided,
misled, and just damned wrong. So, Dev prayed to the real
Man upstairs, the One who'd had her back through the
hardest times. If not for God and Cord, she'd still be raising
Scottie alone.

Please, God. I need a miracle.

Prince Bagani tapped her forehead with that crochet hook
thingee. "Am I boring you?"

"No," she replied quickly, startled that she hadn't been
'ah-huh-ing' at all the appropriate breaks in his rambling.
"You were saying?" she asked, blinking like a fool interested
in his depraved stories before he did anything else with the
instrument twiddling between his slender fingers.

"You're a lot like her, you know," he said as his dark eyes
scrolled over her mostly bare body. "Petite, yet strong. Fierce
like a shrew, but malleable like copper. Teachable. Bendable.
Trainable." He turned to Joachim. "She does know who her
master is, right?"

Joachim ran a finger under his swollen, runny eye, the
one Dev had belted before he'd knocked her out. "She does
now."

The Prince grunted as he traced the cold hook of that long
metal thing on the sensitive skin at the inside of her arm, from
her elbow, down her armpit, and onto the tiny links in the
knitted mesh cup over her left breast. He paused there,

tapping the tip on the peak of her nipple. "Shea Reynolds was a genius I didn't see coming," he murmured, his eyes bright and Dev's heart racing at what he might do next.

"One moment she was in my bed, waiting and ready…" *Yeah, I'll just bet she was waiting and ready for you to torture her.* "…but the next…" His dark brows lifted, and his eyes widened. "Poof. I turned my back, and she was gone. She disappeared just like an angel."

Dev didn't dare take her eyes off her tormentor. When he'd first arrived, the prince had worn a charcoal gray business suit, white shirt, and black tie, almost as if he'd come from a day at the office. But that would've been normal.

Once Joachim had wrestled Dev onto the bed, Bagani had tossed his suit jacket, then swiftly cuffed her ankles to the metal rail at the foot of the bed, and her wrists over her head to the sides of the headboard. She hadn't an inch of leverage to wiggle, they'd stretched her body so tightly between the posts.

Now Bagani's sleeves were rolled up to his elbows, revealing the olive-skin and fine black hairs on his forearms. The man was an attractive male. With his Mideastern heritage, he probably cut a handsome profile that some women would've been drawn to.

Drawn and quartered was more like it.

Repulsed at that very probable outcome in her immediate future, she suppressed a shudder. Falling apart now wouldn't help, and she was afraid it would excite Bagani into acting out his plans for the evening prematurely. He and Joachim seemed to be waiting for someone, Sly no doubt, to join this macabre party. Up until now, all they'd done was stare at her like she was one of those poor butterflies pinned to a poster board for exhibit. Or dissection. So, she listened, and while she listened, she prayed her heart out.

"Where are we?" she asked, hoping to keep him talking.

Bagani leaned back in his chair, crossed his legs, and folded his hands, rotating the instrument between and over his fingers like a baton. "Does it matter?"

"Y-yes," she answered, her teeth chattering. "If I'm going to die here tonight, I'd like to at least know where my final resting place is going to be."

His nostrils flared even as amusement brightened his dark eyes. "Ah, but you're not going to die, my dear little princess. At least, not yet. But as for your final resting place..." He turned his head to ask Joachim, "You're sure the alligators are hungry today?"

God, no!

"Sure, I been feeding them rotten chicken. That's what keeps 'em close to the shallows."

Dev squeezed her eyes shut as her heart sank. Not alligators. No one would ever know what happened to her then. There wouldn't be enough of her body left to make a positive identification. Scottie would grow up not knowing how much she'd loved him. Not even Seth would know what became of her. She closed her eyes even as tears trickled down the sides of her head. *'Help me, Jesus,'* she prayed. *'Please, please help me.'*

Bagani tapped her breast again with that tool, once, twice, then *whip!* He hit her hard, and *God, it stung!*

Dev groaned, fighting the scream climbing up her throat. If she started screaming, she'd never stop, and what good would it do? Nothing!

Still seated, Bagani leaned into her and said, "Open your eyes, my dear. There, there. See how easy that was? You do as I say, and…" *Whip!* "We'll get along just fine. Now then, who am I?"

"Prince Bag—"

Whip! "Try again."

Oh, hell, that hurts! "M-master," she cried, her entire body tensed, hoping that was right. Who the hell knew?

Bagani's brows furrowed. "Better, but…" *Whip!* "…next time, be quick about it. A master…" *Whip! Whip! Whip!* "…hates to be kept waiting on a lowly woman. And who are you?"

"Angelique," she supplied quickly, staring at him through her tears rather than letting him think she wasn't an obedient slave. Oh no. Now was the time to take her beating and survive. Later. If she ever got out of here, she'd kill him later. With relish and with every last tool on the bed beside her.

Chapter Thirty-Six

Seth and Cord raced for East Rockland Key. It had been a long night of failed leads, but he had another hunch, and if this one panned out, Devereaux would be in his arms by daybreak. If not? They'd be back at square one again.

They were nearly off the thin stretch of highway between the islands when his satphone vibrated in the holster on his hip. "McCray."

"Where are you?" Alex bit out.

"Right now, I'm a mile from East Rockland Key. Why? What's up?"

"Cassidy's flying out at noon. Thought you should know."

"Already? Is she well enough to travel?"

"Can't take the chance she won't go back to Cuba and start a war, so yeah. She's going home where Jude can take care of her. What's at East Rockland Key?"

"If I'm right, one of Montego's business associates," Seth answered discreetly. They still had a mile or so to go and there was no sense getting Alex spun up in Alexandria, where he couldn't offer an assist.

"You were right about the woman you saw in the bar. I alerted the police. They found her unconscious in one of Sly Valentine's buddy's vehicles behind the bar, along with another woman. Both had Rohypnol in their systems. The police are looking for Valentine."

"Thanks, Boss, so are we."

"You alone?"

"No, Boss, Cord Shepherd's driving. He's the Marine I told you about."

"Which one of Montego's men?"

"Hopefully, Sly Valentine. Maybe Prince Basheer Bagani." Seth held off mentioning that he no longer knew where Princess Lianna was.

"Bagani's there?" Alex asked.

"Not sure, Boss, but I figure he might be."

That earned him a spiked brow from the driver's seat. "Who you talking to?"

Seth murmured out of the corner of his mouth, "My boss, Alex Stewart."

Cord's brows lifted all the way up to his hairline. "You work for Stewart?" he asked at the same time that Alex asked, "Is Shepherd the idiot who's been running into Cuba rescuing women from Montego without sufficient support?"

Seth glanced sideways at Cord. "Yes, Boss, Cord is that idiot."

Both brows spiked that time.

"Put him on," Alex ordered.

Seth handed the satphone over. "He wants to talk to you."

"Me?" Cord whispered, and wasn't that interesting? The big jock fumbled the phone. It nearly hit the floor before it made it to Cord's ear, and he said, "Yes, sir?"

Seth grinned. Alex might not bite Cord for that faux pas this time, but the day would come Cord would regret having ever addressed Alex with 'sir'.

"Yes, sir, I mean…" Cord's head bobbed as Seth listened to him respond to Alex's rapid-fire questions. "No, sir. I understand. No, I didn't mean that, I meant…"

Whatever had Alex on edge, it was damned funny to watch him put Cord in his place. Maybe there was some truth to that *'once a Marine, always a Marine'* bullshit.

"Umm, sir, that might be a problem." Cord winced as an explosive "Might?" ripped over the connection.

"Yes, sir, you see, she's… she's missing and…" Cord's big head actually ducked into his shoulders. "No, sir, I haven't contacted the authorities yet, but I will." He shot Seth a funny as hell grimace. "I won't? No, sir, I won't. Yes, sir. Right away, sir. Would twenty-four hours be asking too much…? Yes, sir, it's just that I'm a little tied up at the moment and… Absolutely, sir." By the time Cord handed the phone back, he looked stunned and he was out of breath.

"Yes, Boss?" Seth asked, leaned back in his seat and already expecting the G-force of his boss's wrath. Sure enough…

"When the hell were you going to tell me that Princess Lianna is no longer in your custody?" Alex snapped. "Who else is missing?"

"Actually, she was never in my custody, but you're correct. Cord's sister, Devereaux Shepherd, her son, Scottie, and her neighbor, Trish Crawford from North Dakota are missing at the moment, which is why we're going to East Rockland Key. We're fairly certain Sylvester Valentine is behind this, and we suspect he's keeping Devereaux somewhere near—"

"You suspect? You don't know?"

Seth faced the pavement ahead and met his boss's questions head-on. "No, Boss, I'm not sure, but my gut's telling me to follow this hunch. I can't go to the police, remember? Not unless you've smoothed things over with the State Department. Have you?" That would make this day so much easier. Then the FBI would be involved like they should've been all along.

"Yeah, about that…" Alex hissed. "Farraq Khadeem's missing. We suspect he's fled the country, that he's in Europe."

"You suspect?" Seth couldn't help tweaking his boss's bad temper.

"I meant the State Department, smartass," Alex came back with. "Jesus Christ, Seth, I'm not God."

No, but sometimes, you're the next best thing. "Understood. Do we have any idea where Khadeem might be hiding in Europe?"

"Let's get this straight. I said the State Department thinks he's in Europe, not me. I'd bet he's on his way to Cuba, maybe the States. The only thing the State Department knows is Khadeem's no longer in Saudi Arabia. The king made it clear he'll behead Khadeem as soon as his men find him."

"So he knows what Khadeem did to Lianna?"

"And to Prince Bagani," Alex muttered, his voice gone weary. "You need to tread carefully. The king of Saudi Arabia's after Khadeem, but I doubt he'll admit to any indiscretions in the royal line, no matter how distantly related Bagani is."

"Hold a second, Boss," he said as he asked Cord, "Do you know what happened to Lianna's hands?"

Cord shot him a dark look. "Yeah. We found her nailed to a—"

"Rape stand," Seth finished, his mouth gone dry at the thought of the pretty blonde humiliated like that.

"Yeah, if that's what you call it," Cord murmured. "I killed the bastards who did it, and I'd do it again. Why'd you want to know?"

"You hear that, Boss?" Seth asked as he rested a hand on Cord's shoulder.

"Got it," came back terse and low.

Just to be clear, Seth told Alex, "Bagani dumped Lianna on Montego, and Montego's men defiled her hands, but Cord got to her before they had the chance to defile her body. You really want me to let Khadeem, or Bagani for that matter, live?"

"No, but you've got to be damned careful. The world's watching us. Make one mistake and we could be at war. Cover your six."

"I intend to," Seth answered. "I'll be in touch the minute this thing's over."

Alex disconnected. Seth turned to Cord and whined, "Are we there yet?"

Cord rolled his eyes as he pulled into the left turn lane. "Almost. Your boss is quite a guy, huh?"

You could say that. "Yeah, Alex is something all right."

"He, umm, he…" Cord seemed to have trouble speaking as he crossed traffic and they headed north. He tried again. "He, your boss, Alex Stewart, umm…"

"Will you just say it?"

"He offered to fund me," Cord murmured. "Me. My work. Do you believe that? Some guy he doesn't even know.

He offered to fund what I do down here in the Keys. Said he was proud of me, but that I'm a dumbass for thinking I could take on the world and do this all by myself. Said a Marine should know better than to do stupid shit like that, but he also said he'd ante up enough money that I could pay my guys and buy my own building and… Jesus Christ, McCray. He said if I came to work for him, he'd support me every step of the way."

Which was why Seth worked for Alex Stewart. There was no better boss in the world.

By then the scenery had changed from strip malls and residential to backwoods and gravel roads. "I've got twenty-four hours to give him an answer, and, get this. He said it better be the right one."

Seth nearly smiled, but they'd just passed a derelict motel. Damned if there weren't two vehicles parked there, a sleek silver Maserati and a beat-up POS economy car. "Pull over. Now."

Cord parked the Chevelle in the tall reeds and swamp grass, not that Seth minded having to climb out and fight his way through the brush to get to the road. Cord joined him at the rear of the Chevy, his weapon in his hand. "How do you want to do this?"

"Quickly," Seth murmured as he scanned the various points of egress and started forward. The clapboard building faced west, its rear wall against twelve-foot high grass, weeds, and shrubbery. The asphalt parking lot to the front of it was cracked and full of weeds, though these were shorter and worn from travel. The faded sign over the one main door at the south end of the building indicated what might have been the office, but Seth headed for the single door/window combination of the next thirteen rooms. With those two vehicles parked where they were, he bet Sly and Bagani were in the fourth room north of the office.

"Can you believe these guys parking out in the open like this?" Cord whispered as he racked his piece. "Damn, they've got nerve. You think she's here?"

Which was why most people never recognized human trafficking when they saw it. The perpetrators had a helluva lot of nerve and they conducted much of their business in broad daylight.

"One way to find out," Seth muttered, his entire being on high alert, his senses drawing all elements in his surroundings to him. The direction of the slight breeze coming from the north. The angle of the early morning sun to his left. The birdsong from every leaf and branch, and Lordy, Lordy. He'd almost forgotten how much and how loud birds chattered, sang, and chirped at the first glimmer of dawn.

Cocking his head, he tuned his ears on the weathered building ahead, no longer sure he'd heard voices coming from there. Stealthy now, he sidled up to the nearest corner of the building and looked down the length of what had once been a long wooden porch. Straggly tufts of gray Spanish moss clung to the underside of the decrepit overhanging roof. Something rustled in the bushes at his rear, but that something was smaller than a human, so he disregarded it as negligible. Mankind didn't scurry.

"Think you can get past the rear of this motel without being seen?"

"On it," Cord said as he stepped into the weeds.

"We'll go in once you're at the opposite end of this porch, understood? We'll meet in the middle."

"You bet," Cord replied as he rounded the corner and disappeared.

"Hurry," Seth murmured, more to himself than at Cord. "Devereaux's here. I can sense her." *And my gut's churning up a storm.*

Chapter Thirty-Seven

Sweating and in tears, Dev bit her lip in anticipation of another sting from the cruel weapon in Bagani's hand. He struck without warning, and it didn't matter if she'd been paying rapt attention or not. He kept hitting her left breast until the poor swollen mound of flesh twitched and burned as if he'd set it on fire. What was he going to do next?

She tried not to scream and cry, but this was all a game, a contest with him. With each snap of his wrist, she writhed in bitter agony, while he stared and studied her like an insect. There was no escape. Bagani was the big scary cat, and she was the tiny little mouse, caught in a trap from which there was only one way out. Where once she'd prayed for one more chance to see Scottie, now she prayed for the quick death she knew wasn't in her future, not with the other tools Bagani had yet to use.

God! Kill me now, just kill me! Yet simultaneously she prayed, *I'm too young to die!*

Joachim had moved to the heavily curtained window, the edge of it barely pushed aside, watching for someone, hopefully the police. Occasionally, he'd glance over his shoulder at her, but there was no remorse in his eyes and no kindness. Only an odd excitement that made Dev's skin crawl, while she shivered and trembled beneath Bagani's skilled touch. The asses!

What the hell turned men into animals like these guys? What pleasure was there in tormenting another human being? In torturing a defenseless woman?

"Mr. Valentine's here," Joachim said calmly as he walked to the door and opened it.

The last thing Dev needed. Another Inquisitor.

Sly ducked into the room with a hurried, "Sorry I'm late, your Highness." He came to stand behind Bagani, the same freakish glitter in his eyes that gleamed in Joachim's. "I had a little problem at the club last night. One of the girls, you understand," he said as he rolled his long sleeves up to his elbows. "We can start now."

"N-no," Dev whimpered. "Please, s-s-stop. I'll be good. Just don't—" *Whip!* "No! Ahh! Stop!"

But Bagani struck again, and she didn't know how much more pain she could take.

"But you're already a good girl," he purred, as he dragged the hook over the mesh bra and tugged the cup down, exposing her. "In fact, you're perfect. Look, my friend," he said, glancing up at Sly who all but drooled at the sight of her tortured breast. "All I have to do is this…" *Whip!* He struck again, hitting her naked skin, and this time, Bagani chuckled when she shrieked. "You were right, she is a responsive one, and she knows my real name." *Whip!*

"Master!" Dev screamed. "Why are you doing this to me?"

Brushing past Bagani, Sly rounded the bed to stand at her other side. "Because women like you need men like me," he growled as he leaned into her face and squeezed her poor, battered breast.

"Stop!" she squealed, writhing, her wrists and ankles raw and bleeding. She could smell her own blood and sweat, yet this nightmare would not end!

Sly laughed. "Oh, just wait, my lovely, spoiled prima donna. I've been watching since you moved into my turf. Playtime's just beginning. You live for the pain, and I'm here to make sure you get what you like."

BLAM! What was that? It sounded like someone had just kicked the door in.

Dev jerked her head around at that noise, but she couldn't see past Bagani to know for sure. Suddenly as still as a stone, he'd crossed his arms, a weird, detached smile on his face.

Sly pressed a knife under her chin just as someone fired a shot, and Joachim fell to the floor behind the prince. Sly pricked her neck with the tip of the blade and bellowed, "Stop or she dies!"

"Don't listen to him! Help me!" she screamed at whoever'd come to her rescue.

A beat of silence, then a tortured, "Dev? Is that you?"

"Cord? Yes!" she screamed even as Sly pricked her again. "Get me out of here!"

Bagani sat there as silent as a schoolboy, the bloody weapon of choice still in his clean hands.

"Let her up," Cord snapped from somewhere beyond Dev's visual range.

"Not happening," Sly bit out, his dark hair dangling into his face. "Get your ass out of here, Shepherd, or I'll stick her. I swear I will. She'll bleed out before you get to her."

"You think I can't hit you from here?"

"You think I can't cut her throat if you're stupid enough to try?" Sly shot back at him. "Are you willing to take that risk, Shepherd? Are you ready to watch your sister die?"

"No. He's not," a strange woman's voice rang out.

"What the fuck?" Cord growled.

No, no, no! Dev craned her neck to see what was happening. Bagani finally shifted to his left and Dev saw Cord then. He had both hands over his head as the shorthaired woman with the gun in his neck stripped the pistol from his fingers.

"Inside, Mr. Shepherd," she ordered. "I'm not opposed to wasting a good man but trust me. I will."

"Dev, I'm sorry," he bit out as the woman walked him over to the chair Joachim had been sitting in.

This cannot be happening!

"Stab his sister if he makes one move," the woman told Sly while she holstered her pistol, handed Cord a set of metal cuffs, and said, "You know what to do."

Cord sneered at her, but cuffed himself. "Now what?" he asked as he towered over her. Hissing and his teeth chattering, he dropped to the floor. The woman had hit him in the chest with the taser she'd pulled from beneath her jacket.

"Who are you?" Dev asked, her last hope gone, and her heart broken for Cord. This was all her fault.

"Giselle Montego," the blonde replied as she stuck the taser in her waistband.

"You're… you're Roland Montego's wife?"

Giselle winked. "I'm one of many women that he, shall we say, plays with? And now you can be, too."

Chapter Thirty-Eight

Seth had walked halfway along the porch when he'd caught sight of the black sedan rolling toward the motel. Ducking into the first available room, he'd watched while Sly had climbed out of that sedan and entered the same room Seth was headed for.

But once Cord hit the other end of the boardwalk, their plan to meet in the middle went ape shit. He'd seen Sly drive up, too. Fired up and stupid, he'd closed in on door four without coordinating with Seth. Before Seth could get his attention, Cord had entered room four alone, the dumbass. He'd no more than crossed the doorjamb when a shot rang out, but Jesus H. Christ! Yet another car had advanced on the motel by then, this one a sleek silver BMW. *What was this place? Fuckin' Grand Central Station?*

It was Giselle, the dominatrix from the bar, who had unfolded her long legs from the second car. Smoothing her hands over her short black skirt, she'd drawn a pistol from beneath her creamy white suit jacket, and like the rabid dominatrix she was, Giselle followed Cord's dumb ass into room four.

Seth waited, certain Cord had to have fired that shot, that he'd put up a decent fight and that he'd come busting out of that door with Devereaux before Giselle got to him. But when the door closed without so much as a whimper... When things went incredibly quiet...

Damn that Marine! He'd just made everything ten times worse with that pigheaded stunt! Who'd he think he was, John Wayne? Seth would've given anything if a different former Marine had his six at that moment, but the guy he needed was in far-off Virginia, and Shit! Seth was stuck with Cord.

Down to one man, this operation was seriously compromised, but that meant squat. Seth wasn't leaving without Devereaux. Not without Cord now, either.

"Why the hell couldn't you listen? Just once, you pigheaded Marine? Would it have killed you?" Seth muttered as he advanced on room four, his eye on the road in case anyone else decided to show up. Why not? Everyone else had. "I said we'd meet in the middle, but noooooooooooo..."

Shit! He was pissed that Cord had just blown their one and only advantage—surprise. Sucking up a breath of patience and fortitude, Seth steeled himself at room four's door, his weapon ready, his heart locked and loaded.

He'd been down this road more times than he cared to remember. People would die the second he breached the entry. The slightest error at his hand could and would change everything. Things could still go terribly wrong. He could die. Worse, Devereaux could die. He had to time this precisely or—

Devereaux screamed, and to hell with last second strategizing. Cocking his knee, Seth kicked the door open and charged inside. Cord lay flat on his back at Seth's right. Out cold. Bagani looked up from his chair in surprise. Sly and

Giselle stood to the right of the bed with Giselle leaning over Devereaux with, of all damned things, a taser in her hand.

No way! Seth asked no questions as—*BLAM!*—muscle training took over. Down Giselle went, one to the head.

The blade in Sly's hand flashed, but only once. Seth made sure of that, firing automatically as Sly joined the dominatrix beside the bed where Devereaux lay crying.

The poor thing was spread-eagled, bloodied, and half-dressed in metal underwear on the plastic-covered bed at his right. Her one breast was a mound of bloody hamburger. Both wrists and her ankles bled profusely. God, what'd they do to her?

"Seth," she begged, her face mottled red and tearstained, her pretty white hair clumped with sweat and blood.

"I'm here, babe," he told her.

At her side the olive-skinned, arrogant prick of a man in a pristine white dress shirt sat on a wooden chair, one ankle crossed over his knee, and his nose in the air. Had to be his royal bastard highness, Prince Bagani.

Seth wanted to shoot the guy's head off, and he would have if Alex hadn't warned him that the world was watching. Would've shot this dirtbag and walked over his dead body to get to Devereaux. Instead, Seth zeroed down on the asshole behind this dirty business and roared, "Get down! On the floor! Do it! Now! Now! Now!" like he'd done when breaching Taliban strongholds in Afghanistan.

Screaming tended to disorient civilians. Not this guy. The prince dared to stay seated and that just wasn't going to fly. Seth jerked the bastard off the chair by his collar and shoved him to his knees. "I said down!" he roared at the pompous ass.

"I think not," Bagani answered calmly as he sat on his haunches and dusted the single strand of hair that had fallen out of place, off his brow. "You're an American. You have no power over me."

"Like hell I don't! I'll show you power!" Seth spat as he pressed the business end of his pistol to the man's forehead, aching to end this bastard once and for all. "I own your ass, Bagani, don't think I don't. You're a known rapist and murderer. Stay the fuck down!"

"You own nothing," the prince chided, his tone rife with pithy tolerance that Seth had no patience for. "I am royalty, and as such, I have diplomatic immunity. Check with my embassy. Better yet, check with yours. They'll tell you. I. Am. Untouchable." He lifted to his feet, still too damned calm, but, shit—right.

Seth huffed through his nose, pissed at the politics that let this bastard roam free. "Sit your worthless ass down, or so help me—"

"No," Bagani stated, his chin up, his shoulders and back stiff. "My work is done here. Get out of my way. I have a plane to catch."

"Your work!" Seth jerked his head at the bed. "You call that work, you asshat?" It took all of his control to not knock Bagani to the floor and kick his ass. He'd hurt Devereaux. He needed to pay and pay hard. In blood!

But when she whimpered from that frightful bed of horrors, and Cord moaned from the floor, the law of triage demanded Seth get his head back in the game. They needed to live more than Bagani needed to die.

If not for that and Alex's warning, Bagani would never see the light of day. He'd just cleared the doorway on his way to freedom. Seth still had him in his sights, and his heart ached to put the son-of-a-bitch down like the cur he was. But Bagani kept walking, his head held high as if he knew damned well he'd just gotten away with kidnapping, torture, and attempted murder.

Seth kept his red laser dot square on the back of Bagani's skull until the man slid into the Maserati. This was the hardest thing Seth had ever done. The asshole was getting away.

"Seth," Devereaux cried, and Seth lost the war between doing what he knew was right and what he wanted to do. He sent the son-of-a-bitch Bagani one last hate-filled glare before he holstered his weapon and went to her. In no time at all, he jimmied the locked cuffs and pulled her off the disgusting sticky plastic.

"Ow, ow," she cried, cradling one arm over her poor savaged breast.

"I've got you," he murmured as she collapsed against him, crying and shaking so hard that it broke his heart. "Hey, it's over. I've got you and we're going home."

"Scottie," she whimpered. "They said they'd hurt Scottie if I didn't..."

"Shush," he soothed even as he avoided telling her that he had no idea where Scottie was at the moment. First things first.

Seth carried her into the bathroom, where it appeared one helluva fight had taken place. Blood smeared the floor and the walls near the doorjamb. The shower curtain lay half in the toilet, half in the tub. The mirror over the sink was shattered and glass shards were everywhere. Jerking what looked like a clean hand towel off the towel bar, he soaked it in cold water, wrung it out one-handed, then carefully, so as not to hurt her any worse, laid it over her breast.

She shuddered as the cloth met her poor mangled flesh.

"Hang on," he murmured, stepping through the glass and back into the bedroom. The scene in the bathroom explained Devereaux's bloodied feet. "You fought those guys, didn't you?"

Her head bumped under his chin. "Y-yeah. I-I wasn't going easy," she said, shivering so much she could barely speak.

It took a second to dial 9-1-1, give them his location, tell dispatch he needed an ambulance and to step on it. Just then Bagani's vehicle started up. The asshat was getting away and none of this was fair, but Seth had hold of what he treasured most. Let Alex have Bagani. He was welcome to the bastard.

Next, Seth called his boss, thankful this day was almost over. "I've got her," he breathed into the satphone, even as he nuzzled the top of Devereaux's damp head while she clung to him, weeping and hurt and so damned sad that Seth could've cried with her.

"How is she?" Alex asked, his voice soft with uncharacteristic tenderness.

"Alive," Seth answered, the oddest pinch flaring inside his chest. He'd come so close to losing her, so close he could barely breathe now that it was finally done. He couldn't go through that again, not losing the woman he loved. He wouldn't survive. He had to tell her.

"And Bagani?" Alex asked quietly.

"Gone, Boss. I let him go like you said. Man, he's an arrogant—"

BOOM! The too close shockwave of a damned big gun vibrated the air. Even Alex heard it. "What the hell was that?"

"Not sure," Seth muttered as he carried Devereaux with him to find out. "Honey, I've got to set you down while I go check something. Will you be okay outside here on the porch?" he asked her.

Alex chuckled. "Sure hope you aren't talking to me. I like you, son, but not that much."

What an odd thing for Alex to say, but Seth had bigger things on his mind than his boss's uncharacteristic teasing. Bagani's car was still rolling forward, but it had veered into the tall grasses along the right side of the road.

Settling Devereaux against the outside wall of the motel room, Seth ran toward the Maserati to investigate. *Holy hell.* Bagani sat slouched behind the wheel, his seatbelt on, but his eyes wide open, and a neater-than-shit hole in the center of his forehead. Brain matter and blood painted the leather upholstery behind him. Spider webbing decorated the entire rear window, centered around one sure as shit bullet hole.

"Um, Boss?" Seth asked as he looked over his shoulder, sure he'd spy the bad-assed man he worked for standing off in the not too far distance with the butt stock of his sniper rifle on his hip. But there was no one out there, anywhere. Not Alex. Not anyone.

"Where are you?" Seth had to know.

"At my office," Alex replied without one twinge of snark in his tone, which in and of itself was odd considering Seth had asked a rather dumb question, the kind Alex had no use for. "You're the one who called me, didn't you?"

"Yeah, I did, but..." But calls could be forwarded to anywhere on the planet, even to a cellphone or satphone in the middle of the Florida Keys. "But someone just offed Prince Bagani. Head shot, Boss. That's what that noise was."

Canting his head, Seth closed one eye to block the glare of the rising sun, as he looked southward. "Whoever did it is a damned good shot. One to the middle of Bagani's head. Through a darkly tinted windshield, no less. Spot on. I've never seen anything like it."

"Well, damn," Alex muttered, though he didn't sound upset. "I guess that means I'm your alibi, huh?"

Seth's gaze strayed to Devereaux, still sitting on the porch where he'd left her with the wet towel, now stained red, pressed against her chest. "I've actually got two, Boss. Devereaux and you, but…" But this was just plain weird. A sniper had just sniped a member of the Arabian royal family from one helluva long ways off. "I've got to call this into the police. There'll be an uproar, and the press will be all over me and…"

"You do that, Seth. I'm on my way with irrefutable evidence that we were speaking on the phone when Bagani went down. Sit tight. The police can't hold you for a crime you didn't commit. Talk to you soon."

Seth disconnected, still dazed at the turn of events. Bagani was finally dead. Killed by a sniper. If not Alex, then who?

Chapter Thirty-Nine

Dev sipped at the cool mango/orange juice in her hospital cup. She couldn't seem to get enough of it, not after her near-death experience. As soon as she'd been allowed to, she'd showered and washed her hair to get the rank odor of that vile motel off her. Then she'd lounged with an icepack pressed to her poor, battered breast for most of the day, waiting for Seth to return so the hospital would release her. The admitting doctor wanted to keep her overnight for observation, and she still had to wait for the plastic surgeon, but she wanted out of there. Home. She just wanted to go home.

Dressed in the soft cotton nightgown that Seth had bought her—cotton because he'd said nothing felt better than cotton—she waited on his return from the police station. He'd been there most of the day answering questions and offering his assistance in locating Prince Bagani's unseen shooter, but he'd be back. Dev knew he would. She just couldn't wait.

Royal prince, my ass. Knowing Bagani was dead went a long way toward calming Dev's hysteria. Yet every time she thought of what surely would've happened to her and Cord if Seth hadn't shown when he did, her heart still raced, and her throat clamped shut. Her stomach ached, and her head hurt. She could still smell the rank ugliness of Joachim's dead body after Cord had laid him low. A migraine had been threatening all day. Seth said those reactions were normal, but Dev only knew that she felt better when he was there, and she needed him now.

Poor Cord stayed out in the hall, standing guard he said, but she suspected he was avoiding her more than anything else. Her big, tough brother might never forgive himself for blowing Seth's more sensible plan to retrieve her. Yet in the end, it had all worked out, and Seth wasn't angry at Cord. He understood what had driven Cord to ignore his better instincts.

Come to find out, the missing princess hadn't been missing at all, more like relocated by another person who'd followed her gut, Trish. After Cord had left Lianna with Trish when he'd gone to join Seth, she'd taken it upon herself to rent a room at one of the more prestigious hotels on the beach. There she and Lianna had lounged by the pool for the last two days, sipping piña coladas, while Scottie swam and played to his heart's content on a giant watermelon-red floaty. The little guy was as tan as he'd never been before, making his blue eyes seem even brighter.

Dev teared up thinking about how close she'd come to losing her son—and him losing her. Never, if she lived to be a hundred, would she forget the panic in those sad blue eyes when Trish had brought Scottie to visit her at the hospital this afternoon.

Motherhood could be such a bitch sometimes. It was a never-ending job on top of an already never-ending battle of robbing Peter to pay Paul, but seeing how scared he'd been, and feeling that trembling little boy body of his, when he'd run to her and clung to her, sobbing, "Mama!" like his heart was breaking—yeah. There was nothing better, nor sadder, nor more precious in Dev's world.

Even though it had hurt to hold him, she'd had a hard time letting Scottie go. He'd been so frightened for her just because she'd been hurt and should stay in the hospital overnight. The official story he'd been told was that she'd had an accident at work.

But man, what he would've gone through had Bagani accomplished his evil deed. If her body had never been found, and if Scottie'd spent the rest of his life wondering where she'd gone and why she'd deserted him. It was enough to set her heart racing again. He'd never know how close he'd come to losing her, not if she could help it. No, that was one bedtime story Scottie would never hear from her lips.

Then there was her other sweet little guy, Gru. That Seth, out of all the people out and about last night in Key West, was the one who'd found him—twice—was a coincidence too great to ignore. Karma seemed determined that Seth and she be together, and Dev agreed. The sooner, the better.

She glanced at the clock on the wall across from her bed. *Where is he?*

Lianna Khadeem was now under the care of the king of Saudi Arabia, and on her way to his grand palace with an invitation to stay as long as she desired. Earlier this afternoon, he'd graciously and publicly apologized for the inconsiderate suffering she'd experienced at the hands of a distant member of his family. Though he didn't name Basheer Bagani directly, it wasn't hard to make the connection. Better yet, he vowed retribution to the sinister man behind the debacle, aka Khadeem. Lianna now had a home to return to, just not her family.

As usual, the press turned her recovery into a media circus. CNN still hashed and rehashed her narrow escape from a known human trafficker on their thirty-minute recycling of the news timelines. Round and round they went with the details of her journey into Montego's lair, yet not once had they mentioned the guys who'd rescued her, nor what it cost Cord and his men to do what they did.

Not that Cord minded. He'd told Dev about the offer he'd received from Seth's boss, Alex Stewart. But she detected a hint of reluctance when it came to Cord accepting that offer. *This is the offer of a lifetime. What's not to like?*

So, yeah. It was another day living in paradise at the southernmost tip of the United States. Setting her nearly empty glass aside, Dev breathed out a contented sigh and leaned heavily into her pillow. All would be right with the world again—as soon as Seth returned.

Seth sat in his rented truck in the hospital's overflow parking lot. Thinking. Worrying. He now knew Eric hadn't left Florida with Cassidy, which wasn't a good development. If there was anyone who hated Basheer Bagani more than Eric, Seth didn't know the guy.

Years back Eric's wife Shea had encountered Bagani during a dark time in her life. She'd been smart enough to escape his clutches, and as far as Seth knew, Bagani hadn't done anything more than tie her to his bed. But he'd intended to do to Shea what he'd done to Devereaux and more. Whenever Bagani's name came up at the office, Eric lost his focus and his already dark eyes roiled with cold, black intent. It was as if he had internally planned for the day he came face-to-face with Bagani, and Seth couldn't blame him. It had taken all his better senses not to kill the bastard when he'd had the chance.

The question remained. Who killed him? Eric? The vengeful husband who had every right to want Bagani dead? Or Alex, the best ghost in the covert business, and the well-known owner of the most elite covert surveillance company… In. The. World?

But would Alex risk all he'd accomplished to kill a man like Bagani? Seth knew damned well Alex could and would. The man was lethally capable, especially where women, little girls, and boys were concerned. He was one of those rare men who'd never ceased training or grown soft when he'd left the Corps. Even his sweet little wife Kelsey could turn nasty under the right circumstances. Seth hadn't worked for Alex at the time, but he'd heard the stories. He knew who'd shot and killed Kelsey's maniacal ex-mother-in-law during a hard-fought battle for survival, and it wasn't Alex. But that was another story for another time.

After listening to the evidence the Key West police presented, Seth leaned toward Eric Reynolds doing the deed. Bagani had died from one precisely placed round to his head, and that was just one amazingly helluva difficult shot that Alex simply couldn't have made while chatting over the phone as easily as he'd been at the time.

Yes, he could've been using a headset, leaving himself hands-free to manage his rifle. Yes, Alex was smart enough to sound carefree when he wasn't. But no sniper Seth knew or had ever worked with was that dispassionate while zeroing down on a known target, particularly not Alex. The man plain damned cared too much.

Sniping took supreme focus, uncanny attention to detail, and a damned smart man or woman to calculate the mathematics behind distance, windage, and elevation, not to mention the angle of the rising sun. Factor Florida's humidity, the early morning temperature, and spindrift, the bullet's rotation, into that one calculation, and it raised another question. Did Bagani's killer have a spotter, a partner at his elbow who'd watched Bagani through a rangefinder, while he'd coached Bagani's killer as to precisely what Minutes-of-Angle scope corrections to make to achieve said target? Minutes-of-Angle being the standard measure for elevation and windage. Sure seemed like this job had taken two very savvy snipers to get it done.

According to the laws of terminal ballistics and what was left of the back of Bagani's skull, the shot had to have come from nearly a mile south of the motel, through a tinted windshield that would've been nearly impossible to see through at that distance.

Whoever'd done Bagani would've most likely been flat on his belly on a raised platform, a table maybe. He or she— Seth wasn't about to dismiss the fact that this could very well have been a female operator—would've used a thermal imaging scope, possibly one of the new, enhanced Starlights, to have seen his target through the tinted windshield. And… he would've been the steadiest, luckiest son-of-a-bitch on the planet.

The police still hadn't found the bullet, the sniper hide, or any casings. Which meant the shooter knew exactly where Bagani planned to be this morning. Which also meant he'd been following the arrogant bastard for days, possibly weeks, months, or years to get the shot. He might even have witnessed Bagani's depravity, waiting for this perfect opportunity. Didn't that make the tiny hairs on the back of Seth's neck stand up and take notice? Especially since his gut had been warning him for days now that someone had been watching him. Jesus H. Christ. Even in Cuba.

You want to talk about an impossible, scary shot. This one was that—and a helluva lot more. Seth only knew three Americans who'd made similar, record-breaking shots, and they were all either the arrogant owner of The TEAM or working for him.

Had Eric taken the law into his own hands to end the man who'd threatened his wife? Quite possibly—yes.

Given what Seth now knew about Bagani's deviant past and the death toll he'd racked up as he'd traveled from country to country, Seth would've done the same thing if he were Eric—if Eric had indeed offed the son-of-a-bitch. Surely Alex had known about Shea when he'd assigned Eric to accompany Cassidy to Cuba. Surely he hadn't put Eric in close proximity to Bagani for this exact ulterior motive.

Or had he? Was Alex just that—accommodating?

Seth sat there drumming his fingertips on his steering wheel, not sure what or who to believe. The more he pondered the ramifications of Bagani's death, the more he worried the FBI might zero down on his boss or his friend. Alex had a long-running feud with the Bureau. It could happen. They could swoop in with their SWAT, and Alex and Eric would never be heard from again.

Major Delaney's comment came back to haunt Seth: *'...tell that ornery boss of yours to look me up the next time he's in GITMO.'*

By hell, that exact scenario very well could happen. Both Alex and Eric were hands down capable. Both had means, motive, and opportunity. And wasn't it odd that Alex had instantly declared himself Seth's alibi, as if he'd thought that far ahead? As if he'd planned that precise scenario? But if he was Seth's, and Seth was Alex's alibi, who was Eric's?

"Where the hell are you, brother?" Seth whispered, his kneecap jerking against the underside of the steering wheel with every anxious toe tap. "Call me. I'll help you, whatever you need, no questions asked. Just ask. Don't wait for the authorities to hunt your ass down. That'll hurt Shea and your kids, and that's not what you want. I know you, man. You love your wife more than your need for revenge. Call. Me."

But what husband, especially if he were already a military trained sniper, abundantly blessed with the eyesight of an eagle, and employed within a covert surveillance company the likes of The TEAM, wouldn't search out and destroy a known, albeit protected, murderer to keep his wife safe?

A man with morals—like Eric—that was who.

Okay then. Problem solved. That sure knowledge was enough for Seth. Sucking in a gut full of trust in his boss and in his friend, he exhaled as he turned his mind to the problem at hand. Alex was due to arrive at Naval Air Station Key West any moment now, and soon after, he'd be at the hospital. He'd want answers. Hell, didn't they all?

But before that?

Seth had a woman to kiss.

Chapter Forty

'Damn, he's sexy,' Dev thought as she sat in her hospital bed watching the trio of warriors sitting in the corner of her room. Seth had barely lifted her into his arms, when his boss arrived. Darn Alex Stewart. Why'd he have to be so… so… punctual?

All three men, Cord, Seth, and Alex, an impressively younger man than Dev had expected, were seated on molded hospital chairs by the single floor to ceiling window. All leaned forward into each other, their elbows on their knees, and all intent on their muted discussion.

Too tired to eavesdrop on their acronym-filled mumblings, she'd already been served and eaten the blandest food ever. These guys had to be hungry. It was past dinnertime.

Dressed in his customary get-up—black everything—Cord was as handsome as ever. Alex Stewart, on the other hand, had a definite alpha wolf thing going for him. An athletically muscled man in his mid to late thirties, he wore faded jeans and a gray t-shirt under a navy blue casual jacket, its zipper undone. Tall, handsome, and dark-haired with the barest hint of silver at his sideburns, he gave off the powerful vibes of one badassed warrior who was comfortable commanding others.

Yet the man had the bluest eyes. When Seth had introduced him, she could've sworn he'd seen right through her, but she'd glimpsed something, too. Alex could've stayed in far-off Virginia, but he'd chosen to be here with his men, and that told Dev a lot. This guy didn't mind getting his hands dirty. He was one of those *'follow-me-boys'* leaders, the kind that led the charge, instead of the glory seeker who stayed safe in the rear.

Alex reminded Dev of a WWII battleship parting the stormy Pacific like a hot blade slicing through butter. He carried himself proudly and confidently, as if he dared Mother Nature, or anyone for that matter, to stand in his way. Both Seth and Cord were intelligent alphas in their own right, but Alex was another animal altogether. He was that solitary predator at the top of the food chain, and it showed in the ease with which he handled the professionals sitting with him.

But Seth? A smile came automatically to her lips. Seth—well, he glowed. That was the only word for him. His persona seemed to shine above the others. He'd changed clothes since he'd rescued her that morning, but as usual, he'd chosen jeans and a plain white t-shirt that stretched tightly across his impressive chest. Damn, he was one drool-worthy male. But humble. Not once had he lifted his voice like Cord was prone to do, and when Alex spoke, he listened instead of arguing, another Cord trait.

She could've lain there all day studying Seth. The sharp angle of his jaw when he spoke. The way he licked his lower lip. The rapt attention he paid his boss. The way he canted his head when he listened, as if he strived to understand what the others said instead of just waiting for them to finish so he could talk. The straight line of his spine and the width of those tanned, hard as rock shoulders. Very simply, Seth had Cord and Alex beat by miles and miles.

But best of all? The twinkle in those sexy brown eyes, when he sent a wink her way if the other guys weren't looking. Man, they needed to pack it up and leave, so she could get her hands on him again.

She found it interesting that all three men were still geared up and armed, though, even in this gun free hospital zone. Alex sported a double holster underneath his jacket, the slight bulges beneath his arms an easy tell for a woman with a former Marine brother.

Both Cord and Seth wore their pistols on their hips, though Seth also carried another one tucked in the back waistband of his jeans as well. She had no doubt all three also carried knives. These guys knew the way of the real world, and they weren't afraid to face it alone and whip its ass. They must have some special kind of permit or license that allowed them to carry, but what did Dev know? Only that she was surrounded by a company of snipers and had never felt safer.

Alex's head came up, his blues eyes like shards of ice stabbing Cord. "I'm tired of waiting. I need an answer."

Cord leaned into the chair, his arms folded across his chest. "Don't have one. I'm still waiting to hear from one of my guys."

"Not good enough, Shepherd." Man, Alex was like an attack-trained pit bull. He'd gone straight for Cord's jugular. "There are plenty of other men out there who are doing the same—"

"Yes," Cord bit out, the tendon in his muscular neck twitching like it did when he found himself backed into a corner. "I'll take the job, in fact…"

Dev had seen that pissed off glare before, when she'd gotten the best of her big brother. He didn't like to be wrong, but he especially didn't like answering to others.

"In fact, I'm damned thankful you have that kind of faith in me, sir," he finished.

A shadow that Dev could only describe as a thundercloud before one helluva storm shifted over Alex's countenance. "Now that you're going to work for me, Junior Agent Shepherd…" he growled, "stop with the sir bullshit. I work for a living."

Dev knew precisely what that meant. Alex Stewart had never been an officer and he was proud of it. Apparently Cord knew as well. It was comical how he blinked at Alex and said, "Yes, sssssss… I mean—"

"Boss," Seth supplied, nodding pointedly at Cord. "I'm sure you mean, 'yes, Boss,' don't you?"

Dev nearly laughed. She'd never seen Cord backpedal so fast, nor look as dumbfounded as he did then.

"Boss," he finally mumbled like he was trying the word on for size. "Yes, Boss."

Alex slapped both palms to his knees. "Good. I'll be by first thing in the morning with the paperwork and your initial check. Where will you be?"

"Home," Dev spoke up. "He'll be home with me and Scottie, won't you?" she asked her amazingly versatile brother. He'd gone from man in charge to an employee in the blink of an eye.

"You know it," he replied, his brows clenched over his extra dark, extra serious eyes. That had to have been a hard adjustment acknowledging that he just might need another man's help.

Seth cocked his head, measuring her with a heated glance. *'And you are so going home with me,'* she sent to him in her mind, wishing there were such a thing as telepathy. But oh, the naughty conversation they'd be having if it were.

When Alex lifted to his feet, Seth and Cord rose alongside him like two bouncers the guy absolutely didn't need. Seth and Cord must have sensed it, too. Neither had argued with him, though when they'd offered input, he'd listened intently, those icy blue lasers focused on them as if he respected their opinions. Usually Cord just barked orders at his men, and they bucked up and obeyed. But Alex was a different kind of predator. He seemed able to lead his men where they wanted to go. Like Seth had done with Cord.

"Anyone up for breakfast?" Alex asked, looking at her.

Ha! Like she was going anywhere.

"Molly's Marina and Pub serves breakfast until closing," Dev said, holding back her disappointment. Seth would be leaving to eat with his boss. Not what she wanted.

"What can I bring back for you?" he asked as one hand latched onto her wrist.

'Just you,' she would've said, but she settled for, "Molly makes the best blueberry pancakes. A to-go cup of her caramel coffee would be nice, too. Three sugars. Extra cream. Don't forget the blueberry syrup and butter."

Leaning into her cheek, he whispered, "Just you wait."

Delicious shivers raced up her spine. "I've already been waiting," she murmured, sure all eyes were on them. "But go. I understand. I'll be here when you return."

Ever so gently, he cupped her poor battered jaw and placed one melt-in-your-mouth, but too chaste kiss on her lips.

"Hurry," she told him, then added, "I'm hungry," for his boss's and Cord's benefit.

"Damn, Devereaux, don't go telling the world."

"For breakfast," she clarified, the heat from her sexually charged comment creeping up her neck like a small blaze, but yes. She was hungry for every inch of Seth, and he knew it.

Alex cleared his throat like the gentleman he was.

Cord faced the door like he couldn't get out of there fast enough.

But Seth pressed one last kiss to her mouth, sliding his tongue over the seam of her lips like a promise, when he whispered, "Be right back."

Chapter Forty-One

The rich, balmy scent that was Florida met Seth full in the face. Alex was proud of him. Seth could tell. And didn't that make the wreck of the man he used to be, seem like some other guy, as George Lucas would say, *'in a galaxy far, far away'*?

The need to get this middle of the night breakfast over and done with shivered up his spine like the can't-wait excitement of a little boy on Christmas morning. Seth had a lovely present to unwrap. It took all his restraint to tear himself away from Devereaux for the sake of his boss. It just didn't seem right, picking Alex over her.

What a night. Seth took a deep breath of satisfaction for a job well done as he stepped out of the hospital's main entry doors. Life couldn't get any more sublime. The moon shining down on him was now waning in the southern sky. He had his very capable boss at his side, and Devereaux was safe and sound in the hospital.

Better yet, Roland Montego, his dominatrix wife, Giselle, and his dirtbag buddy, Bagani, were dead. Sylvester Valentine and Joachim, whom Seth now knew had worked for Sly at one of his bars, were laid out on stainless steel trays at the morgue, staring at nothing but the righteous comeuppance they'd deserved. May every last one of them linger in hell until the end of time.

The who and the why of the man who'd offed Bagani still toyed at the back of Seth's mind. He glanced at the proud man walking beside him. No way had Alex taken Bagani out. Had to have been Eric.

It wasn't until Seth crossed the street with Alex on one side and Cord on his other, that the hairs on the back of his neck lifted. His gut clenched with an attack of heartburn that he knew better than to ignore. He had that feeling again. Someone was watching.

Glancing over his shoulder, he scanned the lobby and information desk just beyond the entry doors for anything out of the ordinary. Nothing stood out. Not the pleasant gray-haired woman chatting on the phone behind the information counter. Not the police officer walking swiftly down the hall toward the emergency room. Not the older couple he'd passed on the bench outside the hospital doors.

Still…

"Hey, guys," he told Alex and Cord.

Alex cocked his head as if he'd suddenly picked up the same warning rippling through the universe that Seth had. "You need to stay here," he said, not asked.

Seth nodded, acid climbing up his throat. "Something's not right," he told his boss, who was backtracking with him and Cord to the hospital. "I'm going up to Devereaux's room."

Alex pulled a pistol from under his left arm. "Cord!" he hissed, not knowing Cord was already on his six.

"Yes, sir?" Cord breathed. "I'm here."

"Cord, take the stairs," Seth ordered. "Boss—"

"I'm with you. Go!"

They stormed the open elevator while Cord charged the stairwell. "He's here," Seth breathed, his heart pounding like a mother.

"Who?" Alex asked, his eyes on the slow-as-shit floor indicator. Devereaux's room was on the fifth floor, but damn. Nobody knew where she was. How had—whoever—Seth honestly had no idea who was left that might want to hurt Devereaux—how had that person located her so quickly? And why? She was a victim in this mess, not one of the power brokers. She was a single mom, for hell's sake.

"I don't know who's here or if I'm just overreacting," Seth admitted. He couldn't define the sensation that something wicked had zeroed down on Devereaux. "Could be one of Montego's men come for revenge. Or one of his women. Devereaux said Giselle Montego bragged he had more than one wife and they were into game playing, BDSM, and shit."

"Could be paranoia," Alex growled.

"Could be," Seth murmured as the elevator finally chimed at the fifth floor. God knew he'd dealt with plenty of paranoia during his PTSD days. Damn, was that all this was, a flashback?

"One way to find out," he said as he stepped through the elevator doors and ran for Devereaux's room.

Just as Cord cleared the stairs to his right, one damned big behemoth of a man stepped out from a patient room at the other end of the hall. Dressed entirely in black leather, the sniper rifle in this guy's hand displayed an impressive scope on its top rail. Could've been the same one that ended Bagani. The business end of that deadly rifle had just snapped on

Seth. He felt the prick of its laser strike his retina before it danced over the end of his nose.

Returning the courtesy, Seth's pistol sprang automatically on target. His stride lengthened as his laser settled between two black as sin eyes. He'd meet this arrogant asshole head-on with every beat of his heart. No one was getting at Devereaux.

"She's had enough!" he hissed, very aware of Alex at his side and Cord at his six. "I don't care who the hell you are. Back off!"

No answer came back at him, not even a grunt. Just one evil glare from the black-haired stranger closing in on Seth and his team like he owned the place.

Seth would've fired, but Devereaux's door burst open. Another man, this one dressed in the black uniform of one of Key West's finest—that police officer Seth had seen downstairs—dragged her struggling into the hall. The bastard had his hand over her mouth, a pistol in her ribs, and death in his eyes.

Shit. Farraq Khadeem. Unknowingly, he'd put himself and her between the armed man in black and Seth's team.

"Drop your weapon!" Alex ordered, his pistol on Khadeem or the assassin at his back, Seth didn't know which.

Khadeem's face twisted into an evil sneer. He had the balls to bellow, "One move and she dies! I'll take her the same way you took my precious daughter from me!"

"Your precious daughter? You mean the pretty, blonde woman you traded to a known pedophile and rapist, your fuckin' buddy Bagani?" Seth spat as he assumed firing stance, his pistol raised and his eyes on target. He didn't have to look to know Alex and Cord had both done the same, that all three were hellbent on ending this asshole here and now.

"Seth," Devereaux whimpered, her eyes bright with fear and her fingers wrapped around the hard hand clutching her throat.

Seth acknowledged her with one short nod. "Stay cool, baby. This'll be over soon and then—"

"This will never be over!" Khadeem spat. "This is just the beginning of Jihad! The holiest of holy wars!"

"Says the bastard who sold his *precious daughter*," Seth volleyed back. The hairs on the back of his neck bristled and his gut kept telling him to beware, but with two killers in the crosshairs, he hadn't the time to decode that internal warning.

"How'd you get in here?" Cord asked from Seth's far left.

Khadeem's bright eyes shifted. "You American's are so naïve. So trusting. All I had to do was make a few calls. Ask the right questions. It seems everyone in your country wants to help a poor, distraught father."

"You're not... my father," Devereaux wheezed, her blues eyes brimmed with fear and tears.

Enough! Who to kill first, the lethal monster of a man approaching from behind Khadeem, or the most disgusting excuse for a father on the planet? It seemed a no-brainer, until Seth factored in the very real possibility of Khadeem falling at Seth or Alex's hand, clearing the way for the killer in the hall to shoot through Devereaux to get at Seth and his team.

"I'm on the rifleman," Alex murmured out of the side of his mouth. "Don't worry about me. End Khadeem."

Seth grunted his agreement, never more sure of his God-given skill than at that moment. He stepped up. He bucked up. And for Devereaux, he'd die. But his index finger had no more than flexed against the trigger when she elbowed Khadeem in the gut, twisted in his arms, and screamed, "Let me go, you creep!"

After that, the world rolled in slow motion.

Khadeem's mouth dropped open, grimacing in pain. His eyes popped.

Devereaux had hold of his hand, twisting his fingers backward with a vengeance while she screamed, "Asshole! You're behind all of this! You bastard!"

Snarling, he cocked his arm back to pistol-whip her, but just as his fist began its downward swing, he looked over her head and past Seth. He froze, his arm in midair as if he'd seen a ghost. Then...

BLAM!

What the holy hell? Some bastard behind Seth had just fired too close and too damned personal. The blast from the unexpected discharge deafened him. He glanced over his shoulder at—Eric?

"What are you doing here?" Seth asked, though he could barely hear his own voice.

When Eric didn't answer, Seth zeroed back on Khadeem. By then Devereaux had ducked for cover and run for Seth, while the wicked man stood in the hall, dazed and swaying. The tiniest trickle of red dripped from beneath the brim of his stolen police cap into his left eye. His body leaned sideways. Just as Khadeem would've pitched to the floor, the unknown assassin behind him caught his neck in an arm lock, and growled at Eric, "This son-of-a-bitch was supposed to be mine, Reynolds."

To which Eric, now standing alongside Seth, smoothly replied, "And Bagani was supposed to have been mine, Sinclair. Now we're even. Get the hell out of here."

They know each other?

Tugging Devereaux with him, Seth backed against the nearest wall, caught up in the most bizarre tennis match he'd ever witnessed. Apparently, Alex wasn't shocked to see Eric or this Sinclair fellow. Walking straight up to the monster of a man, he extended a hand and said, "Wish you'd declare your presence once in a while, Pagan. Anyone of us could've shot you. How would I explain that to McQueen or Chance?"

Who the hell's McQueen? And who's Chance?

"That'll be the day," Pagan grunted as he jerked the pistol out of Khadeem's limp fingers, while he let the dead man's body slump to the floor. The guy wore nitrile gloves, black like the rest of his gear. Khadeem's pistol went on the floor beside the dead man, along with a single brass casing that Seth knew—he just knew—was the missing evidence from Bagani's murder. "Sorry I can't stay and chat, Mr. Stewart. I've got other places to be. Other lives to save."

"Wait," Seth breathed while Devereaux pressed herself under his chin, her poor heart beating like frantic hummingbirds against his chest. "What the hell just happened?"

"Nothing," both Eric and Pagan growled at the same time, both still staring at each other like gunslingers at the OK Corral.

"Who are you?" Seth asked the man in black.

"No one," he shot back, his upper lip lifted as if he didn't have time for stupid questions.

Seth knew better than to argue, but he turned to Eric and asked, "You've been hunting Khadeem all along, haven't you? You knew he'd be here. That's why you stayed in Florida after Cassidy left."

Eric's dark gaze flittered to Alex, then settled on Seth. "That's my story and I'm sticking to it."

Which meant there was more to this night that Seth might never know.

"And you," Seth directed at Pagan. "You killed Prince Bagani. That was you yesterday, the man who fired that long shot." The sniper who saved countless future lives.

"Goodbye and good riddance," Pagan muttered as he turned and walked back the way he'd come.

Seth wasn't sure if he'd meant that dig for Khadeem or The TEAM. The big guy disappeared into the same patient room he'd come out of. Again, what the hell? Did Sinclair plan to rappel down the side of the hospital and simply walk away? Did he have wings or was someone out there waiting to fly him away? What was he, just another legend in this dark world of covert ops?

Guess so.

Cord ran after the big guy, but returned shaking his head, both shoulders lifting in disbelief. "He's gone. Not a sign of him. Holy fuck."

Seth found that impossible to believe, but he had other things to worry about. Alex was already on his phone, calling 9-1-1 for an assist with an armed intruder that had been shot inside the hospital. "Yes, I'll hold," he growled as he rolled his eyes.

Standing there with Devereaux wrapped up in his arms, Seth took careful notice of the peculiar interaction between

Alex and Eric. Neither seemed surprised to see the other. Neither took notice of the missing—whatever—that Pagan was, either. But wasn't it interesting that Eric was also wearing nitrile gloves, that he'd casually sauntered up to where Khadeem lay, and just as casually, removed the casing that linked Pagan Sinclair to Bagani's murder?

"Who was that guy?" Devereaux asked.

"He's fiction," Seth breathed. "Forget you saw him, and when the police ask what happened—"

"Just tell them that guy…" She jerked her chin at Eric, still standing over Khadeem's dead body, "saved my life, right?"

"It's the truth," Seth told her, and it was. But now he knew precisely who'd killed Bagani. Pagan Sinclair—whoever he was—and that both Alex and Eric were covering for him.

Chapter Forty-Two

Devereaux inhaled deeply, drawing in every last aromatic epithelial of the man she loved into her soul. Making Seth hers on an animalistic, fundamental level. Absorbing the sensual sensation of his hair-roughened skin against her more delicate flesh. Relishing every last angle and hardened contour of his manly body while he held her in his arms, her back to his very impressive front. Snuggled naked together in her bedroom, still in Florida, there was nowhere else she'd rather be.

The admitting doctor had discharged her on the condition that she return for an appointment with a local plastic surgeon. The damage done to her breast and nipple required reconstructive surgery to set things right. For now, that poor little girl was saturated with a numbing agent and wrapped by an abundant bandage that circled Dev's torso and bound both of her breasts. Overall, she was quite comfortable, considering.

The most unexpected surprise of all came when Seth's boss stepped up to pay for her hospital costs. Who did that these days? Tears still sprang to her eyes at Alex's more than generous offer. She'd honestly tried to deny him. She'd never taken charity, not once in her life. She knew how to work, and she had her pride, but when he'd tugged her into his side, and told her, "Get used to it," she'd broken down and cried like a little girl.

He'd told her he was sorry that he'd made her cry, which made her cry even harder. Exasperated, he'd finally handed her off to Seth and told him, "Take her home, for Christ's sake." Which of course Seth did. It wasn't like he had to be asked twice.

Devereaux now knew the rest of the story behind Agent Reynold's drive to wipe the Saudi prince from the face of the planet. Yes, his wife Shea had eluded Bagani at their first meeting, but years later, he'd tracked her down to Ireland with the intention of picking up where he'd left off.

Fortunately, she'd been with another of Eric's and Seth's buddies at the time, an older gentleman, Senior Agent Murphy Finnegan. He'd had the presence of mind to enlist his friends on the Irish police force, who'd apprehended and jailed Bagani. Not that Bagani stayed behind bars that time, either. Once the sly weasel declared diplomatic immunity, away he went to hunt other unsuspecting women.

Damn the politics that had let him slip through too many law enforcers' hands. But thank God for the hard men who weren't afraid to stand up and do the right thing when called upon. Men like Alex and Eric. Like Cord. Like Seth.

"You're awake," he murmured drowsily in her ear. "How are you feeling?"

"Right now?" she breathed. "Like I'm in heaven and wrapped up in the arms of my sexy guardian angel."

"Hmmmmm. Just you wait."

That was Dev's problem. She was tired of waiting. Rolling over carefully so as not to set her poor damaged breast to thrumming, she bumped his forehead with hers playfully and said in her sexiest, sultriest voice, "Hey there."

Two dreamy browns flickered open with a light in them that quickly turned molten. "No," Seth murmured before he shut his eyes again. "You're still healing. Go back to sleep."

"But I'm not tired," she whispered as she planted a kiss between his eyebrows and took in a deep breath of his hair. The scent of warmed up manly spice had become a heady aphrodisiac to her. Running her nose over his hairline, Dev smoothed her palms under the sheets and over his broad chest. Without a doubt, she was in love with Seth's body. Nothing tantalized more than the heat and very masculine sensation of his skin beneath her roving fingertips.

Seth had the grace and sculptured physique of a Grecian god. The latent strength in his pectoral muscles lay coiled and dormant for the moment but running her fingers over the smooth bulges.... Rubbing her palms through the chest hairs that dusted those pecs and narrowed down his centerline to where she wanted to go… How had she gotten so lucky to have this man in her bed?

"What are you doing?" he asked, his eyes still closed.

"Seducing you," she breathed.

"No," he repeated, though his voice didn't sound nearly so groggy now.

Dev lifted his warm hand from under the cover to cup her tender breast, while she dipped under his nose to kiss his lips. "No?" she whispered, her voice breathy and light against his mouth. "Are you sure about that?"

The moment he cracked his lips just the tiniest bit for her, Dev knew she had him. She leaned into him and tongued him so slowly and so thoroughly that he groaned. Their tongues danced, sliding past each other with more and more energy. The callused palm at her breast cushioned her even as she pressed into him, needing the warm, wet haven of his mouth.

Easing into his pillow, he hissed a quiet but firm, "I said no," into her mouth.

But I said yes, she thought as she cupped his jaw, threading her fingers around his ears and into the short hairs of his sideburns. Anchoring him until she was finished with him. This man thought he could tell her no? *We'll just see about that.*

"I love you, Seth," she murmured as she attacked his mouth again. Seth's lips were soft and willing. He didn't mean no. He was just worried he'd hurt her.

"It's too soon, Devereaux," he mumbled around her greedy lips, which only made her giggle.

"It's never too soon, Seth McCray," she said as she nipped his lower lip, then nibbled her way over the two-day stubble on his chin.

Trailing her tongue down his neck, she cocked her head and sucked in a mouth full of a shaving-lotion flavored raspberry until he growled, "You're killing me, Devereaux. No. For the love of all that's holy and right—Ahh."

"Yessssss," she hissed in delight, blowing gentle puffs of air over the sensitive skin she'd just slathered with her lips and tongue. "Yes, yes, yes!"

His back arched, and with one muscled arm, Seth snagged her over and onto his hips. "Trust me. It's too soon, and I don't want to hurt you."

"You would never hurt me," she reminded him as she lifted his hand and repositioned his palm under her still healing breast. "Holding you makes me happy. I just figured if you held me, you'd be happy, too." She cocked her head as she poured on the innocence. "Is it working?"

His eyes turned dark as they scrolled over the bandaged mound now in his palm. She'd never been very large in the boob department, but a woman knew when a man couldn't resist the temptation he'd just been handed.

"I'm so glad he's dead," Seth murmured, his voice gone husky and deep, rippling over her bare body like an intimate caress.

"Me too, but I don't want to talk about that. This is my bed, and you're in it, and when we're together like this, I want…" She took advantage of his compassion to rub her core against his belly like a wanton cat. "… crazy. I don't want to talk about anyone or anything else but you and me, got it? And I want crazy, happy sex. Right now."

He smiled. "Got it, but the answer's still no. It's too soon and—"

She cut him off with a full-on body press, her mouth to his mouth, her knees at his hips, and her core making wild, horny love to the rough hairs on his bare belly. Cupping both his shoulders for balance, Dev began a slow, rhythmic dance of skin-to-skin and heart to heart. To hell with *too soon.* There was no such thing in her book.

"Devereaux," he said sternly. "This is serious, babe. I can't take the chance—"

And enough! If he wanted serious, she'd give him serious—for all of thirty seconds. "No, Seth. Life is not just serious," she told him with a determined, warm, slick bump and grind over his hips. "It's a risk each morning you wake up and smell the coffee, damn it. The only thing we know for sure is that every day's going to be the first of something wonderful and the last of something else. Hurricanes happen, but so do rainbows and new days and second chances. Live, Seth. Just live every second of whatever time we've got left. With me." Dev punctuated with another forward thrust. That was how she was made, one forward thrust at a time, though none had ever felt this sublime.

Most men would've given in by now, but Seth still held her as if she might break. And that was okay. She knew he still carried strong feelings for Katelynn in his heart. What he obviously didn't know was that Dev had no intention of giving in to his past sweetheart. Not this time. Not until he was good and sweaty, totally molested, panting into her mouth, and screaming her name.

"Mhmmm," he moaned, the sweetest smile tweaking the corners of his mouth. "Maybe…"

'Maybe, my ass,' she thought as she eased away from him just enough to slide her fingers down the corded muscles to his waiting cock. Leaning up onto her knees, she took him in hand and gave him a taste of what he was missing. "Maybe?" she teased, growing more aroused by the second as the friction between them heightened.

"Yeah. Maybe," he breathed, his eyes closed and bliss softening the rugged lines of his face. "I might be wrong. It happens."

And maybe was good enough. With one slick slide, Dev impaled her body onto his, swallowing him to the hilt. The man was a goner, and he proved it by not arguing or saying another word. Just smiling. Both hands settled on her hips as the real dance began. There was so much to love about this gentle man, but the way he always pleasured her first meant a lot.

Until he shifted his knees and bucked her off and onto her back.

"Hey," she squealed. "Not fair. I was just getting started."

"But this way will be better for you," he insisted, the light in his eyes gone feral. "With you lying flat, your muscles won't bounce when we do this." He wasted no time entering her as he settled his elbows alongside her shoulders and the dance began again.

"I'm not going to break," she whispered as the first tingle began in the depths of her core. They'd been snuggled like spoons in a drawer for so long, she was well past the need for foreplay. One touch could push her over the edge, and Seth was doing a lot of fine touching and stroking.

"This has nothing to do with you breaking, Devereaux," he murmured, the brown in his eyes swallowed up by the black.

Aww, the tenderness in those words brought tears to her eyes.

"This is about putting you first. Protecting you. Always. I should've told you before I left for Cuba, but I needed to be sure. I don't fall easy, but you—"

She rolled her eyes. "I know. I fall too easy, but—"

"Shush." The pad of his index finger pressed over her lips. "That's not what I meant, and you know it. Let me finish. I don't fall easy, but you need to know that when I do, I fall forever. Understand what I'm saying?"

She could barely see through her tears by then. "Ah-huh," she replied, so damned thankful for the love light gleaming through his rugged countenance, as well as the aching fire clenching her feminine muscles. The heat in his voice cut her to the bone. If he kept talking…

"I love you, Devereaux."

That did it. Those sent every quivering muscle at her core into overdrive. Without trying, her body squeezed him with a warm wet rush and…

"Seth," she gasped, her heart gone crazy happy in her chest. "Seth, I… Seth… Seth!"

"That's it, baby," he murmured, his breath warm in her ear. "Come with me. Stay with me. Love with me… Forever."

"I will. I mean, I dooooooo," she ground out. There was no holding back this time as the most powerful sensation blasted up from her toes and launched her into pure bliss. What a rush! What an extraordinarily excellent ride. Stars. Galaxies. She saw them all.

In seconds, Seth joined her, growling his release into the hollow of her neck, his breath hot on her already feverish skin. "Devereaux."

She clung to him, her legs wrapped around him and her heart pounding against his in a rhythm as old as time. There was no him or her, just them. Just two lost and lonely halves come together in one complete whole. Finally.

She couldn't speak as her happy heart leaked out between her eyelids.

"I knew it. I hurt you."

Dev managed a breathless squeak. "No. I'm fine. Really."

Leaning on his elbows, his eyes went soft and tender as he scanned her chest. "Are you sure? We got carried away. I didn't mean to hold onto you so tight."

"There's no such thing as holding onto the person you love too tight," she whispered as she buried her face in his neck. "Or too soon. Trust me. I know."

She wanted to bawl. No one had ever put her needs first, not even her parents. Cord thought he did, but more often than not, he had ulterior motives or needed something. A place to shelter his guys between missions into Cuba. A resting stop for the women and children he rescued. With Cord there was always something, but Seth wanted nothing more than to please her. To shelter her for a change. And please her he had.

"I love you so much," she told him, her heart pounding. Wow, that orgasm was another first. It thrilled her how quickly they'd come together, both as in this very primal, physical act, but also, how they'd found each other. Maybe there were such things as fate and destiny.

"I'm thinking a year will be long enough," he grumbled as he rolled over and settled her under his arm. "Are you comfortable? I'm not squeezing you too tight, am I?"

"No, I'm fine. Promise." Man, she loved this charming, gentle warrior. "A year? For what?"

"To court you. The only problem is that I live in Virginia, and I don't want another long-distance relationship. I'd never survive it." Sliding her palm over her bicep, he squeezed her ever so gently. "I want this, my arms around you, every night and every morning."

That made her smile. "Are you asking me to move up north with you?" She hoped.

He cocked his head, the whiskers from his chin abrading her forehead. "Would you?"

Dev lifted both shoulders. "I don't know. No one's asked me yet."

Seth's head dipped low as he claimed her mouth until she came up for air. "Well?" he asked as he licked her lips.

"Mmmmmm," she purred. "I'm not sure. Ask me again."

Chapter Forty-Three

"I can't read *that* to him," Seth exclaimed as he slapped the dog-eared copy of Walt Disney's *"Old Yeller,"* with child star Tommy Kirk and his jaunty yellow lab smiling at him, on Devereaux's kitchen table. "It's too sad." Make that downright tragic.

For now, Scottie had a brand-new toy in his backyard, a redwood playhouse, complete with adjoining swing set and climbing ropes. Best yet, Uncle Cord had taken on the supremely detailed job of building it with Scottie's excited assistance. That was where he needed to be, alongside his uncle and outdoors, not dealing with the saddest story Seth had read in a long time.

Cord had already signed on the dotted line. He was taking over Devereaux's bungalow. When Scottie came for a visit, he'd have a playhouse to keep himself busy.

But Seth was *not* reading that book to the kid. No way. Scottie could read it himself when he was old enough. Until then...

Devereaux stepped away from the chocolate cake she was frosting, her head cocked and curiosity sparkling in her all-seeing blue eyes. She didn't come right out and say it, but Seth knew that she knew. Dashing a quick hand over his glistening lashes, he grumbled, "I forgot already. It's been a long time since I've seen the movie or read the book, and… I just forgot how sad it is, okay? There's no way I'm reading that to Scottie. He's too young. It'll break his heart."

Smiling, she set the spatula in the bowl of frosting. "I love you, Seth McCray," she said as she stepped into his arms and snuggled under his chin. "So much that it hurts sometimes, do you know that?"

He bobbed his head in answer. There were no doubts or secrets between them, not anymore. Only love. Blowing out a deep breath, he ruffled her silvery locks as he told her in no uncertain terms, "Scottie needs to be a kid as long as he can, okay? He's seen enough tragedy. Man, who writes that stuff?"

Devereaux's fingertips tapped at his collarbones, settling him like they always did. "Someone who's a lot richer than us. By the way, Alex called. He's coming over, said he had someone you needed to meet."

Alex hadn't left the Keys since the gunfight at the hospital, and Seth knew his boss was still working with, at least communicating with, that Sinclair fellow. Seth just didn't know on what. But he'd heard the way his boss's voice lowered into damned near non-existence whenever his cell phone chimed with the theme song for *"Jeopardy."* Alex wasn't one to spice up his ringtones like that. Something was up.

The police hadn't yet located any trace of the sniper who'd offed Bagani, and for twenty-four hours, they'd thought they had their man—Eric. Guess again. Eric Reynolds was no dummy. He had time-stamped receipts to prove he'd been blocks from the hospital, on assignment from Alex no less, watching for Khadeem. How had Eric known

Khadeem might show? He didn't, but he was there because Alex *had a feeling*.

Thankfully, Trish had moved everyone into the hotel. Those were Khadeem's fingerprints all over her bungalow, not Sly's, Joachim's, or Bagani's. It made sense that Khadeem would come looking for his daughter. He needed to clean up his mess and he needed her dead.

When he didn't find her at Trish's, apparently, he'd found evidence of Devereaux. Tit for tat, he'd hunted Devereaux once the news of Bagani's death hit the airwaves, though how Khadeem tracked Lianna to Trish's bungalow remained a mystery.

Eric had finally gone home after spending a long day with the local police. At the conclusion of their interrogation, they'd had no recourse but to chalk Khadeem's death up to Eric's quick response in saving Devereaux's life.

It was interesting that not one of the hospital's security cameras on that floor had caught a single shot of Khadeem or Pagan Sinclair, though, and that was just plain spooky. Guess they had some kind of an electrical short before everything went down. Sinclair had to be one of the blackest of black operators to have gotten in and out of the hospital like he had. Damn, he was good.

"When's Alex due?" Seth asked, his hands roaming down Devereaux's back, sliding into the waistband of her shorts in case they had time to play. He sighed as his fingers cupped the warm cheeks of her backside. This right here, this ability to intimately touch the woman he adored any time he wanted, grounded him like nothing before.

"Mmmmmm," she purred, rubbing her nose against his chest like a cat marking her territory.

"Are you smelling me?" he asked, though he knew she was. He could tell by the way she inhaled deeply whenever they were wrapped up like they were.

"Ah-huh," she murmured, the tip of her tongue tasting him, too. "You belong to me. I get to nibble on you anytime I want, and" —she growled the most seductive growl— "I want."

Didn't that warm Seth from the inside out? He belonged to her and nothing made him happier than that single truth.

They'd settled easily into domestic life while they packed Devereaux's few household belongings, but there was still time for a break. Unless Alex showed. "Answer the question, woman. Do we have time, or should we wait until later?" he asked, tapping her cheeks with his fingertips.

"He said in an hour, but you know he's always early."

Which meant Seth had better remove his hands from her sweet ass. Seth growled, annoyed at the OCD boss who never seemed to take a day off. "What's he want now?"

Her shoulders lifted. "He didn't say, but I'm sure the anticipation won't kill you," she chuckled.

He squeezed her bottom, relishing the unique softness that was Devereaux. "Is that why you baked? For my boss?"

"Uh-uh. I baked because chocolate cake is Scottie's favorite, and because we need to celebrate. Your realtor called, and—"

He tilted his torso from her to look down into her mischievous blues. "She found a home for us? Already?" He'd only last night called the realtor friend whom his good buddy Taylor Armstrong had recommended. Another jarhead, Taylor restored derelict colonials in his spare time. The man had crazy woodworking and carving skills.

"She did. It's a four-bedroom colonial, and you'll never guess who lives across the street."

His brows pinched. Guessing wasn't his strong suit.

Devereaux tipped far enough back to fiddle with his t-shirt collar. "Ever heard of Taylor and Gracie Armstrong?"

"That dog. I'll bet Taylor set this up. Sweet!"

Devereaux shrugged. "At least I'll have a girlfriend when I show up in chilly Virginia. Brrr. I'm going to miss the ocean and the sunshine."

That was the hard part about moving. Seth had fallen for Florida, too. What was not to love?

A sharp rap at the front door announced Alex's arrival, but Seth didn't recognize the Hispanic male at his side when he opened the door. Of average build and his short dark hair combed to the side with a meticulous part, the stranger didn't crack a smile.

Alex inclined his head to Devereaux as he stepped inside and said, "Seth. Devereaux. I'd like you to meet Special Agent Julio Juarez, a good friend of mine."

Interesting, Alex hanging around with a Fed. "Good to meet you," Seth said as he extended a hand in friendship. "What can I do for you?"

Julio's sharp, black eyes zeroed straight through the bungalow to the kitchen screen door. "It's a pleasure to meet you as well, Agent McCray, but I'm here for him."

Seth looked over his shoulder at Cord and Scottie. "Cord?"

"Yes. We need to talk. Do you mind, ma'am?" he asked Devereaux.

"No, not at all," she said as she gestured him to help himself.

"Ah, you're that Julio," Seth murmured. "You worked with my Uncle George."

Julio nodded. "I have, yes. How is your uncle? I heard he'd had a stroke."

"Still holding his own. He's up and walking now, but his doctor says he might never speak again."

"It was bad then?"

Seth nodded. "Bad enough, but he's a strong old fart. He'll be back, just wait and see."

Julio stepped up to Seth and took hold of his shoulder. "Never doubt the determination of your uncle, Seth. George is one in a million, and you, sir, are just like him."

What an odd thing for a guy who'd never met Seth before to say. "That's very kind of you," he replied, curious as to who'd been talking about him to Julio, and why Julio was really there. "Shall I call Cord for you?"

"No, I'll go to him. Please excuse me," Julio said as he proceeded through the house and out the back door.

"What's going on, boss?" Seth asked once the screen door squeaked shut, and Julio was out of earshot.

"Juarez works for the same man Pagan Sinclair works for. I think he may be asking Cord to team up with him."

"Who does Pagan Sinclair work for?" Seth had to know.

Alex shook his head. "A patriot and another good friend of mine. That's all I can say."

Okay, then. Seth glanced through the house to where Julio and Cord crouched alongside a stack of pre-cut, pre-drilled redwood timbers, their heads tilted together in earnest conversation. It made for an oddly comforting scene, two worthy men in the same line of work, both fighting the good fight to keep America safe, while Devereaux's innocent little boy sat beyond them in the grass, petting one damned handsome iguana.

"This came for you," Alex said as he drew an envelope out from his inner jacket pocket.

Seth could've cried when he opened the seal, and a single black and white photograph fell into his hands. "What's this?" he asked, though he damned well knew.

"Corporal Ritter thought you should have it."

Tears burned at the corners of his eyes. There in western clothing, jeans, and a button-up shirt, stood a young man whose face he recognized instantly. Husam. Three younger girls stood meekly at his side, smiling the widest smiles Seth had ever seen. They had to be Husam's sisters. "But how—?"

Alex stuck his chin at Seth. "You asked me to send someone after these girls, didn't you?"

"But Boss—" It had only been days since Seth made that audacious request. How had Alex gotten Husam out of CIA clutches in GITMO so quickly? And those girls? They lived halfway around the world. Alex had to have put a man on this request immediately after Seth had asked him. *Holy shit.*

"So, wait…" Seth squinted through blurry tears. "You did all this—?" He wanted to say, *'For me?'* but that sounded self-serving and too proud for Seth's tastes.

"Agent McCray," Alex growled, a spark of amusement flashing deep inside those blues. "Don't ever come to me with a problem, and not expect me to handle it. It's your job to perform as you're trained, and it's my job to make sure you have the tools to get the ugly jobs done."

Seth's head bobbed as he stared at the picture. "I know, Boss. I know, but…" This was so much more than just a boss taking care of his employee.

There were no words adequate enough to describe the joy suffusing Seth's heart at the tender reunion depicted in his hands. Husam and his sisters were safe, and damned if that didn't assuage some of the guilt he carried for defending himself against Husam's brothers. They'd deserved better, too, but knowing that this one tiny family was finally safe from the likes of Khadeem's men—helped. Man, how it helped.

But wait. Seth looked closer, blinking to see past his sappy heart. "Who's the old guy standing behind Husam with his hand on Husam's shoulder?" *It can't be. No!* Alex wasn't that good—was he?

"Who do you think he is?" Alex asked, those icy blues warm with kindness.

Seth looked his boss in the eye. "Husam's father? But the man's been in prison for years." *Please say yes.*

Alex nodded. "Of course it's Husam's father. I couldn't leave him behind bars while his children came to America."

"Where are they?"

Alex shook his head. "That I don't know, but they are in the States now, in protective custody. All of them. It took both Maverick and Adam to get him out of that prison. They had to" —Alex cleared his throat— "convince a few guards. He's had a tough time, but he's going to be okay now."

What does one say to an unimaginable gift like this? Seth lurched, grabbing Alex into a guy hug. "Thank you, Boss. You didn't have to do any of this," he breathed, as he squeezed his boss like he'd never—EVER—done before. Alex wasn't what you'd call a huggable guy.

"I don't have to do a lot of things," Alex muttered as he pulled away and took hold of Seth's hand instead. "But that's who we are, isn't it? We do the hard things others can't or won't do. Like your uncle before you, we make a difference in the few years allotted to us to live on this planet. We reach out and we lend a hand. One hand can make a helluva difference."

Seth could only nod, his own hand still in the grip of a most extraordinary man. "Boss, please. I'd love for you to meet Uncle George someday. My mom and dad, too."

"And I want to meet them, but I've got a plane to catch right now." Alex dropped Seth's hand, nodding toward the scene outside the kitchen door. "You two take care of that little guy. He's your mission for the next couple weeks, Seth. We'll talk once your family's settled."

"Thanks, Boss," Seth said as he looked to the backyard, expecting to see Julio and Cord still talking. Only Cord and Scottie were there now, both were on their knees, hammering on the same piece of lumber. *My family. What a sight.*

Scottie's tongue stuck out as he took short, concentrated strokes with his much smaller hammer, his hands up too high on the handle grip to make much of an impact. Cord's brows furrowed as he dealt heavier, more decisive blows. Beyond them, Gru stretched his handsome emerald body in a long shaft of golden sunlight, his eyes closed, and his chin up, posing like iguanas are prone to do when they're happy.

It could've been a slice of paradise, framed the way it was within the confines of Devereaux's aluminum screen door. The peace that surpassed all understanding settled over Seth's shoulders like a warm hug from Heaven. He'd finally come full circle, through tragedy and war, through heartache and misery, and he was—home. Devereaux Shepherd, she was his home.

When he turned to tell Alex goodbye, only she stood at her open front door. "Why do I feel like we've just been visited by two ghosts?" she asked.

There was no need to look for Alex. Seth knew he wouldn't spot him. Like Julio Juarez and Pagan Sinclair, the man disappeared like the ghost he was. Only these three ghosts were nothing like Latoya Franklin. They hadn't come to haunt, whine, or complain. Only to serve. And their special kind of service made all the difference to a world gone bat-shit crazy.

"Because you have," Seth said as he looked at the happy picture in his hand.

"What do you have there? I want to see what had you so upset." Devereaux said, her head cocked and her pretty blues aglow.

"I'm not upset. Just in love," Seth told her as he wrapped one arm around her shoulders and kissed the side of her forehead. He angled the photo so she could see the miracle at his fingertips. "Let me introduce you to a kid I met in Cuba. His name's Husam, and he's one of Lianna's countrymen that her father sent to start his war. These three girls with him are his little sisters, and see that white-bearded guy behind Husam? That's his father. Alex got him out of Khadeem's prison, well, actually Maverick and Adam, two of my good buddies did. But the important thing is that Husam and his family are in the States now. He's going to live happily-ever-after. Like you, Scottie, and me."

Devereaux peered at the picture. "So Alex saved him and his family? Really?"

"Oh, yeah," Seth murmured, his heart stuck up high in his throat all over again. Damn, he hadn't been this emotional in a long while. "Alex does stuff like this," he said, his voice gone hoarse. "He saves people, and sometimes, he even saves them from themselves."

Like me.

Epilogue

"Are you sure about this?" Seth asked as he and Devereaux stopped short of the front door to Jordie's World of Ink.

Despite the fact that this was to be their final day in Florida, the girl was all smiles. The moving truck sat loaded at her curb, ready to take them to Virginia come morning. For one last night, Scottie was sleeping over at Trish's. Cord had turned into a very busy man now that he'd moved his business to Drunken Sailor Island.

Uncle George wouldn't mind, in fact, Seth knew his uncle would want the work he'd begun to continue. After all, it was his little speck-of-dirt island where he'd arranged Cord's *usual* landing place for his rescued ladies and children. It only seemed fair that the island Gru and George loved remained active duty. Yeah. George would want it that way.

Even now, Uncle George was learning to walk again, and Seth's father and his doctors were impressed. He might never talk again, but it seemed George had an extra-large serving of that cocky, *'I'm a Marine. Get the hell out of my way!'* attitude of Cord's.

"Yes, I'm sure," Devereaux answered, a mischievous smile tweaking the corners of her sexy mouth. Her breast had healed from the inside out after her outpatient plastic surgery, and romance was in the air. Just this morning she'd been to Victoria's Secret. And if he knew Devereaux, she couldn't wait to show him. Tonight was the night. Seth just didn't want to ruin it by putting another woman's face inside the empty heart on his arm. It didn't feel right. At all.

"Come on in, worrywart," she cajoled as she tugged him into the tattoo parlor. "You'll survive a few needles."

"I know, but…" Still. One stupid decision could derail the most precious thing in his life.

Three young girls sat at the first station, their eyes wide as the tattoo artist, a shaggy-haired college-aged kid applied a healthy smear of *Aquaphor*® *Healing Ointment* over the artwork on the middle girl's upper thigh. A butterfly. Of course. At least it wasn't a tramp stamp that screamed, 'I'm easy. Come get some!'

"Hi, Jordie!" Devereaux called to the overweight, dark-haired man in denim and a t-shirt that declared: INK is FOREVER, at the rear of the shop. The lettering was a fine example of scrollwork that almost made a believer out of Seth. Almost. He wasn't one of those guys who needed his body adorned with any more ink than what would darken it today. This was it. The end.

"Hey, Dev," Jordie answered. "Haven't seen you since Cord got that Navy Cross. What's your brother been up to lately?"

"Cord received the Navy Cross?" Seth hissed, impressed as hell. "Why didn't you tell me?" *If I'd known that, I might've been nicer to him. Once or twice.*

The Navy's highest award for extreme valor in combat, the Cross singled out very few in the ranks for acts of extraordinary heroism.

"Not *that* Navy Cross," Devereaux muttered. "Cord's is in ink on his chest, not in real life."

"Oh. Okay." That made sense, not that he was jealous of Cord getting the Navy Cross or anything, but the Cross had one hellacious coordination process that normally took years from the initial recommendation to the final presentation by the Secretary of the Navy. Not to mention that receiving the Navy Cross was a substantially big deal.

"That's too bad," he said under his breath. "Cord's a stand-up guy. He deserves something for all he's done since he left the Corps."

Devereaux shrugged. "He could care less about medals. You know how it is."

Seth did. Military service men and women didn't see their heroism in the same light civilians did. Every one of those medals was just another reminder of those who'd borne the ultimate cost of combat and who hadn't come home.

Jordie beckoned him to take a seat and asked, "Whatcha got in mind?"

"He wants his fiancée's face inked into the heart already on his bicep," Devereaux said brightly. "Can you do that for him?"

"Sure," Jordie muttered, his brows furrowed, and his nose wrinkled as he tugged Seth's bared arm beneath the bright lamp at his workstation. "Got a picture of her?"

"I do." Seth drew his wallet out of his back pocket and tugged a two by three photograph out its plastic sleeve. But to Devereaux he said, "Why don't you go shop for a while? Buy something pretty to wear tonight."

She cocked her head at him, the sweeter than sweet pixie smile shining bright in her eyes once more. "I've already done that."

"Well, do it again."

"Are you sure?"

He waved his fingers at her. "Go on, shoo. We'll swing by Molly's when we're done and get some of those pancakes you love."

She winked. "I won't be long."

"Take all the time you need," Jordie said. "This'll take a while."

The moment she trotted out the door, Seth leaned over the desk and told Jordie, "Not that picture. Here. This is the face I want on my arm."

Later that night, Seth kicked in Devereaux's front door. He had to. His hands were full of one intoxicated lady who'd been mauling him the whole drive home. He'd barely turned the key in the lock when she'd attacked him again, tugging his t-shirt over his head, jerking at his pants zipper, and all but undressing him on her front step.

They weren't yet inside when she climbed up his body and clamped those long legs of hers around his hips and sucked his neck like a vampire. A really pretty vampire. "Now, Seth," she ground out, her teeth nipping at his jaw, her nails scraping over his shoulders as she hung on.

"I'd rather do this in bed," he mumbled, licking her lips that tasted of Bud Lite.

Who knew two beers could do this? Although, now that he thought about it, she was a tiny, petite little thing. Probably shouldn't have had that tequila chaser, either. She'd regret those drinks come morning.

"Ah, come on," she whined, thrusting her hips into his belly.

"Shhh," he told her as he made his way down the hall to her room, sans lights. "Almost there. Then I want you naked and ready, understood?"

"Ah-huh," she breathed against his neck, heating him up.

Setting her to her feet, he told her, "Strip."

Quick as a perky little bunny, Devereaux was out of her pants and shirt, and on her hands and knees in the middle of the bed. "Like this?" she teased, facing him but waving her delectable backside. What a delicious sight she was, from her lacy, new, red satin bra to the matching thong. But best of all, she was his.

Tossing his clothes to the floor in a hurry, Seth eased onto the bed behind her. Ah, yes. This was what he'd been waiting for all day, her on her knees, wet, wanton, and waiting. The sexy panties hit the floor, but he left her bra where it was to support her still healing breast. Impatient now, he buried himself in her to the hilt with one slick thrust, angling her hips for deeper penetration, but mostly, just to hear her moan, wiggle her backside, and beg for, "More, Seth. More."

That he could do. Devereaux was a light touch when it came to drinking and things of the heart, so he took their lovemaking slow and easy, intent on her reaching her point of maximum satisfaction first. Little did she know this entire day had been all about her. Since last night, when he'd asked Trish to take Scottie for one last sleepover, to eating

Devereaux's favorite pancakes at Molly's after dark today, Seth had planned for this moment. But now he wished she'd had orange juice with those blueberry pancakes instead of beer.

"More, more," she groaned as her ass met his every move.

"Easy," he murmured, still intent on protecting that delicate breast from them getting rowdy too soon. Still intent on protecting Devereaux in all ways. This very intimate act they shared was only part of their upcoming life together. Little did she know...

Too quickly, her body stiffened, and this was what he'd been waiting for. "Ah, Seth," she ground out, her voice throaty. "Yes. Right there. Yes, yes!"

Pushing forward, he matched her release with his own, grinding his hips into her soft backside, matching his steel to her sheath, and joining Devereaux in the most pleasurable miracle between a man and a woman.

Sated and breathing hard, she dropped her cheek to the sheet, her butt still lifted and his hands hot and sweaty on her hips. He hadn't turned the lights off, and the visual of her willing offering never failed to arouse him all over again.

But she wasn't in the condition for all night sex, not as drunk as she was, and Seth wasn't a user. He'd given her what she wanted and needed for the moment. "I love you, baby," he told her, still holding onto her one hip while he tiptoed his fingers up her spine, just to watch her shiver.

Wiggling against him, she not only shivered but she growled, too. "I never knew it could be like this."

"Like what?" he asked as he gave her one last thrust while he willed his horny body to stand down.

"Like this." Another enticing wiggle. "You never let me down, Seth. I don't know what I'd do without you. You're always here for me."

"I wish I could always be here," he teased, bumping her backside with his hips before he eased out and away from her. "Hold that pose. I'll be right back."

"Ah-huh," she mumbled into the sheets.

Seth hurried to the bathroom off the hall, cleaning himself before he soaked a washcloth in warm water and hustled back to his lady. She'd rolled to her side by then, growing drowsier by the minute. Seth knelt on the bed at her side, loving this final act of caring for his woman.

After he cleaned her, he dropped the cloth to the side of the bed and lay facing her. "Hey, sleepy," he whispered, tapping his index finger gently to the tip of her nose. "Are you too tired for a surprise? Maybe two?" *Maybe three?*

Since her ordeal with Bagani and Khadeem, Seth had come to know quite a bit about Devereaux Shepherd. This woman might be tiny in stature, but her heart was as deep as the ocean, most likely because she gave parts of it away so freely. It all came back to the laws of the universe. What a person sowed, they also reaped, and she'd definitely sown seeds of love wherever she went. Those were what had made her heart so incredibly deep and full. The universe just kept giving back.

Right or wrong, she loved fiercely and freely, which explained the ease with which her brother had used her. Unintentionally, she'd set herself up for that perfect storm, and, like any man on a mission, Cord had simply accepted her generosity because it was there when he'd needed it. It had served both of their purposes, her need to give and his need to provide safe harbor for the women he'd rescued. Neither realized how much those acts of kindness had drained Devereaux, and even today, Seth knew she'd do it all again. That was just the way she was, but it was also what made her vulnerable. That gentle, giving heart of hers.

"Want your surprise now, or should I save it for morning?" he asked, as he ran his fingers over her head and through her short hair, ruffling the silvery blonde strands that he loved.

Her eyes came open to reveal two dreaming pools of blue. "I like surprises."

"Well good, because you're looking at one of them, well, two of them if you look close."

"I am?" She blinked as she pushed up onto one elbow. Those pretty ocean blues scrolled over his bare body, settling below his belly. Her brows arced with mischief. "I really like that surprise."

"Not that," he teased, winking at her salacious grin. "Look higher. Come on. You might have to get up on your knees to see it, so move it."

Devereaux scrambled up, looking over his shoulder to the nightstand, then beyond into the hall. Holding onto his left bicep, she tilted over his side and glanced at the floor.

Irresistible, that was what she was, and Seth couldn't help but cup her bare butt when she leaned over him. "You're hot, baby. Not just getting warmer, but hot." In fact, she was touching her first surprise.

"Hmmm, I don't see anything," she said, her lips pinched in a pout. "Are you teasing me?" Her fingers smoothed over his bicep, stinging the newly inked tattoo that seriously needed another dose of healing ointment.

Seth cringed. Not wanting to draw attention to the new design, he'd held off with the ointment, so it wouldn't stain his t-shirt while it kept the tat covered. That Devereaux hadn't yet asked to see it told him everything he'd already suspected. Yes, she was all for him remembering Katelynn, just not in the same heart with his mother. Little did she know…

"Oh," she yipped, her fingers much gentler on his bicep. Then, softer, "Oh, Seth. You didn't," she murmured as she looked at the heart where her pretty face now smiled. "You put me in your heart. Aww…"

He pulled her against his chest. "I sure did."

"It's beautiful," she whimpered, tears brimming those sexy blues as she studied his new tat.

"Of course, it's you," he teased. "You're the only woman I wanted in this empty heart of mine. Only you, Devereaux."

"B-but Katelynn. You loved her. I know you did."

"Did, baby. Did. Check out my left calf."

Another, "Oh, Seth. You didn't." Devereaux whimpered, her fingers covering her lips. "Why'd you put her on the back of your leg?"

"Because Katelynn's part of my past. She's part of *our* past, and she's behind us. Yes, I loved her then, but I love you now. You're my future. No one else."

"I don't know what to say," she murmured. "I know you loved her, but yeah, you're right. I was a little confused when I left you this morning. Maybe a little jealous, too."

Didn't that make his heart swell? No one had ever been jealous over Seth McCray before. If anything, he'd been a wallflower and a fixture since Katelynn's death. A—ghost.

Son-of-a-bitch. Seth's heart pounded as years of truth hit home. No wonder Latoya hadn't let go of him. It wasn't that she'd refused to leave him all these years. It was him. He'd been holding onto *her*. Holding *her* back. Not the other way around. Somehow in his crazy traumatized brain, her death had mingled with Katelynn's into one desperate need. Letting go of Latoya had translated into losing Katelynn. Only she was already gone. And now, it was Latoya's turn.

Seth thought what he should've said years ago, *'Goodbye, Latoya Franklin. I'm sorry we met like we did, but thanks to you, a whole lot of kids are going to keep getting new shoes. I'm naming the foundation after you. Latoya's kids. I think you would've liked that. Rest easy, sweetheart.'*

He squeezed his eyes shut, so damned thankful for truth and enlightenment. For pixie dust. At last. Seth McCray was ready to fly.

"I've been a little confused, too," he admitted as he scrambled to his knees and reached into his nightstand drawer. "But I'm not any longer." *Because I'm free.* "Hold on. I've got one last surprise."

"Sheesh, I don't have anything to give you." By now, Devereaux sat on her haunches in the middle of the bed. The sight of her sweet naked body reminded him of Eve in the Garden of Eden, only Eve had never looked this sexy. Seth was smitten again. Smitten. Claimed. Owned. All of the above. He was Devereaux's man, now and forever.

Placing the velvet blue ring box between them on the bed, he told her, "This is for you," but he thought, *'Please say yes.'*

"Oh, my," she whispered, blinking at the box like a deer caught in headlights.

"Will you marry me?" he asked, his heart a freight train pounding down the tracks. He couldn't go on living with her without marrying her. He wasn't made that way, and neither was she. Devereaux needed the legal security of marriage. So did Scottie.

Lifting the box between them, her eyes filled.

Seth swallowed hard. That could be a good sign. That could be a bad sign. He held his breath. It was now or never. *Please say yes.*

"I… I don't know what to say," she whispered, not making eye contact.

Oh, damn. Maybe this was too soon. Maybe he was wrong. God knew that happened often enough. Coughing politely, he gave her a way out even as his heart broke around the edges. "You don't have to answer right away." *But I wish you would.* "Sleep on it. You can give me your answer in the morn—"

"Are you nuts?" She lurched off her knees and into his arms, the ring box tight in her hand. "Yes, Seth. Oh, God…" Cue the tears. "Yes, I'll marry you and I'll cook for you and I'll—"

Covering her lips with his mouth, he swallowed all those wifely promises. They could negotiate roles and responsibilities later, but now… "I love you, Devereaux," he vowed with every sinew of his once battered, mixed up heart. "Marry me and I'll make you the happiest woman on Earth. You and Scottie will never want for anything. I swear."

Devereaux always gave as good as she got, even now. She straddled his lap, her knees alongside his thighs and her core pressed tight against his cock. Right where she belonged, peppering his chin and cheeks with kisses, her long slender fingers holding his head as if she would never let him go. "I love you," she said between each fervent, moist kiss to his face, nose, and lips until his heart filled to overflowing.

He knew it then. No man had ever been as treasured as he was. It just wasn't possible.

Rolling onto the bed, he took her with him, her bare breasts to his chest as she straddled him again. This was what he'd been searching for all those lonely years. This connection. This one woman. This brave firecracker who led with a heart full of her private brand of pixie dust—love.

"Mrs. Seth McCray," he murmured as his hands skimmed over her shoulder blades to her warm, bare ass. "Hmmm, I like the sound of that."

"Mr. and Mrs. Seth McCray," she corrected, her fingers dancing over his belly to parts already fired up below. "I like the sound of that better."

"So do I," he whispered, his body ramping up for one more time.

It was oddly comforting that she hadn't yet opened that ring box. She didn't yet have a clue what was inside. She hadn't *'Oooed'* and *'Ahhed'* or displayed the two-carat diamond on her ring finger like most women would have by now. Neither had she asked how much he'd spent or if he'd insured the ring, a roundabout way of determining its value. She hadn't even called Trish to tell her all the latest.

She. Just. Said. Yes.

The End

Thank you for reading Seth's story!

Be sure to check out the rest of the guys and gals from The TEAM in Irish Winters' series: *In the Company of Snipers*

Other Irish Winters' books/series

King of Hearts, Deuces Wild Series, *#1*

Joker Joker, Deuces Wild Series, *#2*

One-Eyed Jack, Deuces Wild Series, *#3*

Smoke, Hearts and Ashes Series, *#1*

Ash, Hearts and Ashes Series, *#2*

Angel, An SOBs Novel, *#1*

Coming soon

Assassin, An SOBs Novel, #2

Ace, Deuces Wild Series, #4

YOU ARE THE KEY TO THIS BOOK'S SUCCESS!

Please tell other readers why you liked Seth and Devereaux's story by leaving an honest review at the retail site where you purchased it. Recommend it to your friends. Lend it. Most of all, enjoy it!

The best way to keep up with my new releases, giveaways, and actionable intel is to sign up for my spam-free newsletter at IrishWinters.com.

About the Author

Irish Winters

...is a best-selling author who, when she isn't writing, dabbles in poetry, grandchildren, and rarely—as in extremely rarely—the kitchen. More prone to be outdoors than in, she grew up the quintessential tomboy on a dairy farm in rural Wisconsin, spent her teenage years in the Pacific Northwest, but calls the Wasatch Mountains of Northern Utah, home. For now. She believes in making everyday count for something, and follows the wise admonition of her mother to, "Look out the window and see something!"

Connect with Irish online:
On Facebook: https://www.facebook.com/author.irishwinters
On Twitter: https://twitter.com/irishwinters1
Or at www. IrishWinters.com